Paul de Ko(

Novels By Paul De Kock

Volume 19

Paul de Kock

Novels By Paul De Kock
Volume 19

1st Edition | ISBN: 978-3-75233-453-1

Place of Publication: Frankfurt am Main, Germany

Year of Publication: 2020

Outlook Verlag GmbH, Germany.

NOVELS

BY

Paul de Kock

VOLUME XIX

THE BASHFUL LOVER

PART I

I

It was the year 1818, I will not say of happy memory, because I do not remember whether that year was happier than other years; probably it was so to certain people, and just the opposite to others; and sometimes, often, I may say almost always, the same cause produces contrary results; that is to say, the thing that causes one person's happiness causes the unhappiness of another person.

But this has been so in all times, and doubtless it will continue to be so till the end of time, assuming that time is to have an end. Nature loves contrasts; I cannot guess why, but that does not prevent me from believing that she is right, for Nature always does perfectly whatever she does.

It was, then, the year 1818.

In an old mansion in Faubourg Saint-Germain, situated on I do not know what street,—and that is of little importance,—a large company was assembled; they were dancing, enjoying themselves—or, at least, pretending to do so, which is not always the same thing; in short, it was a wedding party, the wedding of Monsieur le Marquis de Grandvilain and Mademoiselle Aménaïde Dufoureau.

There was a choice orchestra, in which, however, there were no cornets, because that instrument had not then acquired a commanding position in our ballrooms; there was a select company also; the dancing was marked by that decency, that gravity, that good-breeding which prevents French dancing from being amusing, and which has given rise to the saying that the merriest people on earth dance with the least indication of merriment.

It is true that since that time a certain much more décolleté dance has found its way from the dance hall to the masked ball, and from the masked ball has insinuated itself into some salons; a dance which would be fascinating, and which would have a genuine character of its own, were it not that most of the people who dance it substitute burlesque for grace and indecency for *abandon*. But that dance was not in evidence at Monsieur le Marquis de Grandvilain's wedding.

And then the bridegroom did not set the example for the dancers; he did not run from one to the other, inviting them to dance and offering them his

3

hand. After opening the ball with his wife, he had thrown himself into an immense easy-chair, contented to watch the others, smiling at the ladies and beating time with his head.

You are surprised without doubt at the bridegroom's behavior, and you would like to know the explanation; your surprise will cease when I tell you that on his wedding day Monsieur de Grandvilain was entering his sixty-ninth year. At that age you will understand that a man is no longer one of those inveterate dancers who refuse to leave the floor, one of those dancers who engage partners for six quadrilles ahead.

Perhaps now you will say that monsieur le marquis was as old for marriage as for balls; that it is folly to marry at sixty-nine years.

In the first place, what do you know about it? Has it ever happened to you? And even if it be folly, what harm is there in it, if it makes one happy? The maddest people are sometimes the wisest. Let us marry so long as we are inclined, and let us dance as long as we can. Cato learned to dance at sixty. Plato praises dancing; and you must be well aware that King David gambolled in front of the Ark of the Covenant. I agree that that was a strange way to manifest his faith and devotion, and I am glad to think that, at all events, David did not know the dance which I have just mentioned.

Let us return to the groom. Monsieur de Grandvilain deserved a different name from the one which he bore: he was of medium height and well proportioned; he had once had a fine figure, and he still possessed a well-shaped leg and sufficient calf for a man about to marry. His face, although it was a little like a sheep's, lacked neither dignity nor charm; his features were regular, his eyes had been very fine, and they had retained an amiable expression; lastly, his smile was still passably mischievous.

You see that that gentleman still retained many good qualities, and that it was very excusable for him to have thought of marrying in order to turn them all to some account.

Aménaïde Dufoureau, who had given her hand to Monsieur de Grandvilain, was entering her forty-fourth year and had hitherto remained single.

Single! do you realize the full force of that word? It indicates an inexperienced heart, an inexperienced soul, an untried love, and charms—like all the rest! A single maiden of forty-four, and a flower that has never been plucked! But what a flower, great heaven! and what a long time it has had to go to seed!

For my part, I confess with all humility that I should prefer ten married women at that age to one flower which has been left so long on its stalk.

Probably Monsieur de Grandvilain did not agree with me. Opinions are free, and if we all had the same opinions, it would be very tiresome, because we should no longer have the pleasure of arguing and disputing.

Monsieur de Grandvilain had known Mademoiselle Aménaïde Dufoureau in 1798. At that time she was only twenty-four years old; it is to be presumed that her heart was at least as fresh as at forty-four; and it is certain that her face was more so.

At that time Aménaïde was a very pretty young woman, slender, graceful and ethereal; her black eyes, level with her face, gleamed with health and animation; her mouth, which was a little large, laughed frequently to display a double row of faultless teeth; and although her nose was a little coarse, her forehead a little low, and her complexion a little dark, Mademoiselle Dufoureau might have passed for a very attractive person.

Monsieur de Grandvilain, who was forty-nine at that time, and considered himself still a young man, because he had retained the tastes and the temperament of a young man, had met Aménaïde in society and had paid court to her; but with the frivolity of a man accustomed to making conquests, with the self-assurance of a rake who had never found women cruel, and with the fatuity of a marquis, who thought that he bestowed much honor upon a young woman of the middle class by allowing his eyes to rest upon her.

Mademoiselle Dufoureau was, in fact, only a simple bourgeoise; her parents, worthy tradespeople, had died, leaving her fifteen hundred francs a year and excellent principles.

The fifteen hundred francs a year was but a slender fortune; but combined with the young lady's virtue and innocence, it formed a marriage portion which some very wealthy young women would be sorely at a loss to offer their husbands.

Monsieur de Grandvilain, still proud and magnificent, fluttered about that flower of twenty-four years.

Mademoiselle Aménaïde found monsieur le marquis very agreeable; she was flattered to be noticed by him; and she even allowed him to see that her heart was not indifferent to his homage. But when she discovered that Monsieur de Grandvilain had no idea of making her a marchioness, she proudly repulsed him, saying:

"For what do you take me, monsieur?"

The marquis, offended by her resistance, turned on his heel, humming a tune from *Blaise et Babet*, an opera-comique, then in great vogue; the operas of those days abounded in tunes which were easily remembered, and were sung and whistled on the streets. Other times, other music!

Monsieur de Grandvilain carried elsewhere his glances, his passions, his homage and his heart. Mademoiselle Aménaïde Dufoureau concealed in the depths of her heart her regrets, her sighs, and her ardor.

Think how fortunate men are! A woman resists them, they simply apply elsewhere, and they always end by finding a place for their love, which they offer to every pretty face they see. They are like those people who have their pockets full of money and say to themselves: "I will buy whatever I please, I will have the best and finest things I can find, for I pay cash!" On the other hand, virtuous women are obliged to ask for credit; for they are willing to promise their love, but they do not propose to give it at once.

Six years passed, during which monsieur le marquis, passing constantly from conquest to conquest, spending his time in a life of pleasure, did not again see poor Aménaïde Dufoureau, who led a very tranquil, very modest life, and did not frequent the society in which Monsieur de Grandvilain moved.

At the end of that time, an outdoor fête in the suburbs of Paris brought about a meeting between those two people who had ceased to seek each other. The marquis still found Aménaïde attractive, and Aménaïde could not restrain a sigh or two, which indicated that the past had not been entirely forgotten.

Once more the marquis played the amiable seducer; he thought that the flower of thirty years would be plucked more easily than that of twenty-four; but he was mistaken; he encountered the same virtue, the same resistance, as before, and yet she did not conceal from him that she loved him. She desired to be a marchioness, however, and she did not propose to give herself to anybody but her husband.

Once more our seducer turned on his heel. He travelled; he was away from France six years. When he returned, he was much less active, much less volatile; his bearing was still distinguished, but his step was slow and heavy. However, although he was then sixty-one years old, the marquis believed himself still to be very fascinating; there are people who refuse to grow old; they are perfectly right, but in that case it is time which is in the wrong.

Monsieur de Grandvilain once more met Aménaïde Dufoureau; she was still unmarried, although she had seen thirty-six springs.—We must never reckon except by springs, for that gives an air of youth.—Had she remained unmarried for lack of opportunity to marry, or because she had preferred to keep her heart for the marquis? We are too gallant not to believe that it was for the last reason, and the marquis probably thought the same, because that flattered his self-esteem.

Aménaïde was no longer so slender, so graceful or so willowy as she was at twenty-four, but she was still fresh enough, and her eyes, while losing their vivacity, had become more tender. Monsieur de Grandvilain, always pleased to meet the only woman over whom he had not triumphed, began again to pay court to the flower of thirty-six years. But he was no more fortunate, and that was certain to be the case. After having had the strength to resist him when he was young and good-looking, it was not probable that she would falter when he was old and faded. Monsieur de Grandvilain, still haughty and pretentious, turned on his heel once more, swearing that he would never return again, and that he would carry his homage elsewhere.

Poor old fellow, who had passed his sixtieth year, and who believed himself still capable of inconstancy! The opportunities to forget Aménaïde no longer offered themselves; time passed and brought no distraction; all the ladies became as cruel to the marquis as Mademoiselle Dufoureau, and our old rake said to himself:

"It is amazing how the fair sex changes! women no longer have such susceptible hearts as they used to have!"

At last the marquis decided to return to Aménaïde; she was approaching her forty-fourth spring, and Monsieur de Grandvilain said to himself:

"If I wait until her springs become more numerous, she will strongly resemble a winter. I am beginning to be old enough to settle down. Mademoiselle Dufoureau is not of noble birth, but she is virtuous; for twenty years she has loved me, and that deserves a reward; I will marry her."

And our lover of sixty-nine years at last offered his hand to the maiden whom he might have married twenty years earlier.

When Mademoiselle Dufoureau heard him offer her his heart and his sixty-nine years, she was tempted to reply:

"It is hardly worth while to marry now!"

But she accepted him; and that is why the wedding of those old lovers was celebrated in the hôtel de Grandvilain, in the year 1818.

II

A LITTLE GRANDVILAIN

When a man marries at sixty-nine, can he look forward to having heirs, to living again in his children? It seems to me not; however, it is probable that such men always look forward to it.

When such a thing happens, when an old man's wife becomes a mother, jests rain down upon the husband; but the puns and jocose remarks go astray sometimes; in such a case, even if you do not choose to believe, it is very difficult to prove that you are wrong.

"An ass can deny more than a philosopher can prove."

About five months after Aménaïde Dufoureau had become Madame de Grandvilain, she went to her husband one morning, blushing, with downcast eyes and an embarrassed air, and informed him that she hoped to present him with a pledge of her love.

Monsieur de Grandvilain uttered a cry of joy; he rose, ran about the room, tried to perform a pirouette, and fell to the floor; but madame assisted him to rise, and he began again to indulge in innumerable follies, for the pleasure he felt made him forget his age. He was proud to have a child, and with good reason, especially as his wife's virtue was like that of Caesar's wife: it was absolutely above suspicion.

From that moment, they devoted all their attention to the child that was not yet born.

Monsieur le marquis was persuaded that it would be a boy. And in order to believe that, he said to himself: "Good fortune never comes singly."

Madame la marquise was overjoyed to have a child. Boy or girl, she was certain of loving it equally; but in order to please her husband she too pretended to count on a boy.

"I will nurse him myself!" cried Aménaïde, smiling at her husband.

"Yes, yes, we will nurse him!" repeated the marquis; "we will raise him better than any nurse could do. What the devil! people like us ought to understand such things better than peasants; we will make a hearty blade of him! for I want my son to resemble his father in everything."

As he spoke, the old marquis stuck out his leg and tried to play the exquisite. Since he had known that his wife was enceinte, he fancied that he was twenty years old once more.

They bought a magnificent layette for the little one which was expected; they made great preparations to receive that scion of Monsieur de Grandvilain becomingly; and the intoxication which they felt was perfectly natural: if a young couple celebrate the birth of their child, surely they have much more reason to do so who have no hope of a repetition of such an occurrence.

As the time approached when madame la marquise was to become a mother, the more her old husband overwhelmed her with attentions and care; it went so far sometimes that Madame de Grandvilain lost her appetite with her freedom of action. Monsieur le marquis would not allow her to go out on foot, he was apprehensive of the least fatigue, he watched to see that she ate nothing that might injure her; and his espionage became sheer cruelty to her who was the object of it, for the marquis detected peril in the simplest thing, and it was at once irrevocably forbidden; so that, toward the end of her pregnancy, Madame de Grandvilain was given nothing but bread soup, the only sort of food which, according to Monsieur de Grandvilain, was not dangerous for his wife. There was a physician in attendance on the marchioness who prescribed an entirely different diet; but the marquis depended more on himself than on the physician, and as he grew older, he became very obstinate.

The great day arrived at last; and it was high time, for the poor marchioness was not at all reconciled to eating nothing but bread soup. Aménaïde brought a son into the world.

Monsieur de Grandvilain did not feel strong enough to remain with his wife while she was in the pains of childbirth; but a servant, who had first been a jockey, then a groom, then his master's valet, and who had now reached the age of fifty years, hastened to carry him the great news.

When he caught sight of his old Jasmin, whose red and blotched face wore a more stupid expression than usual, the marquis cried:

"Well, is it all over, Jasmin?"

"Yes, monsieur le marquis, it's done! Ah! we had a very hard time, but it's all right at last."

Everyone knows that the old servants in great families are in the habit of saying *we*, when speaking of their master's affairs, and Monsieur de Grandvilain forgave his former jockey for employing that form of expression.

"What! it is all over, Jasmin? Ah! the poor marchioness! But go on, you villain! what is it?"

"It is something magnificent, monsieur, you will be well pleased!"

"But the sex, you rascal, the sex; hasn't the child any sex?"

"Oh! yes, indeed! a superb sex! we have been delivered of a boy, my dear master."

"A boy, Jasmin? a boy! Oh! what happiness! but I said so; I was sure of it; I would have bet on it; don't I always know what I am doing?"

"You are very clever, monsieur le marquis."

"A boy—I have a son—I have an heir to my name! Jasmin, I will give you a present of ten crowns for bringing me this good news."

"Thanks, my dear master. Vive les Grandvilains!"

"I have a boy—such pleasure—such—Ah! I can't stand it any longer. Jasmin, pass me my phial of salts—no, give me a small glass of madeira; I feel as if my heart were stopping."

"Come, come, monsieur le marquis, pull yourself together," said Jasmin, as he handed a glass of madeira to his master. "This is not the time to be ill."

"You are right; but what can you expect?—the shock, the joy—This is the first time I have ever been a father,—to my knowledge, at least—and it produces such an impression! Pray tell me some details while I recover myself; for I haven't the strength to go to my wife as yet."

"Well, monsieur le marquis, understand that I had stationed myself outside madame's door, so that I might come and tell you as soon as the child was born; for I thought that you would be impatient to know about it."

"Very good, Jasmin; go on, go on."

"After some time I heard cries. I was tempted to run away, but I held my ground, and to give myself courage, I took a good pinch of snuff. Suddenly the door opened; it was the doctor. He was looking for someone; he saw me and motioned for me to go in. I obeyed."

"What! you went into madame la marquise's room, you rascal, while——"

"No, monsieur, I stayed in the little reception room. Everybody was excited; the nurse, the lady's maid,—that great idiot of a Turlurette had chosen to be ill instead of making herself useful——"

"That proves her attachment to my wife; go on."

"I beg pardon, monsieur, I must blow my nose first. Well, I was called to help Turlurette; and as I was much more anxious about madame, I asked:

"'First tell me if we are delivered.'

"'Yes,' the doctor replied.

"'Well then, what have we?'

"'Look, you idiot.'

"As he spoke, the doctor put a little bundle in my arms. Just imagine, monsieur, that at first I thought it was a cheese. It was round and it had a funny smell; but on looking at it closely, I found it was a little boy, just out of his shell."

"What does this mean, Jasmin? What! it was my son that you mistook for a cheese?"

"Bless my soul! when one has never seen a new-born child before, monsieur,—and it was the first one that I ever saw."

"Take my son for a cheese! You are a stupid lout, and you shall have no present!"

"O monsieur le marquis! it isn't that I regret the money, but I didn't think that I had deserved your anger; especially, as on looking at the little boy that I had in my arms, I saw with delight that he has all our features—he is the living image of us!"

"What! the living image of *us*!—Have you been drinking, Jasmin?"

"Pardon me, monsieur le marquis, but it is my affection that carries me away! When I say we, my dear master knows very well that I mean him! In fact, it is your noble face, monsieur, your fine aquiline nose, your pretty little chin; and he will have your fine teeth, which you no longer have. I would bet that he will have them."

The old marquis could not help smiling, and he replied in a milder tone:

"The dear child!—Well, I promised you a present, and you shall have it. I know that you are a faithful servant, my poor Jasmin, but you should be careful what you say when you are speaking of your master's son."

"The little fellow is a real Love, monsieur. Ah! if I could have suckled him, how happy I would have been!"

"I feel strong enough to go to see my wife and my son now. Come, Jasmin, escort me."

"Yes, monsieur, let us go to see our child."

The old marquis, overjoyed to be born again at seventy, rose, took his valet's arm, and tried to run to his wife's apartment; but as both master and servant were heavy of foot, their progress was confined to a rather swift walk, which did not, however, prevent them from being out of breath when they reached the marchioness's room.

Monsieur hastened forward to embrace madame, shedding tears of joy; and in his emotion, he fell upon her bed, from which they had all the difficulty in the world to raise him, because happiness changed his legs and arms to cotton. When they had succeeded in placing Monsieur de Grandvilain in a chair, he asked for a glass of madeira in order to restore his strength and put him in a condition to embrace his son. Jasmin went again to fetch the madeira; he filled a glass for his master, and one for himself also, to drink which he retired behind a long window curtain, finding that he too needed to replenish his strength.

"And now, where is my son?" said the marquis in a trembling voice, glancing about the room.

"He will be brought to you in a moment, monsieur," said the buxom Turlurette; "the nurse is fixing him to show you."

"I don't want him to be dressed," said the marquis; "on the contrary, I want to see him naked; then I shall be better able to judge of his strength, of his constitution."

"Yes, yes," said Jasmin, "we shall be very glad to see what we have made!"

"You hear, Turlurette,—tell the nurse to bring me my son as naked as a worm."

"Yes, let her bring him to us at once, like a savage, without any fig-leaf."

"Jasmin, will you be good enough to keep your tongue quiet for a moment?"

"I beg pardon, monsieur le marquis; it is my impatience to admire our dear love."

Turlurette made haste to perform her errand, and the nurse soon appeared, carrying before her a large basin, wherein the new-born child, entirely naked, moved about and stretched out at pleasure its little pink and white limbs.

The nurse handed the child to the marquis, as the keys of a city used in the old days to be presented to a conqueror.

At sight of his son, Monsieur de Grandvilain uttered a joyful cry, and put out his arms to take him; but his emotion caused another attack of faintness; he had not the strength to take the child, but fell back in his chair. Meanwhile, the nurse, thinking that the father was going to take what she held out to him, had relaxed her hold of the child and the basin alike, and both would have fallen to the floor if stout Turlurette had not luckily caught the child by the part which presented itself first to her grasp.

The bowl fell to the floor and broke into a thousand pieces. When she heard the crash, madame la marquise thought that her son was killed.

"My child! what has happened to him?"

"Nothing, madame," said Turlurette, giving the little boy to her mistress; "he didn't fall; I caught him by—I got hold of him."

"The dear love! I had a terrible fright!—Great heaven! Turlurette, what a very strange way to hold the child!"

"Bless me! it's very lucky that I caught hold of him as I did! If it hadn't been so, he might have fallen with the basin, and God knows if he wouldn't have been smashed like it."

While all this was taking place, Jasmin, seeing his master lying back in his chair, pale and trembling, hastily poured out another glass of madeira for him, and then retired behind the curtain once more.

Monsieur de Grandvilain, having recovered his strength for the third time, took the child whom Turlurette still held, and embraced him heartily; then held him up in the air, exclaiming:

"So this is my son! my heir! Corbleu! I was sure that I should have a son."

But the marchioness, fearing that her husband would faint again, and that he would then drop the child altogether, begged him to sit down beside her bed; Monsieur de Grandvilain complied, and then began to turn the child over and over, scrutinizing every part.

"What a lovely child!" he cried; "and to think that I begot him!"

"Yes, we begot him!" muttered Jasmin, who stood behind his master's chair, with the bottle of madeira in his hand, in case of an emergency.

"How plump and pink he is; what pretty little calves!"

"Faith, I haven't as much calf as that now!" said Jasmin, glancing at his own legs.

"What a pretty little round head!"

"One would swear that it was a Dutch cheese," muttered Jasmin; but luckily for him, his master did not hear his reflection that time, or it would have caused the suppression of his present for good and all.

"He is built like an Apollo!—and he has—why, it is herculean! Look, Jasmin,—see how—how he has developed already!"

"It is marvelous," said Jasmin, who, after examining the proportions of the child, made mentally the same reflection that he had made on the subject of his legs.

After Monsieur de Grandvilain had thoroughly scrutinized his son *per fas et nefas*, he handed him to his spouse, saying:

"By the way, my dear love, what shall we call him?"

"That is what I have been thinking of, my dear husband, ever since he was born."

"My son must have a noble name. My own name is Sigismond; that is a good name, but I don't like the idea of sons having their fathers' names; that leads to mistakes, until you don't know where you are."

"Listen, monsieur le marquis, the most appropriate name for the dear love would be Chérubin. What do you say to that? Isn't it a very pretty name?"

"Chérubin!" said the marquis, shaking his head; "that is very girlish; there is nothing warlike about it."

"Why, monsieur, what's the necessity of giving a warrior's name to our son? That would have been very well in Napoléon's time, but now it is no longer the fashion; let us call our son Chérubin, I beg you!"

"Marchioness," replied the marquis, kissing his wife's hand, "you have given me a son and I can refuse you nothing. His name shall be Chérubin; that rather reminds one of the *Mariage de Figaro*; but after all, Beaumarchais's Chérubin is an attractive little rascal; all the women dote on him, and it would not be a bad thing if our son should resemble the little page."

"Yes, yes," murmured Jasmin, who stood behind his master's chair, swaying from side to side, for the visits behind the curtain had begun to make his legs unsteady. "Yes, Chérubin is very nice; it rhymes with Jasmin."

The marquis turned, and was tempted to strike his servant; but he, finding that he had made another foolish speech, assumed such a piteous expression that his master simply said to him:

"You are impertinent beyond all bounds to-day, Jasmin!"

"I beg pardon, monsieur le marquis, it is my delight, my enthusiasm. I am so happy, that it seems to me that everything in the room is dancing."

At that moment Turlurette appeared and said that all the servants in the house had assembled and requested permission to offer their mistress a bouquet, and their master their congratulations.

The marquis ordered his servants to be admitted.

They arrived in single file, and Jasmin, as the oldest, at once placed himself at their head and began a complimentary harangue of which he could not find the end, because he lost control of his tongue. But he made the best of it, and cut his speech short by crying:

"Long live monsieur le marquis's son and his august family!"

All the servants repeated this cry, tossing their hats or caps into the air. Once more Monsieur de Grandvilain was deeply moved, tears came to his eyes, and, fearing another attack of weakness, he motioned to Jasmin, who, anticipating his command, instantly handed him a glass of madeira.

The marquis drank it; then he thanked his people, gave them money and sent them away to drink to the health of the newly-born. Jasmin left the room with them, carrying a bottle of madeira, the rest of which he drank before he joined his comrades. And that evening, the marquis's valet was completely drunk, and monsieur le marquis had himself taken something to restore his strength so frequently, that he was obliged to retire immediately on leaving the dinner table.

But one does not have a child every day, especially when one has reached the age of seventy years.

III

JASMIN ARRANGES A SURPRISE

Little Chérubin's baptism took place a few days after his birth; on that occasion there were more festivities in the old mansion.

The marquis was open-handed and generous; those qualities are ordinarily found in libertines. He spent money lavishly, and told Jasmin to despoil the cellar. The valet, whose blotched nose betrayed his favorite passion, promised his master to carry out his orders to the letter.

A select and fashionable company came to attend the baptism of little Chérubin. The salons were resplendent with light; the guests chatted, played cards, and then went to see the mother, and to admire her little one—but not more than two at a time, for such was the doctor's order.

The child, who had come into the world so plump and fresh and rosy, was beginning to grow thin and yellow; one could still rave over his pretty face, but no longer over his health.

And yet the marquis's son was the object of the incessant care of his mother, who had the most intense affection for him, who kept him constantly by her side, and would not allow him to be out of her sight for a single moment.

All this was very well; but children are not to be brought up with affection, caresses, kisses and sweet words: nature demands a more substantial nourishment; now, that which madame la marquise supplied to her first-born was evidently of poor quality, and not only was not abundant but was exceedingly deficient in quantity. In short, whether because the bread soup diet had impaired Madame de Grandvilain's health—which was very probable —or for some entirely different reason, concealed or apparent, it was a fact that little Chérubin's mamma had only a very little wretched milk to give her son, who had come into the world with a hearty appetite.

Jean-Jacques Rousseau said that a mother should nurse her child, that it was a crime to put the poor little creatures in the hands of mercenary persons who could not have a mother's affection for them and simply made a business of hiring out their bodies; and in support of that argument he cited the animals, which nurse their young themselves and never seek others to replace them.

But, in the first place, we might remind Jean-Jacques that animals lead a regular life—regular, that is to say, according to their nature and their physical strength. Have you ever heard of lionesses, she-bears, or cats even, passing their nights at balls, giving receptions, and dining out frequently? I think not; nor have I!

We may be allowed then to insist upon a difference between animals and men; and despite our profound regard for the philosopher of Geneva, we will say to him further, that in this world of ours there are positions, trades, branches of business, which make it impossible for a woman to perform that maternal duty to which he insists that all women should submit. When a woman, in order to earn her living, is obliged to sit all day at a desk, or to work constantly with her needle, how do you expect her to take her child in her arms every instant? There is a still stronger reason for her not doing it, if her health is poor and failing.

Nurses sell their milk, you say, and never have a mother's affection for a strange child.

In the first place, it is not proved that a nurse does not love her nursling dearly; there is every reason to believe, on the contrary, that she becomes attached to the little creature whose life she sustains; and after all, even if it were simply a matter of business, has the baker any affection for the people to whom he sells bread? But that does not prevent us from living on that bread.

Philosophers, men of genius, aye, even the greatest men, sometimes put forth propositions which are far from being orthodox; and they make mistakes like other men.

But there are people who take for very noble thoughts everything which comes from the pen of a man who has written great things. Such people are very generous. We rarely find gold without alloy; and can man produce what Nature cannot produce? There are people also, who, when they walk through a cemetery, believe in the truth of all the inscriptions carved upon the tombs, according to which the people there interred were models of virtue, goodness, uprightness, etc., etc. I have infinite respect for the dead, but I do not see the necessity of trying to deceive the living. Those who are no more were no better than we, and we are no better than those who will come after us.

We were saying then that little Chérubin was no longer as beautiful as an angel, although he bore the name of one; but that did not prevent all those who went to pay their respects to the mother from complimenting her upon her child. Honest Aménaïde listened with a sweet smile to all the flattering words which were addressed to her son. Meanwhile, Monsieur de Grandvilain lay back in an easy-chair, patted his legs, and shook his head, and looked at the ladies with an air which seemed almost to say:

"When you want one like him, apply to me."

Luckily for him, none of the ladies was tempted to put him to the proof.

About ten o'clock in the evening, just as the doctor was urging Madame de Grandvilain not to admit any more people to her room, and to try to sleep, there was a sudden uproar in the courtyard, and a bright light shone in the windows; then, something as brilliant as lightning shot through the air.

It was the work of Jasmin, who, to celebrate the baptism of his master's son, had conceived the idea of a display of fireworks in the courtyard, in order to afford the marquis and all his guests a pleasant surprise; and who had just discharged a mortar and then a rocket, to attract everybody to the windows.

In fact, the explosion of the mortar had caused a profound sensation in the house; everyone thought it was the roar of cannon; the mother leaped up in her bed, the child in its cradle, monsieur le marquis in his chair, and all the guests, wherever they were. They gazed at each other with a terrified expression, saying:

"What is it? What a noise! It is cannon! There must be fighting in Paris!"

"Fighting?"

"Great heaven! can it be that the usurper has come back again?"

Remember that this happened in the year 1819, and that in the mansions of Faubourg Saint-Germain, Napoléon was ordinarily referred to as the usurper.

There was a moment of confusion in the salon; some of the men talked of running to arms, others looked about for their hats, the women ran after the men, or prepared to faint, and some talked in undertones, in corners, with young men, whom, up to that time, they had pretended barely to look at.

There are people who make the most of every opportunity and turn every circumstance to advantage. Such people are necessarily those who have the most presence of mind.

Amid the commotion, they heard a shrill voice in the courtyard:

"We are going to discharge a few fireworks in honor of the baptism, and to celebrate the birth, of the son of our worthy master, Monsieur le Marquis de Grandvilain and Madame la Marquise de Grandvilain, his spouse."

No sooner were these words heard, than a sudden change took place on every face, except those of the people who were talking in corners. The men laughed uproariously, the ladies threw aside the shawls and hats which they had hastily donned, and ran to look at themselves in the mirrors, for coquetry is the first sentiment that wakes in the ladies when the others are still benumbed. Then everybody ran to the windows, saying:

"Fireworks! it is fireworks! Oh! what a delightful surprise!"

"Yes," said the old Marquis de Grandvilain, who had been more frightened than all the others together, "yes, it is a pleasant idea of that devil of a Jasmin. But he ought to have notified me that he intended to surprise me, for then I should have expected it, and it would have—have surprised me less."

The guests were all at the windows, the ladies in front, the men behind them, so that they were obliged to lean over a little to see; but everybody seemed well pleased, and nobody would have changed his place for another.

The marquis sat alone at a window in his wife's room.

"You will not be able to see the pieces down below, my dear love," he said, "but I will explain them to you, and you will be able to see the rockets and serpents perfectly from your bed."

"Suppose it frightens Chérubin?" said the marchioness, placing her son's cradle at the foot of the bed.

"Don't be afraid, marchioness; my son will take after me, he will love the noise and smell of powder."

Meanwhile, Jasmin, who had followed his master's orders by levying freely on the cellar, and had made himself, as well as his comrades, very nearly tipsy, seemed to have gone back to his twentieth year; he walked about the courtyard, amid the fireworks, like a general amid his troops.

In the farthest corner of the courtyard the mortars had been placed; they were the heavy artillery, and no more were to be fired until the finale. But as sparks, falling in that direction, might land inside the mortars and set them off before the time for which they were held in reserve, the cook, who was a careful man, and who was acting as Jasmin's second in command, had brought from his kitchen saucepan covers, a frying-pan, and a dish-pan, and had placed them over the mortars, which were made like stove pipes, but of different dimensions, according to the amount of powder they contained: so that the frying-pan was placed on the largest one, the dish-pan on a smaller size, and the saucepan covers on the smallest ones, all to prevent sparks or lighted fragments of rockets from falling into the mortars.

Jasmin glanced from window to window; he waited till everybody was placed before beginning.

The cook, who was no less impatient than the old valet, and whose brain was excited by the marquis's wine, stood near the fireworks with a lighted slow-match in one hand, while with the other he pushed his cotton cap over his left ear.

Meanwhile, stout Turlurette and two other servants were dancing about a transparency representing a moon, which Jasmin declared to be a portrait of young Chérubin.

"They are all there! everybody's at the windows, and we can set them off," said Jasmin, after a last glance at the house.

"Yes, yes, begin," said Turlurette. "Oh! isn't it going to be fine?"

"No women here!" cried the cook in a determined tone; "you will make us do some foolish thing; go up to the second floor, young women."

"Oh! he told me that he would let me fire off one little petard at least; didn't you, Monsieur Jasmin?"

"Yes, yes," cried Jasmin; "everybody must have a good time to-day; it is for our young master! Turlurette shall fire a little rocket; that is the least we can do for her; but not now, later.—Ready, cook, let us begin; to our fireworks!"

The display began with a serpent or two, Bengal fire, and rockets; the guests looked on, and when any piece seemed to be aimed at a window, the ladies drew back with little exclamations of alarm, blended with bursts of laughter; the men encouraged them, taking their hands and pressing them; I am not sure that they took nothing else; however, the ladies consented to be reassured, resumed their places, applauded and were highly pleased; while the old marquis at his window, said to his wife:

"My dear love, it is superb! it is beautiful! it is dazzling! I am sorry that you are so far away."

"But, my dear, suppose it should set the house on fire!"

"Don't be afraid; Jasmin is prudent; he has undoubtedly notified the firemen at the station close by; besides, the courtyard is very large and there is no danger."

The loving Aménaïde was not thoroughly comforted; she would have preferred that there should be no fireworks to celebrate the baptism; but everybody seemed pleased, and she dared not deprive the company of the pleasure which they took in the spectacle.

Soon applause rose on all sides; Jasmin had just lighted the transparency with the moon, calling out as he did so:

"A portrait of our child, young Chérubin de Grandvilain."

At that everybody applauded on trust, although they squinted in vain to discover a face painted in the moon on the transparency; but they ascribed that to the smoke, and several persons went so far as to cry out:

"It is very like, on my word! anyone could recognize it! A very pretty idea! such things as this are not seen anywhere except at the Marquis de Grandvilain's."

While the company was admiring the transparency, Mademoiselle Turlurette, still intent upon her idea of setting off something, went to Jasmin and said:

"Give me your slow-match, it's my turn; what am I going to set off?"

"Here, Mademoiselle Turlurette, set fire to this sun. But aren't you afraid?"

"Me, afraid! oh, no! just show me where to light it."

"See, here is the match."

Stout Turlurette took the slow-match which Jasmin handed to her, and held it to the wick which protruded from the sun. Despite all the courage which she was determined to display, the stout girl was terribly excited, for she had never set off a piece of fireworks before. After she had touched the match which she had in her hand to the place pointed out to her, when she heard the powder hiss and the flame sputter close beside her, a sudden terror took possession of Turlurette; fancying that she was being burned by the sparks from the sun, she ran across the courtyard, holding her dress up with one hand, as if she were trying to make a belt of it, and with her lighted slow-match still in the other. The latter she threw down, without looking, in the first convenient spot.

The sun produced a great effect; it whirled about like a top, and everybody at the windows applauded. Some said:

"It is as pretty as at Tivoli."

Another exclaimed:

"It is almost as fine as the fireworks we have at our house, in my park, on my birthday."

And the old marquis leaned far out of the window, crying:

"Bravo! I am much pleased, my children! You may regale yourselves again after the fireworks."

But Monsieur de Grandvilain had hardly ceased speaking when there was a terrible report, and the old mansion was shaken to its foundation; it was caused by all the mortars, large and small, exploding at the same moment, because stout Turlurette, in her alarm, had thrown her slow-match into the midst of the heavy pieces which were reserved for the finale.

If the mortars had simply been discharged, nothing worse would have happened than the premature occurrence of an explosion held in reserve for the end of the fête; but unfortunately, when they took fire, they were still covered by the various kitchen implements which the cook had placed over them as a precautionary measure; and at the same moment that the sudden report took everybody by surprise, even those who were managing the fireworks, the frying-pan, the dish-pan, and the saucepan covers were hurled through the air with terrific force.

Monsieur de Grandvilain, who had just been thanking his servants, had an ear carried away by the frying-pan, which entered the bedroom and fell at the foot of his wife's bed. Several of the guests were struck by saucepan covers; a pretty woman had four teeth broken, a young dandy who was leaning over her had his nose split in the middle, which gave him later the appearance of a Danish dog; and on all sides there was nothing but shrieks, lamentations and imprecations. Even those who had sustained no injury shouted louder than the others:

"This is what comes of allowing servants to discharge fireworks. The cook put all his cooking utensils in the mortars; it is very lucky that it didn't occur to him to blow up his ovens."

The guests had had quite enough; they all took their leave, some to have their wounds dressed, others to tell of what had taken place at Monsieur de Grandvilain's.

During the disaster, Jasmin had received the dish-pan on his head, after it had made an excursion through the air; and the faithful valet's face was covered with burns and bore a striking resemblance to a skimmer. That did not prevent him from appearing with a piteous air before his master, who was looking for his ear.

"Monsieur," said the valet, "I am in despair; I don't understand how it all came about—but it wasn't finished; there is the bouquet to come—and if you would like——"

The marquis, in a frenzy of rage, raised his cane upon Jasmin, and would listen to no more; while Madame de Grandvilain half rose in her bed and said to the poor valet in an imposing voice:

"In my husband's name, I forbid you henceforth to fire anything of any sort in our house."

IV

A NEW WAY OF BRINGING UP CHILDREN

The display of fireworks for little Chérubin's baptism put an end to all the festivities at the hôtel de Grandvilain. The marquis succeeded in finding his ear, but it was impossible to put it in place again, so that he was obliged to resign himself to the necessity of closing his career with a single ear, a most disagreeable thing when one has worn two for seventy years.

Aménaïde had conceived a horror of fireworks, rockets, in fact, of the slightest explosion; the most trifling noise made her faint; it went so far that nobody was allowed to uncork a bottle in her presence.

Jasmin continued to wear the aspect of a skimmer, but he soon consoled himself therefor; the old valet had long since laid aside all pretension to please the fair sex; the little holes with which his face was riddled did not interfere with his drinking, and to him that was the principal point.

Mademoiselle Turlurette had received no wound, and yet she deserved better than any of the others to be struck by a saucepan cover at least, for she was the author of all the disasters that had happened in the house. But no one suspected how the thing took place, and Turlurette confined herself to expressing the most profound detestation of fireworks.

And so tranquillity had returned to the hôtel de Grandvilain, where they received many fewer guests since the last festivity; for the young women and the dandies feared to lose their teeth, or to have their noses slit.

The marquis was at liberty to devote all his time to the care of his son, and little Chérubin demanded much care; for he became weak and sickly and sallow, and at three months he was vastly smaller than when he came into the world. Turlurette, who had weighed him at that time, was certain of the fact, and one day she said to Jasmin in an undertone:

"It's very funny, but madame's boy is melting away, so that you can see it! He weighs five ounces less to-day than he did the day he was born!"

Jasmin gave a leap when he heard that his master's child was melting away instead of increasing in size, and he said to Turlurette:

"If this goes on, before long he won't weigh anything at all. You must tell madame that the little fellow is falling off."

"Oh, yes! so that madame may torment herself, and so that she won't be able to feed her son at all. No indeed, I will take pains not to tell her."

"But, mademoiselle, it's for the child's good!"

"But I don't choose to make madame feel badly."

Jasmin made up his mind like a devoted servant: he went to his master. Monsieur de Grandvilain was lying on his couch, enveloped in his morning gown; his head was covered with a jaunty green velvet cap, which he was careful to place over the ear which he no longer had. For some time the old marquis had had the habit of moving his jaws, as one does when one is sucking or eating something, and that constant movement gave his face the appearance of a nut-cracker. Those persons who were not aware of this trick of the marquis, waited, before speaking to him, for him to finish swallowing what he was chewing; but they waited in vain, for the jaws continued to make the same movement.

Since the occasion of the fireworks, Monsieur de Grandvilain had treated his valet with less affability. However, Jasmin's face bore so many scars that his master could hardly bear him ill-will for an accident of which he had been the second victim.

"What do you want of me, Jasmin?" said Monsieur de Grandvilain, when he saw that his valet stood before him with an embarrassed air.

"Monsieur, I hope that you will excuse me for what I am going to say, but it is my attachment for you and our young marquis that has decided me to speak."

"I am aware of your attachment, Jasmin, although the proofs of it which you have given me have sometimes had unfortunate results."

As he spoke, Monsieur de Grandvilain scratched the place where his ear should have been.

"Well, what have you to tell me?"

Jasmin glanced about him, walked closer to his master, and said in a low voice and with a mysterious air:

"Let me tell you, monsieur, that your son is melting——"

The old man fell back on his couch and gazed anxiously at his servant, exclaiming:

"Melting! my son! Great heaven! has he fallen into the stove?"

"When I say melting, my dear master, I mean simply falling away, that he has lost five ounces, neither more nor less, since the day he was born."

"The devil take you, Jasmin, you gave me a horrible fright! I wonder if you will never be any less stupid!"

"It was my attachment for you, monsieur, that made me think that I ought to tell you. Turlurette has weighed our little Chérubin, and she is sure of what she says. She doesn't dare to tell madame, but I thought it was better to tell you; for if the child goes on like this, in a few months he won't weigh anything at all."

Monsieur de Grandvilain sadly shook his head.

"In truth," he said, "my son is not making any progress. He is taking on a yellowish color that surprises me, for both his mother and I are very white. Ah! my poor Jasmin, I am beginning to think that we should have children when we are young, because then they inherit our strength."

"Nonsense, monsieur! You are strong enough! You are a perfect horse when you choose! Our Chérubin was magnificent when he was born, as you must remember. If he is doing badly now, it's only because he doesn't eat enough. Madame fondles him and pets him—that's all very well; but perhaps the little rascal would prefer some wine and a cutlet."

"A cutlet! Are you mad, Jasmin? Whoever heard of giving cutlets to children three months old?"

"Perhaps it would be better for them than milk, no one knows. If I was a nurse, I'd try the experiment."

"In truth, Jasmin, you recall to my mind the fact that the grandfather of our good Henri IV gave his son wine to drink a few moments after he was born; and it did the child no harm; far from it, for Henri IV was a regular devil in every way. Judging from that, I believe that my son, who is past three months, might safely swallow a drop of generous wine."

"Surely, monsieur, wine can never do any harm, and you have such good wine! Our little Chérubin, instead of turning yellow, will become a very devil like the great king; and if with that you would venture to let him suck a cutlet ——"

"The wine will be enough, with a little beef juice perhaps. If only madame la marquise will consent to let the child change his food!"

"Why, look you, monsieur, the little fellow is our son, after all! If madame doesn't give him enough to eat, we have the right to do as we please. Deuce take it! A man doesn't have a child every day, and if you should have to try it over again, I think that——"

"Yes, Jasmin, yes, I will be firm. As my heir's welfare is at stake, I will show my strength of character."

And monsieur le marquis, rising from his couch, betook himself to his wife's apartment, leaning on the arm of Jasmin, who repeated constantly on the way:

"Give him wine to drink, monsieur, give him some good strong soups to eat, and I will bet that within a month he will have recovered his five ounces!"

Madame de Grandvilain had not dared to confess to her husband that she had no milk to give their son; she had bought nursing bottles, and when the marquis was not there, the child was given the bottle; but as soon as his father arrived, she played nurse again, and little Chérubin was given a sterile bosom, which supplied him with no nourishment.

When Monsieur de Grandvilain unexpectedly entered madame's chamber, as she was not looking for her husband at that moment, she did not have time to put the bottle out of the way, and Chérubin was still attached to it.

"What's this, my dear love?" said monsieur le marquis, scrutinizing what his son was sucking.

"My dear," said madame, sorely confused, "it's a supplement."

"A supplement! The deuce, my dear love, you use a supplement, and without letting me know?"

"My dear, there are times when my milk doesn't flow freely, and we must not let this dear little fellow suffer on that account."

"Certainly not, madame, but if you had only confessed to me sooner that you use a supplement, I, for my part, should not have hesitated to tell you that I wished to change our son's diet. He is not making progress, marchioness, that is evident. I believe that milk is not what he needs. I am less surprised since I find that it is not yours. In short, I propose to try another method; I propose to give my son wine to drink."

"Wine, my dear! Can you think of such a thing! A child of three months!"

"Who was magnificent when he came into the world, and who is visibly pining away with your bottle. I will give him claret, that is a mild and generous wine. If that works well, later we will try burgundy."

"But, monsieur, on the contrary, the very lightest things, ass's milk, is what Chérubin needs!"

"Ass's milk for my son! Fie, madame! I will not listen to such a thing. Can it be that you would like to make an ass of him? He shall drink wine."

"He shall drink milk."

For the first time the husband and wife quarrelled, and neither of them would give way.

Monsieur de Grandvilain took his son in his arms, carried him to his room, ordered Jasmin to bring a bottle of old claret, and gave some spoonfuls of it to his heir.

The child swallowed the wine without making too wry a face; in a few moments his little cheeks flushed, and the old valet, who was assisting his master to pour wine into little Chérubin, exclaimed:

"Look, monsieur le marquis, look! already our son's color is coming back! He is better already, and recovering his strength. Oh! what an excellent idea it was to give him wine! Let us go on, master. He turns his eyes toward us; I think that he wants some more."

Monsieur de Grandvilain thought that it was better to be prudent the first time and not to make the dose too large; so he returned to his wife and gave her the child, saying:

"Madame, Chérubin is better already; his color has come back and his eyes shine like diamonds. I shall continue what I have begun to-day, and you will see that our heir will be the better for it."

Madame made no reply, but as soon as her husband had left the room, she called Turlurette and said to her:

"Dear Turlurette, just see what a state they have put this poor little fellow in! He smells frightfully of wine, and I believe that he is tipsy!"

"Why, yes, he really is, madame," cried the stout girl, after smelling the child. "That old idiot of a Jasmin is responsible for all this; he's a sot himself, and he would like to make everybody drink, even a nursing child. If you take my advice, madame, you will give the child some syrup of ipecac. That will make him throw up the wine; it will purge him."

"No, Turlurette, no! I am afraid of doing my son an injury, and of angering monsieur le marquis. But I am going to give the dear little fellow some ass's milk, and that will correct the ill effects of the wine."

The ass's milk was offered to the child in the bottle. Little Chérubin drank it without objection, for he had an excellent disposition; he accepted whatever was offered him, so that the important thing was to offer him what would be good for him.

This system of nourishment was continued for several days. The marquis gave his son wine to drink and madame gave him ass's milk. The child was very red when he left his father's hands, but he became very pale again with his mother. They soon discovered that the dear boy was out of order, and stout Turlurette added the syringe to all the other remedies; and Jasmin, determined at all risks to fatten the little Grandvilain, gave him a piece of pie crust, or a slice of sausage, as soon as he was left alone with him.

Before little Chérubin had been on this diet of ass's milk, pie crust and syringes a month, instead of growing fat, he was in a shocking condition. The marchioness wept, and Monsieur de Grandvilain decided to send for a doctor. After examining the child and learning all that they had been doing to nourish him, the doctor exclaimed in a very severe tone:

"Allow me to inform you that, if you go on like this, in a week you will not have any child."

The marchioness sobbed, the marquis turned green, and they both cried in one breath:

"What must we do, doctor, to restore our child's health?"

"What must you do? Why give him a nurse, a good nurse, and send him into the country with her, and leave him there a long while, a very long while; that's what you must do, and at once, this very day; you have no time to waste if you want to preserve the life of this child."

The tone in which the doctor spoke admitted no reply; luckily their love for the child was above all self-esteem, so they were fain to agree that they had done wrong, and to obey in all haste.

The marquis sent all his people in search of a nurse. The marchioness herself went about among her acquaintances, asking for information and advice; but the time passed, and those who were well recommended could not be obtained at once. As evening approached, they had not succeeded in finding a nurse; the marchioness and her husband embraced their child and had no idea what to give him, as they dared not continue to feed him as they had been doing.

Suddenly Jasmin appeared with a fresh, buxom, red-cheeked peasant woman, exclaiming:

"I have found what we want, I think; if she doesn't bring our little one back to life, faith, I will have nothing more to do with it."

The nurse whom Jasmin had brought had such an attractive face and seemed to enjoy such excellent health that they were prepossessed in her favor. Madame de Grandvilain uttered a joyful cry and handed her child to the peasant woman, who presented her bosom to him; he took it greedily, like one who had found what he needed.

The marquis tapped Jasmin on the shoulder, saying:

"You are an invaluable fellow! How did you go to work to discover this excellent nurse?"

"How did I go to work, monsieur? Why, I just went to the office, on Rue Sainte-Apolline, and asked for a nurse; I saw nurses of all colors, and I chose this one. That's all the difficulty there was about it."

What Jasmin had done was the simplest thing to do, but ordinarily the simplest thing is what nobody thinks of doing.

Little Chérubin's nurse was from Gagny, and as the doctor's orders were definite, she returned to her village the next morning, carrying with her a superb layette, money, gifts, strict orders, and her little nursling.

V

THE VILLAGE OF GAGNY

Gagny is a pretty village near Villemonble, of which it is a sort of continuation, and is a little nearer Paris than Montfermeil. When I say that it is a pretty village, I do not mean by that that the streets are very straight and well paved, and that all the houses have a uniform, comfortable, or even elegant aspect; in that case, it would resemble a small provincial town, and would not be the country with its picturesqueness and its freedom from constraint.

What I like in a village is the mixture of architectural styles, the very irregularity of the buildings, which is such a pleasant change from the monotony of the streets of a capital. What I like to see in a village is the farmhouse and all its outbuildings, the pond in which ducks are splashing, the dung-heap with the hens pecking about it; and then the cottage of the well-to-do peasant, who has had his shutters painted green, and who allows the vines to climb all about the windows; the thatched roof of a laborer not far from the fine house of a wealthy bourgeois; the charming villa of one of our Parisian celebrities; the humble dwelling of the market gardener; the schoolhouse, the church and its belfry; and in the midst of all these, tall trees, paths bordered by hedges of elderberry or wild fruit; hens and roosters strutting fearlessly before the house; ruddy-cheeked, merry, healthy children playing in the middle of the streets or squares, with nothing to fear from carriages and omnibuses; and even the odor of the cow barn, when I pass by a dairyman's place; because all these remind you that you are really in the country; and when you truly love the country, you have a sense of well-being, a feeling of happiness, the effects of which you at once realize without any need to try to explain them—effects which you owe to the pure air which you breathe, to the rustic scenes which rest your eyes, and to the pleasant freedom which you enjoy!

Gagny offers you all these things. Situated as it is near Raincy, the forest of Bondy, and the lovely woods of Montfermeil, and only a short distance from the Marne, whose banks are delightful, especially near Nogent and Gournay,—in whichever direction you turn your steps when you leave the village, you find charming walks and beautiful views. The neighborhood is embellished by some lovely estates: Maison Rouge, Maison Blanche, and the pretty little château of L'Horloge, flanked by towers and battlements, which represents in miniature—but in a highly flattered miniature—the abodes of the ancient feudal lords. Such is the village of Gagny, which sees every day one more beautiful and comfortable house built in its neighborhood, where, during the summer, charming women from Paris, artists, scholars or tradesmen, come to seek repose from the constant activity of the capital.

I observe that I have been describing Gagny as it is to-day, whereas it was in the year 1819 that little Chérubin, son of the Marquis de Grandvilain, was taken there. But after all, the aspect of the village has not changed, except for some fine houses which did not then exist, but which are universally admired to-day.

Let us make the acquaintance first of all of the villagers to whose house our hero was taken.

You know that the nurse who had carried Chérubin away was a buxom peasant with a fresh round face, and a solid figure, whose corsets indicated a sufficient supply of food for four marquises and as many plebeians; but what you do not know is that her name was Nicole Frimousset, that she was twenty-eight years old, and had three little boys, and a husband who drove her to despair, although he was a model of obedience and submission to her will.

Jacquinot Frimousset was of the same age as his wife; he was a stout, well-built fellow, with broad shoulders and a sturdy, shapely leg; his round red face, his heavy eyebrows, his bright black eyes, his white, even teeth would have done credit to a gentleman from the city. Frimousset was a handsome youth, and seemed to give promise of becoming a husband capable of fulfilling all the duties which marriage imposes. Peasant women are not insensible to physical advantages; indeed it is said that there are ladies—very great ladies—who attach much value to such bagatelles.

Nicole, who had some property, and a dowry of goodly proportion, could not lack aspirants; she selected Jacquinot Frimousset, and all the women in the village exclaimed that Nicole was not squeamish; which meant doubtless that they too would have been glad to marry Frimousset. But there is an old proverb which declares that appearances are deceitful. There are many people who do not choose to believe in proverbs! Those people make a great mistake. Erasmus said:

"Of all forms of knowledge, there is none older than that of proverbs; they were like so many symbols which formed the philosophical code of the early ages; they are the compendium of human verities."

Aristotle agreed with Erasmus; he thought that proverbs were the remains of the old philosophy destroyed by the wearing effect of time; and that, these sentences having been preserved by reason of their conciseness, far from disdaining them, we should reflect upon them with care, and search after their meaning.

Chrysippus and Cleanthes wrote at great length in favor of proverbs. Theophrastus composed a whole volume upon that subject. Among the famous men who have discussed it are Aristides and Clearchus, disciples of Aristotle; and Pythagoras wrote symbols which Erasmus ranks with proverbs; and Plutarch, in his *Apothegms*, collected the wise remarks of the Greeks.

We might proceed to cite all the authors of modern times who have written in favor of proverbs, but that would carry us too far, and we fancy that you will prefer to return to Chérubin's nurse.

Nicole had never heard of Erasmus, or of Aristotle; we have met people in the city who have no knowledge concerning those philosophers, and are none the worse off for that. As a general rule, we should not carry the study of antiquity too far; what we know about the past often prevents us from being well informed concerning what is going on to-day.

Nicole soon perceived that when she married Jacquinot she did not feather her nest very well. The handsome peasant was lazy, careless; in short, a do-nothing in every sense of the term. Three days after her marriage, Nicole sighed when she was congratulated upon her choice.

But Frimousset had that rustic cunning which knows how to disguise its inclinations, its faults, beneath an air of good-humor and frankness which deceives many people. His wife was lively, active, hard-working; it required very little time for him to learn her character. Far from thwarting her in anything, Frimousset seemed to be the most docile, the most compliant husband in the village; but he carried his servility to a point which finally irritated Nicole, and that was the very thing he counted upon.

For instance, in the morning, while his wife was attending to the housework, Jacquinot, after eating a hearty breakfast, would say to her:

"What do you want me to do now, Nicole?"

And Nicole would reply quickly:

"It seems to me that there's work enough to do! There's our field to plow, and the stones and stumps to be taken out of the piece by the road, and the garden to be planted. Ain't that work enough?"

"Yes, yes!" Frimousset would reply, shaking his head; "I know well enough that it ain't work that's lacking; but where shall I begin—in the field, or the pasture, or the garden? I am waiting for you to tell me; you know very well that I want to do just what you want me to."

"My word! what nonsense! Don't you know enough to know what there's most hurry about?"

"Why no! Don't I tell you that I want you to give me orders as to what I shall do; I want to do my best to please you, my little wife."

"Do whatever you want to, and let me alone."

Frimousset would ask no further questions; when by dint of being submissive he had irritated his wife, she never failed to say: "Do whatever you please and let me alone." Thereupon Nicole's husband would go off to the wine-shop and pass the day there. Nicole would look in vain for him in the pasture and the garden, and at night, when he came home to supper she would ask:

"Where on earth have you been working? I couldn't find you anywhere."

And Jacquinot would reply in a cajoling tone:

"Faith, you wouldn't tell me what work to begin on, and I was afraid of doing something wrong; I didn't want to do anything without your orders."

With a man of Frimousset's stamp, comfort, when it exists, soon gives place to straitened circumstances, and then to poverty; among the small as among the great, there is no fortune which is large enough to withstand disorder. After five years of married life, Nicole was obliged to sell her field and her pasture, all because Monsieur Jacquinot never knew where to begin when it was a question of working.

Meanwhile Nicole had seen her family increased by three small boys, healthy boys with excellent appetites. Three children more and several pieces of land less could not bring comfort to Frimousset's home. Then it was that Nicole conceived the idea of becoming a nurse; and as the peasant was as active and determined as her husband was lazy and shiftless, her plan was soon carried out.

And that was why Jasmin, when he went to Rue Sainte-Apolline, to the Nurses' Bureau, had found the peasant from Gagny, whom he had selected because of her pleasant face, and whom he had carried in triumph to his master, the Marquis de Grandvilain.

Nicole was an excellent woman, and she became sincerely attached to the child that was placed in her charge; she took him as soon as he cried, and was never weary of giving him the breast and of dancing him in her arms; she took care too that he should always be neat and clean. But the peasant woman was a mother too; she had three *gas*—that is what she called them,—and despite all her affection for her nursling, it was to her *gas* that Nicole gave the sweetmeats, the preserves, the biscuit and the gingerbread of which Madame la Marquise de Grandvilain had not failed to give her an abundant supply, urging her not to spare them, never to deny Chérubin anything, and to send to her for other delicacies when those should be exhausted.

Luckily for Chérubin, Nicole did not follow to the letter the instructions that were given her. As one is a mother before being a nurse, the peasant woman necessarily had more affection for her children than for her foster-child. She gave milk to the latter, while the others stuffed themselves with dainties, candy and gingerbread, which soon upset their health, whereas, on the contrary, little Grandvilain became fresh and rosy and plump and hearty.

The coming of the nursling placed the Frimousset household upon its feet once more. Nicole had asked for thirty francs a month, but the marquis had said to her:

"Just let my son get well, let him recover his health, and I will give you twice that!"

And Jacquinot, who had more time than ever to idle away and to spend in the wine-shop, because his wife, being occupied with her nursling, could not keep an eye upon him, exclaimed every day:

"My eye, Nicole, that was a mighty good idea of yours to be a nurse! If you only had three or four little brats like this, we should be mighty well off, I tell you!"

And Chérubin's little foster-brothers, who did nothing but eat sweetmeats and gingerbread, were also delighted that their mother had a nursling who provided them with so many good things, thanks to which they were constantly ill.

Chérubin had been at his nurse's house only six weeks, when, on a fine day in autumn, a fashionable carriage stopped on the public square of Gagny, which square is not absolutely beautiful, although the guardhouse has been built there.

A vehicle which does not resemble a cart is always an object of wonderment in a village. Five or six women, several old men, several peasants, and a multitude of children assembled about the carriage, and were gazing at it with curiosity, when a window was lowered and a man's head appeared.

Instantly a low murmur and a sneering laugh or two were heard among the bystanders, together with such remarks as these, not all of which were uttered in undertones:

"Oh! how ugly he is!"—"Oh! what a face!"—"Is it legal to be as ugly as that, when you have a carriage?"—"Upon my word! I'd rather go afoot!"—"That fellow hasn't been vaccinated!"

There were other reflections of the same sort, which might have reached the ears of him who suggested them, and which it would have been more polite to make in a low tone; but politeness is not the favorite virtue of the peasants of the suburbs of Paris.

Luckily, the man who had put his head out of the window was a little hard of hearing, and, besides, he was not a man to lose his temper for such trifles; on the contrary, assuming a smiling expression, he said, bowing to the assemblage:

"Which of you, my good people, can direct me to Nicole Frimousset's house? I know well enough that it's on a street leading into the square, but that is all I know."

"Nicole Frimousset!" said a peasant about half seas over, who had just come from one wine-shop and was about to enter another; "she's my wife, Nicole is; I am Jacquinot Frimousset, her husband; what do you want of my wife?"

"What do we want of her? Parbleu! we've come to see the little one that we've placed in her charge, and to find out how he is, the dear child."

"The deuce! it's monsieur le marquis!" cried Jacquinot, removing his hat and throwing several children to the ground in order to reach the carriage more quickly. "Excuse me, monsieur le marquis; you see, I didn't know you. I'll show you the way; that's our street over there; it's up hill, but you've got good horses."

And Jacquinot ran ahead of the carriage, shouting at the top of his lungs, and trying to dance.

"Here's little Chérubin's father! Here's the Marquis de Grandvilain, coming to our house! Ah! I'm going to drink his health."

The man who was in the carriage answered:

"No, I am not the marquis, I am Jasmin, his first valet; and mademoiselle who is with me is not madame la marquise; she is Turlurette, her maid. But it's all the same, our masters or us, it's absolutely the same thing."

"What a stupid thing to say, Jasmin," said Turlurette, nudging her companion; "the idea! our masters or us being the same thing!"

"I mean so far as the child we have come to see is concerned. They have sent us to find out about his health; can't we see that as well as our masters? And even better, for we have better eyes than they have."

"You speak of your masters with very little respect, Monsieur Jasmin."

"Mademoiselle, I respect and venerate them, but that doesn't prevent me from saying that they are both of them in a miserable state. What wretched carcasses! They make me feel very sad!"

"Hush, Monsieur Jasmin, here we are!"

The carriage had stopped in front of Frimousset's house, and Jacquinot's shouts had put the whole household in commotion.

"Those are Chérubin's parents," was heard in every direction. The little boys rushed to meet the carriage; Jacquinot went to draw wine to offer to his guests; while Nicole, after hastily washing her nursling and wiping his nose, took him in her arms and presented him to Jasmin and Turlurette, just as they alighted from the carriage, and called out to them:

"Here he is, monsieur and madame; take him, and see how well he is! Ah! I flatter myself that he wasn't as pretty as that when you gave him to me!"

"True; he's superb!" said Jasmin, kissing the child.

"Yes, he is as well as can be!" said Turlurette, turning little Chérubin over and over in every direction.

But while they admired her nursling, Nicole, who had had time to recover herself, looked closely at Jasmin and Turlurette, and then exclaimed:

"But I say, it seems to me that monsieur and madame ain't the child's father and mother. Pardi! I recognize monsieur by his red nose and his peppered face; he's the one who came to the bureau and picked me out."

"Yes, nurse, you are not mistaken," replied Jasmin, "I am not my master; I mean that I am not the marquis, and that is what I shouted to your husband, but he didn't listen. But that doesn't make any difference; we were sent here, Turlurette and I, to satisfy ourselves about young Grandvilain's health, and to report to monsieur le marquis and his wife."

"You will always be welcome," said Nicole.

"And then you won't refuse to taste our wine and refresh yourselves," cried Jacquinot, bringing a huge jar, full to the brim of a wine perfectly *nif*, which means new in the language of the country people.

"I never refuse to taste any wine, and I am always glad to refresh myself, even when I am not warm," replied Jasmin. "But first of all, I must fulfil to the letter my dear master's orders. Nurse, undress the child, if you please, and let me see him all naked, so that I can judge if he is in good condition from top to toe—inclusively."

"Oh, bless my soul! drink and let us alone! That is my business!" said Mademoiselle Turlurette, still keeping the child in her arms.

"Mademoiselle, I will not prevent you from looking at the child too, but I know what my master ordered me to do, and I propose to obey him. Give me Chérubin, and let me make a little Cupid of him."

"I won't give him to you."

"Then I'll take him!"

"Come and try it!"

Jasmin leaped upon the child, but Turlurette would not let him go, and each of them pulled him; Chérubin shrieked, and the nurse, to put an end to this imitation of the judgment of Solomon, adroitly took the child from both of them. In the twinkling of an eye she undressed him, and, handing him to the two servants, bade them kiss her nursling's plump little posterior.

"There! what do you think of him?" she cried; "ain't he fine? You'd like to be as fresh and plump as that, wouldn't you?—but I wish you may get it!"

The nurse's action restored general good-humor and peace between the servants of the house of Grandvilain. Turlurette did not tire of kissing her master's child. As for Jasmin, he took a huge pinch of snuff, then seated himself at a table, and said:

"Yes, yes, everything is all right; we have a superb scion. And now, let us taste your wine, foster-father."

Jacquinot made haste to fill the glasses, drink, and fill again; and Jasmin was as well pleased with the foster-father as with the nurse.

"But why did not monsieur le marquis and madame come themselves?" asked Nicole.

"Oh!" Turlurette replied with a sigh, "my poor mistress isn't very well; when she tried to nurse the child, she didn't get along well, and now that she's given it up, she's worse than ever!"

"But I offered to take our Chérubin's place, in order to relieve my excellent mistress!" murmured Jasmin, tossing off a great bumper of sour wine.

"Mon Dieu! Monsieur Jasmin, you're forever saying stupid things," said Turlurette; "the idea of madame feeding you."

"Why not, when it was the doctor's orders? I once knew a lady who nursed several cats and two rabbits, because she had too much milk."

"Oh! we've had enough of your stories!—In short, my mistress is very weak; she can't leave her room, or else she'd have come long ago to see her dear child; she talks about him all the time."

"As for monsieur le marquis," said Jasmin, "he has the gout in his heels, which makes it very hard for him to walk. I suggested a way to do it, and that was to walk on his toes and not touch his heels to the ground; he tried it, but after taking a few steps that way, *patatras!* he fell flat on the floor, and he has never been willing to try again. But they sent us in their place, and never fear, we will make a good report of what we have seen. You have restored our son's life! You are excellent people! Here's your health, foster-father; your wine scrapes the palate, but it isn't unpleasant, and it has a taste of claret."

While Jasmin drank and chattered, Turlurette went to the carriage to fetch what her mistress had sent to the nurse. There were presents of all sorts: sugar, coffee, clothes, and even toys for Chérubin's foster-brothers. The room in which the peasants usually sat would hardly hold all that came out of the carriage. The little Frimoussets jumped and shouted for joy, and rolled on the floor, at sight of all those presents, and Nicole said again and again:

"Madame la marquise is very kind! but she can be sure that her son will eat all these nice things; my *gas* won't touch 'em! Besides, they prefer pork."

Jasmin enjoyed himself exceedingly with Jacquinot, and Turlurette was finally obliged to remind him that their masters were impatiently awaiting their return. The domestics bade the villagers farewell. They kissed little Chérubin again, but on the face this time, and returned to their master's carriage, which quickly took them back to Paris.

The marchioness awaited the return of her servants with the anxiety of a mother who fears for the life of the only child that Heaven has granted her. And despite his gout, Monsieur de Grandvilain dragged himself to the window from time to time, to see if he could discover his carriage in the distance.

Turlurette, who was young and active, ran ahead of Jasmin and entered the room with a radiant air; her face announced that she brought good news.

"Magnificent, madame! magnificent health! A superb child! Oh! no one would ever know him; he was so pale and thin when he went away, and now he's as fat and solid as a rock."

"Really, Turlurette," cried the marchioness; "you are not deceiving us?"

"Oh! just ask Jasmin, madame; here he comes."

Jasmin appeared, puffing like an ox, because he had tried to go upstairs as quickly as Turlurette. He walked forward, bowed gravely to his masters and said:

"Our young marquis is in a most flourishing condition; I had the honor to kiss his posterior; I ask your pardon for taking that liberty, but he is such a lovely child and so well kept! I assure you that the Frimousset family is worthy of our confidence, and that we have only praise to give the nurse and her husband."

These words filled the atmosphere of the hôtel de Grandvilain with joy. Chérubin's mamma promised herself that she would go to Gagny to see her son as soon as her health was restored, and Monsieur le Marquis de Grandvilain swore that he would do the same as soon as the gout should be obliging enough to leave his heels.

VI

TIME AND ITS EFFECTS

The old marquis and his wife were very happy when they knew that their son was in good health; they forgot that their own health was poor, and they made great plans for the future.

There is an old song that says:

> "To-day belongs to us,
> To-morrow belongs to no one."

All of which is very true; and it means that we must never rely upon the morrow; but that does not prevent us from often making plans in which we stride over a great number of years, which is much more than a morrow! And most of those same plans are destined never to be executed. We are wise to make them, however, for in them consists the better part of our happiness; what we actually have in hand never seems so sweet as what we expect; it is with that as with those landscapes which seem charming to us at a distance, but very commonplace when we come close to them.

A month after receiving the assurance that her son was well, and that he had entirely recovered his health, Aménaïde, feeling somewhat better, determined to go out and take the air, in order that she might sooner be in a condition to go to Gagny. But whether it was that she went out too soon, or that a new disease declared itself, the marchioness was feeling wretched when she returned; she went back to bed, and a fortnight later little Chérubin's mother was laid in her grave. However, she had not realized that she was dying, and up to the last moment had retained the hope of going to embrace her son.

The old marquis was in despair at his loss; but at seventy years a man no longer loves as at thirty; as it grows old, the heart becomes less loving, and that is the effect of experience no less than of years; men are so deceived in their affections during the course of their lives, that they inevitably end by becoming selfish and by concentrating upon themselves the affection which they once offered to others.

Moreover, the marquis was not left alone on earth; had he not his son to comfort him? His faithful retainer said to him one day:

"My dear master, think of your little Chérubin; he has no mother now; you certainly ought to have died before her, for you were much older, but things don't always go as one expects! Madame la marquise is dead and you are alive; to be sure, you have the gout, but there are people whom it doesn't carry away at once; you are a proof of it. Be a man, monsieur le marquis, and remember your son, of whom you will make a lusty blade, such as you used to be; for you were a famous young rake, monsieur, although no one would suspect it to look at you now."

"What do you mean, Jasmin? Am I very much changed? Do I look as if I were impotent now?"

"I don't say that, monsieur, but I do think that you would find it difficult to keep five or six appointments in the same day; and that is what often happened in the old days! Ah! what a lady-killer you were! Well, I have an idea that your son will take after you, that he too will send me with billets-doux. Ha! ha! I will carry them with great pleasure; I know all about slipping notes into ladies' hands."

"In other words, my poor fellow, you were forever making mistakes and blunders, and it wasn't your fault that I wasn't surprised and murdered a hundred times by jealous husbands or rivals."

"Do you think so, monsieur? Oh! you are mistaken; it was so long ago that you have forgotten all about it."

"After all," rejoined Monsieur de Grandvilain, after a moment, "even if I should weep for the poor marchioness all the time, that would not bring her back to me. I must preserve myself for my son. Ah! only let me see him when he is twenty years old! That is all I ask."

"The deuce! I should say so! You are not modest!" said Jasmin; "twenty added to the seventy you are now, would make you ninety!"

"Well, Jasmin, don't men ever live to that age?"

"Oh! very seldom; but it may happen."

"How old are you, you rascal, to venture to make such remarks?"

"Why, monsieur, I am fifty," replied Jasmin, straightening himself up and putting out his leg.

"Hum! I believe that you take off something; you look much older than that. But no matter, I will bury ten like you!"

"Monsieur is at liberty to do so, certainly."

"And as soon as my gout has left me, I will go and embrace my heir. Of course I could send for the nurse to come here; but the doctor says that children mustn't have change of air; and I would rather deprive myself of seeing mine than expose him to the danger of being sick again."

"Besides, monsieur, whenever you want me to go to see our young man, you know that I am always ready; and there's no need of sending that fat Turlurette with me; I know how to tell whether the child is well. I will go to Gagny every day if you want; it doesn't tire me a bit."

Jasmin was very fond of going to see Chérubin; in the first place, the faithful retainer was already devotedly attached to his master's son; and in the second place, he always emptied several jars of wine with the foster-father, who also had become his friend. The marchioness had been dead five months, when Monsieur de Grandvilain at last got relief from his gout and was able to leave his great easy-chair. His first thought was to order the horses to be harnessed to his carriage; then he climbed in, Jasmin scrambling up behind, and they started for Gagny.

Little Chérubin continued in excellent health, because it was not he who had the delicacies that Turlurette continued to send to Nicole. One of the nurse's little boys had already died of inflammation of the bowels; the other two, who were larger and stronger, still held out against the biscuits and sweetmeats; but their complexions were sallow, while Chérubin's glowed with health and freshness.

On the day when the marquis started for Gagny, Jacquinot Frimousset had begun his visits to the wine-shop in the morning, and he was already quite drunk when one of his friends informed him that the Marquis de Grandvilain's carriage was in front of his door.

"Good!" said Jacquinot, "it's my friend Monsieur Jasmin come to see us. He ain't a bit proud, although he's a valet de chambre in a noble family; we'll empty a few jugs together."

And the nurse's husband succeeded, although staggering and stumbling at every step, in reaching his own house; he entered the room where Monsieur de Grandvilain was at that moment occupied in dandling his son, who was then a year old; and who seemed much amused by his dear father's chin, which did not remain at rest for an instant.

"Who's that old codger?" cried Frimousset, trying to open his eyes and leaning against the wall.

"It's Monsieur le Marquis de Grandvilain himself," cried Nicole, making signs to her husband to assume a more respectful attitude; but he roared with laughter, and said:

"That, Chérubin's father? Nonsense! Impossible! It's his grandfather, his great grandfather at least! As if a shrivelled and shrunken old fellow like that could have such young children!"

Monsieur de Grandvilain turned purple with rage; for a moment he was tempted to take his son away and never again set foot inside the house of that vulgar peasant who had said such unpleasant things to him; but Nicole had already succeeded in pushing her husband out of the room, and Jasmin, who was engaged in refreshing himself at a little distance, went to his master and said:

"Don't pay any attention to him, my dear master, the foster-father has been drinking; he's drunk, he can't see straight; but for that, he would never have said such things to you; he might have thought them, perhaps, but he wouldn't have said them."

"My husband is a drunken sot and nothing else," said Nicole. "I ask your pardon for him, monsieur le marquis; the idea of thinking that you ain't your son's father! Mon Dieu! it's plain enough that his eyes are blinded by drink. Why, the dear child is the very image of you! He has your nose and your mouth and your eyes and everything!"

This language was absurdly exaggerated, and far from flattering to little Chérubin; but the Marquis de Grandvilain, who did not choose to grow old, took it all for gospel truth; he looked at his son again and murmured:

"Yes, he looks like me, he will be a very handsome boy."

He rose and put a purse in the nurse's hand, saying to her:

"I am well pleased; my son is well; continue to take good care of him, for since the air of this neighborhood agrees with him, I think that I shall do well to leave him with you a long while, a very long while, in fact. Children always have time enough to study; health before everything! eh, Jasmin?"

"Oh yes! health indeed, monsieur! You are quite right; for what good does it do to know a lot when one is dead?"

Monsieur de Grandvilain smiled at his valet's reflection; then, after embracing Chérubin, he returned to his carriage. Jacquinot was cowering in a corner of the yard, and did not dare to stir; he contented himself with bowing to the marquis, who, as he passed the peasant, drew himself up and did his utmost to impart to his gait the ease and firmness of youth.

Several months passed. Monsieur de Grandvilain often said: "I am going to Gagny." But he did not go; the dread of meeting the foster-father again, and of being greeted with fresh compliments after the style of the former ones, restrained the marquis, and he contented himself with sending for his son, who had become large enough to take such a short journey without danger.

At such times Nicole passed several hours at the mansion; but Chérubin did not enjoy himself there; he always wept and asked to be taken back to the village. Whereupon the marquis would embrace his son and say to his nurse:

"Go at once, we must not thwart him; perhaps it would make him ill."

Two more years passed in this way. Chérubin was in excellent health, but he was not stout or robust, like the children of most peasants; he was a merry little fellow, he loved to play and to run about; but as soon as he was taken to

Paris, as soon as he found himself with his father at the hôtel de Grandvilain, the boy lost all his merriment; to be sure, the old mansion in Faubourg Saint-Germain was not a cheerful place; and the old marquis, who was almost always suffering from the gout, was rather a dismal object himself.

However, they did what they could to make his visits to his father's house pleasant to the youngster; they had filled a room with toys, and they always covered a table with sweetmeats; Chérubin was at liberty to eat everything, to break all that he saw; he was left free to do whatever he chose; but after looking at a few of the toys and eating a cake or two, the child would run to his nurse, take hold of her apron, gaze at her affectionately and say in an imploring voice:

"Mamma Nicole, ain't we going home soon?"

One day the marquis assumed a solemn expression, and beckoning his son to his side, said to him:

"But, Chérubin, you are at home here. When you are at the village, you are at your nurse's home; here you are in your father's house and consequently at your own home."

"Oh, no!" he replied, "this ain't to home."

"You are an obstinate little fellow, Chérubin; you don't think that you are at home here, because you are not used to being here; but if you should stay here no more than a fortnight, you would forget the village; for after all it is much finer here than at your nurse's house; isn't it?"

"Oh no! it's ever so much prettier to our house!"

"To our house! to our house! this is most annoying. However, as it is so, as you are not happy at your father's house, you are going to stay here, Chérubin; you shan't go back to your nurse's again; I am going to keep you with me; you shall not leave me after this; and at all events I will teach you to speak French, and not to say 'to our house' anymore!"

The child did not dare to reply; the stern tone which his father assumed to him for the first time, terrified him so that he was speechless and dared not move; but in a moment his features contracted, his tears gushed forth and he began to sob.

Thereupon Jasmin, who, in an adjoining room, had heard all that had been said, rushed at his master like a madman, crying:

"Well! what does this mean? So you make our child cry now, do you? That's very nice of you! do you propose to become a tyrant?"

"Hold your tongue, Jasmin!"

"No, monsieur, I won't allow you to make our little one unhappy! I should think not! I say that you shall not! Look, see how he is crying, the dear boy! For heaven's sake, what is the matter with you to-day, monsieur? Has the gout gone to your heart?"

"Jasmin——"

"I don't care, monsieur; beat me, discharge me, send me to the stable, make me sleep with the horses; do whatever you choose, but don't make this child cry; for if you do, why—I——"

Jasmin paused; he could say no more, because he too was weeping.

Monsieur de Grandvilain, when he saw his faithful servant cover his eyes with his handkerchief, held out his hand instead of scolding him, and said:

"Come! come! don't lose your head. I was wrong, yes, I was wrong, since I have made this poor child unhappy. After all, my company is not very lively; the gout often makes me cross. What would he do in this great house, poor boy? He is too young to be made to study. And then he no longer has any mother, so we must leave him with his nurse as long as possible. Besides, the air in Paris is not so good as that which he breathes in the village. So take back your foster-child, nurse; as he loves you so dearly, it must be that you make him happy. Come and kiss me, Chérubin, and don't cry any more; you are going back to your good friends; they do not love you any more than we do, but you love them more. I will try to be patient, and perhaps my turn will come some day."

"Bravo! bravo!" cried Jasmin, while his master embraced his son. "Ah! that is what I call talking; I recognize you now, monsieur. Why, certainly your Chérubin will love you, he will adore you,—but later; you can't expect that all at once; let him grow a little, and if he doesn't love you then, why I shall have a word to say to him."

So the nurse took Chérubin back to the village. Nicole was well pleased to keep a child who was a fortune to her; but she promised the old marquis to bring his son to him the next week, for the old man seemed more depressed than usual at parting.

They say that there are presentiments, secret warnings, which enable us to divine that some disaster threatens us; that our heart beats more violently when we part from a dear one whom we are destined never to see again. Why should we not believe in presentiments? The ancients believed in omens; men of sense are sometimes very superstitious; it is infinitely better to believe in many things than to believe in nothing; and strong minds are not always great minds.

Had the Marquis de Grandvilain a presentiment, that he was so loath to allow his son to go? That is something that we cannot tell; but it is a fact that he was destined never to see him again. Three days after the scene which we have described, an attack of gout carried the old nobleman off in a few hours; he had only time to whisper to Jasmin the name of his notary, and to breathe that of his son.

The grief of the marquis's valet was more intense, more touching, more sincere, than that of a multitude of friends and relations would have been. When our servants love us, they love us dearly, for they know our faults as well as our good qualities, and they forgive us the former in favor of the latter, which our friends and acquaintances never do.

Jasmin was especially distressed because he had reproved his master for wanting to keep his son with him.

"I am responsible for his not being able to embrace his son again before he died, my poor master!" he said to himself. "He had a presentiment of his approaching death when he didn't want to send the child back to the country; and I presumed to scold him, villain that I am! and he did not strike me as I deserved; on the contrary, he gave me his hand! Ah! I would die of grief if I had not Chérubin to look out for."

Thereupon Jasmin recalled the fact that his master, before he closed his eyes, had stammered the name of his notary; and presuming that that functionary was instructed concerning the wishes of the late marquis, he made haste to go to him and tell him of his master's death.

Monsieur de Grandvilain's notary was a man still young, but of a serious and even somewhat severe aspect; he had, in fact, the marquis's will in his keeping, and was instructed to carry out his last wishes. He lost no time in opening the document which he had in charge, and read what follows:

"I possess thirty thousand francs a year. All my property descends to my son, my sole heir. I desire that he be put in possession of his property at the age of fifteen. Until then I beg that my notary will undertake to manage it. I desire that no change shall be made inside my house, and that none of my servants shall be discharged. I appoint Jasmin, my faithful valet de chambre, steward of my household. Every month my notary shall hand him such sum as he shall require for the household expenses and for the education of my son.

SIGISMOND VENCESLAS, MARQUIS DE GRANDVILAIN."

The notary could not help smiling after reading this extraordinary testament, and Jasmin, who had listened with all his ears, gazed at him with an air of amazement, and faltered:

"In all this, monsieur le notaire, I didn't understand who is to be the child's guardian."

"There isn't any, Jasmin, his father hasn't appointed any; he relied upon you and me; upon me to administer his fortune, and upon you to superintend his conduct. It seems that Monsieur de Grandvilain had great confidence in you; I have no doubt that you deserve it, but I urge you to redouble your zeal with respect to the young marquis. Remember that it is your duty now to watch over him. As for his fortune, his father wished him to be placed in possession of it at the age of fifteen. That is making him rich at a very early age; but since it is his father's will, see to it, Jasmin, that at all events, when fifteen, the young marquis is already a man in knowledge and strength of character."

Jasmin listened to this speech with the greatest attention; he attempted to reply, but got confused, lost his way in a sentence which he could not finish, and finally left the notary, after receiving a sum of money with which to begin to manage his master's household.

On returning to the house, Jasmin had grown three inches and was puffed up like a balloon; vanity perches everywhere, among the small as well as among the great, and it is likely to be even more powerful among the former who are not accustomed to grandeur.

All the servants gathered about the valet, curious to learn the contents of the will. Jasmin assumed a peculiarly idiotic expression, and replied, speaking through his nose:

"Never fear, my friends, there is to be no change here; I keep you all in my service."

"You, Monsieur Jasmin! are you our master's heir?"

"No, no, I am not the heir, but I represent the heir; in fact, I am the steward of the household. I will keep everybody: cook, coachman, housekeeper, because Monsieur de Grandvilain wished it; otherwise I should have discharged you all, for servants without a master are useless things. But I forget, our master now is the young marquis, and whenever he chooses to occupy his house, he will find his household all arranged; that was his late father's wish, no doubt, and we must conform to it."

All the servants bowed before Jasmin, who had become a man of weight, and he, after receiving the congratulations of those who were now his inferiors, withdrew to his chamber, and, reflecting upon what the notary had said, cudgelled his brains to decide what it was his duty to do with Chérubin, in order properly to carry out his master's designs.

After passing several hours at this occupation, without result, Jasmin exclaimed:

"Faith, I believe the best thing to do is to leave little Chérubin out at nurse."

VII

LITTLE LOUISE

Chérubin was still at the village, still living with his nurse Nicole Frimousset, and yet Chérubin was ten years old. Although of small stature, his health was excellent, and the attentions of a nurse had long since ceased to be necessary to him. But the marquis's heir had retained undiminished his affection for the place where he had passed his childhood, and he lost his temper when it was suggested that he should leave it.

Meanwhile Jacquinot, the foster-father, had become more of a sot than ever; and as she grew older, Nicole, being obliged to scold her husband incessantly, was rarely in good humor. And then her two boys had left the village: one was a mason at Orléans, the other was apprenticed to a carpenter at Livry.

In spite of that, Chérubin still enjoyed life at his nurse's house, where he had for his companion a little girl who was only two years younger than he. It was a few days before the Marquis de Grandvilain's death, that one morning, a very young lady from the city, fashionably dressed, alighted from a cab in front of Nicole's cottage. This young lady, who was beautiful and bore a look of distinction, was very pale and seemed much excited; she had in her arms a little girl of about a year old, and she said to Jacquinot's wife, in a voice broken by sobs:

46

"This is my daughter; she is only a year old, but she has been weaned for some months; I wish to leave her with some kindhearted people who will take great care of her and treat her as their own child. Will you take charge of her, madame? I cannot keep her with me any longer; indeed, it is possible that I may not be able to take her for a long while. There are three hundred francs in this roll; that is all that I can raise at present; but within a year I will send you the same amount, if I do not come before that to see my child."

Nicole, who had profited much by bringing up one child, thought that a second fortune had fallen into her lap, and eagerly accepted the proposition which was made to her. The young lady handed her the little girl, the money, and a large bundle containing the child's clothes; then, after embracing her daughter once more, she hurriedly entered her carriage, which instantly drove away.

Not until then did Nicole reflect that she had not asked the young lady her name, or her child's name, or her address; but it was too late, for the cab was already a long way off. Nicole soon consoled herself for her forgetfulness, thinking:

"After all, she will come again, she certainly can't mean to abandon her child. She has given me three hundred francs; that is enough for me to be patient; and then the child is a sweet little thing, and I believe I would have kept her for nothing. What shall I call her? *Pardieu!* Louise; for this is the feast of Saint-Louis. When her mother comes back, if she don't like that name, she can tell me the child's own name. What a fool I was not to ask her! But she seemed in such a hurry, and so excited.—Well, Louise,—that is decided; she will be a playmate for my Chérubin, and in that way the dear child won't get tired of living with us. Bless my soul! the longer we keep him, the better off we are."

And the little girl had, in fact, become Chérubin's inseparable companion; she had grown up with him, she shared all his games, all his pleasures. Chérubin was not happy when Louise was not with him; the little girl's activity was a foil to the little marquis's natural mildness of character; and when he began to show signs of becoming a charming young man, Louise gave promise of being a very pretty young girl. But the young lady who had brought to Nicole that child whose mother she claimed to be, had not returned to Gagny; once only, a year after her visit, a messenger from Paris had appeared at Frimousset's house and had handed them a paper which contained only one hundred and fifty francs, saying:

"This is from the mother of the little girl who was brought here a year ago; she requests you to continue to take care of her child."

Nicole had questioned the man, had asked him for the name and address of the lady who sent him; but the messenger had replied that he did not know, that she had come to his stand in Paris and had given him the errand to do, paying him in advance, after making sure that he had a badge.

Nicole had not been able to learn anything more, and since then she had received neither money nor information. But Louise was so attractive that the idea of sending her away had not once occurred to her. Besides, Chérubin was devoted to her, the little girl was a new bond which kept him in his nurse's family; and when by chance Jacquinot made any reflection upon the child whom they were bringing up for nothing, his wife would reply:

"Hold your tongue, you drunkard; it isn't any of your business; if the girl's mother doesn't come to see her, it must be because she is dead, or else because she is a bad mother; if she is dead, then I must take her place with the child; if she is a bad mother, Louise would be unhappy with her, and I prefer to keep her with me."

While Chérubin grew up beside his little friend, Jasmin continued to govern the Marquis de Grandvilain's household; he was careful in his expenditure; the servants were not permitted to indulge in any excesses, and he himself got tipsy only once a week, which was very modest in one who had the keys to the cellar. But Jasmin thought constantly of his young master; he went to see him often, and sometimes passed whole days at Gagny; and he always asked Chérubin if he wished to go back to Paris with him, to his own house. The little fellow always refused, and Jasmin always returned to Paris alone, consoling himself with the thought that the young marquis was in excellent health, and that that was the main point.

When Jasmin went to the notary to ask for money, which he never did without presenting an exact statement of what he had to pay out, the notary, after praising the faithful valet for the honesty and economy with which he regulated the household expenditure, never failed to ask him:

"And our young marquis, how does he come on?"

"He is in superb health," Jasmin would reply.

"He ought to be a big fellow now, he is nearly eleven years old."

"He has a very pretty figure and a charming face; he will be a little jewel, whom all the women will dote on, I am sure, as they doted on his late father; but I presume that they won't be the same women."

"That is all very well; but how is he getting on with his studies; have you placed the little marquis at a good institution?"

"Excellent, monsieur; oh, yes! he is in a very good house indeed; he eats as much as he wants."

"I have no doubt that he is well fed, but that is not enough; at his age, what he wants above all is food for the mind. Does he give satisfaction?"

"They are enchanted with him; they would like never to part with him, he is so attractive."

"Has he had any prizes?"

"Prizes! he has whatever he wants; he has only to ask, they refuse him nothing."

"You don't understand me; has he obtained any prizes for his work, I mean; is he strong in Latin, Greek, and history?"

Jasmin was slightly embarrassed by those questions; he coughed, and faltered a few words which could not be understood. But the notary, who attributed his embarrassment to other causes, continued:

"I am talking about things you don't understand, eh, my old Jasmin? Latin and Greek and such matters are not within your scope. However, when I have a few moments to myself, I will come to you, and you must take me to see your young marquis."

Jasmin went away, muttering:

"The deuce! the deuce! if he goes to see my little Chérubin some day, he won't be very well content with his studies; but it isn't my fault if monsieur le marquis refuses to leave his nurse. That notary keeps talking to me about food for the mind; it seems to me that when a child eats four meals a day with a good appetite, his mind ought not to be any more hungry than his stomach, unless it doesn't want to be fed."

One day, however, after a visit to the notary, when he had again urged the old valet to commend the young marquis to his teachers, Jasmin started at once for Gagny, saying to himself on the way:

"I am an old brute! I leave my master's son in ignorance; for after all, I know how to read myself, and I believe that Chérubin doesn't even know that. Certainly this state of things can't be allowed to go on. Later, people will say: 'Jasmin took no care of the child who was placed in his charge. Jasmin is unworthy of the late marquis's confidence.'—I don't propose that people shall say that of me. I am sixty years old now, but that's no reason for being an idiot. I propose to show my strength of character."

When Jasmin arrived at Nicole's, he found her at work in the house, while Jacquinot sat half asleep in an old easy-chair.

49

"My friends," said Jasmin, entering the room with a very busy air, and rolling his eyes about, "things can't remain like this; we must make a complete change."

Nicole gazed at the old servant and said:

"You want to change our house over; you think this room is too dark? Dear me! we're used to it, you see."

"Ain't we going to drink a glass?" said Jacquinot, rising, and rubbing his eyes.

"In a minute, Jacquinot, in a minute.—My friends, you don't understand me. I am talking about your foster-child, my young master, to whom you only give such food as you yourselves eat; do you not?"

"Ain't he satisfied, the dear child?" cried Nicole. "Bless my soul! I will give him whatever he wants; all he has got to do is to speak. I will make him tarts, cakes——"

"It isn't that, Nicole, it isn't that sort of food that I'm talking about. It's Chérubin's mind that needs a lot of things."

"Mind? Something light, I suppose? I will make him some cream cheese."

"Once more, Dame Frimousset, allow me to speak. My young master must become a scholar, or something like it; it isn't a question of eating, but of studying. What does he learn here with you? Does he even know how to read, to write or to figure?"

"Faith, no," said Nicole; "you never mentioned those things, and we didn't think they were necessary, especially as Chérubin is going to be very rich; we didn't think there was any need of his learning a trade."

"It isn't a question of learning a trade, but of becoming a scholar."

"Ah yes! I understand, like the schoolmaster, who always stuffs his conversation full of words that nobody knows what they mean."

"That's the very thing. Oh! if Chérubin could say some of those fine sentences that no one can understand, that would be splendid.—So you have a learned schoolmaster in this village, have you?"

"To be sure,—Monsieur Gérondif."

"Gérondif! the name alone indicates a very learned man. Do you think he would consent to come to your house and give my young master lessons? For it is impossible for monsieur le marquis to go to school with all the young brats in the village."

"Why shouldn't Monsieur Gérondif come here? He has educated two or three children for people who come to Gagny to pass the summer. Besides, he ain't very well fixed, the dear man, and to earn a little money——"

"There is no difficulty about that; I will pay him whatever he asks. Do you suppose that I could talk—that I could see this Monsieur Gérondif?"

"That's easy enough; Jacquinot will go and fetch him. It's after five o'clock, so his school is over. Jacquinot, you will find the schoolmaster at Manon the baker's, because he goes there every day to bake potatoes in her oven while it's still hot."

"Go, my dear Jacquinot; bring me this scholar, and then we will empty a few bottles; I will treat Monsieur Gérondif too."

That promise roused Jacquinot, who went out, promising to make haste, and Jasmin asked Nicole:

"Where is my young master?"

"My *fieu?*"

"My master, the young Marquis de Grandvilain. He is eleven years old now, my dear Nicole, and it seems to me that he is rather large for you to keep on calling him your *fieu.*"

"Oh! bless my soul! habit—what do you expect?—He's in the garden, under the plum trees."

"Alone?"

"Oh no! Louise is with him, always with him. As if he could get along without her!"

"Ah! is that the little girl who was left here, and whose parents you don't know?"

"Mon Dieu! yes."

"And you are still taking care of her?"

"*Pardi!* one child more. When there's enough for three, there's enough for four."

"That is what my father used to say, when he cribbed my share of breakfast; and in our house, on the contrary, when there was four of us, there was never enough for two.—Never mind, Dame Frimousset, you are an excellent woman, and when Chérubin leaves you, we will make you a handsome present."

"Oh! don't speak of that; I should rather not have any present, if my *fieu*

51

would never leave me."

"Oh yes! I can understand that; but still, we can't leave him out at nurse until he is thirty; that isn't the custom. I am going to present my respects to him, while I am waiting for Monsieur Gérondif; and I will inform him that he must become a scholar."

Chérubin was at the farther end of the garden, which ended in an orchard. There, trees which were never trimmed extended at pleasure their branches laden with fruit, as if to prove to man that nature does not need his help to grow and bear.

The Marquis de Grandvilain's son had attractive, regular features; his great blue eyes were exceedingly beautiful, and their soft and languorous expression made them resemble a woman's eyes rather than a man's; long dark lashes shaded those lovely eyes, which, according to appearances, were destined to realize Jasmin's prophecy, and to make many conquests some day. The rest of the face was agreeable, although not especially remarkable, except his complexion, which was as white as that of a girl who has a white skin; life in the country had not tanned the young marquis, because Nicole, who had always taken the greatest care of her foster-child, never left him exposed to the sun; and because the little fellow, who was not employed in the arduous labor of the fields, always had leisure to seek the cool shade.

Little Louise, who was then nine years old, had one of those pretty faces, gay and sad by turns, which painters delight to copy when they wish to represent a young maiden of Switzerland or of the neighborhood of Lake Geneva. It was a lovely face, after the style of Raphael's virgins, in which however there was a melancholy and charm distinctly French. Louise's eyes and hair were jet black, but very long lashes tempered their brilliancy, and gave to them a sort of velvety aspect which had an indescribable charm; a high, proud forehead, a very small mouth, and white teeth set like pearls, combined with her other features to make her one of the sweetest little girls whom one could hope to meet; and when she laughed, two little dimples which appeared in her cheeks added a new charm to her whole person; and she laughed often, for she was only nine years old. Nicole treated her as her own child, Chérubin as his sister, and she had as yet no suspicion that her mother had abandoned her.

When Jasmin walked toward the orchard, Chérubin and Louise were eating plums. The little girl was plucking them and throwing them to her companion, who sat at the foot of a tree so heavily laden that its branches seemed on the point of breaking beneath their burden.

Jasmin removed his hat, and humbly saluted his young master, uncovering his head which was almost bald, though the few hairs which still remained above the ears were brought together and combed with much care over the forehead, and made the old servant look, at a distance, as if he had tied a bandage around his head.

"I present my respects to Monsieur le Marquis de Grandvilain," said Jasmin.

At that moment the girl shook a branch which extended over the old valet's head, and a shower of plums rained down upon Jasmin's skull.

Thereupon there was a roar of laughter from behind the tree, and Chérubin mingled his laughter with it; while the old servant, who would not have kept his hat on his head in his master's presence for anything in the world, received with resignation the rain of plums that fell on him.

"My young master still seems to be in flourishing health," continued Jasmin, after throwing to the ground a few plums which had lodged between his coat collar and his stock.

"Yes, Jasmin, yes. But just see how handsome they are, and good too; eat some, Jasmin; you have only to stoop and pick some up."

"Monsieur is very kind, but plums—sometimes they occasion inconvenience.—I have come, first of all, to ask if monsieur wishes to return to Paris with me at last; his house is, as always, ready to receive him and ——"

Jasmin was unable to finish his sentence, because a fresh shower of plums fell upon his head. This time he glanced angrily about, but the mischievous girl had hidden behind a tree; meanwhile Chérubin exclaimed:

"No, Jasmin, no, I don't want to go to Paris, I am so happy here; I have told you already that I should be bored in Paris, and I have such a pleasant time at my dear Nicole's."

"Very good, monsieur le marquis, I don't wish to thwart you on that point; but if you stay here, you must not pass all your time in playing any longer; you must study, my dear master, you must become a learned man; it is absolutely necessary and——"

A shower of plums, heavier than the other two, once more cut Jasmin short; and he, finding that he had two breaches in his band of hair, turned round and exclaimed angrily:

"Oh! this is too much; do you want to make marmalade of my head?—Ah! it is that little girl who is playing these tricks on me. It is very pretty, mademoiselle; I advise you to laugh; there is good reason for it."

Louise had run to hide behind Chérubin, laughing heartily; and he, laughing also at the grimace made by his old servant, said to him:

"It is all your own fault, Jasmin; leave us in peace. Louise and I were eating plums, and having a good time; why did you come to disturb us, to tell me a lot of foolish things? that I must study, that I must be a learned man. I don't want to study! Go and drink with Jacquinot; go, go! I don't need you."

Jasmin seemed sorely embarrassed; at last he replied:

"I am sorry to annoy monsieur le marquis, but you are too big now not to know how to read or write; in fact, there are a lot of things which you ought to know, because you are a marquis and—in short, your venerable father's notary says that you ought to have prizes in Latin and Greek, and it seems that it is customary to study in order to get prizes. I have just sent after the schoolmaster of this village, Monsieur Gérondif; he is coming here, and he is to teach you, for Nicole assures me that he is a good scholar, although he is obliged to have his potatoes baked in the baker's oven."

Chérubin's brow darkened, and the little fellow replied with a very pronounced pout:

"I don't want the schoolmaster to come here; I don't need to be a scholar. You tire me, Jasmin, with your Monsieur Gérondif!"

It pained Jasmin greatly to have to vex his young master. He did not know what to say or to do; he twisted his hat and twirled it in his hands, for he felt that after all it was necessary to compel the young marquis not to be a dolt, but he did not know what course to pursue to that end; and if at that moment he had received another shower of plums it would not have roused him from his stupor.

But Nicole had followed the old servant at a distance; the nurse realized that if Chérubin refused to learn anything at her house, they would be obliged to make him go to Paris to learn. Dreading lest she might lose a child whom she loved, and who had brought ease to her household for eleven years, Nicole felt that some way must be found to induce the boy to consent to take lessons of the schoolmaster.

Women, even those in the country, speedily divine where our vulnerable point is. Nicole, who had gradually drawn near, and was then standing behind Jasmin, who had ceased to speak or move, advanced a few steps nearer the children, and, taking Louise by the hand, said:

"Look you, Monsieur Jasmin, I see the reason plain enough why Chérubin don't want to work; it's because he plays all day with this girl. Well! as I too want my fieu to be a scholar, I am going to take Louise to one of our relations two leagues away; she'll be taken good care of there, and then she won't prevent Chérubin from studying."

Nicole had not finished when the little boy ran to her and taking hold of her dress, cried in a touching voice, and with tears in his eyes:

"No, no, don't take Louise away; I will study, I will learn whatever you want me to with Monsieur Gérondif; but don't take Louise away, oh! please don't take her away!"

Nicole's ruse had succeeded. She embraced her foster-child, Louise leaped for joy when she found that she was not to be sent away, and Jasmin would have done as much if his age had not made it impossible; he threw his hat in the air, however, exclaiming:

"Long live Monsieur le Marquis de Grandvilain! ah! I knew perfectly well that he would consent to become a learned man!"

At that moment Jacquinot appeared at the garden gate and shouted:

"Here's Monsieur Gérondif; I've brought him with me."

VIII

MONSIEUR GÉRONDIF

The new personage who had arrived at Nicole's was a man of about forty years of age, of medium height, rather stout than thin, with an ordinary face, in which could be detected the desire to give himself an air of importance, and the habit of bending the knee in servile fashion to all those who were above him in social rank or in fortune.

Monsieur Gérondif had long, thick, greasy brown hair, which was cut straight in front, just above the eyebrows, and which hid his coat collar behind; on the sides it was held in respect by the ears. The teacher had gray eyes, the size of which it was difficult to discover, because he kept them lowered all the time, even when speaking to you. He had a very large mouth, which was abundantly furnished with very fine teeth, and whether for the purpose of displaying that attractive feature, or to afford a favorable idea of the affability of his disposition, he smiled almost continually when he talked, and never failed to open his mouth so far that one could see his whole supply.

A nose much too large for the rest of the face, and almost always adorned by a number of small pimples, impaired infinitely the general aspect of the professor's countenance; and the habit which he had adopted of scratching it, and of stuffing it with snuff, gave to that protuberance a very conspicuous red and black appearance, which would have been in some degree repellent, if Monsieur Gérondif's soft and honeyed voice had not lessened the unfortunate impression produced at first by his nose.

The schoolmaster's costume was rather severe, for it was supposed to be all black; the coat, trousers and waistcoat were in fact originally made of cloth of that color; but time had wrought such ravages upon them all, that it had often been necessary to apply patches upon each of those garments; and whether from carelessness on the part of the person who had made the repairs, or because black cloth was scarcer than any other color in the neighborhood, blue, green, gray, and even nut-colored pieces had been used to patch Monsieur Gérondif's coat, trousers, and waistcoat; so that he bore some resemblance to a harlequin; add to all this, socks and wooden shoes, and a generally dirty aspect, and you will have an idea of the individual who had been sent for to act as tutor to the young Marquis de Grandvilain.

As for what he wore on his head, we have not mentioned that, for the reason that Monsieur Gérondif never wore hat or cap, and that no one could even remember having seen him with any sort of head covering in his hand. He had an old umbrella, which boasted of but three ribs, beneath which our schoolmaster bravely sheltered his head when it rained, without fear that the old thing would collapse, because it was divided into several pieces.

The schoolmaster suffered terribly from chilblains and corns on his feet, so that he had been obliged to lean heavily upon Jacquinot's arm, which was doubtless the reason that Nicole's husband had announced that he had *brought* Monsieur Gérondif. When he learned that he had been sent for on the part of Monsieur le Marquis de Grandvilain, the professor had not taken the time to remove his potatoes from the baker's oven, nor had he deemed it necessary to wash his hands, a task which he performed in fact only on Sundays and holidays.

Jasmin pushed his young master in front of him. Chérubin did not release Louise's hand, as if he still feared that they proposed to separate him from his dear companion. The old valet followed him, still holding his hat in his hand; Nicole walked behind; and they all went to receive the professor, who had halted on the threshold of the street door, sorely embarrassed to know whether he should remove or retain his wooden shoes before presenting himself to the distinguished persons who had sent for him; at last he decided to appear in socks.

When he perceived the bald head of Jasmin, whose respectable costume had nothing about it to indicate the servant, Monsieur Gérondif rushed to meet him, smiling in the fashion best adapted to show his molars and his incisors, and saluted him with:

"Honor to whom honor is due! *Salutem vos.* Monsieur le marquis, I consider myself very happy to be before you at this moment."

While Monsieur Gérondif made his complimentary address, bowing to the ground, Jasmin, who saw that the professor had made a mistake and had taken him for the marquis, hastily changed places with his young master; Chérubin did not release Louise's hand, so that when he raised his head, Monsieur Gérondif found himself with the two children in front of him; he thought that he had made a mistake, and pushed the little boy and his friend aside with little ceremony, to place himself once more in front of Jasmin, who was at the other end of the room, saying:

"Pardon the blunder; *errare humanum est.* I place myself at your commands, monsieur le marquis. I did not even take the time to finish my slight collation, in order that I might be instantly ready for your orders."

While the schoolmaster was speaking, Jasmin once more left his place and stepped behind his master; Monsieur Gérondif seemed inclined to follow him into every corner of the room, when Nicole said laughingly:

"But you are making a mistake, Monsieur Gérondif; the marquis is my *fieu*, my foster-child, this pretty boy here."

"And I am only his very humble servant, former valet to monsieur le marquis, his father, who deigned when he died to entrust the care of his heir to me," said Jasmin, saluting Chérubin.

Monsieur Gérondif took the thing very well; he smiled anew and hastened to place himself in front of Chérubin, saying:

"I make my excuses *ut iterum*, and that does not prevent me from saying once more that I am the very humble servant of monsieur le marquis *junior.*"

"Not Junior! de Grandvilain," said Jasmin solemnly.

"One does not prevent the other," replied Monsieur Gérondif, with a sly smile, "permit me to inform you, brave Eumæus; for you remind me much of that virtuous and royal retainer of Ulysses, King of Ithaca. I do not know whether he was bald too—Homer does not say, but it is very probable. I am at the orders of Monsieur le Marquis de Grandvilain, who can now tell me what he wants of me instantly."

The schoolmaster's long sentences, and the quotations with which he seasoned his discourse, produced the best effect upon Jasmin, who, like most fools, placed a high estimate on whatever he did not understand; so he nodded his head to the nurse, muttering:

"He is a learned man! a very learned man, in fact; he will do very well for us."

As for Chérubin, who was not of his old servant's opinion, and who found Monsieur Gérondif very tiresome, he answered without hesitation:

"I don't want you at all; it was Jasmin who insisted on sending for you, to make me study—I don't know what! I am perfectly willing to learn, but Louise must stay with me during my lessons."

Having said this, Chérubin abruptly turned his back on the schoolmaster; Louise did the same, laughing heartily at Monsieur Gérondif's nose; and the two children ran from the room, to return to the garden and eat more plums.

The others deemed it best to let them go, and Jasmin asked Monsieur Gérondif, with a respectful air, if he were willing to give lessons to his young master, who had learned nothing as yet, and to whom it was high time that some attention should be paid if they wished him to have any education.

Monsieur Gérondif received the proposal with delight; he shook Jasmin's hand warmly and said:

"Trust me, we will make up for lost time. I will make the young marquis work like a horse."

"Oh, no!" cried the old servant, "my young master is very delicate; he isn't used to studying and you will make him ill; you must go gently with him."

"Of course, of course!" replied Gérondif, scratching his nose. "When I say like a horse, I use a figure of speech—a metaphor, if you prefer; we will go *piano et sano—ecce rem!* In addition to writing and mathematics, I will teach monsieur le marquis his own language, root and branch, so that he may speak it as I do; that is to say, with elegance; also Latin, Greek, Italian, philosophy, history, ancient and modern, mythology, rhetoric, the art of versification, geography, astronomy, a little physics, and chemistry, and mineralogy, and ——"

"Oh! that is enough, monsieur le professeur!" cried Jasmin, bewildered by all that he heard, and aghast with admiration at Monsieur Gérondif's learning. "When my young master knows all those things, he will be quite learned enough."

"If you wish for anything more, you have only to speak; I venture to say that so far as learning is concerned, I am a well, a genuine well. At the age of five, I took a prize for memory, and at seven I had three wreaths on my head, wreaths of oak, like the Druids, ancient priests of Gaul, who worshipped Teutates, or Mercury, and the mistletoe, a parasite which, according to them, cured all diseases. I don't agree with them, for I have corns which pain me

58

terribly; I put mistletoe on them, and they hurt me worse than ever."

Jasmin dared not breathe while Monsieur Gérondif was speaking; the nurse and her husband shared his admiration, and the schoolmaster, well pleased with the effect that he had produced, was listening to himself with much complaisance when the old servant interrupted him to say:

"A thousand pardons, monsieur, if I venture to slip in a word, but it seems to me necessary to agree upon terms; how much will you take a month to teach my young master all these things, it being understood that you will come every day except Sunday?"

Monsieur Gérondif reflected a few moments, and replied at last in a hesitating manner:

"For imparting to Monsieur de Grandvilain as much knowledge as it is possible for me to impart, it seems to me that if I charge you fifteen francs a month I——"

"Fifteen francs!" cried Jasmin in a tone of disgust; "fifteen francs for all that; why, you must be joking, monsieur."

Monsieur Gérondif ceased to smile; he lowered his eyes and muttered:

"Well, then, if you think that is too much, we will reduce the amount and ——"

"Think that it's too much!" replied Jasmin; "on the contrary, monsieur, I think that it isn't enough! Thank heaven, my young master is rich, he is able to pay those who give him lessons. What! I, a valet de chambre, earn six hundred francs a year, with board and lodging, while a man as learned as you, who is going to teach my master so many fine things, receives less than that! Oh, no! I offer you a hundred and fifty francs a month, monsieur, and I consider it none too much for all that you know."

"A hundred and fifty francs—a month!" cried Monsieur Gérondif, whose features expressed indescribable bliss. "A hundred and fifty francs! I accept, Monsieur Jasmin, I accept with gratitude, and I will prove myself worthy. I will pass almost the whole day with my pupil—my school will not prevent, for I have a sub-master, to whom I pay three francs a month; I will increase his salary if necessary, and at need I will give up my school entirely, to devote my whole time to the interesting child whom you entrust to me."

The schoolmaster seized Jasmin's hands and shook them effusively; then he shook hands with Jacquinot, then with Nicole, and finally, finding no more hands to shake, he began to clap his own, crying:

"Hosanna! Hosanna! *applaudite cives!*"

Jasmin whispered to Jacquinot:

"I think that Monsieur Gérondif said: 'Apportez du civet.' Bring some jugged hare."

"We haven't got any jugged hare," replied Jacquinot, "but we've got some of our wine to drink, and the schoolmaster will drink with us, I know."

Nicole brought wine and glasses. Monsieur Gérondif gladly accepted the invitation to drink, but he asked the nurse for a crust of bread, because, as he had not had time to have his potatoes baked, he was conscious of a void in his stomach. Nicole fetched what provisions she had and placed them on the table, whereupon Monsieur Gérondif began by cutting an enormous slice of bread, then attacked a dish of beef and beans with a vehemence in which there was something appalling.

But while eating, the schoolmaster found time to talk; he said to Jasmin:

"We have talked about knowledge, but there is another subject upon which we have not touched,—I mean morals. In that matter too you may rely upon me. I am extremely rigid upon that point; for you see, Monsieur Jasmin, morals are the curb of society. I venture to say that mine are beyond reproach, and I propose that it shall be the same with my pupil."

"Oh! as for that," said the old servant with a smile, "it seems to me that we have no reason to fear as yet, considering my young master's age. Later perhaps! for look you, a young man is not a girl!"

"He's much worse, Monsieur Jasmin, much more dangerous! Because the young man, being more free, can do more wrong things. But I will inculcate in him principles which will keep him in the right path; I will be the Mentor of this Telemachus!—But I beg pardon, it just occurs to me that in order to begin monsieur le marquis's studies, I shall have to buy some elementary books, grammars and dictionaries; those that I use in my school are worn out, and I believe that I have not enough money at this moment to make these purchases. If Monsieur Jasmin could pay me a month's salary in advance, why then——"

"With pleasure, Monsieur Gérondif; I always bring money when I come here, in case my master should ask me for some. See, here are a hundred and twenty francs in gold, and thirty in five-franc pieces."

The schoolmaster gazed with a covetous eye at the money which was counted out to him. He took it, and counted and recounted it several times; he put it in his pocket, then took it out to count it once more. He did not tire of handling that gold and silver, for never before had he been in possession of so large a sum. They spoke to him, he did not hear, he did not answer, but he jingled his gold pieces and his silver pieces, and after he had finally placed them in a pocket of his trousers, he put his hand over them and kept it there all the time.

Meanwhile, as it was late, Jasmin, having taken leave of his master and received from him renewed promises that he would study, returned to the carriage which had brought him thither and drove back to Paris, delighted that he had found a way to make a scholar of Chérubin.

As for Monsieur Gérondif, having saluted his future pupil and informed him that he would come on the morrow, he left the nurse's house, and went home, still keeping his hand in his pocket and jingling the money which was there.

PART II

IX

We will pass rapidly over the years following that during which Monsieur Gérondif became the young marquis's tutor. Chérubin had kept his word; he had consented to study, but he had insisted on Louise's presence during his lessons; at first, Monsieur Gérondif had tried to keep the little girl from the room, but Chérubin had shrieked and wept and refused to listen to his tutor; so that it was found necessary to yield to him. By slow degrees Louise's presence had evidently come to seem less inconvenient to Monsieur Gérondif, for if she were not there when he arrived, he was the first to send for her.

The fact is that Louise had grown too, and that she had improved even more rapidly. At thirteen, she seemed at least fifteen; she was slender, well-built, and possessed of many graces; not studied and affected ones such as so many young ladies in Paris assume, thinking that they will be deemed natural; but those naïve, simple graces which one recognizes instantly but vainly tries to imitate.

Monsieur Gérondif was not a genuine scholar, but he might have passed for such in the eyes of many people. He had tried everything, having in his youth essayed a number of professions, but having fixed upon none; after making a pretence of becoming a doctor, a druggist, a chemist, an astronomer, a geometrician, a tradesman, and even a poet; after stuffing his head with the first rudiments of many forms of knowledge and succeeding in none, he had ended by turning schoolmaster. The man who knows one branch thoroughly has much more merit than he who talks glibly about all branches, and yet, in the world, the preference is often given to the latter.

At fifteen, Chérubin knew a little of a great many things; in the eyes of the village, in the eyes of the Frimoussets, the young man was a phenomenon who had learned with extraordinary ease. As for Jasmin, he opened his eyes in amazement when he heard his young master use a Latin word, or mention some historical or mythological fact, and he bowed before Monsieur Gérondif, exclaiming:

"He knows as much as you, and that is a great deal to say."

Monsieur Gérondif puffed himself out, for he had purchased an entirely new costume; he no longer resembled a harlequin, and he was seen now with a hat and a real umbrella.

But with well-being ambition had come; that is usually the case. When a man has nothing, he becomes accustomed to forming no wishes, to not looking above himself; he remains in his shell and tries to be happy there forever; he even succeeds sometimes. But when he becomes well-to-do, then he indulges in a multitude of little luxuries hitherto unknown; but they are no longer enough; every day he desires others, forms a thousand new aspirations, becomes ambitious, in short; and it often happens that he is less contented than when he possessed nothing.

Such was substantially Monsieur Gérondif's story; when he had nothing to live upon but the paltry profits of his school, he wore clogs, went without hat or cap, very often dined upon nothing but potatoes baked in the oven, and yet seemed perfectly contented with his position.

Since he had become young Grandvilain's tutor and was earning eighteen hundred francs a year, a sum which it is rather difficult to spend in the village of Gagny, the schoolmaster had formed new desires; and first of all he hoped not to remain forever in a village where he could not even find means to spend his money, a state of affairs which is very annoying to one who has not been accustomed to having money to spend.

Monsieur Gérondif had been shrewd enough to obtain his pupil's confidence, and even to inspire affection in him; for Chérubin's heart was easily won; he flew to meet all those who showed the slightest attachment to him. While enjoining virtue and good morals upon the young man every day, Monsieur Gérondif, whose eyesight was very good although he constantly kept his eyes lowered, had perceived that Louise was growing, developing, and becoming a charming girl; and more than once, as he looked at the sweet child, he had thought:

"What lovely eyes! What an exquisite oval face! What a correct chin!"

And then, whether to make sure that Louise's chin was in fact correct, or for some other reason, the tutor would pass his hand over the young girl's face, and sometimes go so far as gently to pinch her cheek, which did not amuse Louise at all; whereas Chérubin, on the contrary, was very glad to hear a complimentary remark addressed to his faithful companion.

"Isn't Louise lovely, my dear master?" he would say at such times.

And Monsieur Gérondif would hasten to assume a sanctimonious air, and would reply, lowering his eyes:

"Yes, this girl has the type of Jael in all its beauty; she seems to me to have the very appearance of a Madonna."

Thereupon Chérubin would smile again, as he glanced at Louise, and Monsieur Gérondif, thinking of something very different from madonnas, would say to himself:

"This girl will be perfectly bewitching! but if my pupil remains much longer with her—hum! The flesh is weak, the devil is very powerful, especially when he takes the face of a pretty girl. I am not always here; Jacquinot is almost always drunk, and Mère Nicole allows these children to run about together in the fields, looking for flowers among the grain, playing together in the grass,—all very hazardous amusements. I absolutely must look to all this. The best way would be to induce my pupil to return to Paris. I should go with him, there is not the slightest doubt, for his education is not yet complete enough for him to do without a tutor. I shall take care that he needs one for a long time yet, forever, if possible. I shall live in my pupil's mansion at Paris. That will be infinitely pleasanter than to live in this village; and then I can continue to keep an eye on little Louise at a distance; I will protect her, I will push her on in the world. As for Chérubin, after a few months in Paris, he will have forgotten his little friend of the fields.—All this is reasoned out with the wisdom of Cato, and it only remains to put it into execution."

And to attain his object, Monsieur Gérondif for some time past had not failed to talk constantly of Paris while giving Chérubin his lessons; he drew a fascinating, enchanting picture of that city; he praised its theatres, its promenades, its monuments, and the innumerable pleasures which one finds there at every step.

Young Chérubin was beginning to listen to these observations. The idea of going to Paris terrified him less; and his tutor would say:

"At least, come and spend a little time in the capital, to see your mansion, the house of your fathers, it is all so close at hand, and we will come back at once."

But Louise always wept when she saw that Chérubin was on the point of consenting to go to Paris; she would take her playmate's hand and exclaim:

"If you go to Paris, I am very sure that you won't come back here again; you'll forget Gagny and those who live here."

Nicole said the same, as she lovingly embraced her foster-child, whereupon Chérubin would instantly cry out:

"No, no, I won't go, since it makes you feel sad; I am happy here, and I shall always stay here."

At that, Monsieur Gérondif would bite his lips, trying to smile; but in the depths of his heart, he consigned nurses and childhood friends to the devil.

As for Jasmin, when the professor reproached him for not seconding him and urging his young master to go to Paris, he would reply, with that air of good humor which was natural to him:

"What do you expect me to do about it? My dear monsieur le marquis has passed his fifteenth birthday; he is his own master; he can do whatever he chooses; he can even dispose of his whole fortune, thirty thousand francs a year. But if it's his choice to remain with his nurse, I have no right to oppose him."

"When a man has such a handsome fortune as that, it's perfectly ridiculous for him to pass his best years out at nurse!" cried the tutor; "and then what good does it do my pupil to become learned, to learn so many useful things, if he continues to live with peasants? Monsieur Jasmin, history offers no example of remarkable men who have remained at nurse until they were fifteen. It is all very well to love the woman who reared us, but *est medius in rebus*."

"Monsieur le professeur, I am not good at guessing rebuses; but I am my master's very humble servant, and I have no right to give him orders."

At Paris, too, Jasmin had frequent discussions with Mademoiselle Turlurette on the subject of his young master. The former lady's maid had become housekeeper; she had grown so stout, although she was not yet forty, that it was very difficult for her to walk from one room to another; that state of corpulence nailed her to her chair, and prevented her from going to see her young master at Gagny. And Jasmin was not at all anxious to take her with him, because he always feared that Mademoiselle Turlurette would usurp a part of his authority, which he did not propose to stand. The bulky housekeeper asked the old servant every day why their young master did not leave his nurse; and sometimes sharp quarrels arose between them on that subject; but Jasmin always put an end to them by saying in a morose tone:

"Mademoiselle, after all, I am the one that the late Monsieur le Marquis de Grandvilain intrusted with the care of his son; in fact, I have the right to turn you out of the house if I choose; so be kind enough to allow me to guide young Chérubin as I please."

Thereupon Turlurette held her peace, although she knew perfectly well that Jasmin was not capable of discharging her.

"A foster-child of sixteen years!" she would mutter between her teeth; "that's a funny thing!"

Things were at this point when a servant appeared at the hôtel de

65

Grandvilain one morning, asked for Jasmin, and told him that the late monsieur le marquis's notary desired him to call at his office during the day, because it was very important that he should speak with him.

The old valet wondered what the notary could have to say to him; then he remembered that his young master had long since passed his fifteenth birthday, and that that was the time that his father had desired that he should be put in possession of his fortune. All this worried Jasmin, who said to himself:

"Thirty thousand francs a year, to say nothing of the additions due to the savings that I have made in fourteen years! It is a fact that it would be a pity to waste that at his foster-father's. But still, if Monsieur Chérubin insists on staying with Nicole, I can't use violence to compel him to return to Paris, for after all, he is his own master."

Jasmin decided to comply with the notary's wish. He put on his best coat, pulled a bit of his ruff out beneath his waistcoat, donned his silver buckled shoes, although they had long since ceased to be in style, and in that garb, worthy of the confidential valet of a great family, he betook himself to the office of Monsieur d'Hurbain, the notary.

When Jasmin appeared at the office, the notary was not alone; two persons were with him.

One of them, by name Edouard de Monfréville, was a man apparently thirty-six or thirty-seven years of age, who still had the bearing, the manners and all the dandified aspect of a young man. He was tall, well-built, as slender as if he were but twenty, and wore with much grace the costume of a young exquisite. His face was handsome and attractive at the same time; his features were regular, and his brown hair of a fineness and gloss which a lady might have envied; but in his great eyes, which were black and piercing, one could read sometimes a mocking expression which harmonized perfectly with the faint smile that played about his mouth; and upon his brow, which like his face bore signs of weariness, there were lines which indicated that ennui and grief had passed that way.

The other person was a man of twenty-eight, a faded blond, with a very fair complexion, light-blue eyes, a nose with dilated nostrils, and a large mouth with thick lips. That assemblage of features did not make what could be called a handsome man; but his face exhibited a constant succession of expressions which enlivened it wonderfully; it was a combination of gayety, raillery, cunning, libertinage, indifference, and shrewdness, all accompanied by most distinguished manners; and although his costume was a long way from the elegance of Monsieur de Monfréville's, and although, in fact, certain parts of his dress were too much neglected, he wore his soiled and shabby coat with so much ease of manner, he held his head so straight in his faded cravat, that it was impossible not to recognize in him a man of birth. His name was Comte Virgile Daréna.

When a clerk entered the private office and announced that old Jasmin had obeyed the summons that he had received, Daréna burst out laughing.

"Jasmin!" he said; "who in the devil can have such a name as Jasmin? Can it be, my dear notary, that you have clients named Jasmin? Why, that name is only fit for a stage servant!"

"No, Monsieur Daréna," replied the notary, with a smile, "this man is a servant in a most excellent family; he is one of that race of old retainers such as we used to see; unfortunately the race is almost extinct in our day."

"Ah! he must be an amusing character; an old groom, eh, Monfréville?"

The person to whom this question was addressed barely smiled as he replied:

"I don't see what there is so amusing in all this!"

"Oh! nothing amuses you when you are in one of your *days of humor*, as the English say.—Well, tell me, will you buy my little house in Faubourg Saint-Antoine? I will sell it to you for thirty thousand francs."

"No, I should blush to accept such an offer. Your house is worth nearly twice that, and I do not care to take advantage of your need of money to buy it at a low price."

"Oh! mon Dieu! that isn't the question at all! If the bargain is satisfactory to me, why shouldn't you take advantage of it? I make you the offer before a notary, and it seems to me that your conscience should be tranquil. I don't like the house; it is occupied by water carriers, Savoyards, the commonest of the common people! What the devil do you suppose I can do with it? They move without paying, or else they stay and don't pay; they insult whoever goes to ask them for money, or they threaten to beat you! Such tenants are delightful!"

"But you have a principal tenant who looks after all those details."

"No, no, I tell you that I want to sell, that is the quickest way out of it; it's too much of a nuisance to me! And then, there's another inconvenience: if I have among my tenants a pretty grisette or two, or a pretty face, why, you understand—I give them a receipt after obtaining, not their money, but something else. Upon my honor, I am not fitted for a landlord, my heart is too susceptible!"

"You are arranging your affairs in such a way that you won't be a landlord much longer," said the notary, shaking his head, "you are not reasonable, Monsieur Daréna. Only six years ago your father left you a very pretty fortune!"

"Of which I have nothing left but the little house that I want to sell," said Daréna, laughingly. "Well, that is the fate of all fortunes; they vanish, but one constructs another! I am never disturbed, for my part!—Well, Monfréville won't take my house, and so Monsieur d'Hurbain must sell it for me. But pray admit your old Jasmin! I am curious to see this fossil!"

"In whose service is this model retainer?" asked Monfréville.

"He was in the service of Monsieur le Marquis de Grandvilain, who died ten or eleven years ago."

"The Marquis de Grandvilain!" cried Daréna, throwing himself into a chair and laughing until the tears came. "What delicious names they have!"

"Grandvilain!" muttered Monfréville, "why, I knew the old marquis; my father was a friend of his. He used often to speak of a party at his house, of a display of fireworks to celebrate the birth of a son; of a frying-pan that was thrown into the air, and of saucepan covers that wounded several people."

"Nonsense! nonsense! it is impossible! Monfréville is making fun of us!" said Daréna, stretching himself out in his chair.

"It is all true," replied the notary; "what Monsieur de Monfréville says really happened. But the Marquis de Grandvilain is dead, and so is his wife; nobody is left now of the old family except a son, who is sixteen years and a half old, and who already has more than thirty thousand francs a year; I manage his property. But his father, obeying a whim, a most incredible piece of folly, provided that at fifteen years his son was to have control of his whole fortune, and he left him no guardian except old Jasmin, his valet de chambre."

Daréna straightened up in his chair and assumed a singular expression, as he exclaimed:

"Thirty thousand francs a year at fifteen! That deserves consideration."

"Was the poor old marquis mad?" asked Monfréville.

"No, but he was very old when the child was born, and he wished him to be his own master early in life."

"Pardi! that doesn't strike me as so foolish, after all!" said Daréna. "In fact, why shouldn't one be reasonable at fifteen, when one is so far from it at sixty? But how does the heir manage his fortune? He is consuming it doubtless in cakes and *marrons glacés?*"

"Thank heaven, so far as I know, he has given his time thus far only to his rhetoric and the humanities. But it was with a view to learning something about him that I sent for the faithful Jasmin. With your permission I will have him come in."

"We beg that you will do so. For my part, I am very curious to know how this little Grandvilain behaves himself. Oh! what a devil of a name! But no matter, I would gladly change with him now, if he would throw in his father's coin with the name.—What do you say, Monfréville? Oh! you are a philosopher; and besides, you are rich, which makes philosophy come very easy."

Jasmin's arrival put an end to this conversation. The old servant bowed low to all the company, then said to the notary:

"Has monsieur any questions to ask me?"

"Yes, my dear Jasmin. I want first of all to hear about our young marquis."

"He's very well, monsieur; he is in excellent health, and he's a very fine-looking boy."

"That is well; and his studies?"

"Well! so far as I can learn, monsieur, he seems to be a great scholar."

"Do you know, Jasmin, that your young master was sixteen more than six months ago?"

"Oh yes, monsieur, I know it very well."

"Does he know the terms of his father's will?"

"Why, yes, monsieur."

"I fancy that he is too sensible to think of entering into possession of his property yet; but for all that, it is my duty to go to him and render an account of my administration of it, and to ask him if it is his intention that I should continue to handle it. Moreover, I have long desired to see the young marquis, and I do not propose to postpone that pleasure any longer. At what college is he?"

Jasmin opened his eyes in dismay and looked toward the door.

"Don't you hear me?" continued the notary. "I ask you to what college I must go to find Monsieur Chérubin de Grandvilain?"

"The model valet seems to me as if he were deaf," said Daréna, laughing at Jasmin's expression; while Monsieur de Monfréville, who had been scrutinizing the old servant closely, walked toward him and fastening his eyes upon him, said in a half-serious, half-mocking tone:

"Do you mean that you don't know what you have done with your young master?"

"Yes, yes!" replied Jasmin; "monsieur le marquis is at Gagny."

"At Gagny! Is there a college there?" demanded the notary.

"Gagny, near Villemonble. Oh! I know that place," said Daréna; "it's a small village; there are some fine estates in the neighborhood, but not a restaurant in the whole region. I went there with two dancers from the Opéra, and we could not even obtain a rabbit stew, the inevitable dish in the country. But there never was a college at Gagny; I don't even know of a boarding-school there."

"Tell us, Monsieur Jasmin," said the notary in a stern tone, "where is young Grandvilain staying at Gagny?"

The old servant made up his mind and replied with an almost proud air:

"At his nurse's, monsieur."

At those words the notary was speechless, Monfréville began to laugh, and Daréna rolled about in his chair.

"At his nurse's!" repeated the notary at last. "Is it possible, Jasmin, that the young marquis is still at his nurse's, at sixteen years and a half?"

"Yes, monsieur; but never fear, he is none the less well educated; I found a teacher for him, the village schoolmaster, Monsieur Gérondif, who teaches him all that it is possible to teach."

Daréna roared with laughter anew, when he heard the name of the tutor.

"Educated at his nurse's!" he cried; "that is delicious; it's a new method, and perhaps it will become fashionable. I am tempted to return to my nurse myself."

"Monsieur Jasmin," said the notary, "I cannot understand how you can have left your master's son with peasants up to this time. I consider you very reprehensible; you should at least have consulted me."

The old servant, who was sorely vexed, began to shout at the top of his lungs:

"Monsieur, I am my master's servant! I am not the man to thwart him and to use force upon him, and it is not my fault if Monsieur Chérubin does not want to leave Nicole, his nurse, and his little foster-sister."

"Aha! so there's a little foster-sister, is there? I begin to understand the

70

young man's obstinacy," said Daréna; "and how old might the foster-sister be?"

"Two years younger than my young master,—about fourteen and a half."

"And is she pretty?"

"Why, yes, monsieur, she's a fine slip of a girl."

"Monsieur Jasmin," continued the notary, "things cannot go on like this; it is my duty to straighten out this affair; my friendship for the late Monsieur de Grandvilain imposes that duty upon me, and you too must understand that a child of a good family, the son of your former master, ought not to pass his best years in a village."

"I assure you, monsieur le notaire, that I tell my master so very often. I say to him: 'You have a house at Paris, a beautiful apartment with crimson hangings, solid mahogany furniture, a night table with carved corners, and the inside of gilded porcelain.' But all that doesn't tempt him. He turns his back on me and won't listen."

"I should think not!" cried Daréna; "the idea of the old fool expecting to tempt his master with a night table and all its accessories! If you wish, Monsieur d'Hurbain, I will undertake to persuade the young marquis to return to Paris."

"You, Monsieur Daréna; by what means, pray?"

"That's my business. Will you trust me?"

"I shall be very much obliged to you if you will assist me, but I propose to act for myself also. Monsieur de Monfréville, will not you lend us your assistance too? Won't you go to Gagny with me, as your father was a friend of the old marquis?"

"I am very much inclined to join you. Indeed, I am already trying to think how we can induce the young man to come back with us; for after all, this is not a case for resorting to violence. The young man is his own master, by his father's express desire; and if he should persist in remaining at his nurse's, we should be obliged to leave him there."

"But it is impossible that the marquis should not give way to our arguments, to our entreaties."

"Arguments! ah! my dear Monsieur d'Hurbain, I fancy that we shall need something stronger than arguments to captivate a boy."

"Messieurs," cried Daréna, "I suggest a wager. A magnificent dinner at the Rocher de Cancale, to be given by two of us to the one who triumphs and who brings young Chérubin to Paris. Is it a bargain?"

"With all our hearts."

"When do we start for Gagny?"

"I will arrange to leave my office at noon to-morrow, messieurs. Will you call for me? Shall I expect you?"

"No," said Monfréville, "let us go each on his own account; we shall be able to find this nurse's house."

"Nicole Frimousset," said Jasmin; "a narrow street leading into the square. Anyone will point out her house."

"Very well," said Daréna; "Nicole Frimousset; the names are engraved on my memory. Monfréville is right, it is better for us to go each on his own hook."

"But take care, messieurs," said the notary; "if you delay, you may make the journey for nothing, and I shall already have started for Paris with Chérubin."

"Oh! I don't think so," said Monfréville.

"As for me, messieurs, I am a bold player," said Daréna, "and I will give you the start. I will not leave Paris until a full hour after you, and even so I am sure that I shall arrive in time."

Jasmin, who was bewildered and somewhat alarmed by all that he heard, exclaimed with an air of dismay:

"I say, messieurs, I hope that you won't do my young master any injury in all this; I mean, I hope that you won't make him unhappy?"

"Ha! ha! ha! this old fellow is enchanting with his innocence!" said Daréna.—"Never fear, venerable retainer! We shall employ only pleasant methods! As for you, all there is for you to do is to find a way to get Monsieur Chérubin's little foster-sister out of the way to-morrow morning. That is indispensable for the success of our excursion."

"You hear, Jasmin?" said the notary. "Remember that the happiness, the future of your young master is at stake, and that you will be very blameworthy if you do not try to help us."

The old servant bowed and went out, saying that he would obey.

Monfréville and Daréna also left the notary's, saying to each other:

"Until to-morrow, at Gagny."

X

THE ARMS OF ACHILLES

Jasmin returned to the house utterly upset; the old servant did not know whether he ought to rejoice or to grieve; he would be very glad to see his master at Paris, so that he might be always with him, and serve him as he had served the old marquis; but he was afraid that that would grieve the youth whom he called his dear child; and he was also afraid that life in Paris would not be so good for Chérubin's health as life in the village.

While making these reflections, he summoned all the servants in the house. It will be remembered that Jasmin had kept all those who had been in the employ of his former master, and that is why Chérubin's household consisted entirely of mature persons. The cook had passed his sixtieth year; the coachman was approaching his sixty-fifth; there was a little jockey of fifty; and Mademoiselle Turlurette, who was a child compared with all the rest, was in her thirty-seventh year, none the less.

"My children," said Jasmin to the servants, "I think it my duty to inform you that our young master will come among us to-morrow."

"To-morrow!" cried Turlurette, with a joyful exclamation; "is that certain?"

"It is very certain—perhaps. However, arrange everything so that Monsieur Chérubin will be pleased; see that everything is rubbed and polished with more care than ever. Cook, prepare a dainty dinner. Coachman, let the carriage and horses be ready, in case he should want to use them. Have flowers placed in the hall, as on the days when my late master gave a ball."

"Are we going to have a display of fireworks?" asked Turlurette in a quizzical tone.

"No, mademoiselle, no, I have had enough of fireworks!" replied Jasmin, passing his hand over his face; "and unless Monsieur Chérubin orders, not even a rocket will ever be fired in this courtyard again. But still, we must see that it is very lively here. By the way, we will have some music—three organ grinders, and as many violin players, who will be stationed in the courtyard; they must play their best pieces when our young master enters the house; that cannot fail to be agreeable to him."

"Do you want singers too?" asked the old jockey.

"Well! if you can find any singers, men or women, it seems to me that they will not do any harm. You understand, all this for the afternoon."

The next morning, Jasmin started early for Gagny, where he arrived about ten o'clock. First of all, he asked for Chérubin, and Nicole informed him that he had gone to walk with Louise toward Maison Rouge. The old servant was about to go in search of the young people when he met Monsieur Gérondif in the square, and hastened to inform him as to what was to happen during the day.

The professor clapped his hands, tossed his new hat in the air, and seemed inclined to cut a caper.

"*Tandem! Denique! Ultima cumæi venit jam carminis ætas! Jam nova progenies cœlo demittitur alto!*"

"Why no, that isn't it," replied Jasmin; "I tell you that the notary and two of his friends are coming."

"Very good! perfect! more than perfect! We must now find my pupil at once."

"I was going to look for him; he is walking with little Louise in the direction of Maison Rouge."

"With little Louise, who is already large. How imprudent it is! It is high time to separate the man from the serpent!"

"Did you see a serpent?"

"The serpent, my dear Jasmin, is woman, the apple, sin! You don't seem to understand; I will explain it to you some other day, but now we must find the child at once."

"Especially as those gentlemen requested me to send the little girl away this morning, while they were talking to my master."

"You see, those gentlemen think as I do; they understand that this little girl is now a dangerous companion, most certainly. We will get her out of the way, virtuous Jasmin, we will find a pretext, a subterfuge. Come, take my arm and let us run."

"Run! the devil! that's very easy to say! However, I'll try."

"Men run at all ages, worthy Jasmin, and you were built for a runner."

As he spoke, the professor took the old servant's arm and hurried him away in the direction where they hoped to find Chérubin. As they walked rapidly along, Jasmin asked Monsieur Gérondif:

"Have you thought of any excuse for sending the girl away?"

"No; have you?"

"No, I have not."

"Let us go on, that will come in due time."

That rapid march lasted for three-quarters of an hour. Jasmin could hold out no longer, he was entirely out of breath. But the professor still pulled him along, saying:

"*Macte puer! macte animo!* Our dear Chérubin's happiness is at stake. Look out, excellent Jasmin, you are stumbling; you are putting your feet in the ruts, in pools of water!"

The excellent Jasmin's breath was exhausted, and he decided to fall in the middle of the road.

"I can't go any farther," he stammered; "I must get my breath."

But at that moment Monsieur Gérondif glanced at a clump of trees a short distance from the road and exclaimed:

"There they are! the little girl is eating apricots; she offers one to my pupil, who stands lost in admiration before his apricot! It is time that we arrived."

Chérubin had gone out early with Louise that morning; they had taken a basket containing bread and fruit, and looked forward to eating their luncheon in the woods; that frugal collation seemed most delicious to them. And, in sooth, what more could they desire? they were together, and they loved each other; that is the most enjoyable repast to which one brings a contented heart.

The relations between Louise and Chérubin at this time were so pleasant, so pure, that they were happy to be together and aspired to no other happiness. It may be, however, that young Louise's affection was more eager, more expansive, because there was already a tinge of sadness in it. She was afraid that Chérubin would decide to go to Paris; she was afraid that she was going to lose her friend; and that fear made her love him even more, for our affections are strengthened by the sorrows that they cause us.

The two young people were greatly surprised when the professor and Jasmin suddenly appeared in the midst of their open-air repast.

"We were looking for you, attractive youths," said Monsieur Gérondif; "we were perturbed in spirit. The adventure of Pyramus and Thisbe has been running in my head; I have mistaken every dog I met for a lioness. I am well aware that my pupil has no inclination to fly, like the young Assyrian, with any Thisbe; but anyone may make a false step."

"Tell me, why did you come to look for us?" said Chérubin; "I have time enough to study, I should think. I know enough already. Is anyone sick? Has anything happened, that Jasmin comes with you?"

Monsieur Gérondif seemed struck by a sudden thought; he glanced at Jasmin and said:

"In truth, my noble pupil, there has been an accident—not at all serious, I trust. Your nurse's oldest son has hurt himself; he is at Montfermeil—he has written; and Nicole would like to have Louise go to him at once; she will come too very soon."

"We'll go with Louise," said Chérubin.

"No, we had better go back to poor Nicole, who is in grief—she doesn't know where to go for a doctor. Louise can go to Montfermeil alone; you can see the first houses from here."

"Oh, yes! yes! I will be there in a few minutes," said Louise; "but where is dear mother Nicole's son?"

"At Madame Patineau's, on the main street. Here, here is her address, and a line for her."

Monsieur Gérondif scrawled a few words in pencil, wherein he requested the lady to whom he was sending the girl to keep her at her house, and not to let her go until she was sent for. The girl took the note, bade Chérubin adieu and ran off toward Montfermeil. The professor rubbed his hands and glanced at Jasmin, who said to himself:

"I should never have thought of that."

They returned to Gagny; as they approached the square, they saw a carriage stop and a gentleman alight: it was Monsieur d'Hurbain, the notary.

"Here's a visitor for you," said Jasmin to his master. "This gentleman is your notary, in whose care your venerable father placed his testament."

"And it was to prevent your attention being distracted so that you might receive some gentlemen who are coming from Paris to see you, that we sent little Louise to Montfermeil," said Gérondif with a smile.

"What? the accident to Nicole's son——"

"Was all a joke."

Before Chérubin had time to reply, Monsieur d'Hurbain came up and bowed low to him. The notary's solemn manner made an impression on the young man, who faltered a few words in reply to the flattering remarks that were addressed to him. They walked toward the nurse's house, and for the first time Chérubin had a feeling of something like shame when the notary said:

"What, monsieur le marquis, is this where you are studying? You are sixteen and a half years old, you belong to a noble family, you have a handsome fortune, and you pass your life beneath the roof of these village folk! I honor the laboring man, I esteem all honest persons, but everyone should keep to his own rank, monsieur le marquis, otherwise society would fall into confusion and anarchy; and there would no longer be that desire to rise, to succeed, which, by implanting in men's hearts a praiseworthy ambition, makes them capable of noble efforts to attain the end at which they are eager to arrive."

"Bravo! *recte dicis!*" cried Monsieur Gérondif, smiling at the notary; "monsieur talks now as I used to talk."

Chérubin blushed and did not know what to reply. Monsieur d'Hurbain continued his efforts to make the young man listen to reason, displaying the utmost amiability and suavity in his arguments. He was careful, however, to dwell on the marquis's rank and wealth, and he always ended with these words:

"You agree with me now, do you not, and you are coming back to Paris with me?"

But Chérubin, although he seemed to listen with great deference to the notary's speeches, replied in a very mild tone:

"No, monsieur, I prefer to stay here."

"It certainly isn't my fault!" cried Monsieur Gérondif, raising his eyes heavenward. "Every day I say to my pupil the same things that you have said, monsieur; but I reinforce them by example from history, ancient and modern; it's as if I were teaching a blind man to draw!"

Monsieur d'Hurbain was beginning to doubt the success of his visit, when they heard a horse's footsteps. They ran to the door to see what it was, and discovered a very stylishly dressed gentleman in a dainty tilbury, accompanied by his groom only.

It was Edouard de Monfréville, who was driving himself. He stopped, jumped lightly to the ground and approached the party, bowing courteously to Chérubin, to whom the notary said:

"Allow me to introduce the son of one of your father's old friends, Monsieur de Monfréville, who has come to add his entreaties to mine, to induce you to go to Paris."

Monfréville took Chérubin's hand and pressed it; and after scrutinizing the young man for some time, he said:

"When, in addition to a name and a fortune, a man also possesses such a charming face, it is really inexcusable for him to hide in a village."

"Most assuredly!" murmured Gérondif, smiling at Monfréville; "if Helen had hidden, we should not have had the siege of Troy; if Dunois had remained with his nurse, he probably would not have been called 'le beau Dunois.'"

Monfréville bestowed an ironical glance on the professor, and continued to address Chérubin:

"My dear monsieur, my father was a friend of yours, and that made me desire your acquaintance; it rests entirely with you whether we shall be friends as our fathers were. Oh! I realize that the difference between my age and yours may make my suggestion seem absurd to you, but when you know the world, you will find that such differences vanish before congenial tastes and temperaments; I am certain even now that we shall get on very well together. But deuce take it! what sort of costume is this? A good-looking young fellow, with a fine figure, rigged out in such style! It is pitiful!"

"My young master employs his late father's tailor," murmured Jasmin; "I thought that I ought not to take him anywhere else."

"You were wrong, my faithful servant; a tailor is not a relic to be preserved with respect; evidently this particular one is out of touch with the styles of the day.—Franck! bring what I told you to put under the seat of the tilbury."

Monfréville's servant soon appeared laden with clothes; he laid out on a table a beautiful coat made in the latest style, a waistcoat of bewitching material, black satin stocks, dainty cravats, and a little blue velvet cap, with gold lace and tassel.

Chérubin could not restrain a cry of admiration at sight of all those things. Without asking his permission, Monfréville removed his jacket and waistcoat and made him put on what he had brought; then he put a richly embroidered cravat about his neck and tied it rakishly; and lastly he placed the charming little velvet cap on his head and arranged the curls which it did not hide. Then he led the young man in front of a mirror and said:

"Look at yourself! Aren't you a hundred times better-looking?"

Chérubin blushed with pleasure when he saw how comely he was; and in truth his new costume did impart a wholly different expression to his pretty face. He was so handsome that Nicole, although distressed to find that her *fieu* was to be taken away from her, could not help crying out:

"Jarni! how fine he is! Why, he's superb in that rig! He's a hundred times better-looking than he was!"

"He doesn't look at all like his late father," murmured Jasmin.

"He resembles the son of Jupiter and Latona, Diana's brother, otherwise called Apollo,—Phœbus, if you prefer," cried Monsieur Gérondif, still smiling.

Monsieur d'Hurbain glanced at Monfréville with an air of satisfaction, as if to congratulate him on having discovered the means of seducing Chérubin, who, in truth, seemed delighted with his costume. He constantly gazed at and admired himself; and Monsieur de Monfréville, to encourage his favorable disposition, made haste to say to him:

"I was told that you lived in a village, but I was loath to believe it! The son of the Marquis de Grandvilain, who ought to be noted for his style, his dress, his manners, who, in short, was made to be a shining light in Parisian society, cannot remain buried in a peasant's house! It is an anomaly—a crime! These trifling specimens of clothes will give you an idea of what you would have in Paris. I have come in my tilbury to fetch you, and I propose that within a week you shall be the best dressed, the most stylish young man in the capital. You will set the fashion; you are rich enough and handsome enough for that."

Chérubin seemed to be captivated by Monfréville's words, and the latter, assured of his triumph, said in a moment:

"Let us start, my young friend, let us not delay any longer. The tilbury is waiting for us, and Paris is beckoning to you."

But at that Chérubin's face became clouded, and instead of following Monsieur de Monfréville and the notary, who had risen, he resumed his seat, saying:

"No, I don't want to go away, for I want Louise to see me in these clothes."

The two gentlemen from the city were in despair; they believed that they had fully persuaded the young marquis to accompany them, and again he refused.

The notary argued, Monfréville put forth all his eloquence and drew fascinating pictures of the pleasures of Paris, but Chérubin refused to go with them.

Monsieur Gérondif was in dismay, Nicole was triumphant, and Jasmin muttered under his breath:

"I had an idea that these men wouldn't be any smarter than me."

No one spoke, for no one knew what course to adopt. Suddenly they heard another carriage approaching. Thereupon a gleam of hope shone in Monfréville's eyes, and Monsieur d'Hurbain exclaimed:

"Faith! it's high time that Monsieur Daréna arrived, but I doubt very much his having any better success than we have had."

"Perhaps he will," murmured Monfréville; "Daréna is one of those people who dare to do anything."

The carriage stopped in front of the nurse's house, and Nicole's guests ran to the door to see who alighted.

The cab, for it was a vulgar cab that had arrived, seemed to contain a number of people, to judge by the noise inside. Several voices could be heard speaking at once, and continual bursts of laughter. At last the door opened. Monsieur Daréna alighted first, dressed even more shabbily than on the previous day; which fact did not deter him from exhibiting the most distinguished manners, as he assisted his companions to alight.

First came a young woman dressed as a Spaniard, then one dressed as an Odalisk, a third in a Swiss costume, and a fourth in the piquant garb of a Neapolitan. And they were all young, pretty, graceful and shapely; their eyes were bright, mischievous, and most alluring; and there was in their manner of jumping from the carriage, a surprising lightness and grace, and in their general bearing an uncommon absence of restraint.

The villagers gazed at them in wide-eyed amazement. Monsieur Gérondif affected to lower his eyes, but he hazarded a glance nearly every minute. The notary glanced at Monfréville with an air of surprise, muttering:

"What does all this mean?"

Monfréville laughed heartily, as he replied:

"Faith! I believe that he is cleverer than we are."

Meanwhile, Daréna took two of the ladies by the hand.

"Come, Rosina and Malvina; follow us, Cœlina and Fœdora. We have come to pay our respects to the young Marquis de Grandvilain. Where is he? Ah, yes, I see him; this charming young man with the melting eyes is he. *Peste!* be on your guard, mesdames; those eyes will make terrible havoc in your ranks."

As he spoke, Daréna entered the house with his companions. After ushering in his four ladies, who seemed not in the least embarrassed, and who scrutinized laughingly the interior of the rustic dwelling, Daréna saluted Chérubin as if he were an old acquaintance, and said:

"My dear marquis, your notary, Monsieur d'Hurbain, is mine as well; your friend Monsieur de Monfréville is also a very intimate friend of mine; so you see that I too should be your friend—that is a title which I should deem myself fortunate to deserve. Shake hands, marquis—men like us understand each other instantly. You are young, but we will form you."

Chérubin was bewildered by all that he saw and heard; moreover, the Spaniard and the Neapolitan were already flashing glances at him of a sort to which he was not accustomed; while the Odalisk smiled at him in a most enticing fashion, and the Swiss constantly passed the tip of her tongue over her lips and winked at him. All this caused him a perturbation which he could not define.

"Marquis Chérubin," continued Daréna, "I have ventured to bring with me four fascinating ladies; they are artists, dancers of the greatest talent, connected with the Grand Opéra in Paris; they had a most eager desire to see you and to drink milk in the country.—Is it possible to obtain milk here, virtuous villager?"

While Daréna put this question to Nicole, who ran off at once to the dairy, the little woman dressed as a Swiss jumped up and down on her chair, crying:

"Yes! milk's splendid! I'm going to drink it hard."

Daréna walked to where she sat and nudged her with his elbow, saying in her ear:

"Be kind enough to keep quiet, Malvina, for you can't say anything but nonsense."

And Monfréville, biting his lips to avoid laughing, whispered to Daréna:

"You have the face to say that these women are from the Opéra!"

"Three of them are, my dear fellow; I swear that those three are *figurantes*. The Swiss is at one of the boulevard theatres, it is true, but she has a bewitching leg.—I have brought these ladies in their stage costumes," Daréna continued, addressing Chérubin, "because they promised to give you a slight specimen of their talent. Come, my goddesses, give us a pretty *pas de quatre* for the young marquis, who has no idea of what is to be seen at the Opéra. I realize that this isn't as convenient a place for dancing as the stage; the floor isn't parqueted; but you will have all the more credit."

"It isn't even tiled!" cried the Swiss, looking at her feet; "how do you expect us to slide on such a floor? No, thanks! it's too much work! We shall come down on our backsides!"

"Ha! ha! very pretty! very pretty!" cried Daréna, affecting to laugh heartily in order to lessen the effect produced by the Swiss girl's expression; "you must excuse madame; she isn't a Parisian and she doesn't know our language very well; she doesn't understand the comparative value of words."

"Tibullus, Petronius and Ovid sometimes employed the equivalent," said Monsieur Gérondif, perpetrating an immense smile, so that the four dancers might see all his teeth.

"I ain't a Parisian!" cried Mademoiselle Malvina; "well, upon my word! I was born on Rue Mouffetard—just where my mother sells Brie cheese."

Daréna trod on her foot and whispered to her:

"If you don't hold your tongue, Malvina, I'll put you in the cab, you shan't have any milk, and you shan't come to the dinner."

The Swiss held her tongue, and the count, taking a kit from his pocket, prepared to play.

"I'll be the orchestra," he said; "I have thought of everything, you see. Come, mesdames, ready."

Meanwhile, Monsieur d'Hurbain went to Monfréville and said to him in an undertone:

"Really, Monsieur le Comte de Daréna has employed an expedient which —I don't know whether I ought to assent to this. His scheme seems to me rather shady."

"Why so?" rejoined Monfréville. "Daréna is cleverer than we are. I think that his method of seduction is all right. After all, the young fellow would go to the Opéra, if he went to Paris; so what is the harm of letting him see here what he would see on the stage? In fact, it seems to me that the illusion is much less."

"Very well," said the notary, resuming his seat; "after all, the end justifies the means."

The four dancers were on the point of beginning their performance, when Nicole appeared with milk and cups. They pounced upon the latter and declared that they proposed to have something to drink first.

While they were drinking, Chérubin kept his eyes constantly on those four women, who were so utterly unlike all the women he had ever before seen. Monsieur Gérondif poured the milk for the dancers with his own hands.

"Assuredly I bear a resemblance to Ganymede at this moment," he said to them. "He served Jupiter, I serve Terpsichore and her sisters."

"I say," said Malvina, snatching the pail from the professor's hand, "you make us sick, pouring it out so, drop by drop! I'd rather drink as much as I like—it's a quicker way."

"It's amazing how thirsty they are, for fashionable ladies," said old Jasmin, rolling his eyes in wonderment.

When the milk was exhausted, the four dancers took their places. The others were seated, Daréna with his kit. He played the air of the *Jota Arragonaise*, and the ladies began to dance with much grace and lightness of

83

foot.

The peasants were lost in admiration. Jasmin applauded; Monsieur Gérondif no longer lowered his eyes, and his whole face was as red and inflamed as his nose.

Monfréville and the notary watched Chérubin; he seemed fascinated, enchanted by the novel spectacle presented to him, and his eyes did not grow weary of gazing at those young and pretty women, whose steps, whose attitudes, whose slightest movements were instinct with pleasure and licentiousness. Daréna, observing the effect produced by the dance, played a livelier air, then another in even quicker time. The dancers followed the change of tempo, and their dance became more rapid, more seductive. They seemed to vie with one another in grace and litheness; their eyes, enlivened by the violent exercise, shone brighter and with more fire. Jasmin applauded wildly, Monsieur Gérondif scratched his nose as if he would demolish it, and Chérubin became much moved. At that moment, excited by the zest with which she danced, Mademoiselle Malvina began to hurl her legs into space with such vigor that it was impossible for the spectators to avoid seeing that she wore no drawers.

"They are bayadères!" cried Monsieur Gérondif, whose eyes were almost out of his head; "it's the Mozambique dance! it's very interesting!"

Monsieur d'Hurbain, considering that the Mozambique dance went altogether too far, rose and said:

"Very good, mesdames, but that will do; you must be tired."

"Bah!" cried Mademoiselle Malvina, "I'd like to dance the cancan myself! I'm rather good at the cancan."

Daréna, who was desirous that the effect produced by the dance should not be wasted, ran to Chérubin and took his arm, saying:

"Now we are going back to Paris; we are to dine at the Rocher de Cancale with these ladies, and they hope that you will join us, for the party would not be complete without you."

Chérubin was excited, and he hesitated. Daréna made a sign to the dancers, who at once surrounded the youth, saying:

"Oh, yes, monsieur, come to Paris with us!"

"You must go to the Opéra to-night; you will see us dance there, and it will be rather different from what it was in this room."

"It would be very mean of you to refuse us."

"And then," cried Malvina, "at the Rocher de Cancale! That's the place to get a good dinner! I'm going to stuff myself, I am!"

"Come, come, you must be one of us!" exclaimed Daréna.

The Spaniard and the Neapolitan each seized one of Chérubin's arms; he let them drag him away and they carried him, almost dancing, to the cab, which he entered with Daréna and the four dancers.

"But I have a carriage," cried the notary; "you will be too crowded with six in there! Let some of the ladies come in my carriage."

"No, no!" said Daréna; "we'll sit in one another's laps—it's all the more fun!—Off you go, driver; founder your nags—we'll pay you for them. To the Rocher de Cancale!"

The cab drove away with Chérubin, who had not even had time to bid his nurse good-bye.

"Daréna has succeeded!" said Monfréville; "the bird has left his nest."

"Yes," replied Monsieur d'Hurbain, "but this sort of thing must not go too far. And this dinner—with those women; really, I can't be there. I, a notary, dine with ballet dancers!"

"Oh! bless my soul! just once; you can go *incog*. Besides, it's for a good motive, and your presence will prevent the dinner from being too indecent. Let us take my tilbury, we can follow them better."

Monsieur d'Hurbain entered the tilbury with Monfréville, and Monsieur Gérondif and Jasmin jumped into the carriage.

"They are taking my young master to the Rocher de Cancale," said the old servant, "and I have ordered a sumptuous banquet at the house, and a reception, with music and flowers and——"

"Never mind, worthy Jasmin," rejoined the tutor, "all those things will serve as well later; my pupil will have to go home eventually. As for myself, I am Mentor, and I must not abandon Telemachus, even when he goes to dinner at the Rocher de Cancale."

XI

MONFRÉVILLE.—DARÉNA.—POTERNE

A handsome salon had been engaged and a sumptuous banquet ordered at the Rocher de Cancale, by Comte Daréna, who had said to himself before he started for Gagny:

"Whatever happens, we shall surely come back to dinner; to be sure, if I happen to be one of those who are to pay, it will be rather hard for me just at this time; but that doesn't worry me much; I'll order the dinner none the less."

To give no thought to anything but pleasure, to pay no heed to the future, to be, in truth, often indifferent concerning affairs of the present, such was Daréna's nature. Born of a noble family, he had received an excellent education and had studied diligently. His father, a man of a proud and stern character, having observed in his son early in life a decided taste for independence and dissipation, had thought that he could correct him by depriving him of those amusements and that liberty which are the ordinary means of relaxation after toil and study. Thus, when Daréna was nineteen years of age, he had never had a franc that he could call his own, or a half hour of freedom. At that time his father died; his mother had died long before, and he suddenly found himself his own master and possessed of a very pretty little fortune. He plunged recklessly into pleasure and dissipation, trying to make up all the time that his father's severity had caused him to lose, and bade adieu forever to study and to serious things.

Cards, women, horses, the table, became his idols. At first he frequented the best society, to which his name and his wealth gave him access; from the very beginning he had a multitude of love intrigues; but Daréna was not sentimental, he looked for nothing but pleasure in such affairs, and broke them off as soon as he foreshadowed the slightest exaction or annoyance.

As ladies in good society are not always disposed to form a liaison of a few days only, and as Comte Daréna's behavior was no secret, since he plumed himself on not becoming attached to any woman, his amatory triumphs gradually became less numerous in the fashionable world, and he was compelled to pay his addresses to *petites bourgeoises*, then to ladies of the theatre, then to grisettes, then to courtesans; and finally he had grown to be so unexacting on that point that he had been known to take his mistresses from the most humble ranks of society.

Daréna's fortune, like his love-affairs, had sunk constantly lower and lower. At last, at the age of twenty-eight, the count had squandered his whole patrimony and had nothing left save the house in Faubourg Saint-Antoine, which he desired to sell, and upon which he had already borrowed more than it was worth.

But, far from worrying concerning his present plight and his future, so long as he was able to dine well, to drink champagne with a ballet dancer, a figurante, a lace-maker, or even a lady's maid, Daréna snapped his fingers at all the rest. To obtain those enjoyments, he was often obliged to resort to doubtful expedients; but the man who is not particular in choosing his acquaintances is not always particular as to his means of existence.

A person named Poterne had seconded Daréna's dissipation and ruin to the utmost of his power. This Poterne was a man whose age it was impossible to guess, he was so ugly and unshapely. A gaunt, bony, angular body, supported by thin, knock-kneed legs, was surmounted by an oblong head of excessive length, a nose broken in the centre and hooked at the end, a mouth without lips, a protruding chin, and small eyes of a dull green hue, shaded by bushy eyebrows, and turning incessantly in every direction. Add to these an enormous quantity of thick, dirty brown hair, always cut like the quills of a hedgehog, and you have a faithful image of Monsieur Poterne.

This man had become attached to Comte Daréna when he was still wealthy; he had offered his services in any capacity; he knew all the places in Paris where a young man of family can ruin himself with the least difficulty. If Daréna spied, at the play or on the street, a woman who attracted him, Poterne undertook to follow her, and to hand her a letter containing information concerning him. Later, Poterne made it his business to find usurers, money-lenders, accommodating tradesmen; so that he had become indispensable to the count, who treated him sometimes as his friend, sometimes as his servant, cajoled him occasionally, despised him always, and could never do without him.

The reader will assume perhaps that it had been this gentleman's aim to enrich himself at the expense of the person whom he was assisting to ruin himself. That was Poterne's idea at first; but his own vices prevented him from taking advantage of another's failings. As inveterate a gambler and libertine as Daréna, while the latter was losing thousand-franc notes in a fashionable salon, Poterne was gambling away, in some wine-shop or low resort, the money he had extracted from his intimate friend. While Daréna entertained some charmer at Véfour's or Véry's, Poterne betook himself to a gin-shop to squander what money he had with a street peddler, and he was too ugly not to be compelled to be open-handed. And when Daréna was without a sou he sometimes abused his friend, and accused him of being the author of his ruin. At such times he unceremoniously appropriated all that Poterne possessed; and that worthy, who was also a coward, allowed himself to be despoiled without a murmur, promising himself that he would have his revenge ere long.

It may seem strange that the refined Monfréville should be on intimate terms with a man whose tastes, whose conduct, whose very dress, proved his disorderly mode of life. But there are people who, after knowing a person when he was rich and fortunate, dare not turn their backs on him when they meet him with a soiled coat and dingy hat. Moreover, Daréna still had intervals of prosperity; when the cards had been favorable to him, or when his friend Poterne had discovered some new resource, he instantly reappeared, elegantly and stylishly dressed; he frequented the theatres, the ballrooms and the best restaurants in Paris; and a few days later, a perceptible falling off in his toilet, a certain lack of neatness in some part of his costume, indicated that the situation had changed. But even with a wretched hat and dirty linen, Daréna succeeded so well in retaining the manners of good society, that it was hard to believe that he consorted with the very lowest.

Indeed, does anyone know aught of the private life of the great majority of the persons with whom he has only a passing connection? Meeting Daréna arrayed as in the days of his prosperity, seeing him squander money madly in some pleasure resort, no one asked him by what blessed change of luck he had become rich; and for the same reason, when he was seen, in shabby garments, slinking into a wretched twenty-two sou restaurant, no one took pains to inquire what hard luck he had had. In Paris, people do not try to worm themselves into other people's secrets; and in this respect, discretion very often resembles indifference.

Monfréville, who had known Daréna when he was rich, was well aware that he had squandered his fortune, but he did not believe him to be entirely without resources, having no idea that he would resort to indelicate methods of obtaining money. The count had frequently borrowed a thousand-franc note of him, however, none of which had he ever returned; but Edouard de Monfréville was wealthy and attached little importance to those trifling services. And then, too, Daréna's society amused him; his sallies, his indifference, sometimes carried to the point of cynicism, made him laugh and banished the melancholy humor which now and then took possession of his mind.

Sometimes people wondered what could be the cause of that pensive air, of that smile, rather bitter than mocking, which often played about Monfréville's mouth. He was rich, he had everything calculated to attract. In society he was sought after, women schemed to gain his notice; he had been known to have a great number of love-affairs, and he was still at an age to have more. But his merriment rarely seemed genuine, and in his conversation he avoided speaking of a sex of which he could hardly have had reason to complain. Some thought that Monfréville had reached the point of being surfeited with all sorts of pleasure, and attributed to that fact the clouds that sometimes darkened his brow; others, when they heard him sneer at those of his friends who believed in the constancy of their mistresses, concluded that the handsome and fascinating Monfréville had had some unfortunate passion, had been the victim of some treachery. Finally, when he was seen to pass his thirtieth year, and even to approach his fortieth, without apparently thinking of marriage, all sorts of conjectures were indulged in.

"He must have a very low opinion of women," people said, "as he doesn't choose to do like other men, and settle down, under the yoke of hymen."

But Edouard de Monfréville paid no heed to what people might think or say of him; he continued to live according to his taste, to do exactly as he chose; sometimes after passing a month in a succession of uproarious debauches, surrounded by a jovial, dissipated crowd, all whose follies he shared, he would hold himself aloof from society for weeks at a time, finding pleasure only in solitude. His friends had finally become accustomed to the eccentricities of his humor, because in society a rich man is always entitled to be original; only the poor devils are denied that privilege.

Now that we are better acquainted with the people whom we are to join, let us enter the Rocher de Cancale, where Chérubin had just arrived with the priestesses of Terpsichore.

XII

A DINNER AT THE ROCHER DE CANCALE

Chérubin found himself in Paris, and at the Rocher de Cancale, before he had had time to collect his thoughts. All the way to town the ladies had talked so much nonsense, their conversation was so lively, their remarks so amusing, that the boy had not ears enough to hear, and he glanced constantly from one to another of the dancers, to make sure that he was not dreaming.

When they entered the cab, the ladies enveloped themselves in ample cloaks, which concealed their costumes, and pulled hoods over their heads, so that their headdresses could not be seen.

"Why do these ladies all disguise themselves in hoods?" Chérubin asked Daréna in an undertone.

"My dear marquis," the latter replied aloud, "they do it so that their stage costumes may not be seen when they go into the restaurant, for the Carnival hasn't come yet.—A modest dress is the correct thing in Paris."

"Bah! I don't care a fig for your correct thing!" said Mademoiselle Malvina; "for my part I'd just as lief walk about Paris in a Swiss costume. I say, why mightn't I be a real Swiss?"

"If you wore an oyster woman's costume, my dear girl, it's much more probable that no one would think that you were disguised."

"Well! well! that's a joke, I suppose! how ugly you are! When you're out-at-elbows the way you sometimes are, you don't look any too much like a count yourself!"

Daréna laughed heartily and tapped Malvina on the cheek, saying:

"Come, come, hold your tongue, and above all things behave decently, mesdames; in the country a mild sort of freedom is permissible, but at the Rocher de Cancale, and in the honorable company with which you are to dine, remember, my little shepherdesses, that if you are not discreet I shall be obliged to turn you out of the room."

"Bless my soul! we know how to behave, monsieur! Do you think we never go into swell society?"

"Why, I often dine with my friend and his brother, who's one of the biggest butchers in Paris!"

"And I sometimes keep my cousin's desk; she's a baker and sells pastry, and only gentlemen with canary-colored gloves come to her little place to eat."

"Very good, mesdames, very good; we are certain now that you are worthy to go into good society, and that you know how to behave decorously. Oh! if Monsieur d'Hurbain had not come to dine with us! But he has come, for I see him and Monfréville getting out of the tilbury. We have arrived; come, my young marquis, hand out the ladies."

The carriage stopped and the door was opened; a porcupine's head appeared, surmounting a body clad in an old nut-colored box-coat, the collar of which was marred by some very extensive spots of grease. It was Monsieur Poterne, who had stepped forward to assist the ladies to alight.

Malvina drew back, crying:

"Great God! what sort of thing is that? An owl, a hedgehog?"

"It is my—my business agent," replied Daréna; "he has looked to it that everything is properly prepared, and now he has come to assist you to alight; he is an extremely obliging man."

"He may possibly be obliging, but he is very ugly; isn't he, Rosina?"

"Yes. Oh! how stupid it is to be ugly like that!"

"And when you look from him to our charming little Monsieur Chérubin!"

"Gad! there's as much difference as there is between the sun and a flea!"

"Come, mesdames, get out of the carriage; you can talk upstairs."

The company soon assembled in the salon where the table was laid. Messieurs d'Hurbain and Monfréville had arrived at the same time with the cab containing Chérubin and the dancers. The notary went to Daréna and said in his ear:

"I trust, my dear count, that your dancers will behave properly here. I agree that by their graceful dancing and their bright eyes they have fascinated this young man; but he is still a mere child, who ought not to consort with ballet dancers——"

"Mon Dieu! don't be alarmed! You surprise me! It is due to me that this baby of sixteen years and a half consented to leave his nurse, and, instead of thanking me, you preach at me. Be of service to people—exert your imagination—so that they may lecture you afterwards!"

"I say, Daréna," said Monfréville, scrutinizing Monsieur Poterne, who was sidling by the ladies, casting furtive glances at them, to which they replied by wry faces, "is that horribly dirty person a friend of yours? Do you expect us to dine with him? I must confess that I am not charmed by the prospect of his company. Who is the fellow? He looks very like a hawk."

"He is my steward."

"Ah! so you still have a steward? I thought that you had ceased to keep up an establishment."

"I have kept nobody else. This man looks after my affairs—he's an invaluable fellow for expedients."

"In that case, he would do well to devise an expedient for obtaining another coat."

"Well! aren't we ever going to dine?" asked Malvina, trying a *pas de seul* in a corner of the salon.

"Yes, indeed, madame. Come, Monsieur Chérubin, be kind enough to take your seat."

Monsieur d'Hurbain was about to sit beside Chérubin, but Monfréville stopped him, saying in an undertone:

"Let these girls sit by our pupil, or else we may lose all the fruit of our trouble. I have been watching Chérubin among all these people; he sighs sometimes, and if he should have an attack of homesickness, he might absolutely insist on returning to his nurse, and we should have much difficulty in keeping him in Paris."

Monsieur d'Hurbain submitted; he allowed Mesdemoiselles Rosina and Cœlina to seat themselves on each side of Chérubin; Malvina, who was too late to obtain a seat next the young man, attempted to force Rosina to give up her chair to her and threatened to strike her; but a stern glance from Daréna put an end to the dispute, and Mademoiselle Malvina seated herself at the other end of the table, humming:

"You shall not take him away, Nicolas! 'Tis I whom he will love, tradera!"

There was one vacant place, for Monsieur Poterne had ordered the table laid for nine, and, despite Daréna's signs, the gentleman in the box-coat seemed to be on the point of taking the vacant chair, when the door opened and Monsieur Gérondif appeared, accompanied by Jasmin.

The professor bowed to the company, saying:

"I humbly salute the gentlemen, and I lay my homage at the feet of the ladies simultaneously."

"What is the man doing to our feet?" Malvina asked Daréna, who was seated beside her, and whose only reply was a violent blow with his knee.

But Chérubin's face lighted up when he saw the new arrivals, and he cried:

"Ah! here you are, my dear tutor! How glad I am that you came to Paris too! What a pity that—that you——"

Chérubin did not finish the sentence; he was thinking of Louise, and something which he could not define told him that his innocent playmate would not be in her proper place in the company of those young ladies who danced so prettily. Monsieur d'Hurbain, who was greatly pleased by the tutor's arrival, because he saw therein an additional safeguard for Chérubin, saluted Monsieur Gérondif with a gracious smile, and said:

"You did well to follow your pupil, monsieur, and we relied upon your doing so. Pray take a seat at the table—there is a place awaiting you."

"Yes, yes, sit there, Monsieur Gérondif," cried Chérubin, pointing to the vacant seat. "And you, my good Jasmin, stand by me."

"I know my duty, monsieur le marquis, and I will take my proper station."

As he spoke, the old retainer put a napkin over his arm and planted himself behind Chérubin's chair. As for Monsieur Gérondif, he did not wait for the invitation to be repeated; he pushed Monsieur Poterne aside, took his seat at the table and swallowed the soup that was placed before him, crying:

"This is the banquet of Belshazzar! It is the feast of Eleusis! the wedding festival of Gamache! Never assuredly was there a more sumptuous repast!"

"I say! that gentleman is talking in poetry," said Malvina to her neighbor.

"Yes," replied Daréna, "I believe that it was monsieur who wrote the tragedy called the *Earthquake of Lisbon.*"

Monsieur Gérondif smiled graciously at the count, murmuring with an air of modesty:

"I write verse rather easily, but I never wrote a tragedy, that is sure, certainly."

"I beg pardon, monsieur, I took you for Master André; you have much affinity with him.—But let us drink to monsieur le marquis's health, and to the pleasure of having him in Paris at last."

Daréna's proposition was eagerly welcomed; the glasses were filled with madeira, and emptied in Chérubin's honor; the four dancers drank without heel-taps, and poured down madeira in a way to arouse an Englishman's envy.

Meanwhile Monsieur Poterne, having been cheated out of the seat to which he aspired, had decided to remain on his feet and to assist Jasmin, in preference to retiring. So he took his stand behind Daréna; but while making a pretence of passing him a plate now and then, he asked him in undertones for whatever he saw on the table. Daréna passed him well filled dishes, and Poterne, instead of serving them to the guests, turned his back and rapidly made away with the contents.

The beginning of the repast was lively, but free from anything offensive to the proprieties; the young women, upon whom Daréna had enjoined the most rigidly correct behavior, gave their whole attention to doing justice to the dinner, and maintained an irreproachable demeanor, although they bestowed an amiable smile on Chérubin from time to time. Malvina alone let slip an occasional remark or jest of a somewhat obscene flavor; but Daréna always made haste to cover it by beginning to talk. His conversation, which was always piquant or rambling, Monfréville's, who was in an unusually cheerful mood, and the quotations of Monsieur Gérondif, who, while eating for four, found time to display all that he knew, did not leave Chérubin a moment for reflection. Surprised to find himself the hero of that impromptu fête, he was dazzled, fascinated, taken captive; the glances that were darted at him, the witty remarks that he heard on all sides, the flattering things that were said to him, and the delicious, dainty, toothsome dinner, which gratified his sense of smell and of taste alike, prevented him from giving a thought to the village; for when his face became grave and indicated the arrival of a memory, his companions redoubled their attentions, their gayety and their pranks, to banish the cloud that had dimmed his eyes.

"I say," suddenly exclaimed Malvina, who, as she turned her head, happened to see Monsieur Poterne taking away a plate that Daréna passed him, "so your man of business waits on you at table, does he? Is he your servant too?"

"He serves me in every capacity," said Daréna; "I tell you he is an invaluable man; I make whatever I choose of him!"

"Then you'd better make a good-looking man of him!"

"Socrates, Horace, Cicero and Pelisson were hideously ugly," said Gérondif, filling the little Swiss maiden's glass; "a man may be very plain and still have a brilliant intellect."

"Ah! you fox, you have your reasons for saying so," retorted Malvina, tossing off her champagne.

The tutor, who did not expect that reply, scratched his nose and called for truffles.

The crash of a breaking plate interrupted the conversation; Jasmin, while trying to remove his young master's plate, had dropped it on the floor; it was the fourth which had met that fate at his hands, together with two bottles and a carafe.

"I say, is that old fellow Jocrisse?" cried Malvina, with a roar of laughter.

"Such a valet de chambre must be very expensive!" said Monfréville, with a smile.

"Excuse me, my dear master," said Jasmin, who turned scarlet at each new mishap caused by his awkwardness. "You see, it is a long while since I have waited at table; but I shall soon get used to it—it is simply a matter of renewing an old habit."

"The devil!" said Daréna, "if he means to go on until he gets used to it, it will be very fine!"

"But why do you stand behind me, my good Jasmin? It is altogether too fatiguing for a man of your years. Sit in the corner yonder; I will call you if I should need you!"

"The idea of it!" said Jasmin, trying to stand erect. "Does monsieur think that I do not know my duty? I will not quit my post, monsieur; I will die first!"

"In other words, all the landlord's crockery will die!" said Daréna, laughingly.—"Honor to unlucky pluck!" he added aloud, raising his glass.

"This old servant's attachment is greatly to his credit and to his master's," said Monfréville, "I propose a toast to fidelity; it is so rare that we cannot do it too much honor, in whatever guise it appears."

The toast was drunk with enthusiasm by the company. Monsieur d'Hurbain proposed a toast to the late Monsieur de Grandvilain, and Daréna to the ballet dancers at the Opéra. Monsieur Gérondif rose and exclaimed with great earnestness:

"To the progress of the culinary art in France! The old Romans may have had more dishes than we on their tables, but probably they were less satisfying."

Mademoiselle Malvina, determined to propose a toast of her own, raised her glass and cried:

"I *toast* for very long ballets and very short skirts, in the interest of the dancers and of everybody who likes a high kick."

None of the ladies chose to lag behind; Cœlina drank to her squirrel's health, Rosina to her cat's, and Fœdora to her cousin's, who was in the Chasseurs d'Afrique. Monsieur Poterne drank to nobody's health, but he kept his back turned to the table, and swallowed an appalling quantity of champagne. A terrible crash interrupted the toasts: Jasmin had dropped a pile of plates that time, and the floor was strewn with débris of crockery.

"This will be rather an expensive dinner," said Daréna; "one must needs be very rich to indulge in such servants as this old Jasmin."

Meanwhile the frequent toasts had excited the guests to some extent. Malvina, who could not keep still, began to dance a very pronounced cancan; Cœlina and Rosina attempted the Cracovienne; Fœdora waltzed with Daréna, and Monsieur Gérondif, finding that everything about him was in a whirl, although he did not leave his chair, called loudly upon Malvina for a second performance of the Mozambique dance, with all its accessories.

Monsieur d'Hurbain, who had retained his presence of mind, thought that it was time to take Chérubin away; he took the young marquis's arm, motioned to Monfréville, and to the tutor, who left the table with regret, and, picking out a path through the broken crockery, they left the restaurant and entered a carriage which took them to the hôtel de Grandvilain, not observing that Jasmin, who had followed them, had succeeded in climbing up behind, with the assistance of a messenger.

"Aren't we going back to Gagny?" inquired Chérubin, when he found himself in the carriage.

"It is impossible to-night, my dear friend, it is much too late," said Monsieur d'Hurbain. "To-morrow, or a few days hence, you will think about it. Since you are in Paris, you should at least get acquainted with the city."

"Yes," mumbled Monsieur Gérondif, whose tongue was very thick, "*Cras*, to-morrow; *cras mane*, to-morrow morning; *perendinus dies*, day after to-morrow—no matter when!"

"And with your permission," said Monfréville, "I will undertake to be your guide, and to show you all that a young man of your rank should know."

Chérubin made no reply; he would have liked to return to Gagny; but the delicious repast of which he had just partaken had aroused a new train of ideas in his mind, and he had heard so much of the pleasures that awaited him in Paris, of which he had already had such a pleasant specimen, that he finally said to himself:

"After all, as long as I am in the city, I may as well see at once all the wonderful things I have heard so much about; and when I go back to Louise I shall have lots of things to tell her, at all events."

The cab arrived at the mansion in Faubourg Saint-Germain; the porte cochère was thrown open. The equipage had no sooner entered the courtyard than the ears of the young marquis and his companions were assailed by some most extraordinary music. They heard the strains of several barrel-organs, several violins and two or three clarinets, playing at the same time, but playing different tunes. Male and female voices too, shrill and false, roared ancient airs, laments, or vaudeville choruses. The general result was a horrible medley of sounds.

The occupants of the carriage were asking one another what it could mean, when they heard a dull thud on the pavement, as if caused by the fall of a heavy body. They recognized Jasmin, who, when he attempted to climb down from behind the cab, had fallen in the middle of the courtyard. But the dauntless retainer was already on his feet, crying:

"It's nothing; I just slipped.—Monsieur le marquis, I ordered this concert —musicians and singers—in honor of your return to your paternal mansion. Long life to the new Marquis de Grandvilain!"

Chérubin thanked Jasmin for his kind intentions, but begged him instantly to dismiss those people, who were making such a horrible din. Monsieur d'Hurbain and Monfréville bade the young man good-night, commending him in whispers to the care of his tutor, who was not in a condition to understand what they said; then they left him to enjoy the repose which he was likely to need.

When the strangers had gone, Jasmin asked Chérubin if he wished to pass his servants in review; and Mademoiselle Turlurette, who was overjoyed to see her young master, proposed that he inspect the linen closets and the servants' quarters, so that he might become acquainted with his establishment and see how things had been managed since his father's death. But Chérubin had no desire to take all that trouble; pleasure is fatiguing when one is not accustomed to it, and the young marquis wanted nothing except to go to bed.

When he saw the immense room which was to be his bedroom, where there was an old-fashioned bed, reached by a set of steps, and surrounded by enormous curtains of crimson velvet, Chérubin made a wry face and exclaimed:

"Oh! how ugly it is here! I liked my little room at my nurse's much better; it was more cheerful! I am going back there to-morrow, for it seems to me that I can't sleep well here."

But at sixteen years and a half, after a tiresome day, one sleeps well anywhere; and that is what happened to Chérubin.

As for Monsieur Gérondif, after bestowing an affable smile on Mademoiselle Turlurette, whom he called "mesdames," because, his eyesight being a little blurred, he took her for two persons, he was escorted to his apartment, and was radiant with delight when he saw the fine room that had been prepared for him. He stretched himself out luxuriously in a soft bed, and gently laid his head on a pile of pillows, saying:

"I never slept in such a bed as this! I sink in, I drown! It is enchanting! I would like to pass my life in bed, and dream of the Mozambique dance!"

XIII

TO-MORROW

Chérubin woke late; he gazed about him in amazement and tried to collect his thoughts. He asked himself why he had left Gagny, his dear Nicole, and Louise, whom he loved so dearly. Then he thought of the magnificent dinner of the day before and of those four young women, who were so pretty and gay and amusing, and who danced so gracefully, casting soft glances at him the while. It was all well calculated to engross so inexperienced a head and heart.

Suddenly the crash of breaking furniture made Chérubin start; he turned his head and saw Jasmin standing in dismay beside a washstand that he had overturned.

"What is all this?" cried the young man, who could not help laughing at the grimace made by his old valet.

"It's I, monsieur—it was because I didn't want to make a noise and wake you."

"So you call that not making a noise?"

"I was walking so carefully that I ran into that little piece of furniture, and it fell. But no matter; you can find those things at all furniture shops."

"Oh! I am not at all alarmed, Jasmin. I am going to dress and go back to Gagny."

"What! already, my dear master? Have you examined your cash-box?"

"No; why should I?"

"That is all full of gold, monsieur," said Jasmin, pointing to the cash drawer in the secretary; "and it's all yours. And when it's all gone, there is plenty more; you have only to apply to your banker. And one can enjoy so much in Paris with money."

"Jasmin, you know that I don't like to be thwarted. Where are my clothes and my shoes?"

"I threw them all out of the window, monsieur, except what Monsieur de Monfréville brought you yesterday."

"What does that mean? Do you mean that I haven't any trousers to put on? Are you mad, Jasmin?"

"It was Monsieur de Monfréville who advised me to throw away all monsieur's old things. But there's a tailor waiting outside, and a boot-maker and a shirt-maker and a hatter, who have brought some things that are more in style. It was Monsieur de Monfréville again who sent them all here; they've been waiting an hour for you to wake."

"Let them come in then."

The tradesmen were admitted. Each of them was attended by a boy laden with merchandise. While Chérubin selected those things which pleased him and which he was told were the most fashionable, Comte Daréna was announced.

Daréna wore his old ragged coat, his shapeless hat, and his rumpled cravat of the night before; but he appeared with his usual charming and playful manner, and shook the young man's hand with great heartiness, crying:

"Here I am, my dear fellow; I intended to be here to salute you when you woke. I have come to breakfast with you.—Ah! you are making purchases? You should have left that to me; I would have sent my tradesmen to you. You left very suddenly last night, did you not? The ladies were all terribly surprised when they found that you were no longer there."

"Monsieur d'Hurbain told me it was time to go—that we ought not to stay any longer at a restaurant," replied Chérubin artlessly.

"Ah! charming! delicious!—In Paris you stay at a restaurant as late as you choose—you even pass the night there when the fancy strikes you. Your Monsieur d'Hurbain is a most estimable man, but he is not of our time, nor on the level of the age we live in. Luckily he won't always be with you, for he would be a terrible bore.—Aren't you going to take this blue coat?"

"I have already selected two sack coats and two frock coats."

"Then I'll take it; I can see at a glance that it will look well on me. I am also attracted by this little polonaise—it's a whim. Parbleu! I like the color of these trousers; I'll take them and these two waistcoats. When I am once started, there is no good reason why I should stop. Here are some shirts which should fit me perfectly. They make shirts now that fit as tight as a coat; I will take this dozen. These boots look as if they were well made.—You have a very pretty foot, Chérubin, of the same type as mine. I will take this pair of boots. Are they the same size as the ones selected by monsieur le marquis?"

"Yes, monsieur," the boot-maker replied, with a bow.

"Then I will keep them.—I am curious to see if my head is the same size as yours, also. Let me see the hat you have chosen."

Doing his utmost to squeeze his head into a hat which the hatter handed him, and which was much too small for him, Daréna cried:

"It will fit me—oh! it will end by fitting me. Have you another one like it there, hatter—but a little larger?"

"Yes, monsieur."

"Let me see—that is just right; I will take it."

The tradesmen glanced at one another with some uneasiness; one could see in their eyes that they were wondering whether they ought to trust this gentleman, who selected so many things without even asking the price, and whose costume did not inspire unbounded confidence. Daréna put an end to their uncertainty by adding:

"By the way, here I am buying and buying, and I have no money with me! Parbleu! my friend the young Marquis Chérubin will pay for my purchases with his own; it is useless to make two bills. Then I will settle with him.— Will that inconvenience you, my young friend?"

"No, monsieur, it will give me great pleasure," replied Chérubin, as he proceeded to dress; "I am delighted to accommodate you!"

And Jasmin whispered to his young master, as he assisted him to put on his waistcoat:

"It's very good form, too, very noble, to lend to your friends; the late Monsieur de Grandvilain, your father, did it all the time! I will settle with monsieur's tradesmen."

Jasmin paid the various accounts.

Daréna gave the dealers his address, so that they might send him what he had selected, and they took their leave, greatly pleased.

While the old servant went out to give orders for breakfast, Daréna said to Chérubin:

"Now you are dressed in perfect taste—that is very good so far; but it isn't enough; I propose that my young friend shall have all the little trifles, all the jewelry that is absolutely essential for a Parisian lion."

"What do you say? a lion?"

"That is the name given to-day to a young man of fashion. Have you a

100

watch?"

"Yes, this one; it belonged to my father."

As he spoke, Chérubin showed Daréna a gold watch as thick as it was broad. The count roared with laughter as he glanced at it.

"Why, my dear fellow, if you should be seen carrying such an onion, people would laugh in your face."

"What's that? Why, it's gold!"

"I don't doubt it; and I may add that it is a most respectable watch, as it came from your father; but such watches are not worn now. Put it away carefully in your desk and have a stylish one, as thin as a sheet of paper. I have instructed my steward to find one for you, and to bring you this morning all the jewelry that you ought to have. Stay, I hear him asking for you now in your reception room.—This way, Poterne, this way; monsieur le marquis is visible."

Poterne's villainous face appeared at the bedroom door, and Chérubin invited him to come in. As he passed Daréna, he said to him rapidly and in an undertone:

"The dealer wouldn't trust me with anything; he's waiting at the door."

"All right, you will be able to pay him. They're not false, of course?"

"No, they're genuine stones."

"How much does he want for them?"

"Eight hundred francs."

"Call it two thousand."

Monsieur Poterne took a pasteboard box from his pocket, containing a very pretty, flat watch, a gold chain, which looked very light but was of beautiful workmanship, and a diamond pin. Chérubin uttered a cry of admiration when he saw the baubles.

"These, monsieur le marquis, are the finest and most stylish things to be had," said Poterne, passing the chain about the young man's neck, and doing his utmost to assume an honest expression.

"Yes, they're in the latest style," said Daréna. "My dear Chérubin, you must have these things; a well-dressed man cannot do without them. I have several chains myself; they are all broken just now, but I am having them mended."

"Oh! I will buy all these jewels," cried Chérubin. "Who would believe that there was a watch inside of this? What a pretty pin!—How much for them all, monsieur?"

Observing the young man's enthusiasm over the jewels, Poterne thought that he might add a little more to the price.

"Twenty-five hundred francs in all," he said.

Daréna turned his face away and bit his lips, while Chérubin ran to his cash drawer.

At sight of that drawer filled with gold pieces, Monsieur Poterne turned blue, his brow became wrinkled, his eyes increased in size and his nose shrunk. Daréna, observing his excitement, took advantage of the fact that Chérubin's back was turned to administer a kick to his friend, muttering:

"I trust, you villain, that you have no detestable intentions; if I thought that you had, I would break every bone in your body."

Poterne had no time to reply; he rubbed that portion of his anatomy which had been attacked, received the amount which Chérubin counted out to him in gold, and hastily took his leave. But he had hardly passed through the bedroom door when Daréna ran after him, saying:

"Excuse me, my young friend, I will return in a moment; I forgot to give my steward an important order."

Hurrying after Poterne, who seemed anxious to avoid being overtaken, Daréna caught him on the stairs and seized him by his coat collar.

"Don't go so fast," he said; "you're in a great hurry, you old scoundrel. Come, give me two thousand francs, in a hurry."

"Two thousand francs!" muttered Poterne; "why, I've got to give eight hundred to the jeweler, who is waiting downstairs."

"You can give him five hundred; he will be satisfied to wait for the rest."

"But I——"

"I'll break you into six pieces, if you argue. Come, Poterne, be decent! You know that when I am in funds, you never lack anything."

Monsieur Poterne complied, looking as if he were about to weep. Daréna pocketed the gold and returned to Chérubin, who was admiring himself in the mirror. Jasmin came to say that breakfast was served, and the gentlemen took their seats at the table. They were hardly seated when Monsieur de Monfréville was announced.

When he saw Daréna at table with their young friend of the preceding day,

Monfréville moved his head imperceptibly and said to the count:

"Here already? The deuce! you must have come quite early."

"When I am fond of my friends, I am always in haste to see them," replied Daréna.—"What wine is this, faithful Jasmin?"

"Beaune, monsieur," replied the old servant, bowing.

"It is very good; but I like sauterne and chambertin at breakfast. You must have a fine cellar here?"

"Oh, yes, monsieur; and all old wines."

"I imagine so, if they were laid in by our young friend's father.—Come, O model of old retainers, go and bring us several more bottles. When a cellar has been left in peace for a generation, it seems to me that it is high time to empty it."

Jasmin hastened to do as he was requested, and Monfréville said to Daréna:

"But you give orders without even consulting the master of the house!"

"My friend has given me carte blanche, and I am making the most of it."

"Yes, monsieur," said Chérubin; "pray do whatever you choose in my house."

Daréna leaned toward Monfréville and said in his ear:

"He was already talking of going back to Gagny this morning; if we don't make the young fellow giddy, he is capable of returning to his nurse, and that would be downright murder!"

"Aren't you going to breakfast with us, monsieur?" Chérubin asked Monfréville.

"Thanks, my young friend, but I have breakfasted. Were you satisfied with the tradespeople whom I sent to you this morning?"

"Oh, yes, monsieur; everything was beautiful. I bought a lot of things, and so did monsieur le comte."

Monfréville glanced at Daréna, who pretended not to hear and seemed busily occupied helping himself to partridge pie.

"And look at my watch and my gold chain, and this pin. Monsieur Daréna sent them all to me by his steward. How pretty they are, aren't they?"

"Did you pay much for them?" Monfréville inquired.

"Why, no, only two thousand five hundred francs; I don't call that dear!"

Monfréville looked again at Daréna, who continued to stuff himself with partridges.

"Why, yes, it was quite enough," he said; "in fact, it was very dear. In the future, with your permission, I will advise you in your purchases; I fancy that I know at least as much about such matters as monsieur's steward."

Jasmin returned with a number of bottles; he broke one when he attempted to put it on the table, and dropped a cream cheese on Daréna's head. Chérubin was terribly distressed by his servant's awkwardness; and the old fellow, overwhelmed with confusion by what he had done, slunk out of sight behind a screen. Daréna was the first to laugh at the accident.

"It's of no consequence," he said; "I am not dressed yet.—For all that, my dear marquis, if I may venture to give you a piece of advice, I advise you to relieve your old Jasmin from the duty of waiting at table. His services will be ruinous to you and fatal to your friends. The excellent fellow has abundantly earned retirement and you must give it to him. I will go home to dress, and come back for you; for we will pass the day together, eh, Monfréville?"

"That is my wish, if it will not annoy our young friend."

Chérubin hesitated a moment, then said falteringly:

"But I intended to—to go to Gagny—to see my—my nurse."

"Oh! to-morrow! to-morrow!" cried Daréna; "we have too many things to do to-day; I will hurry home to dress and return at once."

Daréna took his leave. Monfréville would have liked to hint to his young friend that he would do well not to place too much confidence in the count's manifestations of friendship for him; but if he attempted so soon to destroy the young man's illusions, if he told him to be on his guard against false friends, selfish affections, the wiles of shopkeepers, and all the perils of Paris, would he not run the risk of disgusting him with that city, which he had consented to visit only with regret?

"After all," said Monfréville to himself, "Daréna is jovial and bright; he has the art of inventing some new pleasure every day, and even if his friendship should cost Chérubin a few thousand-franc notes, the youngster is rich, and one must needs pay for one's apprenticeship in everything. Besides, I will keep an eye on our pupil, and I will try to see to it that his inexperience is not over-abused.—By the way, my young friend," he said aloud, "what have you done with your tutor? He is to remain with you, is he not? Is he not well?"

"Dear me! you are right!" cried Chérubin. "I had entirely forgotten Monsieur Gérondif!—Jasmin, go and inquire what my tutor is doing; ask him why he doesn't come to breakfast."

Jasmin went to Monsieur Gérondifs room. The ex-schoolmaster was buried in his bed, sound asleep, and entirely hidden by the bedclothes and the pillows, which had fallen over his head. There was nothing save his snoring to indicate that the bed was occupied.

The old servant put out his hand toward the pillow; it came in contact with Monsieur Gérondifs prominent nose, which he laid hold of and pulled violently, crying out:

"Come, monsieur le savant, wake up; my master is asking for you."

Monsieur Gérondif opened his eyes and rescued his nose from the fingers that had grasped it.

"What's the matter?" he muttered; "what's the meaning of this violence, and why wake me by the nose? That's a new way, surely; rosy-fingered Aurora doesn't treat the fair-haired Phœbus so."

But, on learning that his pupil had breakfasted, Monsieur Gérondif decided to rise; he made a hasty toilet and went down to pay his respects to the marquis.

"The delights of Capua enervated Hannibal's soldiers," he said, eying the remains of the breakfast, which were very appetizing. "My dear pupil, I became even as a woman on my downy couch. Accept my apologies; hereafter I will certainly rise with the chanticleer."

And Monsieur Gérondif seated himself at the table to make up for lost time, while Chérubin, to content Mademoiselle Turlurette, went to cast a glance at the different parts of the establishment. Monfréville, who had declined to accompany him, went to the tutor and said:

"Monsieur, you have a most important duty to perform; I doubt not that you will do your utmost to succeed."

Monsieur Gérondif looked up at Monfréville, opened his enormous mouth, apparently annoyed at having to reply instead of eat, and said at last:

"In truth, monsieur, I have a very hearty appetite at this moment; but I hope to succeed in satisfying it with what is on the table."

"That is not what I referred to, monsieur, but to your pupil, to this young man who should be the object of your utmost care here in Paris, because, although it was absolutely necessary that he should come here, we must see to it that he is not made the dupe of his innocence and his amiable disposition."

After taking time to swallow a chicken wing, the tutor replied in a magisterial tone:

"In that respect, young Chérubin could not be in better hands! Never fear, monsieur, I will draw for my pupil a most appalling picture of the seductions in which people may seek to ensnare him. Morals before everything! That is my motto. St. Paul said: *Oportet sapere ad sobrietatem!* But I say that, at the marquis's age, one must be virtuous first of all."

"No, no, monsieur, that isn't what I mean," rejoined Monfréville, with a shrug; "it isn't a question of terrifying the young man and trying to make a Cato of him. Let him enjoy such of the pleasures suited to his years as his means will allow; but prevent his abusing them, and see to it that he is not made the dupe of the schemers and swindlers with whom Paris is overflowing."

"That is just what I say, monsieur; I will be constantly on the lookout; I will keep my eyes and ears open and my nose in the air, and it will not be my fault if the child succumbs to temptation. Moreover, I have an entirely novel system of education—always in the interest of good morals.—Pardon me if I continue my breakfast."

"Clearly the man is either a fool or a hypocrite," thought Monfréville, as he turned on his heel. "I trust that he is not both!"

Chérubin concluded his inspection of his family mansion, which seemed to him old, dark and dismal. Monfréville advised him to have it painted, furnished and decorated according to modern ideas.

Daréna returned, arrayed in the latest fashion; he had donned a part of the purchases he had made that morning without untying his purse strings, and with the money received from Poterne he had bought what he still lacked. So that his costume was beyond reproach, and he wore it with as much ease and unconstraint as he displayed in his old coat.

Chérubin admired Daréna's elegant appearance and the grace with which he wore his clothes. Monfréville made similar reflections, regretting that a man possessed of so many advantages sometimes descended so low and frequented such wretched company.

"Here I am, at your service," said Daréna. "We must take Marquis Chérubin somewhere. I can't make up my mind to say 'Grandvilain'; indeed, the name doesn't fit our young friend at all, and if he takes my advice, he will be content with Chérubin alone, which is a most gallant name."

"What!" murmured Jasmin, "is monsieur going to drop his father's name?

I tell you, I object!"

Nobody paid any heed to the old servant, and Daréna continued:

"First of all, our friend must see everything in Paris that deserves to be seen. That will take time; for a shrewd observer there is a great deal to see."

"And then," said Monfréville, "Chérubin will do well to give a few hours every day to the masters who are quite indispensable; for his education is far too incomplete for him to go into society."

Monsieur Gérondif's fork stopped in the act of conveying food to his mouth, and he cried:

"Who says that my pupil's education is incomplete? He will surely know as much as I do very soon."

"Come, come, learned Master André, don't get excited," said Daréna, with a laugh; "I have no doubt that you are very strong in the dead languages,—and in the art of carving a chicken; yes, you're very good at that. But can you teach our friend music, dancing, riding, fencing, boxing?"

"Boxing?" muttered Jasmin, with an air of stupefaction.

"Yes, boxing, and all the fashionable sciences which a young man of rank and fortune must know, unless he wishes to be laughed at."

"Trust me," said Monfréville, taking Chérubin's arm; "my father was a friend of yours, and even without that, your youth and innocence would be sufficient to awaken my interest and to arouse in me a wish to make an accomplished gentleman of you."

"And to begin with," said Daréna, "a short ride in the saddle; there is nothing pleasanter in the morning. Do you know anything about riding?"

"Oh! I can ride very well, and I'm not afraid," Chérubin replied; "at the village I used to ride all our neighbors' horses."

"Good! there's a livery stable close by where there are some very good horses; let us go there and hire, pending the time when you have horses in your stable—another indispensable thing."

Chérubin went out with his two friends; he was beside himself with delight at the thought of a riding party. Being still a novice in all sorts of pleasure, Nicole's foster-child had never before ridden anything but plough horses.

They went to the stable-keeper, who ordered his three best horses saddled. Just as the gentlemen were mounting, they heard a voice calling:

"Well! isn't there a horse for me too?"

Thereupon they discovered Jasmin, who had followed his master, after tightening the waistband of his breeches as much as possible, covering his head with a long-vizored cap, which entirely concealed his eyes and nose, and arming himself with a hunting crop.

Chérubin and his friends could not help laughing at the aspect of Jasmin in the garb of a groom, and Monfréville exclaimed:

"This old servant's devotion is becoming very painful."

"But I don't need you, Jasmin," said Chérubin; "go back to the house; you can't come with me, it would tire you too much."

"I know my duty, monsieur," replied Jasmin; "my place is always in your rear."

"Yes, yes, he is right," said Daréna; "and as he insists on coming with us, why, let him come.—A horse for this faithful retainer—a good little trotting horse. Jasmin has the look of an excellent rider."

"He will certainly be thrown," said Chérubin, in an undertone.

"That is what I expect too; but it will do him good. This fellow needs a lesson; he is extremely pig-headed; he insists on breaking your dishes, capping your friends with cheese, climbing up behind carriages, and riding horseback; we must try to cure him of this exuberant zeal."

A horse was saddled for Jasmin, and, with the aid of two hostlers, he succeeded in climbing to its back. The cavalcade started; in the streets of Paris they went slowly and the old servant was able to follow his master, which he did with much pride, sitting erect in his saddle and bearing heavily on his stirrups; but when they reached the Champs-Elysées, Chérubin and his two companions started off at a gallop. Jasmin, seeing his young master disappear in a cloud of dust, was determined to follow him, and began to strike his steed with his crop. The beast, desiring nothing more than to join his stable companions, sprang forward and darted in pursuit.

But his old rider had presumed too much on his strength; in a few seconds the horse was galloping alone and Jasmin was rolling in the dust.

When they reached the Bois de Boulogne, Chérubin turned and said:

"Well! where on earth is Jasmin?"

"I was certain that he couldn't keep up with us," said Daréna.

"If only he has not fallen and hurt himself!"

"Don't be alarmed; at his age one falls gently. Somebody must have picked him up, and we must hope that this lesson will correct the old fellow a little, for his attachment needs to be toned down."

They rode on, the two gentlemen admiring the confidence of their young companion, who needed only a few lessons in grace and style to become an excellent horseman.

After their ride they returned to Paris, sauntered along the boulevards, visited several cafés, then went to one of the best restaurants in the Palais-Royal, and after dinner to the play. About midnight Chérubin returned home, not having had a single moment during the day to think of the village.

He found that Jasmin was not hurt by his fall, but he admitted to his young master that he should not try again to attend him to the Bois de Boulogne.

The following days were no less thoroughly occupied; Monfréville and Daréna were almost constantly with Chérubin; the former sent him teachers in all the social accomplishments; the second talked to him incessantly of the lovely little dancers with whom they had dined.

"Which of the four do you prefer?" he would ask.

And Chérubin would reply, lowering his eyes:

"They are very pretty, all four."

"I understand, you liked them all. That can be arranged, and I will take you to see them whenever you choose; you will be received with open arms."

At that suggestion Chérubin would turn as red as a cherry and stammer:

"Oh, yes! in a few days."

And while his pupil was being taken about and entertained and dazzled, Monsieur Gérondif lay idly in his bed, sat for hours at a time at the table, showed his teeth to Mademoiselle Turlurette, and said to Jasmin every day:

"Above all, worthy Eumæus, do not forget the orders to the concierge: if anybody from Gagny, even Madame Frimousset, should call and ask to see monsieur le marquis, she must be told that Monsieur Chérubin de Grandvilain is absent, that he is travelling; for if my pupil should see her again, above all if he should see little Louise, although he is beginning to like the city, he might allow himself to be lured away again, and all the fruit of our efforts would be lost! And that would be the greater pity, because, thanks to the advice of his two friends and the lessons I give him, he must necessarily become ere long a most preponderating cavalier."

Jasmin, who always humbled himself before the tutor's learning, did not fail to do exactly what he recommended, saying to himself that it could not be wrong to send the nurse away without allowing her to speak with his master, because a man who educates children must be perfectly familiar with the rules of courtesy.

And the days and weeks and months passed in that life of enjoyment, of constant occupation, and of dissipation, which Chérubin led at Paris. Whenever he spoke of going to the village, his new friends said:

"Yes, to-morrow; you haven't time to-day."

But when Daréna proposed to Chérubin to take him to see one of the little ballet dancers who he thought so attractive, the marquis replied, blushing to his eyes:

"Yes, to-morrow, to-morrow!"

XIV

A CHILD'S LOVE

While Chérubin was enjoying himself in Paris, making merry and thinking of nothing but pleasure, at Gagny his friends were dismal and bored, and shed frequent tears. It is often so in life: the happiness of one is acquired only at the expense of others' misery. Is it not too high a price to pay? If we always reflected upon causes and effects, we should sometimes regret being happy.

On returning from Montfermeil, where, it will be remembered, she was sent by Monsieur Gérondif, Louise, who had discovered that he had had no other object than to get her out of the way, asked anxiously where Chérubin was; and Nicole, weeping bitterly, told her that the youth whom she still delighted to call her fieu had gone to Paris with several gentlemen, and some charming ladies, evidently foreigners, judging from their costumes, who had danced in her house in a style utterly unlike any village dance.

Louise wept a long while; her heart was torn. There was one pang more cruel than all the rest in her suffering; at fourteen and a half a girl may well know what it is to love; and with love jealousy had made its appearance.

"You let him go!" said Louise, sobbing; "but he promised never to leave me; those people must have taken him by force."

"No, my child, Chérubin went away of his own free will, in high spirits, in fact, and almost dancing with those little hussies, who twirled round and round longer than the tops my boys used to spin when they were little."

Louise wept more bitterly still.

"Why did you let those horrid women come into your house?" she cried.

"Oh! I detest them!"

"Bless my soul, child, it was one of the gentlemen who brought 'em; they drank milk just like cats; and then they danced like kids."

"And Chérubin went away with them!—But he'll come back to-morrow, won't he, mother dear?"

"Let us hope so, my child."

But the morrow and several more days passed without bringing Chérubin back to the village. Louise was so depressed that Nicole forgot her own grief to comfort her.

"But something must have happened to him!" the girl constantly exclaimed. "Probably they are keeping him in Paris against his will; for, if not, he would have come back. Let's go after him, mother, let's go after him."

Nicole tried to make Louise listen to reason.

"Listen, my dear," she would say, "it's a long, long while since Monsieur Jasmin began to tell me: 'My young master will have to go to Paris some time; he can't pass his whole life out at nurse! If it was known that he's still with you, I should be scolded.' And a lot of things like that. The fact is, my child, that they usually take children away from a wet-nurse when they begin to talk, unless—unless——"

And the good woman stopped, for she was on the point of saying:

"Unless they do like your mother, and don't take 'em away at all."

Louise had that instinct of the heart which enables its possessor to read one's inmost thoughts; she divined the words that died on Nicole's lips, and she said, sobbing and pressing her hand convulsively:

"Nobody came for me, I know that. My mother didn't want me, and yet I couldn't have been naughty then—I was too young. And if it hadn't been for you, for your kindness, what would have become of me? Oh! dear Nicole, how can a mother ever abandon her child? I would have loved my mother so dearly, and she didn't want to take me back, or even to kiss me! Oh! she must have died, I am sure, or else she'd have come after me, or at least have come to see me sometimes."

"Yes," said Nicole, kissing Louise, "you are right, my child, your mother must have died and not had time to send for you; perhaps she wasn't able to tell where her child was. Bless my soul! people die so sudden sometimes! That's the way it must have been. But let's not say any more about it; you know, I don't like to get into that subject, for it always makes you sad."

"That is why I so seldom mention it, my dear Nicole, although I think about it almost all the time; but when Chérubin was with me, I used to forget sometimes that I don't know who my parents are. He told me that he would always love me—and now he has abandoned me too."

After this conversation Louise went to the end of the garden, where she could weep at her ease. In vain did Nicole say to her:

"He'll come back, my child, he'll come back!"

Time passed and they saw nothing of Chérubin.

At last, yielding to the girl's entreaties, Nicole started with her for Paris one morning; and all the way Louise kept saying:

"We are going to see him. I'll tell him how sad I am when I am away from him; I'll tell him that I cry almost all the time, that there's nothing to amuse me in the village, and he'll come back with us, mother; oh! I am sure that he'll come back with us."

Nicole shook her head with a doubtful expression, and murmured:

"At any rate, we shall find out whether he's happy and well; that's the main thing."

In due time they reached the old mansion in Faubourg Saint-Germain.

"This is his house," said Nicole; "I recognize it all right! This is the very house where I came to get him when he was a spindling little thing, as thin as a rail. I made a fine boy of him, thank God! And then I came here two or three times to bring him to his father, when the old gentleman was alive."

Louise gazed wonderingly at the old structure, whose severe aspect and time-blackened walls almost frightened her. Meanwhile, they had entered the courtyard, and Nicole said to the concierge:

"Monsieur, I've come to see my *fieu*—my nursling, young Chérubin, your master. He left us to come here, but we don't like not having a chance to kiss him for so long; we couldn't stand it any longer, so here we are."

The concierge, who had his orders, replied:

"You can't see monsieur le marquis, my master, for he isn't in the house."

"Gone out, has he? Oh well! he'll come back! We'll wait, won't we, Louise?"

"Oh, yes, mother, we will wait; for we must see him when we came to Paris on purpose."

The concierge rejoined with exasperating indifference:

"It won't do you any good to wait; Monsieur de Grandvilain is travelling and he may not come home for ten days or a fortnight."

"Travelling!" cried Louise; "oh dear! it's very annoying! Where is he travelling, monsieur? in which direction? Has he gone far?"

"My master didn't tell me."

"But tell us at least whether he's well?" said Nicole; "is he happy? is he enjoying himself in Paris?"

"Monsieur le marquis is in perfect health."

"Thank God! But why does he go travelling without coming to see us?—Monsieur, are those young foreign ladies who dance so well travelling with—with Monsieur Chérubin?"

"I couldn't tell you."

Nicole and the young girl returned to Gagny, sadly disappointed that they had not been able to embrace Chérubin; but the nurse said to Louise:

"Never mind, we know he's well, and that's a great deal."

"Yes, dear mother, and no doubt he'll come to see us when he returns from this journey; if he doesn't, we'll go to Paris again, for he won't always be away."

But once more the days and weeks passed without a word or a sign from the youth whom they loved so dearly and whom they were always expecting. Conquered by Louise's tears and entreaties, Nicole consented to go to Paris again, but the second trip was no more fortunate than the first. That time, however, the concierge said that monsieur le marquis had gone to pass some time at the château of one of his friends.

The two women returned to Gagny more depressed than ever.

"My dear child," said Nicole, weeping with her, "I believe that the little fellow I nursed doesn't mean to see me again. You see that he's forgotten us, for he doesn't come to the village or send us any word. And when folks in Paris don't want to see anyone, why they just say that they're out."

"O mother! do you really think that Chérubin doesn't want to see us, that he would be ashamed of us?"

"I don't say that, my child; but this much is certain: that I won't go to his house in Paris again; for they must have told him that we came, and if he still cared anything about us, it seems to me that he wouldn't have lost any time before coming to see us."

Louise could think of nothing to reply; she longed to defend Chérubin in Nicole's mind, when in the depths of her own heart she retained only a glimmer of hope. After the second trip to Paris, the girl's depression became more and more marked; in the presence of her foster-mother she tried to conceal her distress, her sorrow, but when she was alone she gave way to them with a sort of enjoyment; for, in extreme unhappiness, it is almost a consolation not to be disturbed in one's musings, one's regrets, one's memories.

Louise did like all those who have lost a beloved object—she haunted all the spots which she had often visited and admired with him. When we revisit the places where we have been happy, it seems that we must be happy again; our memory recalls all the circumstances of our previous visits, and the most trivial and futile things become of inestimable value when they have some connection with the one we love. By dint of identifying ourselves with our memories, we fancy that we are still living in that bitterly-regretted past—our heart dilates with a thrill of joy. But alas! how brief its duration! The present returns with its overwhelming truth; we look about—we are alone, all alone— we find in the depths of our hearts naught save a ghastly void, and no unalloyed joy in the days to come.

One morning Nicole was working, Jacquinot sleeping, and Louise in the garden, where she was thinking of Chérubin as usual, when a gentleman entered the rustic dwelling.

"O *agrestis* and *rusticus* abode!" he cried; "I salute thee, but I do not regret thee. My tastes do not agree with Virgil's, I prefer the city to the country."

Nicole uttered a joyful exclamation at sight of Monsieur Gérondif, and she made haste to call Louise, saying:

"Come quick, my child, here's the schoolmaster come back; no doubt Chérubin will soon be here too."

It was in fact the tutor, who wore a hat so shiny that it looked as if it were varnished, with his hair carefully oiled beneath it; his gloves were glazed and his handkerchief drenched with Portugal water, but his nose was redder than ever.

Louise rushed into the house. Never had Monsieur Gérondif's presence caused her such pleasure; she longed, yet feared to speak to him, but at last she gave him her hand and said in a hesitating tone:

"Ah! what happiness, monsieur! You are going to tell us about *him*."

Monsieur Gérondif, for his part, was speechless with admiration at sight of the girl, for it was eight months since he had left Gagny, and in that period a tremendous change had taken place in Louise, altogether to her advantage. She was no longer a child, a little maid; she was a tall, well-built, charming girl, who had every qualification to attract, and to whom anybody would have given credit for seventeen years and a swarm of suitors.

"It is most extraordinary!" cried the tutor; "it is sorcery surely! What a gratifying change!"

"You find Louise grown, don't you, monsieur?"

"Grown at least twelve centimetres, and her figure much more solid, more palpable!"

"But Chérubin, monsieur, tell us about Chérubin! Never mind me. Is he coming, monsieur? Shall we see him soon? Does he think about us? Does he speak of us sometimes?"

"Is he very fat and healthy, and happy, the dear *fieu*? And when shall we have a chance to embrace him? Why don't he come to Gagny?"

"Monsieur le marquis is very well indeed," replied Gérondif, still ogling Louise. "You ask why he doesn't come to see you? Why, my dear Madame Frimousset, it's plain that you know nothing of life in Paris, and especially the life led by a young man in fashionable society! My pupil hasn't a moment to himself: in the morning he fences, rides horseback, dances, sings and boxes; why, he hardly has time for his meals. Then he has to go into society— theatres, concerts, balls! How in the devil do you expect him to find a moment to come to this village? It's impossible! Even I had infinite difficulty in making the trip to-day; I was obliged to hurry my breakfast, and I don't like to eat fast."

"So we shan't see him any more?" murmured Louise, whose heart had grown heavy again, and whose eyes were filled with tears.

"I do not say that, adorable lass! but I say that you must be sensible and not expect monsieur le marquis to interrupt his important occupations for you."

"Oh! I don't expect anything! We'd have gone to Paris again to see him, but they always tell us he's away."

"Don't come to Paris, you will simply waste your time; how do you expect to catch a young man on the wing who has five hundred things to do in the day?"

"Five hundred things! Bless my soul! but the poor boy must get all tired out!"

"As if he went on foot! He's always in a carriage or on horseback; and he rides at full speed."

"And he can't come as far as this!" said Louise, with a profound sigh. "And those lovely ladies who dance so well—he goes to see them, of course?"

"The ballet dancers! fie, fie! What about morals! We used those mountebanks just as we use the magnet to attract a lot of things; but afterward —*retro, Satanas!*"

"But I hope he still thinks of us!" said Nicole.

"The proof that he thinks of you, Dame Nicole, is that he has instructed me to hand you this; for he wants you to be happy and to have everything you need. And he's very generous, is my pupil. Here, take it; there's a thousand francs in it. That's a very pretty sum."

As he spoke, Monsieur Gérondif handed Nicole a bag of money. She took it, exclaiming:

"A thousand francs! Oh! that's too much, a thousand francs. It's a handsome present, but if I could have given him a kiss at the same time, I'd have enjoyed it much better."

Jacquinot, who had just waked up, looked at the bag of money and muttered sleepily:

"A thousand francs! How many casks does that make at six sous the litre?"

"And didn't he give you anything for me, monsieur?" inquired Louise. But in a moment she added hastily: "Oh! it's not a present, it's not money that I mean; but a kind word, a remembrance, a word to show me that he hasn't forgotten me. Pray try to remember, monsieur."

Monsieur Gérondif scratched his nose and replied:

"No, my sweet girl, the marquis gave me no message for you in particular, but he told me to wish you all the best of health."

Louise turned pale and averted her eyes. Whereupon the tutor went to her side and said in an undertone:

"Pray do not grieve, *mia cara bella*. Although the marquis forgets you, there is one who will never forget you, who will watch over your future, and will not allow you to vegetate in obscurity in this village. Patience; you are still very young, although perfectly developed already. Let us wait a bit; Penelope waited a long while for the return of Ulysses, but he came at last and killed all her suitors. That man shot perfectly with the bow!"

Louise gazed at Monsieur Gérondif in surprise, as if to ask him what he

116

meant; but he had turned to Nicole.

"Now, I must bid you adieu," he said.

"What, already, Monsieur Gérondif, without eating a mouthful, and without taking a drop to drink?"

"Have a glass of wine," said Jacquinot; "nobody ever refuses that."

"Pardon me, my dear Frimousset, but it's very easy to refuse it, when you are in the habit, as I am, of drinking fine wines; your *sour* stuff would make me sick now."

"But why are you in such a hurry to go?"

"Excellent Nicole, I know that there are potted quail for dinner to-day,—Mademoiselle Turlurette told me so,—and it would be uncivil to myself not to take my share of them. Au revoir, virtuous country folk; Nicole, watch over this little pearl—*margarita*; I commend her to your care. And you, sweet Louise, do not give way to sorrow; you have a grand future before you assuredly! *This oracle is more reliable than the oracle of Calchas.* I wish you all the best of health, and I fly to Villemonble to take the diligence."

As he spoke, Monsieur Gérondif bestowed an expansive smile upon each in turn; he added to the young girl's smile an exceedingly ardent glance, and took his leave, resuming his shiny hat and his glazed gloves.

"He tells me not to give way to sorrow," thought Louise, when he had gone; "and Chérubin gave him no message for me!"

XV

MONSIEUR POTERNE'S TRADE

Chérubin must inevitably appear ungrateful and fickle in his affection, for he seems to have forgotten very quickly good Nicole, who had reared him, and little Louise, his playmate, whom he said that he loved so dearly. But such ingratitude and inconstancy are too natural in man for us to be surprised at finding them in a mere boy. Chérubin had just entered his eighteenth year; he was surrounded by people whose only aim was to make life in Paris attractive to him, who were constantly occupied in affording him new pleasures, and who did not fail to make sport of him and rally him on account of the time he had passed at his nurse's. Ridicule is a very potent weapon among the French; grown men fear and do everything to avoid it; could a child of seventeen be expected to set it at naught?

However, Chérubin was not so forgetful as one might suppose. He had often longed to go to see Nicole and Louise; but, in order to divert him from that design, they had, in the first place, carefully concealed from him the nurse's two visits to the house; then they had told him that Madame Frimousset had sent Louise away to a kinswoman in Bretagne, in order to help her to forget the grief caused by her young friend's departure.

The prospect of not finding Louise at Gagny had considerably cooled the young man's longing to revisit the village. But, as he was still desirous that his nurse should be happy, he had, as we have seen, despatched Monsieur Gérondif to her with money, begging him also to inquire about Louise, to ascertain whether she was likely to return to Gagny soon—in short, to satisfy himself concerning her future.

On returning from his visit to Nicole, Monsieur Gérondif did not fail to inform his young master that Louise was still in Bretagne, in the family of a respectable, well-to-do farmer, who treated her like his own daughter; and that she was very happy there.

Chérubin smiled faintly at the thought that his former playmate had entirely forgotten him so soon; he felt a pang of sadness and regret, and for a moment he thought of going to Bretagne, to reproach Louise for changing so and for ceasing to love him.

For we are like that at every age: we are quite ready to forget other people, but we are not willing that they should forget us; we are inconstant and unfaithful, but we hope that others will be constant and faithful to us; in short, we have no hesitation in deceiving, but we do not wish to be deceived.

Daréna's arrival always brought animation to the hôtel de Grandvilain; and, while seeking to divert Chérubin, he availed himself of the acquaintance to turn Monsieur Poterne's talents to account.

For instance, the ugly hanger-on brought the young marquis two saddle horses one morning, and, assuring him that it was a magnificent opportunity, which he must not let slip, induced him to pay three thousand francs for a pair of nags that were worth five hundred at the very most.

At another time, it was a tilbury which Poterne had bought from a Russian prince; at another, some fine hunting dogs of a very rare breed; in short, Monsieur Poterne had reached the point where he dealt in everything; he never appeared at the house without offering Chérubin something at a bargain; he even brought canes, silk handkerchiefs, parrots and cats. The young man bought everything, and paid with the most absolute confidence. But Jasmin, who was beginning to consider that Monsieur Poterne's bargains were terribly extravagant, was in very ill humor whenever he saw him enter the house; and he tried to devise some means by which he could rid his master of his visits. Unfortunately the old servant had never had a brilliant imagination, and as he grew old that faculty had become more confined instead of developing.

Monfréville might have thwarted Daréna's schemes and Poterne's little commercial ventures; but he had been obliged to go for some time to an estate that he owned in the neighborhood of Fontainebleau, where considerable repairs were necessary. When he left Paris, however, he urged his young friend to distrust Monsieur Poterne's services and obliging disposition; but Chérubin was too young not to be trustful; and moreover, Daréna always seemed amazed at the good bargains which his steward found for the young marquis.

While Monfréville was absent, the mansion became crowded with horses, hunting-dogs, birds of all varieties, gothic vases, and objects said to be rare or curious, which Monsieur Poterne brought thither every day.

At last, Jasmin said to his young master, one morning:

"If this goes on, monsieur, your house will look like a bric-à-brac shop! You can't turn around here! This Monsieur Poterne induces you to buy too many things; these antique, rare vases look very ugly to me; the hunting dogs make a frightful noise, and when they are let go, they bite everybody's legs. And then the parrots shriek so, and you have five of them! That so-called Spanish cat he sold you has changed color, and is nothing but a common white cat now. And you have nineteen canes, my dear master; I have counted them. What do you mean to do with nineteen canes? Monsieur le marquis, your father, had only one, and he never carried more at one time."

"Hush, Jasmin," Chérubin replied, laughing at his old servant's distress; "am I not rich? haven't I the means to gratify my whims?"

"Excuse me, my dear master, but you buy all these things because Monsieur Poterne tells you they're magnificent, great bargains, and a thousand other things to tempt you; why, you would never have taken it into your head to have ten dogs, nineteen canes, five parrots and a turtle, and to fill this house with old vases and strange looking jugs, which I call hideous, as I do the turtle, which frightens me."

"Because you don't know about such things. Monsieur Daréna always congratulates me on my purchases; he thinks everything is very fine and not dear."

"Oh! as to Monsieur Daréna," said Jasmin, shaking his head, "I don't call him economical! By the way, my dear master, has he ever repaid the money that you paid the tailor, the shirt-maker and the boot-maker for him?"

"No; but that isn't very important. He has probably forgotten it. Besides, Jasmin, you told me then that it was very good form to lend money to one's friends, and that my father often did it."

"That is true, monsieur, but all the difference is that your father's friends paid back what they borrowed."

This conversation was interrupted by Poterne's arrival; he still wore his shabby box-coat, beneath which he carried something of considerable size, which he kept carefully out of sight. Jasmin made a very significant grimace at the appearance of the very person of whom he had been speaking. But Monsieur Poterne came forward with a most humble air, bowing to the ground, and trying to assume a pleasant expression.

"Ah! it's Monsieur Poterne!" said Chérubin, laughing at his old servant's pantomime. "I was just talking about you with Jasmin, who declares that my Spanish cat is turning white."

Monsieur Poterne replied, with a sneering laugh that sounded like the rattling of copper sous in a saucepan:

"Monsieur Jasmin is joking! The cat that I had the honor to sell you is very valuable; he used to belong to a Spanish grandee. It is possible that he may turn white temporarily; he may not be well; but the color will all come back if you take good care of him."

"Do you mean that you think that animals aren't well fed in our house?" demanded Jasmin haughtily.

"I didn't mean that, my dear monsieur; but Spanish cats are very delicate, and——"

"All right," said Chérubin, "we have talked enough about a cat. Doubtless you have come to offer me something new, Monsieur Poterne? for you are an invaluable man! With you one has no time to form a wish."

"Monsieur le marquis is too kind; as it happens, I have something."

As he spoke, Monsieur Poterne bestowed a savage glance on the old valet, whose presence embarrassed him; but Jasmin did not budge, and as his master did not tell him to go, Monsieur Poterne was fain to make up his mind to exhibit before him what he had under his coat.

"Well, what have you brought me to-day?" asked Chérubin.

"What I have brought you, monsieur le marquis,—is a bargain."

"Always bargains," muttered Jasmin; "we know all about that."

"I have just come from the sale at an ex-minister's house; he was a great epicure. At your age, monsieur le marquis, young people like sweetmeats—good things—especially those that are hard to get. Faith, when this was put up for sale, I thought that you might like it."

As he spoke, Monsieur Poterne produced from beneath his coat a huge jar of blue china, carefully sealed with parchment.

"What is there in that, Monsieur Poterne?"

"Indian preserve, monsieur le marquis; it's a very popular sweetmeat in hot countries, and very rare in France, on account of the difficulty of bringing it here; this is made of pineapples."

"The deuce!" muttered Jasmin; "he's taken to bringing us eatables now! This is the finishing touch!"

"A jar of this size is ordinarily worth a hundred francs at Chevet's, when he has any. I got this for fifty, and I bought it with the intention of offering it to you."

"Thanks, Monsieur Poterne; pineapple preserve should be delicious, in very truth.—Jasmin, give Monsieur Poterne fifty francs, then take this preserve to the pantry."

Jasmin took the jar which the ugly knave handed him.

"We don't need preserves," he muttered. "Mademoiselle Turlurette makes very good ones, and it wasn't worth while——"

A glance from Chérubin imposed silence on the old retainer, who walked, still grumbling, to the secretary and took out the money, while Poterne said to the young man:

"I shall soon have something very interesting to offer to monsieur le marquis. It's a monkey of the large species, extremely bright and intelligent, whose owner would not dispose of him except that he has failed in business. I mean to seize the opportunity, and you will have a monkey worthy of a king."

"A monkey!" cried Jasmin; "that would be the bouquet! Our house would be a complete menagerie then!"

"Hush, Jasmin," said Chérubin; "and do you, Monsieur Poterne, bring me the monkey as soon as you obtain it. I am very anxious to own it."

Monsieur Poterne bowed, took the fifty francs which the old servant, with a horrible grimace, counted out to him, and left the room, repeating that he would try to get the monkey at a reasonable figure.

Chérubin, who had an appointment with Daréna and several other young men to breakfast at the Café de Paris, hastily completed his toilet and dismissed his old servant, who was in despair at the idea of having a monkey. He left the room, after casting an angry glance at the jar for which his master had just paid fifty francs.

A few minutes later, Chérubin, attended by a genuine groom, entered his tilbury and drove away, paying no heed to Jasmin, who shouted to him from a window in the pantry:

"He's taken us in, monsieur! It's grape jelly and nothing else!"

XVI

MONSIEUR POTERNE CONTINUES HIS LITTLE TRICKS

At the Café de Paris, Chérubin found Daréna and two young dandies whose acquaintance he had made in the foyer of the Opéra. Intimacies are quickly formed at eighteen years; we proffer and give our friendship as if it were the most commonplace thing in the world. As we grow older, we often discover that we gave nothing and received nothing.

Chérubin's two new friends were only a few years older than he. One of them, whose name was Benoît Mousseraud, called himself *de* Mousseraud, and never mentioned his Christian name, which he considered vulgar. The other, on the contrary, whose name was Oscar Chiponard, used his Christian name only, and never mentioned his family name.

The former was a tall, slender young man of twenty-two, not ill-looking, although his eyes lacked expression and his hair, which he declared to be blond, bordered closely on the red; he was a brainless chatterbox, who boasted of making a conquest of every woman he saw, and of being the best dressed man in Paris.

The other was twenty-four years of age; he was small, dark, yellow-skinned, and would have been decidedly ugly, except that his black eyes were so full of fire and animation that they imparted much expression to his countenance. He might have passed for a clever fellow, if he had not had the folly to blush for his family and to lose his temper whenever anyone mentioned the name of his father.

Both these gentlemen belonged to wealthy families. Mousseraud was the son of a provincial notary and proposed to purchase a brokerage business in Paris; Chiponard, whose father was a retired watchmaker, proposed to do nothing at all.

They both displayed great friendliness to Daréna because he was of noble birth, and he reciprocated because they were rich. In society there is an almost constant interchange of these selfish sentiments.

"Come, come, Marquis Chérubin," said Daréna, "we are waiting for you; the breakfast is all ordered, and it will be rather fine; I understand such matters."

"You're a little late," said Oscar.

"He has probably been to bid one of his mistresses good-morning," added the tall Mousseraud, stroking his chin.

"My mistresses!" repeated Chérubin artlessly; "oh! I haven't any."

"Hasn't any, indeed!" cried Daréna, nudging him; "I trust that you don't believe that! The fact is that he has them in all quarters; he is a downright villain with the women already.—Don't say that you have no mistresses," he added in Chérubin's ear; "people will laugh at you and point their fingers at you as a curiosity. And it's a fact, my dear fellow, that for a young man of eighteen, you are very backward."

Chérubin blushed and hastily took his seat at the table. During the breakfast Mousseraud talked incessantly of his *bonnes fortunes*, while Oscar from time to time made malicious comments upon what his friend said. Daréna ate, drank, and laughed at their speeches. Chérubin listened to everything with the utmost good faith, simply uttering exclamations of wonder when their adventures seemed to him extraordinary.

"Yes, messieurs," said the tall red-blond, "at this moment I have five mistresses, without counting two others who are on the waiting list."

"Waiting for what?" sneered Oscar.

"Parbleu! that is plain enough: waiting for the intrigue to be consummated; it will be arranged this week, or next at the latest."

"Then you will have seven mistresses, just like a rooster!"

"Oh! you may pretend to joke, Oscar, but it's the truth. Indeed, I sometimes have more."

"You are getting to be a terrible fellow, Monsieur de Mousseraud!" said Daréna; "however, if your conquests are pretty, accept my congratulations."

"Four of them are enchanting, two very nice, and one passable. But I shall let the last three go; I intend to keep only the first quality."

"What's that! can you let a mistress go?" inquired Chérubin with a surprised expression.

"I say, marquis, where have you come from? One would think, to hear you, that you are a novice in love; whereas monsieur le comte assures us that you are his pupil. That would not do him credit."

Daréna emptied his glass and cried:

"Do you mean to say that you believe our young Adonis? Don't you see that he's making sport of you—a man who keeps a damsel three days at most? He takes us all in with his little innocent expression! And if he deceives us men, tell me whether the women are not likely to fall into his toils?"

"Monsieur Chérubin is favored in every respect," said Oscar.

"Monsieur is not the only one!" rejoined tall Mousseraud, with a conceited air; "I only say this, because it's a fact, but, on my word of honor, I have never met a woman who could resist me."

"Oh! that's not surprising with you!" retorted Oscar, in a mocking tone; "you have such an ardent nature—anyone can see that from the color of your hair."

"What do you mean by that?" demanded the tall young man, while his cheeks became as red as his locks. "Do you dare to say that I have red hair?"

"It seems to me that there is no need for me to say so."

"Come, come, messieurs; are we going to quarrel?" said Daréna. "We met here to breakfast, to laugh and talk nonsense; and we lose our temper, and sulk! That is most execrable form—and all about a matter of hair! Mon Dieu! I wish that mine were red; I should be delighted! It is much less common in France than dark or fair hair. And it proves too that the hair is not dyed.—Fill my glass, Oscar, and you, de Mousseraud, serve what is on that dish."

"Yes, yes!" cried Chérubin; "instead of losing your temper, tell me what you do with your seven mistresses?"

"Parbleu! what you do with yours, I presume."

"I? Why, I haven't——" A glance from Daréna checked Chérubin, and he continued: "I don't do anything at all with mine."

"In that case they must play some amusing tricks on you."

"I," said Oscar, "have a fascinating little grisette just now; I give her a cap every week and a dress every month, and she is perfectly satisfied."

"Among my seven mistresses," said Mousseraud, "there is an Englishwoman who costs me a lot of money; but she is an admirable creature!"

"What a braggart he is with his seven mistresses! He reminds me of Blue

Beard. Take them all out walking some day—you'll look like a boarding-school master."

"I give women nothing but my heart now," said Daréna; "and they are much more fond of me since I put them on that diet."

"And you, Chérubin, do you squander money on your charmers?"

"I—I don't know—that depends," stammered Chérubin, playing with his knife.

"Really, you are too close-mouthed," said Mousseraud; "one can get nothing out of you."

Chérubin, who was much embarrassed by the turn that the conversation had taken, drew his watch, pretending that he had an appointment.

While he was looking at the time, Oscar Chopinard, who was beside him, examined his watch.

"It's very pretty, very thin, isn't it?" asked Chérubin, holding the watch for his neighbor to see.

That gentleman took it, scrutinized it again very closely, and exclaimed:

"This is very strange! Is it a wager? Let me see the chain. Parbleu! the chain too. It would be curious if the pin—Allow me, my dear Chérubin."

And Monsieur Oscar, who, after examining Chérubin's watch, had scrutinized and weighed in his hand the chain that he wore about his neck, turned his attention to his diamond pin.

"What makes you stare at me like this?" queried Chérubin; "what is there about me that is so extraordinary?"

"You have upon you objects that I am much surprised to see you wear," replied Oscar; "a young man as rich as you are. You certainly didn't pay much for your watch and chain and pin?"

"Why, no, not too much—twenty-five hundred francs in all. To be sure, I got them at a bargain."

"Twenty-five hundred francs!" cried Oscar, bringing his hands together violently; "well, my dear fellow, in that case, you have been robbed! yes, absolutely robbed! The three articles are worth about sixty francs; the stones are imitation, and the watch and chain are gilded copper."

"Copper!" cried Chérubin; while Daréna muttered between his teeth:

"Ah! the villain! I almost suspected as much!"

"Why, it's impossible! Monsieur Daréna's man of business sold me all these things."

"I promise you that I am sure of what I say."

"Parbleu!" cried tall Mousseraud, in a sneering tone, "Oscar ought to know: his father was a watchmaker, and he was brought up in the shop."

"How can this be?" said Chérubin, addressing Daréna. "You are well aware that it was Poterne who brought me all these things."

Daréna broke a plate with his glass, crying:

"If it is true, Poterne is a miserable villain who has deceived me outrageously; but I will shatter him like this plate."

Chérubin could not believe that they had told him the truth. They left the restaurant and entered the first jeweler's shop they saw. The jeweler had no sooner examined the objects produced by the young man than he said in a most courteous, but slightly sarcastic tone:

"Oh! how can you wear such trash, monsieur? I would not give fifteen francs for the whole lot."

Chérubin took off his chain, his pin and his watch, and dashed them all on the floor, in a passion which was due, not to the loss of his money, but to his vexation at being deceived. Then he gave the jeweler his address.

"Please bring me to-morrow," he said, "all that I believed that I really owned—the handsomest things that you have; you will see, monsieur, that I have the means to pay for genuine jewels."

The jeweler bowed, assuring him that he should be obeyed; and they left the shop.

"As for your Monsieur Poterne," cried Chérubin to Daréna, "I advise him not to show his face at my house again."

Daréna, making a show of being furious, seized Chérubin's hand and shook it violently.

"My friend," he said, "I am the involuntary cause of all this; that rascally Poterne deceived me as he did you. I am sure that he is robbing me shamefully too. But it is for me to punish him; I am going to find him now and give him a thrashing."

With that, he hastily took his leave of the three young men and went home.

Daréna at this time occupied a small, but attractive apartment on Rue Neuve-Bréda. Thanks to Poterne's transactions with the young marquis, of which Daréna received a share of the profits, he had been in funds for some time. His man of business occupied a small room above his apartment.

"Is Poterne in my rooms?" asked Daréna, as he passed the concierge.

"In yours or else in his, monsieur," was the reply; "he's upstairs. I just saw him go in with the little boy who's been coming to see him every day for a fortnight."

"Aha! so a little boy comes to see him every morning? About how old a boy?"

"Oh! perhaps ten or twelve years old; but he's got a very sharp face. He ain't handsome, but in spite of that, he's got such a sly expression that you'd almost call him good-looking."

"What in the deuce can Poterne be doing with this boy?" said Daréna to himself as he went upstairs. "Can it be his son? Oh, no! a man like him never acknowledges a child; he would have to take care of him. It's probably some urchin whom he has hired to do his errands and polish his boots; but I supposed that he did all that himself."

Daréna entered his room, and, not finding Poterne there, went up another flight and knocked at the door of his agent's chamber.

Instantly there was a great commotion inside; it was as if chairs were being upset, and closet doors opened and shut. At last Monsieur Poterne's shrill, unmusical voice inquired:

"Who's there?"

"Parbleu! it's I. Let me in, you old scoundrel."

"Why don't you let me know who it is at once?" asked Poterne, as he opened the door. "I was very busy—your knock disturbed me—as I didn't know who it was."

Daréna glanced about the room, which was in great disorder; then, fastening his eyes on Poterne, who seemed to be anxious to set things to rights, he said:

"You weren't alone here, you had a small boy with you. What devilish mystery are you brewing now, with this child? Come, answer quickly; I am in no joking mood, I promise you!"

Monsieur Poterne's only reply was to call out:

"Come, Bruno, come; you can show yourself; it was my intimate friend, there's no danger!"

Instantly a closet opened and a small boy of twelve years or more emerged and rolled across the floor, uttering a shrill noise not unlike the cry of a savage. The singularity of his behavior was intensified by the fact that he was clad from head to foot in a sort of greenish skin, hairy in spots; that that skin, which covered his hands and feet as well, ended at those extremities in something like claws; and that a very slender and exceedingly long tail depended from his posterior. His face alone was uncovered.

"What in the devil is this?" asked Daréna, examining the boy, who went through a multitude of leaps and capers on the floor, and seemed perfectly accustomed to walking on his hands.

Monsieur Poterne emitted a hollow rumble, as if he were laughing internally, and replied:

"This is a monkey I am training."

"A monkey! For whom, pray?"

"For our young marquis. I wanted to sell him a large and handsome monkey, but I had no desire to put out the money for one. I had noticed this little bootblack at the corner; the rascal always did what errands I gave him, to my entire satisfaction; I saw that he was a bright little devil, so I proposed to him to play the monkey, for a handsome remuneration. I bought this orang-outang's costume, which is very lifelike; Bruno comes here every morning and puts it on; then he practises jumping and capering. He is doing very well, and he's more amusing than a real monkey. I have a mask, but I haven't made up my mind whether to have him wear one. As he is horribly ugly, I think that, by staining his face and gluing hair on his eyebrows and chin, I could make a fine monkey of him! Ha! ha!"

Daréna threw himself into a chair; he could not help laughing with his agent, as he rejoined:

"This is shocking! it is horrible! and yet I cannot help laughing! Really, this idea of manufacturing a monkey—Poterne, it's a pity that you are such a vile knave, for you have much imagination. But let us suppose that Chérubin has bought this counterfeit monkey—is Monsieur Bruno inclined to remain an animal all his life?"

"Why, no," replied Poterne; "once in the house, he will cleverly choose the moment to take flight; he will escape in one way or another—by the chimney, if need be; for he has been a sweep, and he is perfectly at home climbing chimneys. That part of it doesn't concern me, you see; I sell a monkey and get my money; it isn't my fault if you let him escape. Ha! ha!"

The boy, hearing Poterne laugh, followed his example, imitating anew the monkey's wild chatter, and leaping over all the furniture in the room in order to develop his talent.

"Well," said Daréna, after a moment, "you will lose the expense of educating him, Poterne; this little scamp may play the monkey on the boulevards, but he won't do it in our young pupil's house!"

"Why not, pray?"

"Why not? Because you are a villain, a swindler, a thief!"

Monsieur Poterne looked at the count with an expression which said plainly enough: "You've known that a long while; why pretend to be so surprised?"

"I have no objection to your selling things at rather a high figure to my young friend, because tradesmen always get as much as they can. That is business and nothing else. But I do not propose that you shall abuse Chérubin's confidence to the point of cheating him outrageously; and that is just what you have done, master thief!"

Poterne rolled his eyes in amazement, muttering:

"I don't see where the great harm comes in! I told him they were preserved pineapples, and they're turnips; but they can't hurt him; on the contrary, they're less heating."

"I am not talking about turnips—I don't know about that episode, you must tell me about it!—I am talking about the watch and chain and pin; they are all sham, horribly sham; and you had the face to tell me that they were worth eight hundred francs! You robbed me too, you villain!"

"It's very lucky that they weren't worth as much as that!" replied Poterne coolly; "for, out of the twenty-five hundred francs I got for them, you left me only five hundred to pay the dealer on account, and you've never given me the rest since."

"Because I had a sort of presentiment of your knavery! The idea of selling trash, gilded copper, to my young friend! it is infamous!"

"Bah! look you, it seems to me that you've been living comfortably at your young friend's expense for eighteen months past."

"Hold your tongue, Poterne, hold your tongue. I am tempted to break every bone in your body, and you deserve it. See what a fine thing you have done in not being content with the honest profits you might have made on such things as you sold Chérubin; now you can never go to his house again. I had thrown open an excellent house to you, and you have closed it by your thirst for gold—and as a result you have injured me considerably. I have derived some profit from your little transactions—and that was no more than fair; as it was I who made you acquainted with this rich youngster."

"Some profit! In other words, you took the whole!" muttered Poterne, with a horrible grimace.

"Once more, hold your tongue, or I cannot restrain myself!—Now, how shall I maintain my position, my life of luxury? I can borrow of Chérubin occasionally, to be sure, but that resource will soon fail me: the most obliging people get tired of lending, especially when they are never paid. I have tried to instil into my young friend a taste for cards, telling him that it was the passion of fashionable people; but I could not do it, cards are a bore to him; and then that devil of a Monfréville has strongly advised him not to touch them. So that there is but one way left for me to feather my own nest by making myself useful to Chérubin, and that is—love. When a wealthy young man is in love, he usually does all sorts of foolish things for the woman he loves. If there are obstacles, he spends money lavishly to overcome them,—and we should have had no difficulty in placing obstacles in his path whenever we chose. Well! by some fatality which I cannot understand, Chérubin, who exclaims in admiration at sight of a pretty face, who seemed to be dead in love with my four little ballet dancers, who cannot look at a grisette without a thrill, who, in short, acts as if he were tremendously in love with all women, hasn't yet engaged in any intrigue or taken a mistress. I have proposed twenty times to take him to Malvina, or Rosina, or Fœdora; he will agree at first, then refuse, saying: 'Later; we'll see about it; I don't dare!' And my sarcasms, my jests, fail to overcome his timidity.—That is where I stand now, monsieur; I was justified, you see, in saying that your knavery has placed me in an unpleasant position."

Poterne, who had listened very attentively to Daréna, reflected for some moments on what he had heard, and replied at last:

"If the young man has no love-affairs on hand, it is probably because he has not yet met a woman who has really attracted him. Those dancers of yours who seemed to be throwing themselves at his head—that's not the way to captivate a wholly inexperienced heart, which wants illusions, ardent passion. Never fear, I'll find what he needs, and before long I will involve him in a most romantic and complicated intrigue."

"Remember that you cannot show your face before Chérubin, who is quite capable of kicking you downstairs. He is in a terrible rage with you, I warn you."

"Oh! don't be alarmed; if I appear before him, I will take good care that he doesn't recognize me."

"Poterne, if you succeed in arousing a passionate love in our young man's heart, I will give you back my esteem."

"Oh, yes! I shall succeed! But first, you must give me time to find a pretty girl, and then to learn whether—I say, Bruno! Bruno! where are you going, you little rascal?"

During the foregoing conversation between Daréna and Poterne, the small boy, who had understood that he was not to play the part of a monkey, as he had been led to expect, had resumed his ordinary garb; but, when he had finished his toilet, Monsieur Bruno, presuming that no one was paying any heed to him, rolled the monkey's skin around the mask, put it under his arm, and left the room.

"My skin! my monkey's skin, Bruno!" cried Monsieur Poterne, running out to the landing. "Ah! you little vagabond! don't you mean to give it back to me?"

But Monsieur Bruno, who had become very skilful in gymnastic exercises, thanks to the lessons he had taken in playing the monkey, ran down the stairs so rapidly that he was at the foot before Poterne had covered three stairs. The latter ran after the little thief none the less; and while Daréna returned to his room, laughing at the episode, Monsieur Poterne ran through the street after the bootblack, crying:

"My skin! my skin! stop that little scamp—he's stolen my skin!"

XVII

ADVICE OF A FRIEND

On returning home, Chérubin sent for Jasmin and said to him:

"If Monsieur Poterne should ever dare to appear here again, I order you to have him thrown out of doors; you may even go so far as to order the concierge to thrash him; but you must not undertake it yourself, for you are too old and he would return the compliment."

Jasmin uttered a joyful exclamation, and said:

"What! really, monsieur? And without taking the monkey?"

"Oh! I forbid you above all things to take anything whatever from him."

And Chérubin told his old servant what had happened.

"You see, monsieur," said Jasmin, "that Poterne is an outrageous swindler —I was sure of it. His so-called Indian preserves—I gave 'em to Mademoiselle Turlurette to taste; they gave her a very bad stomach ache, and she's been out of order ever since. I'm very much afraid, monsieur, that everything you have bought of that Poterne is like your watch!—And this Monsieur Daréna whose man of business he is—hum!"

"Daréna was even more furious than I with that man; he swore that he'd thrash him. He was deceived too; it isn't his fault."

"All the same, my dear master, I very much prefer your other friend, Monsieur de Monfréville. Ah! such a difference! he doesn't borrow your tailor; he doesn't induce you to buy things; he doesn't let his steward loose on you."

Chérubin smiled at Jasmin's reflections, but it did not enter his mind that Daréna could be a confederate in his agent's wrongdoing. His heart was too frank, too trustful, to suspect cunning and perfidy, and he would have been unable to believe in Monsieur Poterne's shameless rascality had it been less abundantly demonstrated to him.

As for Monsieur Gérondif, who passed a large part of his time in sleep, and another large part at the table, and who had adopted the habit of reading Voltaire or Racine to Mademoiselle Turlurette of an evening, telling her that he had composed the lines that morning, when he learned what Monsieur Poterne had done, he exclaimed:

"That man never read *Deuteronomy*, where it says: *Non furtum facies*; or else he mistranslated it."

A few days after this adventure, Monfréville, returning from the country, came at once to see Chérubin. When he spied the pack of hounds, the parrots, the turtle, the canes, the gothic vases, and all the alleged rare objects with which his young friend's house was filled to overflowing, he uttered an exclamation which was not of delight, and said to Chérubin:

"Mon Dieu! what on earth induced you to buy all this stuff?"

"They are all bargains. I was told that they were very fine."

"Fine! Why, they are all horrible, in wretched taste, and of no value whatever. Your parrots are wretched cockatoos, your dogs are miserable curs that I would not have to guard chickens! Even your canes are common sticks of wood; this rattan is an imitation, it was never what it pretends to be."

"What did I say?" cried Jasmin; "that Poterne is an infernal pickpocket; he has taken us in with everything, just as he did with the jewels.—Tell monsieur the story of our watch, my dear master."

Chérubin told Monfréville what had happened to him.

"If it was Monsieur Poterne who sold you all this," said Monfréville, "I am surprised no longer! But Daréna—do you still see him?"

"Yes," replied Chérubin; "he was indignant at his agent's conduct, and he has told me since that he had beaten him and dismissed him from his service."

Monfréville smiled faintly; then he took Chérubin's hand and said:

"My friend, you are still very young, and you cannot be expected to understand men; the knowledge of the world which one acquires only by experience and familiarity, unless one is blessed in youth with a most observant mind, that knowledge is rather melancholy than agreeable! For men are rarely what they choose to appear; frankness is not esteemed as a virtue in society; on the contrary, the man would be considered a fool or a boor who should say frankly what he thought, at the risk of wounding the self-esteem of this one or the susceptibility of that one. We consider those people delightful who never have any but agreeable and flattering words in their mouths, and we do not worry as to whether they mean what they say. In the world, every man acts as his interest or his passions impel him, and they who make the most parade of their virtues, their honor, their good faith, are the ones whom we should trust least; for people who are really virtuous and upright deem it perfectly natural to be so, and quite unnecessary to proclaim it. I have not said all this to you earlier, for I regret to deprive you of the illusions which make a large part of the charm of youth, and with which we begin life; but I take too deep an interest in you not to try to put you on your guard against the snares which may be laid for you."

"What, my dear Monfréville," said Chérubin sadly, "can't we trust anybody in the world?"

"I don't mean to go so far as that. I do not want to make a misanthrope of you—God forbid! But I warn you that you must be particular in the choice of your friends."

"Monsieur Gérondif has often told me that when a man became learned he became a man to be feared, because a learned man can never be cheated by anybody, as he knows more than other men."

"I don't know whether your tutor is very strong on his authors, but he is rather weak in knowledge of the human heart. In the first place, a person may be very learned without a spark of wit—we have proofs of that every day; and in the second place, those who have the most wit are almost always the ones who are most easily cheated; doubtless Providence so ordained as a recompense to fools."

"So you feel sure that people will try to cheat me?"

"You are young and rich, and you have had very little experience. There are numbers of people who would like to take advantage of that combination. All this that I am saying is very sad—but you will realize later that I am right."

"Have you been caught often, Monsieur de Monfréville?"

This artless question brought a smile to the lips of him to whom it was addressed; he heaved a sigh, however, as he replied:

"Like other men, my friend. Take my advice and do not form an intimacy with Daréna. I dislike to speak harshly of anyone; but the more I observe the count, the more strongly I feel that his acquaintance is not at all suitable for you."

"But he is very amusing, very agreeable, very clever."

"I know it, and that makes him all the more dangerous. He has already borrowed money from you, has he not?"

"Why, yes—sometimes."

"He will never pay you."

"Do you think not?"

"I am sure of it. He will urge you to play."

"Yes, he has often proposed it."

"It is the most fatal of passions. He is a gambler and he has ruined himself. When a man has reached that point, he tries too often to ruin others; for an unlucky gambler is sometimes far from delicate in the methods to which he resorts to obtain money, in order to gratify his passion. Daréna has reached that point."

"As you have so bad an opinion of Daréna, how does it happen that he is a friend of yours? Why did he come to Gagny with you?"

"Your question is perfectly just; but in society one accepts a man's good qualities and does not concern oneself enough about his bad ones. Daréna bears an honorable name; he is able to behave most becomingly when he chooses; in fact, he has most agreeable and fascinating manners; and nobody asks for anything more in society. But, I tell you again, one should look for something more in a friend."

"And the women, my dear Monfréville, the women—must I distrust them too? Ah! that would be a great pity, women are so pretty!"

"It's different with women! As a general rule, men are too fickle to be exacting in the choice of their mistresses, and for that reason such liaisons are not at all dangerous. What does it matter that you are in love with a coquette, with a woman whose reputation is more than shady, with an actress who will make a fool of you? That love will soon be replaced by another, which, in its turn, will be as quickly forgotten! A man's reputation has nothing to fear from all that; on the contrary, the more love-affairs you have, the more flattered the ladies will be to win your love; that fact says more for their self-esteem than for their hearts."

"What do you say? to attract the women, one must deceive them?" cried

Chérubin, gazing at Monfréville with an incredulous expression. "Do you mean that it is all the same to them whether we forget them and abandon them?"

Monfréville turned pale, his brow darkened, and he kept his eyes on the floor for a long while; not for some moments did he reply:

"There are women who never forgive inconstancy, but they are not ordinarily the ones who love you the best; for true love makes one indulgent. It forgives, provided that you return in all sincerity. I tell you, Chérubin, that the shrewdest man knows nothing about a woman's heart. There has been much discussion of the subject, and no two persons ever agreed. Tertullian declares that the devil is not so spiteful as woman, and Confucius says that a woman's soul is the masterwork of creation. Cato maintains that wisdom and virtue are incompatible with the female mind, and Tibullus that woman's love brings us back to virtue. How are we to form an opinion about it?—But I believe that at this moment I am too much like your tutor, who overwhelms you with his learning. I conclude, my young friend, by informing you that the best way to be happy is to form no attachment. Love all women! Your life will glide along amid pleasures and folly. But if you love only one, you must expect much sorrow in exchange for a little happiness."

"Love all women, you say! I ask nothing better! I fall in love with all I see —when they are pretty."

"But I believe that you have not yet formed any liaison? I have not heard that you have any mistress!"

"No—you see—it seems to me that I shall never dare to tell a woman that I love her. A man must be very bold to say that, do you know?"

"Ha! ha! this is the result of a sojourn of sixteen years with your nurse. But you must cast off this timidity, which will be much more injurious than advantageous to you, especially with the fair sex. You are more than eighteen years old—you must make a start, show yourself in society. You must not serve your apprenticeship in love with grisettes or supernumeraries from the theatre. You will find something better than that. In the fashionable society to which I propose to introduce you, a thousand women will contend for your favor, and they will do you credit, at all events. Moreover, it is high time that you should know something besides the theatres, cafés and restaurants of Paris; the salons are where a man gets his training, and I will take you to those where refined manners are the rule. With your name you will be welcomed everywhere. This is the season for receptions; Madame Célival has resumed her assemblies, which are very brilliant affairs; the best people in Paris go there. I will introduce you to her house."

Chérubin trembled at the idea of going into society; he was afraid of being awkward and clumsy, and of being unable to talk. But Monfréville encouraged him, promised to be his guide and to stay with him, and the young man consented to allow himself to be taken to Madame Célival's reception.

The day arrived too quickly for Chérubin, who, having never attended any such function, was greatly excited at the mere thought of finding himself in the midst of a large company, exposed to everybody's glances and remarks.

"What shall I say?"—That was always the result of Chérubin's reflections; and, pending Monfréville's arrival, he went to Monsieur Gérondif, to consult him as to what a young man may find to say when he makes his first appearance in society.

Monsieur Gérondif was learning some of La Fontaine's poetry by heart, intending to recite it to Mademoiselle Turlurette as his own. The tutor was not enamored of the housekeeper; he considered her over-developed for him, and he had views elsewhere; but Mademoiselle Turlurette's functions included the department of preserves, sweetmeats and liqueurs, and Monsieur Gérondif was very fond of all such dainties.

When he saw his pupil enter his room, the tutor was thunderstruck; it was the first time that Chérubin had paid him a visit since they had been in Paris. He imagined that he wished to resume his studies, and he said:

"Everything is ready, my noble pupil. I am always expecting you. I have prepared abstracts of history, mythology and geology for you. I am always at work in your service. At this moment, as you are taking lessons in *savate*, I am trying to find the origin of that form of exercise in Plutarch's lives of illustrious men. I find the *cestus*, boxing and wrestling, but I haven't yet found *savate*."

"I thank you, Monsieur Gérondif," replied Chérubin, "but that is not what I have come about. This evening Monsieur de Monfréville is to take me into society; he declares that it is necessary for me to go there, that I shall acquire refined manners there; he is probably right, and I have promised to let him take me. But what do people say at a fashionable reception? How should one behave? Do you talk with people whom you don't know?—I thought that you could tell me that, you know so many things; for as yet I haven't been anywhere except to the theatre and concerts, and to cafés; and I must confess that I am terribly afraid of cutting a foolish figure in company."

"Foolish!" cried Gérondif; "that is impossible! You forget that you are my pupil; you are not equal to me in Horace and Virgil, but you know some passages—you must repeat them when you are talking with men. With the ladies, it is different; employ those figures of speech, those metaphors, which embellish discourse; compare them to Venus, Diana, Juno, Hebe, and you will certainly win a surprising triumph. But, if you wish me to go with you, I will stand behind you and prompt you."

Chérubin did not consider it necessary to be attended in company by his tutor; he believed that Monfréville would keep his promise and would not leave him.

Monfréville called for his young friend at the hour appointed. He was dressed in the most perfect taste; his slender and shapely figure was encased in an exquisitely fitting coat, which he wore with much grace. His youthful bearing, his beautiful dark hair and his still charming face made him seem barely thirty years old, although he was near forty.

Chérubin, who was dressed in the latest style, still retained a trace of the awkwardness characteristic of village youths; but as he was well-built and had a most attractive face, the awkwardness of his carriage sometimes resembled the innocent coquetry of a schoolboy.

They entered the carriage, and Monfréville said:

"I am taking you into fashionable society, but, in order to dispel any feeling of shyness, that may injure your prospects, say to yourself first of all that you are of as good family as any of the people you will see there; say to yourself in the second place, that, thanks to your fortune and your rank, you need no support. When a person can say that to himself, my dear Chérubin, he should be perfectly self-possessed in society; indeed, some people are too much so. In default of the advantages which you have, and which everybody cannot have, a philosopher would say: 'Why should I allow myself to be awed by this man's title, or by that man's fortune? Are they not men like myself, after all? Imagine all these vain, proud people in the costume of our first parents in the Garden of Eden; strip them of these decorations, these jewels, these costly clothes, in which their whole merit often consists,—will they be so imposing to me then? No, indeed; it is probable that they will make me laugh, and that is all.'—My dear fellow, a few such reflections are enough to put one entirely at his ease in the most exalted company."

"You encourage me," said Chérubin; "I shall talk Latin with the men, and with the ladies I shall talk about Venus, Diana and Phœbe. Monsieur Gérondif advised that."

"If you want to make people laugh at you, that would be the best of all ways. I suspected that your tutor was a fool, now I am sure of it."

"Mon Dieu! what shall I say then, if anyone speaks to me?"

"Reply to what they say."

"But suppose I don't know what to reply—suppose I can't think of anything to say?"

"Keep silent then. A person is never stupid in society when he knows how to keep silent; indeed there are people who owe their reputation for wit to their silence."

"But suppose I see any lovely women, who take my fancy?"

"Tell them so with your eyes; they will understand you perfectly."

"But if I want to make their acquaintance, to pay court to them?"

"Say whatever comes into your head; but above all things don't try to be bright, for you would make yourself a terrible bore."

"But suppose nothing comes into my head?"

"You still have the resource of silence and eloquent glances; there are many people who stop there."

"But this lady to whose house you are taking me?"

"True, I must tell you something about her. Madame Célival must be about thirty-six, but she is very good-looking; she is an alluring brunette; her eyes are most expressive, she has a lovely figure and graceful outlines; there is something fascinating, something voluptuous in her whole aspect, which seduces all the men. Madame Célival is a coquette, too, and is not supposed to be too cruel to those who sigh for her; but that is whispered only. She is her own mistress, however; she is the widow of a general, yes, a real general, who actually lived and left her a handsome fortune and no children. You may judge that the lovely widow does not lack adorers.—But, attention; here we are."

PART III

XVIII

In an elegant, brilliantly-lighted apartment on Rue Saint-Lazare, a fashionable company, already quite numerous, was engaged in conversation that was rarely of a private nature, but often piquant and satirical. At intervals, some witty person interjected a word or two, while the undaunted chatterers, who never had anything clever to say, persisted in holding the floor.

Madame Célival was just as Monfréville had described her: lovely, amiable, coquettish, glancing at a mirror from time to time, to be sure of the effect of her gown; paying due attention to all her guests, with the talent of a woman accustomed to society, but reserving softer and tenderer smiles for the men who were paying court to her.

Near the couch on which the mistress of the house had just taken her seat sat a young and pretty blonde, dressed in muslin and crêpe, and entangled in veils and scarfs that almost concealed her charming features; it was all pink and white and formed so becoming a frame for this lady that at a distance she resembled one of those engravings of a woman's face surrounded by clouds.

Madame Célival thanked the pretty blonde for consenting to come to her reception, despite the torture caused by her nerves. A few steps away was a tall gentleman wearing a decoration; he was very thin and very ugly; his chin was surrounded by a sparse necklace of jet-black beard; moustaches no less glossy, and carefully waxed and twisted at the ends, made his face resemble a cat's in some measure. He was addressed as colonel.

A young man whose hair was parted and curled with as much care as a woman could possibly take, and whose regular, but somewhat harsh features recalled the faces which our historical painters love to give to the heroes of ancient Rome, was standing by the fireplace; he rarely removed his eyes from the ladies who were talking on the divan, but he seemed not to be observing either of them more particularly than the other.

Near the piano, for there was necessarily a piano in the salon, several young persons were assembled, turning over the leaves of albums, or looking at the music; they were not all good-looking, but they were all dressed with so much taste, there was so much reserved grace in their manners, that even those who were not pretty were not without charm.

In another part of the room the mammas were chatting together; some were dressed with a coquetry which seemed to indicate a purpose to outshine their daughters; others displayed a simple but tasteful elegance, suited to their age, which made them the more attractive when they were still young enough to attract.

Some young men were fluttering about the younger ladies, while others contented themselves with standing very straight and stiff in order to call attention to the finished elegance of their clothes and the good taste with which their hair was arranged. Some had assumed a smile which remained as if stereotyped on their faces throughout the evening. Then there were men of uncertain age standing and talking in the middle of the room; among them a gentleman, whose gray hair, very scanty over his forehead, curled luxuriantly about his temples. He possessed a distinguished and intellectual face, but there was an over-curious, over-inquisitive expression in his little eyes, which gleamed with the vivacity of youth, although his face indicated that he was in the neighborhood of sixty. This gentleman talked incessantly, with much energy, and while carrying on a conversation in one part of the salon, managed to hear what was said elsewhere, and thus took part in most of the other conversations, sustaining his share of the discussion on several different subjects at the same time, with the same facility with which Caesar dictated several letters at once in different languages.

Another salon, smaller than that where the ladies were sitting, and reached by passing through a lovely little room furnished with the most delicious luxury, was set aside for those of the guests who wished to play cards. Whist and bouillotte tables were prepared, but there were as yet no players.

Monsieur de Monfréville and the Marquis Chérubin de Grandvilain were announced. All eyes were turned toward the door. The names Chérubin and Grandvilain formed such a strange contrast that everybody was curious to see the person who bore them.

"Monsieur de Grandvilain!" said one; "Gad! how ugly he must be! He must be an elderly man."

"But the footman said Chérubin too; that's a very pretty name."

"They can't belong to the same man."

"Probably there's a father and a son."

While the guests indulged in these reflections, Madame Célival said to those who were nearest her, but speaking loud enough to be overheard by everybody:

"Monsieur de Monfréville did ask my permission to introduce a young man who has never been out at all; and I granted it the more willingly because this young man, who is the last of a noble family, deserves, so it is said, all the interest that Monsieur de Monfréville takes in him."

"Ah! very well done!" murmured the gray-haired gentleman; "a little announcement preceding the introduction."

At that moment Chérubin entered the salon with Monfréville. Despite all that his mentor had said to him, he was far from self-possessed, and the deep flush that covered his cheeks sufficiently betrayed his embarrassment. But his eyes were so lovely and soft, his features so refined, his face so interesting, that a flattering murmur greeted his entrance into the salon, and everyone felt prepossessed in his favor at once. The young men who were standing stiffly erect to display their fine points were the only ones who did not seem to share the general feeling.

"He has a very awkward manner," said one.

"He carries himself badly," said another.

"He looks like a woman in man's clothes," murmured a young dandy, bristling with beard, moustache and side-whiskers.

And Monsieur Trichet, the gray-haired gentleman, smiled maliciously and said:

"Chérubin! a most appropriate name. He is Comte Almaviva's little page to the life! He still lacks the gallantry and self-assurance of his namesake; but those will soon come. The ladies will ask nothing better than to train him."

Madame Célival greeted the young man with a charming smile when Monfréville presented him. She made several of those complimentary remarks which captivate instantly the person to whom they are addressed. Chérubin tried to reply to her compliments, but he went astray and tangled himself up in a sentence which he was unable to finish. Luckily Monfréville was at hand and interposed to relieve his embarrassment, and Madame Célival was too well-bred not to do her best to put him at his ease. So that, after a few moments, Chérubin began to venture to look about him.

"What a lot of pretty women there are here!" he whispered to his sponsor. "I say, my friend, do you mean to say that one can love them all?"

"You are perfectly at liberty to love them all, but I cannot promise that they will all love you."

"The mistress of the house is very beautiful; she has eyes that—I don't dare to say it."

"Say on."

"That dazzle one, intoxicate one—excuse me, but I can't think of the right word."

"Intoxicate isn't at all bad; in fact, you have unwittingly hit upon the most apt expression; for if wine deprives us of our reason, a pretty woman's eyes produce precisely the same effect. I am tempted to tell Madame Célival what you just said about her eyes; she will be flattered by it, I'll wager."

"Oh! my dear fellow, don't do that—I shouldn't dare to look at her again. But the lady opposite is very pretty too! That blonde almost hidden by pink and white muslin."

"That is Madame la Comtesse Emma de Valdieri; she is a fascinating creature, in very truth; she has something of the sylph about her, something of a daughter of the air. She is perfectly proportioned: small feet, small hands, small mouth, small ears; only her eyes are large. She is the perfect type of tiny women. But she is exceedingly nervous and flighty, and, above all, capricious; to-day she will greet you with a tender glance, to-morrow she will act as if she did not know you; adulation has spoiled her. Comtesse Emma is French, but her husband is a Corsican. He is that stout gentleman with whiskers, who is singing at the piano. He has a superb bass voice, so that he is always anxious to sing; and, although he's a Corsican, he seems to be very little disturbed by the homage paid to his wife."

Monsieur Trichet, who was at some distance from Monfréville, succeeded none the less in overhearing what he said to Chérubin; and he approached the two friends, saying in a sarcastic tone:

"True, true. Valdieri, the handsome singer, is not at all jealous; but it isn't safe to trust him! With these Corsicans, there is always the vendetta to guard against. Is your health good, Monsieur de Monfréville?"

"Very good, monsieur, I thank you."

"It is some time since you have shown yourself in society."

"I have been obliged to pay a long visit to my estate near Fontainebleau."

"Oh, yes!—So you are introducing monsieur in society? He could not find a better guide."

Chérubin bowed and attempted to say a few words in reply; but after a vain effort, he deemed it more prudent to hold his peace. Monsieur Trichet was about to continue the conversation, when he saw, at the other end of the room, three gentlemen talking with great earnestness; he instantly ran toward them, crying:

"That isn't so—you're wrong! I know the story better than you do, and I'll tell it to you."

Monfréville smiled at Chérubin and said:

"I need not tell you that that gentleman, whose name is Trichet, is the most inquisitive and loquacious mortal whom it is possible to meet. He can't see two people talking together without joining their conversation, which is not always agreeable. However, as Monsieur Trichet is a very wealthy old bachelor, who gives very handsome fêtes, and as, aside from his curiosity, he doesn't lack wit and tells a good story, he is made welcome everywhere, in salons and at the theatres."

Chérubin was still engaged in looking about at the assembled company, when the door opened and the footman announced:

"Monsieur, Madame and Mademoiselle de Noirmont."

A lady above middle height, but of dignified and refined bearing, entered first, with a girl of some fourteen or fifteen years. The lady, whose dress, although rich, was almost severe in its simplicity, seemed to be rather more than thirty years of age; her features were beautiful, but grave; her large dark eyes, surmounted by heavy eyebrows, wore a vague and thoughtful expression which might lead one to think that her thoughts were often busy with something different from what she was saying; her lips, somewhat too tightly closed, hardly ever parted in a smile. That cold and haughty face was framed by beautiful tresses of black hair, which fell very low.

The young lady had the winning charm of her age; although she was not very pretty, her features attracted one by their fascinating expression of playfulness and mischief, which was often moderated by her mother's stern glances.

Monsieur de Noirmont, who came after them, was a man of fifty; he was very tall and stooped a little; his temples were shadowed by a few dark hairs, but the top of his head was entirely bald. His appearance was stern, supercilious and far from attractive; his regular features had probably been handsome, but his steely glance, his sharp voice and his shortness of speech inspired neither affection nor confidence.

The arrival of these three persons seemed to cause Monfréville profound emotion; his brow became wrinkled, his eyebrows drew together, and a veil of melancholy covered his eyes. But in a moment, surmounting his sensations, he succeeded in resuming the amiable and unruffled air which he wore on his arrival; indeed one would have said that he made it a point to seem more cheerful than before.

Monsieur Trichet, who had returned to Chérubin's side, did not fail to comment on the new arrivals:

"That's the Noirmont family; they have left their estate in Normandie, and they live in Paris now. They must have found it very dull in the country. They are not a very hilarious family. That De Noirmont is stiff and sour and overbearing! Just because he was once in the magistracy, you would think that he was always sitting in judgment on you. However, he's a man of the strictest probity; he deserves his reputation, but he's not an agreeable companion. As for his wife, she is a worthy mate to her husband—she talks very little and never smiles. I don't know whether she has any wit, but at all events she never compromises it. As for her virtue—oh! that is intact, as far beyond reproach as her husband's probity. And yet Madame de Noirmont, who is very handsome still, although she may be thirty-three or thirty-four years old—yes, she must be quite that—must have been an enchanting creature at eighteen, assuming that she deigned to smile occasionally then. Their daughter, young Ernestine, is a mere child still. She is a nice little thing, merry and playful—which proves that she takes after neither father nor mother. But that is often seen.—Stay, colonel, I knew the person you are talking about, and I will explain the matter under discussion."

At that, Monsieur Trichet joined the tall gentleman with the waxed moustache, who was talking with two ladies; and Chérubin, turning his head, saw that Monfréville was no longer by his side.

Finding himself alone, in the midst of that numerous assemblage, the young man felt sorely perturbed and lost the assurance which he derived from his friend's neighborhood. As he preferred not to stand there, awkward and embarrassed, by the fireplace, where he was exposed to every eye, he succeeded in extricating himself from the circle by slipping behind an easy-chair, and thence made his way to a window recess, where he was prevented from going farther by several persons who were seated there. He tried to retrace his steps, but Madame de Noirmont and her daughter had seated themselves in front of him and closed the way by which he had come; so that he was blockaded in a very confined space, which he could not leave except by compelling the ladies in front of him to rise. As he was incapable of such an audacious act, he decided to remain in the corner where he was, until it should please chance, or Monfréville, to release him from his prison.

The ladies who were seated in front of the recess in which Chérubin stood had no suspicion that there was anybody behind them. The conversation continued in the salon; the guests walked hither and thither, laughing and chatting. Chérubin alone could not stir, and he was at a loss what to do in his little corner. Several times Madame Célival passed the people who were blockading him, but she did not see him. He congratulated himself that she did not, for he would not have known what reply to make, if she had asked him what he was doing there. Monfréville too had reappeared in the salon, but he did not see the suppliant glances which his young friend cast at him, and, instead of approaching him, he seemed to avoid that part of the room in which Madame de Noirmont had seated herself.

Nearly an hour passed thus. Poor Chérubin was terribly fatigued by standing so long, and terribly bored in his little nook. He could hear what Madame de Noirmont said to her daughter; but that lady did not enter into any sustained conversation; she simply replied in few words to Ernestine's questions.

"Mamma," said the latter, after a young lady had sung a ballad, "don't you want me to sing?"

"No, my child, you are too young to put yourself forward; besides, unless your father insists upon it, you will never sing in company."

"Why not, mamma?"

"Because I prefer in a young lady the modesty which keeps itself concealed, to the vanity which makes itself conspicuous."

"But in that case, mamma, why did you give me a music teacher?"

"Such accomplishments are more useful in solitude than in society."

"Oh!—But, mamma——"

"That is enough, my child."

A glance from Madame de Noirmont imposed silence on the girl; but, after a few moments, she returned to the charge.

"Don't they dance here, mamma?"

"Of course not. Did I tell you that we were going to a ball?"

"Oh, no! but sometimes they dance at receptions; it's much better fun then."

"You think of nothing but pleasure and dancing!"

"Oh! I am so fond of it! Father told me that he would give a great ball next winter."

"A great ball! Oh! I hope that he will change his mind."

"Why don't you want to give one, mamma?"

"No matter; hush!"

The girl held her peace, but indulged in a pretty little pout; whereupon her mother seized her hand and pressed it, and said in a gentler tone and with an expression of the deepest melancholy:

"I distress you, Ernestine; you don't love your mother."

The girl replied by putting her mother's hand to her lips and murmuring:

"Oh! you know that I do!"

Suddenly, happening to turn her head, Mademoiselle de Noirmont caught sight of Chérubin, who did not know which leg to stand on. When she saw that young man standing behind her and cutting such an amusing figure, young Ernestine only half restrained her longing to laugh.

"What is the matter?" her mother asked her; "what has happened to you? You should not laugh so in company—it is not proper."

The girl replied by nudging her mother gently and whispering:

"Look—behind us—there's a young gentleman."

Madame de Noirmont turned and saw Chérubin, who, having no idea which way to turn, bowed low to her. Amazed to see the young man in hiding in a window recess, Madame de Noirmont was about to move so that he might pass; but at that moment, Monfréville, having just discovered his young friend, for whom he had been searching the salons in vain, drew near to assist him in escaping from his prison.

When she saw Monfréville coming straight toward her, Madame de Noirmont seemed to experience a nervous convulsion; but her face changed very slightly.

"Pardon me, madame," said Monfréville, "and permit me to release a young man who, I am sure, has stood here a long while, afraid to stir because he was unwilling to disturb you."

Madame de Noirmont's only reply was to motion to her daughter to rise, which she instantly did. Chérubin thereupon took advantage of the path thus opened, apologizing profusely to young Ernestine; then he walked quickly away with Monfréville, not remarking the extreme pallor that covered Madame de Noirmont's face, and his friend's forced gayety.

"I have been there for more than an hour," whispered Chérubin to his mentor. "Oh! I was awfully uncomfortable! such torture!"

"Well, my dear fellow, why do you creep into little nooks like that? Did— did Madame de Noirmont speak to you?"

"That lady in front of me, who looked so stern? No, indeed; she had only just discovered me. Oh! I should never fall in love with her, although she is very handsome! I don't think she looks at all agreeable. How different from Comtesse Valdieri, and Madame Célival, and that one, and that one."

While Chérubin turned his amorous glances upon those ladies who attracted him, Monsieur de Noirmont, who was talking with Monsieur Trichet, left that gentleman and walked to meet the young marquis, to whom he made a solemn and ceremonious bow, saying:

"I have just been told that the son of the late Monsieur le Marquis de Grandvilain is here, and I wish to say to him that I am delighted to meet the son of a person whom I esteemed and honored in every respect. Yes, monsieur, I was well acquainted with monsieur your father; he was a most excellent man; I have no doubt that his son resembles him, and I trust that he will do me the honor to call at my house. Here is my card, monsieur; I look forward to the pleasure of a visit from you."

Chérubin, bewildered by this unexpected invitation, bowed and muttered a few commonplace words; but Monsieur de Noirmont took his hand and led him away, saying:

"Allow me to present you to Madame de Noirmont."

Chérubin made no resistance; he allowed himself to be led back, shuddering, to the little recess where he had stood so long; but that time he was not compelled to enter it. Monsieur de Noirmont introduced him to his wife, saying:

"Monsieur le Marquis de Grandvilain, son of a man who honored me by calling me his friend."

Madame de Noirmont, recognizing the young man who had been her prisoner, repressed a gesture of surprise, bowed coldly to Chérubin, and seemed to hesitate to look at him, as if she dreaded to see Monfréville with him again.

Little Ernestine bit her lips to keep from laughing, when she heard her father give the name of Grandvilain to the young man whom he presented.

At last Chérubin found himself at liberty once more, and returned to Monfréville, who said to him:

"You have been introduced to Madame de Noirmont?"

"Yes, my friend."

"What did she say to you?"

"Nothing; indeed her greeting was decidedly cold."

"Shall you go to her house?"

"Faith, I have no inclination to do so; it seems to me that it must be a horribly dull place. That Monsieur de Noirmont has a stiff sort of courtesy that turns one cold. After all, I am not obliged to visit all my father's friends; they are hardly of my age."

"You must leave your card at his door, that will be enough; I think with you that it will be as well for you not to go to that house. But Madame Célival is looking for you, she was asking just now what had become of you; I think that you have made a conquest of her."

"Really! Oh! if that were true!"

"Look, there she is yonder. Go and say something to her."

"What shall I say?"

"Whatever you choose; she will help you to keep up the conversation. Don't be bashful, my dear fellow; that isn't the way to get ahead in the world."

Chérubin made an effort to overcome his diffidence, and resolved to join Madame Célival; she, when she saw him coming toward her, bestowed a charming smile on him and at once motioned him to a seat by her side. Encouraged by this greeting, Chérubin took his place beside the lovely brunette, faltering some words which it was impossible to hear, but to which Madame Célival replied as if she had heard them. A clever woman always finds a way, when she chooses, to impart assurance to the most bashful man, by taking upon herself substantially the whole burden of the conversation. Chérubin gradually felt bolder, better pleased with himself; he had almost reached the point of being entirely at ease with his companion, when the inevitable Trichet planted himself in front of them and exclaimed:

"I don't know what you are talking about, and yet, I'll wager that I can guess."

Madame Célival, who appeared to be not at all pleased that Monsieur Trichet had interposed in her conversation with Chérubin, answered the old bachelor:

"You always try to guess what people are saying, but in this case you are quite likely to be mistaken. Tell me, what was monsieur saying to me?"

"That you are bewitching, adorable; for no man can say anything else to you."

Madame Célival smiled, with a less irritated air, while Chérubin, blushing to the whites of his eyes, exclaimed:

"Why no, I didn't tell madame that!"

"At all events, you thought it," rejoined Monsieur Trichet, "and that amounts to the same thing."

Chérubin did not know what to say; he lowered his eyes and made such a comical face that Madame Célival, taking pity on his embarrassment, rose and said:

"Nonsense, my dear Trichet; you are an old idiot! That is why we all have to forgive you."

The old bachelor did not hear these last words; he had run off to join a gentleman who was declaiming at the other end of the salon, and whom it gave him great pleasure to interrupt. Madame Célival left Chérubin, saying, with a glance at once amiable and affectionate:

"I trust, monsieur, that you find my house agreeable; you will prove that you do if you come to see me often."

"Well," said Monfréville, as he joined Chérubin once more, "your business seems to be progressing."

"Ah! my dear fellow, that woman is delightful! In her company, it seemed to me that I actually had some wit. I have never been so well pleased with myself."

"It is always so!

"'A great man's friendship is a boon of the gods;' but an agreeable woman's love is the greatest blessing on earth! Come; you don't play, nor I; it is time to go."

They left the salon, which the Noirmont family had quitted just before.

XIX

THE COMTESSE DE GLOBESKA

It was nine o'clock at night, and two men, who seemed to be waiting and watching for somebody, were walking back and forth on Rue Grenétat. One of them, whose beat was from the centre of the street almost to the fountain at the corner of Rue Saint-Denis, wore a long frockcoat which fitted his figure perfectly and was buttoned to the chin, together with straw-colored gloves and the general outfit of a dandy; but when he passed a lighted shop, one could see that his coat was worn and spotted in many places, and that his gloves were no longer perfectly fresh. This gentleman was smoking a cigar with all the grace of a regular customer at Tortoni's.

The second individual, who was enveloped in an old nut-colored box-coat, with which we are already familiar, wore a round hat, with so broad a brim and so low a crown, that at a short distance he seemed to be arrayed in the headgear of a coal man. He walked only a few steps from a house with a dark passageway, the gate of which was open, to the second or third house on each side of it; but his eyes never lost sight of the passage.

In these two individuals the reader will already have recognized Daréna and his worthy friend Monsieur Poterne.

Since his agent had been unable to do business with the young Marquis de Grandvilain, Daréna had fallen off lamentably from his former magnificence; as his profits had been squandered in a very short time, he had fallen back into what is called *noble indigence*; "completely cleaned out," was Monsieur Poterne's way of stating it.

Daréna still had recourse to his young friend's purse from time to time; but he was afraid of ruining himself entirely in Chérubin's estimation, if he abused that method; for, despite his ingenuous candor, the young man was possessed of some natural common sense which enabled him to divine what was not in accordance with propriety; and Daréna did not wish the doors of the hôtel de Grandvilain to be closed to him.

"By God! is that beast of a Poterne making a fool of me?" said Daréna, stopping at the street corner to shake the ashes off his cigar. "The idea of doing sentry-go on Rue Grenétat, where it's always muddy! It's like the country! I ought to be in the foyer of the Opéra now! But I forget that my costume is a little seedy! What a beastly cigar! Pah! there's nothing decent in this region!"

Daréna threw away the end of his cigar, retraced his steps, and, halting beside Poterne, who was leaning against a post, with his eyes fixed on the dark passageway facing him, nudged him with his elbow and said:

"Are we going to say here long, old tom-cat? Do you know that I am beginning to be deucedly bored?"

"When you want to carry an undertaking through to a good end, you must be patient," rejoined Poterne, without turning his head.

"To a good end! I fancy that your end won't be very good, you old rascal. But why does the damsel keep us waiting? Doesn't she know that you are here? Come, Poterne, answer your friend."

Poterne turned quickly and said in an undertone:

"Don't call me by name, I beg you; there's no need of the girl's knowing my real name; she might repeat it by accident, or from stupidity, and my whole plan would be overboard."

"You ought to be overboard yourself! But come, tell me what scheme you have thought up, and let me see if it has any sense; for I didn't listen to you very carefully this morning."

"It is very simple; we propose to try to make young Chérubin fall in love, in order to entangle him in an intrigue which may prove lucrative for us."

"Alas, yes! for although 'gold may be a mere chimera,' all these rascally tailors refuse to make coats for me without some of that same chimera!"

"To make sure that our Adonis becomes deeply enamored, we must first of all find a pretty girl."

"That is true; it's the same way with jugged hare—first catch your hare."

"Well, I have discovered what we need; here, in this house, on the third floor back, there is a rose, a genuine rose!"

"A rose in this vile hovel—and on the back! I am terribly afraid that your rose is only a hip!"

"You will be able to judge for yourself directly. This is the time when the work-girls leave their work; indeed, I am surprised that they haven't come out yet."

"And what does this blush rose do?"

"She makes Italian straw hats."

"Very good; and she is virtuous?"

"Oh! I don't hold her out as a prize-winner; but she makes a very modest appearance; she is very fond of a little *pays*[A] of hers, who was obliged to go into the army as a simple *tourlourou*,[B] and it would make her perfectly happy to be able to save up enough money to marry her little pays when he comes home. So she won't listen to any of the young men who run after her every night, because she knows that they're ne'er-do-wells, who won't help her to set up housekeeping with her little pays."

"Bravo! the young woman has excellent principles. How did you make her acquaintance? by treating her to chestnuts?"

"By defending her against a young wig-maker's apprentice, who, when he pretended to take her arm, always took hold of something else."

"Those wig-makers are sad villains. This is what the habit of making curls leads to!—What proposition have you made to this rose-bud?"

"In the first place, I represented myself as a Polish noble, the Comte de Globeski."

"You sinner! to presume to take the title of count!—What next?"

"I told the girl that, if she chose, I would put her in the way of making a very neat little sum. As she thought at first that I was in love with her, she answered that I was too ugly."

"That's good, I like that outspokenness."

"I reassured her by telling her that I wasn't talking about myself, but about a very comely young man, whom, for family reasons, we desired to become amorous of her."

"I adore family reasons! Go on."

"My pretty working-girl did not seem to have a very alert imagination; however, she almost understood. She's an Alsatian, and her name is Chichette Chichemann. She has a slight accent, but it is not at all disagreeable and will pass for a Polish accent, especially as Polish is very like German. I have an appointment with her for this evening; we will take her to a café, and there we will agree on our movements; you will see that she is extremely pretty, and that she has a little virginlike way about her that is most deceptive. When she is dressed as a Polish countess, the young marquis must inevitably fall madly in love with her."

"We will hope so, and then we must act in all haste, for Monfréville is taking Chérubin into society now. Our real marchionesses and countesses will find the youngster very attractive; and he, in his turn, will fall in love with one of them; and if his heart is once fairly caught——"

"We should be our expenses out of pocket!"

"Bah! that won't make any difference, if your damsel is really pretty; there's always room for a new love in the human heart. At eighteen years and a half, I could have loved all four quarters of the globe.—Attention! I think the flock is coming out."

As he spoke, several young women in little caps and modest aprons came from the dark passage; some of them were soon joined by young men who were waiting for them; others walked away alone. Daréna and Poterne, stationed on the other side of the street, let them all pass. The last of all leaped the gutter with agility and walked up to Poterne, who tried to impart an amiable tone to his voice as he said:

"Did you recognize me, Mademoiselle Chichette?"

"I should say so; you look like a coal man with your big hat."

Daréna laughed aloud, and the girl stepped back, saying:

"Ah! there's someone with you, Messié Globeski?"

"Yes, an intimate friend of mine, who is employed to manage the affair I spoke to you about. We will go somewhere and talk it over."

"Yes, my dear child," said Daréna, taking the girl's arm and passing it through his, "we will go and have a chat and a glass of punch. Do you like punch?"

"Oh, yes! ever so much!" the Alsatian replied, looking at Daréna.

"Very good; I see that we shall be able to come to an understanding! I am not quite so ugly as monsieur; take my arm, I shall frighten you less than he will. Is there a decent café hereabout? Let us go to Rue Saint-Denis. I haven't looked at you yet, but I am told that you are enchanting; however, I must satisfy myself. Here's a drug store."

Daréna led the little hat-maker in front of the drug store, and, placing her under one of those blue globes which cast a sickly light into the street, he scrutinized her, then exclaimed:

"Excellent! Very pretty, on my word! And if we are like this, seen through a colored bottle, what shall we be in a moment? Here's a café, let's go in."

The gentlemen entered the café with Mademoiselle Chichette; they chose a table in the corner, so that they might talk with less constraint, and Daréna said to the waiter:

"A bowl of rum punch—the very best that can be made."

Poterne made a wry face and whispered to Daréna:

"The little one would be perfectly satisfied with beer; it isn't worth while to——"

"What's that? We are growing stingy, are we? Poterne, my friend, you know that I don't like that sort of thing."

"Don't call me Poterne, I tell you."

"Then be quiet, and don't annoy me with your foolish reflections."

Mademoiselle Chichette had taken her place at the table, where she seemed to pay no heed at all to anything that was said by the gentlemen who were with her. The Alsatian seemed about twenty years of age; she was very small, but she had a very becoming measure of *embonpoint*; her face was round, with dark eyes, not very large, but well-shaped and surmounted by gracefully arched light eyebrows; a tiny mouth, pretty teeth, a plump little chin adorned by a faint dimple, chubby cheeks, and an extremely fresh complexion combined to form a charming village girl's face; but there was no character to it, no expression in her eyes; always the same placidity and the same smile.

Daréna scrutinized the Alsatian anew, then said to Poterne under his breath:

"She's very pretty, and as fresh as a rose. She looks respectable; in fact, she has rather a stupid air; but that will pass for innocence. Do you know, you have made a genuine find; when she is handsomely dressed, Chérubin cannot possibly help falling in love with her.—Ah! here's the punch—let's have a drink! Drink, young Chichette. Alsatians generally have a well-developed gullet."

Mademoiselle Chichette smiled and took a glass, saying:

"Oh, yes! I don't object."

"The accent is a little pronounced," muttered Daréna. "However, it doesn't matter, it's Polish—that's understood.—Some macaroons, waiter! What! you see that we have a lady with us, and you forget the macaroons! Haven't you any? If not, you should make some."

"I have sent for some, monsieur."

"That's lucky for you. Meanwhile, give us some cakes, or gingersnaps— whatever you have."

During this dialogue Poterne heaved a succession of stifled sighs. At last a dish was brought and placed by Daréna in front of the young work-girl, and he himself stuffed himself with cakes as if he had not dined. Whereupon Monsieur Poterne also decided to attack the plate, and to devour all the gingersnaps.

"You see, Comte de Globeski," said Daréna, in a serio-comic tone, "that I did well to order these trifles. But now let us talk business, and come to the point.—Mademoiselle Chichette, you have one of the prettiest faces to be met with in Paris or the suburbs. We desire a young man to fall violently in love with you. That will be easy to bring about; but we wish his passion to encounter obstacles. Why? That does not concern you; the essential thing is that you should do exactly what you are told to do. In the first place, you are Monsieur le Comte de Globeski's wife—consequently you are the Comtesse de Globeska. That is the usual custom in Poland: the man's name ends in *i* and his wife's in *a*."

"Oh, no! I want to be my little pays's wife! I've promised him."

"Sacrebleu! this is only a joke; it's part of the comedy we want you to play."

"Oh, yes, yes! a joke! I'll do it."

"You are the Comtesse de Globeska, then, a Polish refugee; and your friend here—this gentleman who is so ugly—is horribly jealous; stuff all that in your head. We will give you a pretty costume; that can't offend you; and you will live with monsieur for a few days, except at night; but with honorable intentions!"

"Oh, yes, yes!"

"And when the young man is dead in love, you may love him too, if you please; in fact, he is well worth the trouble—he's a charming fellow. You don't dislike charming fellows, do you?"

"Oh, yes, yes!"

"And for all this you shall have twenty-five napoleons; in other words, five hundred francs."

"That's too much! it's too much!" whispered Poterne, nudging Daréna, "she would have helped us for two or three louis."

"Yes, you shall have five hundred francs," continued Daréna, "six hundred, in fact, if the affair goes off well. I will guarantee you that amount, and monsieur here will pay it.—Isn't that rather pleasant, eh?"

"Oh, yes, yes!"

"Sapristi!" said Daréna, turning to his companion, "she strikes me as being stupider than a flock of geese! However, it makes no difference; Love is blind, and he is entitled to be deaf too.—Let's have a drink! Another bowl, waiter."

"But—but——"

"Be quiet, Comte de Globeski! you are at liberty not to drink any more, but you will still have the privilege of paying."

The second bowl was brought; the young Alsatian's color became more brilliant than ever; even her eyes began to show some life and Daréna exclaimed:

"*Fichtre!* if only Chérubin could see her now! What a conflagration she would kindle! Comte de Globeski, see to it that Chichette has such eyes to-morrow evening; make her a little tipsy."

"Yes, with brandy!" muttered Poterne, blowing his nose.

"Attention! as it is easier to become acquainted at the theatre than anywhere else, the Comte de Globeski will take his wife to the theatre to-morrow evening—to the Cirque; that is the favorite theatre of foreigners."

"Very good," said Poterne, "we will go to the Cirque; we will sit in the second amphitheatre."

"And why not in paradise, at once? Hum! you make me blush for you, Globeski! You will take seats in the first balcony—in a box."

"But——"

"No buts!—Madame must be dressed in perfect taste."

"I will do my best."

"And you, count, will look to it that you bear no resemblance to a certain hound named Poterne."

"There's no danger."

"We will sit in your box, behind you; the Comtesse de Globeska will assassinate my young friend with her glances.—Do you understand, my girl?"

"Oh, yes, yes!"

"And above all things she must not seem to know me."

"Yes, yes!"

"Comte de Globeski will go out during the entr'acte without his wife, who will answer the sweet speeches my young friend will make to her. She will not talk much, for fear of making a slip, but she will be loving and passionate."

"Oh, yes, yes!"

"After the play the count will take his wife away, and we will follow them. He will take a cab, we will do the like. The rest will go of itself. It's all agreed and understood. There's no more punch; pay the bill, count, and let's be off."

Poterne paid with a groan; Daréna even compelled him to give the waiter six sous; then they left the café. Mademoiselle Chichette lived on Rue Saint-Denis; they escorted her home and she promised not to go out on the following day, but to await Monsieur de Globeski's coming. Then Daréna went to stroll in the Palais-Royal, and Poterne went home to bed.

Daréna had taken his measures in advance; he knew that Monfréville was to attend a large dinner on the following day, so that Chérubin would be free. He had seen him in the morning and had said to him:

"I want to pass the evening with you to-morrow; surely you will sacrifice your great ladies to me for one evening! You are always in the fashionable salons now—they monopolize you. Monfréville is never away from you; but my friendship demands its turn, and as I do not go into society—for the moment! I have such seasons—why, we will go to the theatre."

Chérubin had agreed. But he was beginning to enjoy large parties; the pleasant welcome that he received everywhere gradually dispelled his shyness. Madame Célival was more amiable with him than with any other man; which fact seemed to annoy several gentlemen, among others, the colonel who resembled a cat, and the young dandy who had the look of a Roman.

Nor was this all: the fascinating Comtesse Valdieri, that fanciful, nervous, ethereal creature, who often received as if by special favor the homage that was addressed to her, had supposed at first that Marquis Chérubin would speedily help to swell the crowd of her adorers; but the young man had contented himself with admiring her at a distance, and in this case his shyness had served him well. The little countess was deeply offended by behavior which she attributed to indifference; for in these days it is not to be presumed that young men are bashful, and Madame Valdieri, seeing that Chérubin talked a great deal with Madame Célival, did her utmost to steal that new conquest from her. With women anger sometimes leads to love, and any other than Chérubin would already have taken advantage of the rivalry he had caused.

The pretty countess had invited the young marquis to come to her receptions. Monsieur Valdieri, like a complacent husband, had seconded his wife's invitation; and Chérubin waited upon the flighty Emma, who was most affable to him and seemed to forget her nerves.

And then, in a street near the hôtel de Grandvilain, there was a rather pretentious linen-draper's shop, and in that shop, among a number of young women who were always at work at the counter, there was one fair-haired damsel, somewhat red about the eyes, with a little turned-up nose *à la*

Roxelane, and an extremely wide-awake air. When Chérubin passed, she always found a way to be at the door and smile at him; or to go out into the street for a moment on the most trivial pretext; and several times, as she passed the young man, she had said:

"I come out at nine o'clock every night; if you would like to speak with me, wait at the end of the street; my name is Célanire."

And lastly Chérubin had met Mademoiselle Malvina several times, no longer dressed as a Swiss, but very alluring with her little pink tucker, her short skirt, and the black silk scarf, which was wound so lightly about her waist that it caused her hips to stand out in a very pronounced fashion. And Malvina had halted in front of the young man, shot a burning glance at him, and said:

"So you don't mean to come to see me, Monsieur Chérubin? Do you know that that is very bad of you, and that you are an ungrateful wretch not to cultivate my acquaintance? You know my address—come and breakfast with me. I get up late, but I give you leave to come very early."

Thus Chérubin was exposed to a rattling fire from a number of fair ones, when Daréna, who had found a way to freshen up his costume, called for him and took him to the Cirque, on Boulevard du Temple.

On the road the young man did not fail to tell Daréna all that had happened to him; and he, having listened attentively, said:

"It seems to me, my dear fellow, that you are a regular Faublas—all women adore you! And how is it with yourself?"

"Oh! I adore them too!"

"So you love Madame Célival, eh?"

"Why, yes, I think so; I find her very fascinating."

"And the languishing Comtesse Valdieri?"

"Oh! I like her very much too."

"And the grisette—otherwise called the linen-draper's apprentice?"

"I think that she's very nice."

"And Malvina, who dances so well?"

"She is very much to my taste."

"Well! if that is so, how do you stand with all these women? Men don't make any secret of such things among themselves, parbleu!"

"How do I stand? Why, no farther ahead than I was."

Daréna roared with laughter, to the great annoyance of Chérubin, and rejoined at last:

"Then, my dear fellow, it's because the will was lacking! and, according to that, I am bound to think that all these ladies have made very little impression on your heart. However, I understand that: salon conquests—grisettes—lorettes—there's nothing interesting in any of them! Sometimes chance brings us into contact with something better. But here we are at the Cirque."

Chérubin purchased the tickets—Daréna always left that duty to him—and they entered the theatre.

"This is a very good place," said Chérubin, stopping at the entrance to the balcony.

But Daréna, who had caught sight of the persons he was looking for in a box, answered:

"We shall be more comfortable in a box; besides, it's better form. Come—let us go in here, for instance."

And Daréna bade the box-opener admit them to the box in which he had recognized Poterne and Mademoiselle Chichette Chichemann.

One must have had Daréna's keen sight to recognize those two individuals, and must have been certain that they were there, for they were perfectly disguised, especially Poterne, who was absolutely unrecognizable.

Daréna's intimate friend had sacrificed the bristly hair that covered his head; he had been shaved, and so closely that he resembled a poodle returning from Pont Neuf. He wore on his nose green goggles, the sides of which were screened by silk of the same color; and he had stuffed something in his mouth, which transformed his hollow cheeks into chubby ones. The change was complete. The false Comte de Globeski was suitably attired in a blue frockcoat with frogs, buttoned to the chin, so that it almost made a cravat unnecessary.

Mademoiselle Chichette wore a silk dress of faded pink, a long cloak trimmed with fur, and a sort of little toque of green velvet, with silk tassels and bows of the same color, which fell over her left ear. Her costume was not new, but her plump face was prettier than ever under the velvet toque, and her astonishment at finding herself in such fine array gave an almost piquant expression to her eyes.

Daréna grasped all this at a glance.

"That miserable Poterne bought everything at the Temple!" he muttered.

"However, the little one is very pretty, luckily, and if my young Cupid doesn't take fire, I shall begin to believe that there's something wrong in his make-up."

Poterne nudged Mademoiselle Chichette with his knee, calling her attention with his eyes to the young man who had seated himself behind her. The supposititious Pole turned, and after eying Chérubin, she murmured:

"He's very pretty—almost as pretty as my little pays!"

Chérubin, on his side, glanced at the lady in front of him, and whispered to Daréna:

"Pray look at that pretty creature, my dear fellow!"

Daréna put his head forward, pretended to be moved to admiration, and replied:

"Upon my word, I never saw anything so perfect! The freshness of the rose and the splendor of the lily! She's a pearl! At your age I would have stormed the moon to possess that woman."

Chérubin made no reply, but he paid much more attention to the young lady in the green cap than to the play that was being performed. For her part, Mademoiselle Chichette, faithful to her instructions, turned constantly to look at Chérubin. Her glances lasted so long sometimes that Poterne was compelled to pull her dress, and whisper:

"That's enough, you're going too far! Anyone would think that you did nothing else on the boulevards."

After some time Daréna said to his young friend:

"It seems to me that you are making progress, and that your business with this rose-bud is in a fair way to end in a bargain."

"Why, it is true, she does look at me rather often. I don't know whether I ought to hope."

"You don't know! What in the devil more do you expect a woman to do at first sight than to return your glances—yes, and with big interest! You have made a conquest of her, that is evident.—Gad! what a lucky fellow you are! I have an idea that she's a foreigner; that man isn't a Frenchman; he must be her husband."

"Do you think so?"

"However, he has a very respectable look."

"Do you think so?"

"It seems to me that nobody can help seeing it."

During the entr'acte Monsieur Poterne did not fail to leave the box, alone; Daréna followed him at once, saying to Chérubin:

"Here's an excellent opportunity to start a conversation. Go at it boldly."

"Do you think that I might?"

"I promise you that the lady wishes it too. You see it is hard to be more hideous than that man who was with her, and she would not be his wife if she did not deceive him."

Chérubin, when he was left alone with the charming person with whom he felt that he was very much in love, wondered how he should begin the conversation. Meanwhile she was making eyes at him in a fashion which invited him to speak, with an accompaniment of the most melting smiles. The young man ventured at last.

"Is madame fond of the theatre?"

"Yes, *messié*."

"Does madame come often?"

"No, *messié*. But I used to go ever so much with my cuisine."[C]

[C] *Cuisine* means 'kitchen' or 'cooking'. She intended to say *cousine*.

Chérubin opened his ears, trying to understand.

"My *cuisine* liked the theatre ever so much."

"Ah! you are speaking of a *cousine*, no doubt?"

"Yes, yes, my *cuisine*."

"And this gentleman with you—is he your husband?"

"Yes; Comte Glo—Globe—Oh dear! I have forgot his name! I am stupid!"

"You are not French, madame?"

"Oh, no! I am from Alsa—No, no, I'm from some other place! I have forgot again; I am awful stupid!"

Mademoiselle Chichette said all this so comically, and rested her eyes on Chérubin so often, that the young man paid no heed to the incoherency of her speech, but became more and more enamored of the lovely stranger.

"Do you enjoy Paris, madame?"

"Oh yes! I enjoy it; but I am always thinking of my little pays!"

"Ah! you regret it?"

"Yes! I would like to see my little pays again!"

"You love your country—pays—that is perfectly natural."

"Ah, yes! he's a *tourlourou* now."

Here Chérubin again failed to understand, but Poterne returned, luckily for Mademoiselle Chichette, who was beginning to forget her part and to talk at random.

Daréna soon returned also; he asked Chérubin whether he had carried forward his affair with his pretty neighbor.

"Yes, we talked; she seemed to ask nothing better. You were not mistaken; the gentleman is her husband; she's a foreigner, she has a very strong accent."

"They're Poles; I found that out in the foyer."

"She seems to be very much attached to her country—pays,—for she sighs for it and talks about it all the time!"

"Her country! oh, yes! Poland.—Did you make an appointment with her?"

"An appointment? Oh! we didn't get so far as that!"

"How did you amuse yourselves then? A woman who is mad over you, who fairly eats you with her eyes!"

"Do you think so? What good fortune! She is so pretty, and her accent is so fascinating!"

"Yes, the Polish accent has much charm."

"I am quite mad over her, my dear fellow."

"And you are right. It would be downright murder not to carry that rose-bud away from that old caterpillar!"

"Carry her away! What! do you think that it will be necessary——"

"Hush! let me act; I will arrange the whole business."

The play came to an end. Monsieur Poterne donned his umbrella-like hat, and gave the fair Chichette his arm. She, although sorely embarrassed in her costume, succeeded in holding her hand out straight behind her.

Daréna and his companion walked on the heels of the Poles, who took care not to turn around. Daréna almost compelled Chérubin to seize the hand which the lady obligingly held behind her back, and the young man turned crimson as he whispered in his friend's ear:

"Ah! she squeezed my hand! she is squeezing it again! she keeps squeezing it!"

"Parbleu! what did I tell you?" rejoined Daréna. "Sympathy—I believe that you were made for each other."

As he spoke, Daréna kicked Poterne's legs viciously, to make him walk faster and force Mademoiselle Chichette to drop Chérubin's hand, which she seemed to have resolved never to release.

The so-called foreigners entered a cab. Chérubin and Daréna took another and told the driver to follow the first, which stopped in front of a modest, furnished lodging house on Rue Vieille-du-Temple.

"Good," said Daréna; "we know where they live, and that is enough for to-night. To-morrow you must write an impassioned letter to that Pole; I will undertake to see that she gets it without the knowledge of her husband, and I promise you that she will reply to it."

Everything being agreed between them, Chérubin went home, where Daréna left him, congratulating himself on the success of his stratagem.

XX

LOUISE IN PARIS

Although fairly launched in fashionable society, although he had become the object of the allurements of several women whose conquest was desired of all; despite the ogling of grisettes and the assignation proffered him by lorettes, Chérubin had not wholly forgotten the village of Gagny, and little Louise, with whom he had passed his earliest years.

He often spoke of going to Gagny to see and embrace his dear Nicole; he had several times despatched Monsieur Gérondif to bring him news of her, accompanying the commission with little gifts for the people of the village, and bidding him inquire concerning Louise's position and prospects. The tutor always half performed his errand: he went to Gagny, delivered the presents, devoured with his eyes young Louise, who improved every day, then returned and told his pupil that his former playmate was still in Bretagne, where she was so happy that she did not intend ever to return to Nicole.

But on the day preceding his visit to the Cirque with Daréna, Chérubin had once more spoken about going to Gagny, and he had stated positively, in Monsieur Gérondif's presence, that he should not allow the week to pass without going to see and embrace his old nurse.

At that the tutor was greatly disturbed.

"If monsieur le marquis goes to Gagny," he said to himself, "he will find young Louise there, and consequently he will see that I have lied to him. He is quite capable of discharging me; for, notwithstanding his usual mildness of manner, there are times when he is extremely quick to take fire. I am not at all anxious to lose a place worth fifteen hundred francs, in a fine house where I am boarded, lodged and coddled; where my duties are confined to sleeping, eating and reciting poetry to the mammoth Turlurette. Moreover, if my pupil sees young Louise again, it is probable that his love for her will revive; and that would interfere with my plans, for that girl has kindled a conflagration in my insides. My designs are honorable, I propose to make her my wife, to raise her to the honor of my name. But, in order to marry, I must obtain some advance in my pay. If I stay with the marquis two years longer, I can save money, for I can put aside almost all that I earn; the only thing is to put little Louise in a safe place, so that she can't be whisked away from me."

Monsieur Gérondif mused upon this subject all day, and in the evening he went to pursue his meditations in the company of the kindhearted Turlurette, who fed him on brandied fruits which she prepared to perfection; and while the professor was smacking his lips over his third plum, old Jasmin, who became less active every day, but was sorely aggrieved because his master had hired a young groom, entered the housekeeper's room and said to her:

"Do you happen to know a lady's maid who is out of a place?"

"Why do you ask, Monsieur Jasmin?" queried Mademoiselle Turlurette.

"Because not long ago I was waiting for my master at some reception.— He always forbids me to do it, but that day his little groom was sick, and I seized the opportunity to drive his cabriolet in the evening. In fact, I ran into two booths; some people won't get out of the way."

"Well, Monsieur Jasmin?"

"Well, I was talking in the antechamber with the servants who happened to be there—and we had time enough to talk; people stay so late at these parties nowadays! To cut it short, one of them says to me: 'We're looking for a lady's maid for mademoiselle. Her mother's gone to the country for a while; monsieur insisted on keeping his daughter at home with him; and just at that moment they had to dismiss the lady's maid, because she talked too much with a floor-washer. As monsieur is very strict, it didn't take long; but we are looking for another maid.'—At that I proposed a person I know, who's as intelligent as can be; but when I told them that she was sixty years old, they informed me that it wasn't worth while to send her. It's surprising the way people act nowadays; they want children to wait on them."

"I don't know anybody who wants a place," Mademoiselle Turlurette replied.

Monsieur Gérondif, who had not lost a word of what Jasmin said, interposed at this point, with an affectation of indifference.

"Who were the people who wanted a lady's maid? I might be able to oblige some acquaintance of mine in Paris by offering her the place; but before I do anything about it, you will understand that I want to be sure that it's with respectable people."

"Oh! as to that, you needn't be at all afraid, Monsieur Gérondif," replied Jasmin. "It's in the most honorable family you can imagine. Monsieur de Noirmont, an ex-magistrate, a man who never laughs, and who wouldn't wrong a bird. He was a friend of the late Monsieur de Grandvilain, our marquis's father."

"What does the family consist of?"

"Monsieur de Noirmont, his wife, their daughter, who is fifteen years old, a cook, monsieur's servant, and the maid they are looking for."

"Is the man-servant young?"

"Yes, he's the one I talked with. He's only fifty-six, but he seems to be a very sensible fellow."

Monsieur Gérondif smiled as he inquired:

"Do they receive much company, give balls? Are they the sort of people who pass their life in *varietate voluptas*?"

"Never a ball, and no *volupétas*, as you call them. The lady doesn't care for society, and Monsieur de Noirmont passes his life in his library. So our young marquis doesn't care to go to the house, although he has been invited."

"Ah! he has been invited there, has he?"

"Yes; but I've often heard him say when he's dressing in the morning: 'I've no desire to go to that house; it must be horribly dull there.'"

"Are you sure that Monsieur Chérubin said that?"

"Yes; and I've heard Monsieur de Monfréville answer: 'You are very wise; it's a house which has little to offer that is attractive to a man of your age.'"

Monsieur Gérondif rubbed his hands and asked no more questions. The next day, after procuring Monsieur de Noirmont's address, he went to his house, asked to speak to his servant, introduced himself as coming from old Jasmin and as having to suggest a lady's maid for Mademoiselle de Noirmont.

Jasmin was the Nestor of servants; his recommendation was most influential, and that of so serious-minded a man as Monsieur Gérondif seemed to be could only confirm the favorable opinion which was sure to be entertained of Jasmin's protégée.

The young servant of fifty-six informed the tutor that madame was absent, and that, as monsieur never interfered in any domestic details, the choice of another lady's maid was left to him; that he was perfectly content to accept the one whom the venerable Monsieur Jasmin was kind enough to send, and that his only wish was that she should arrive as soon as possible.

Sure of success in that direction, Monsieur Gérondif thanked the servant, promised to bring the girl soon, and set out at once for Gagny and Nicole's house.

The tutor's presence always brought joy to the humble abode of the villagers; for he brought news of Paris, and with him they talked constantly of Chérubin.

After answering the questions of Nicole and Louise, who inquired first of all for the health of the object of their affections, Monsieur Gérondif turned to the girl and said:

"My child, it is principally on your account that I have come to Gagny, for I am thinking about your future, your lot in life. You are seventeen years of age, you are tall, and well-developed physically as well as mentally; I mean by that that you have intelligence beyond your years; and you have profited by being present at the lessons which I gave to my pupil; you read and write very fairly and speak quite correctly. Moreover, you handle the needle with facility, and you seem to be apt at all the tasks suited to your sex; isn't that so, Mère Nicole?"

"Why, yes, it's all true," replied the good woman, staring at the visitor. "What scheme have you got in your head for our Louise; do you mean to make a duchess of her too?"

"No, not exactly; but I tell you again, I mean to assure her future. What would it be if she remained in this village? She has no relations, no fortune; so she must think herself very lucky if some uneducated country clown should want to marry her."

"Oh! never! never!" cried Louise; "I won't marry!"

"Bless my soul, my dear child," said Nicole, "you know very well that nobody'll force you to, and that I'll never turn you out of our house."

"That is all very well," rejoined Gérondif. "But if Louise should find a good place in Paris, in a respectable family, where she could lay by a little money, and then find a good match, it seems to me that that would be worth thinking about."

"In Paris!" cried Louise, with a joyful exclamation; "go to Paris! Oh! what bliss! how glad I should be! Oh! yes, yes! you'll let me go, won't you, mother?"

"What, my child, do you want to leave me too?" said Nicole sadly.

But Louise kissed her again and again, crying:

"Why, just think that *he* is in Paris! If I live in the same city with him, it seems to me that I may see him, meet him sometimes; and that thought is the only thing that makes me want to go to Paris. Isn't it true, Monsieur Gérondif, that people are sure to meet when they live in the same place, and that I should see him sometimes if I was in Paris?"

"See him? whom?"

"Why Chérubin—monsieur le marquis. Whom do you suppose I am talking about, if not him?"

The tutor realized that the hope of seeing Chérubin was the sole reason that led the girl to welcome his suggestion so joyously, and he was careful not to undeceive her.

"Certainly," he replied, "when two people live in the same place, there is much more probability of their meeting than when one is at the north and the other at the south—or, if you prefer, when one is *per fas* and the other *nefas*. —Well, my interesting young friend Louise, I have found what I wanted to find for you; the place of lady's maid is offered you in a first-rate family; and when I say 'lady's maid,' it's as if I said 'companion;' and when I say 'companion,' it's as if I said 'friend,' to a young lady of fifteen who is said to be as amiable as she is kindhearted. You will assist her to dress, and she will not assist you; but we see that every day between friends: there's one who does everything, while the other one strolls about. Lastly, you will be well dressed; the friend who strolls generally gives the gowns and fichus that she doesn't want to the friend who dresses her. And then you will earn money, which is never a bad thing to have; for with money—silver—you get gold, which is the purest of metals, when there's no alloy in it.—Well! what do you think of my proposition? tell me."

"Oh! I ask nothing better—if my adopted mother consents!"

"Dear me! my child," said Nicole, "if it will make you so happy to go to Paris, I won't stand in your way; besides, I don't think that Monsieur

Gérondif, who's been the village schoolmaster, could propose anything that wasn't for your good."

"You are as wise as Æsop, Dame Nicole, although you are not hunchbacked! My only desire is to assure a happy lot for this *puella formosa,*—and the future will prove it."

"And—Monsieur Chérubin?" ventured Louise, who no longer dared to say "Chérubin" simply, when she spoke of the young man she loved; "does he know of this plan that you propose to me? does he want me to go to Paris?"

Monsieur Gérondif scratched his nose a moment, then replied with assurance:

"Does he know it? why, of course he does; and he is very anxious that my offer should please you."

"Oh! in that case, there must be no hesitation; must there, dear mother?—I accept, monsieur; I will start whenever you choose; I am ready."

"Then we will start at once."

"What!" cried Nicole, "do you mean to say you're going to take the dear child right away like this?"

"I must, Dame Frimousset; the place I have secured for her is wanted by a great many people; if we delay, it may be given to somebody else. We are not flooded with good places in Paris, so that I must introduce her and have her engaged to-day."

"Oh, yes! let me go, mother! I know that it will make you unhappy not to have me with you, and it makes me unhappy too to leave you. But, on the other hand, I am so glad to be near—Monsieur Chérubin. Besides, he wants me to come to Paris, and we mustn't vex him. But I will come to see you; oh! I won't do as he did, I shall never forget the village and those who have taken the place of my parents."

Nicole embraced the girl lovingly, and said at last:

"Go, my child; I am not your mother; I haven't any rights over you, and even if I had, I wouldn't stand in the way of your future good. But do at least come to see me sometimes. She'll be allowed to, won't she, Monsieur Gérondif?"

"Oh! certainly. She will enjoy a reasonable liberty, on condition that she doesn't abuse it.—Come, sweet Louise, make a bundle of your belongings—only those that are most necessary. You needn't carry your wooden shoes—you won't wear that kind where you are going. Make haste; I will wait for you."

Louise hastily made a bundle of her clothes; she was so surprised, so bewildered by what had happened to her, that it seemed to her that it must be a dream. Her heart leaped for joy at the thought of going to Paris. But the pleasures of the great city were not what she was thinking about, nor beautiful dresses, nor a less laborious life than she had led; in that journey she saw but one thing—that she was going to live in the same city with Chérubin.

While Louise was making her preparations for departure, Monsieur Gérondif took the nurse aside and said to her in a grave and imposing tone:

"Now, virtuous Nicole, I must disclose a secret to you. My main purpose in taking Louise to Paris is to remove her from the seductions which it is proposed to employ in order to triumph over her virtue and pluck the flower of her innocence. In two words, here are the facts: your foster-child Chérubin has become a great libertine in Paris; he will not endure resistance. Not long ago he remembered Louise, the playmate of his boyhood, and he exclaimed: 'She must be a charming girl by now! I am going to make her my mistress.'"

"Great God! is it possible?" cried Nicole, opening her eyes to their fullest extent. "My little Chérubin has got to be such a rake as that?"

"It's as I have the honor to tell you. In Paris, with lots of money, a man soon learns to be what they call a *lion*, and lion means seducer."

"Chérubin, a lion! And he used to be a perfect lamb!"

"I tell you there are no lambs in Paris now. To make a long story short, I thought that you wouldn't lend a hand to the ruin of your adopted daughter, and that you would approve my putting the child beyond the reach of any attempt at seduction."

"Oh! you did just right, monsieur le professor, and I approve of it."

"Now, when Chérubin comes to see Louise, you must tell him that she's been in Bretagne a long while, with a relation of yours, and that she's very happy there."

"All right, I'll tell him that! Great God! Chérubin a rake! so that's why he's forgotten the village altogether!"

Louise soon had her parcel ready. She put on the little hat of coarse straw, which she sometimes wore to walk about the neighborhood, and beneath which, although it was not of fashionable shape, her face was as lovely as possible.

She threw herself into Nicole's arms and whispered in her ear:

"When I see him, I'll tell him that it's very wicked of him not to come to see you!"

Nicole covered Louise with kisses.

"If by any chance you should get sick of it, my child," she said, "if you ain't happy there, you know that there's always a place for you here, and that we'll be very happy if you conclude to come back."

Monsieur Gérondif speedily put an end to these farewells by taking the girl's arm. Jacquinot was at the wine-shop as usual. Louise cast a last glance at her adopted mother and went away with Monsieur Gérondif, who had incurred the expense of a cab by the hour, in order to take the girl to Paris more quickly.

On the way he said to her:

"I must give you some preliminary instructions, my lovely child, as to your behavior in the place you are to fill. In the first place, if they ask you what you know how to do, answer boldly: 'everything!'"

"Everything! But that would not be true, monsieur, for I know how to do very few things."

"You can learn the others; you are saturated with intelligence, therefore you will learn very rapidly; so that it's the same as if you already knew. Do what I tell you—it is essential, to inspire confidence; in the world you must never act as if you were uncertain of yourself. Secondly, you must understand that you must not speak of the young Marquis Chérubin and say that you were brought up with him. The world is very unkind! people might think things; and you mustn't trifle with your reputation."

"What, monsieur? What could people think, pray? Is it wrong to love one's foster-brother, then?"

"Foster-brother! foster-brother! as much as you please! I must make you understand me better: my noble pupil does not want it to be known now that he remained out at nurse until he was sixteen; that annoys him terribly. And then you must see that a marquis can't be the friend of a—a—a lady's maid; if you should talk about him, it might make him blush."

"Blush!" cried Louise, putting her handkerchief to her eyes. "What! monsieur le—Chérubin blush because of my friendship, my acquaintance? Oh! never fear, monsieur; I shall never speak of him, I shall never mention his name."

"That is very well, *O flavia*!—No, you are not a blonde.—Come, come! don't weep any more about that; what I say doesn't prevent the marquis from still being interested in you, and myself as well. I will say no more now, young Louise, but be virtuous and prudent; do not joke with the young men; if anyone should presume to take any equivocal liberty with you, scratch the insolent knave's face; for you must keep yourself free from stain, like the Paschal Lamb, until—But, mum's the word! I will go no farther now."

Louise had ceased to listen; she was thinking of Chérubin, who was ashamed of knowing her; and that idea destroyed all the pleasure she had enjoyed in the fact of going to Paris.

Meanwhile, the cab had entered the city; Monsieur Gérondif told the driver to take them to Faubourg Saint-Honoré, whereupon Louise exclaimed:

"Is it near Monsieur Chérubin's house?"

"Not very far, my child; in fact there are no distances in Paris now; the six-sou carriages take you to all quarters of the city, and you don't even need to know the way, which is very convenient for strangers."

The carriage stopped in front of a handsome house which Monsieur Gérondif pointed out to the driver, very near Rue de la Concorde. The tutor helped Louise to alight and carried his gallantry so far as to offer to carry her bundle.

"Follow me," he said; "it's in this house, on the second floor; a magnificent apartment; they're very swell people. See how this staircase is polished! It doesn't look much like our village hovels, which are floored with mud."

As he spoke, the professor slipped down two stairs and nearly broke his neck on the waxed staircase; perhaps it was a punishment from on high for his ingratitude to the village. But he clung to the rail, muttering: "*Ne quid nimis!* They put on too much wax."

Louise followed Monsieur Gérondif; she was slightly tremulous and covered with confusion at the thought that she was about to appear before people whom she did not know, and that she must remain alone amid those surroundings which were so strange to her. She heaved a profound sigh and invoked the memory of Chérubin to sustain her courage.

It was Comtois—that was the name of Monsieur de Noirmont's servant—who received Monsieur Gérondif when he introduced his protégée. Louise's aspect could not fail to prepossess everybody in her favor, and the valet smiled with satisfaction as he said:

"Ah! mademoiselle seems to have every quality likely to give pleasure here: a gentle, unaffected manner. I am sure that she will please our young Mademoiselle Ernestine, who has said to me several times: 'Above all things,

Comtois, I want a young lady's maid, because if I have an old one, I shall not dare to give her any orders, or to laugh in her presence!'—Mademoiselle is a very merry young person; a little quick-tempered, a little whimsical; but that is perfectly natural at her age, and she isn't the least bit unkind with it all. When she loses her temper, she asks our pardon; that isn't common with masters, I tell you!"

"This servant is very talkative!" thought Monsieur Gérondif, as he blew his nose.

Comtois, after looking at Louise again with a satisfied air, continued:

"I will present mademoiselle at once.—By the way, what is your name?"

"Louise, monsieur," replied the girl timidly.

"Louise—very good; that is your Christian name. And your family name? sometimes one is very glad to know that."

The girl blushed and lowered her eyes, without replying; but Monsieur Gérondif made haste to say:

"Louise Frimousset; Frimousset is the name of this young woman's parents."

Louise glanced at the tutor; but he had assumed a solemn air, which seemed to indicate that it would not be proper to contradict him, and that it was only after mature reflection that he had replied; so the girl said nothing.

"Frimou—Frimousse—Friquet," said Comtois. "That's a queer name; however, I only asked so that I might know it; for you understand of course that mademoiselle will always be called by her baptismal name here. As I was saying, I am going to present you now. If madame was here, I should naturally take you to her first; but madame has been absent a fortnight; she has gone to see an aunt of hers, who's sick. She wanted to take her daughter, but monsieur insisted on keeping Mademoiselle Ernestine with him; for, although he looks very stern, monsieur is very fond of her—he never refuses her anything; and sometimes I've even known him to be angry with madame, because he claimed that she spoke to mademoiselle too sharply, and that she didn't love her. But, to be just, I must say that monsieur is mistaken; I am sure that madame's very fond of her daughter. However, it's true that sometimes she hardly speaks to her, she responds coldly to her caresses; but we all have days when we're in ill humor, more or less."

Monsieur Gérondif blew his nose at great length, saying to himself:

"Is this never going to finish?—My worthy man," he said to Comtois, "excuse me if I interrupt you; but it seems to me that it is not necessary for me to be present at the introduction of our young Louise, as you tell me that the business is settled. So I will take my leave, urging you to watch over this child, as if she were your niece."

"Never fear, monsieur; mademoiselle is in a good family; I am quite sure that she won't be unhappy here."

"Adieu then, Louise, adieu! I shall come to inquire for you, to learn how you are getting on; in short, I shan't lose sight of you; you will always be my guiding star, my object, my—my polygon!"

The girl offered her hand to Monsieur Gérondif, who seemed inclined to kiss her, and said in an undertone:

"You will tell him that I am in Paris; won't you, monsieur? that I didn't hesitate to come, as he wished it, but that it makes me very depressed not to see him, and that my only desire——"

"I shall say all that it is my duty to say," replied the tutor, showing his teeth, although he had no desire to smile. Then, turning quickly on his heel, he saluted Comtois and went out.

The valet escorted him to the door, and Monsieur Gérondif said in his ear:

"This girl is very pretty, and the men in Paris are terribly licentious. I need not urge you to watch over her innocence and not allow her to converse with floor-washers."

"Monsieur," Comtois replied rather stiffly, "none but respectable people are received in this house, and no young girl will ever be ruined here. If the last lady's maid was a giddy creature, it wasn't our fault; and at all events she was discharged at once, as well as the floor-washer."

"Your reply scatters all the clouds which might have obscured my firmament. Adieu, excellent Comtois, I repeat my assurances of esteem."

Monsieur Gérondif took his leave, and Comtois returned to Louise, who was standing, lost in thought, in the hall; he motioned to her to follow him, led her through a salon, then opened the door of another room, and said, standing in the doorway:

"Mademoiselle, this is the lady's maid I was expecting; she has just arrived."

A voice replied at once from within the room:

"Oh! let her come in, show her in at once! I am waiting so impatiently for her!"

Comtois let Louise pass him; she stepped forward, trembling and afraid to raise her eyes; but she soon felt reassured when young Ernestine exclaimed:

"Oh! how pretty she is! I like her very much!—Come, mademoiselle; don't be afraid of me; I am not a bit terrible, am I, Comtois? I am not stern, like mamma! But, for all that, mamma's very kind, and papa too.—What is your name?"

"Louise, mademoiselle."

"How old are you?"

"Seventeen, mademoiselle."

"Seventeen! Why, how tall you are! and so strong! I am fifteen—I am rather small for fifteen, am I not?"

Louise could not help smiling; and as she looked at her who was to be her mistress, she felt a thrill of joy at the aspect of that dainty creature, so like a child, whose sparkling blue eyes were fixed on hers with a kindly expression that instantly dissipated the terror that she had felt on entering.

"Am I not very small for fifteen?" repeated Ernestine, after Louise had looked at her.

"You still have plenty of time to grow, mademoiselle."

"Oh, yes! that is my only consolation. Have you been in service in Paris before?"

"No, mademoiselle, I am just from my village; I have never been in service anywhere, and I have no doubt that I shall be very awkward at first; but I promise to pay close attention to whatever you tell me, so that I may learn quickly and be able to satisfy you sooner."

Young Ernestine began to leap and dance about the room; she seized Louise's hand and pressed it, crying:

"Oh! I like to hear you talk like that! I feel that I shall love you dearly; indeed I love you already. I either like a person instantly, or never! You will like me too, won't you?"

"That cannot be very difficult, mademoiselle, you seem so kind and sweet!"

"Ah! I am very happy, Comtois. But has Louise brought her bundle, all her clothes? Can she stay here now?"

"Yes, mademoiselle," said Louise, "I have brought all my clothes and I can stay with you now, if you care to keep me."

"Certainly; I don't mean to let you go.—Comtois, see that her chamber is prepared—the little one behind mine, you know. Be sure that she has everything that she wants or needs."

"Never fear, mademoiselle."

"At all events, I will go myself to see if everything is all right.—You see," continued Ernestine with comical gravity, "during mamma's absence I have to look out for everything and take her place here.—Go, Comtois, and take Louise's things to her room; meanwhile I will take her to my father. Is he in his study?"

"Yes, mademoiselle."

"Come, Louise, don't be afraid; he has rather a stern manner, but he isn't unkind."

"Suppose that monsieur your father should not like me?" murmured Louise timidly; "suppose he should think me too young to be in your service, mademoiselle?"

"Oh! don't worry about that; as soon as I tell him that you suit me, father won't think of sending you away."

Ernestine led the way through her mother's bedroom, then through another smaller room, and knocked at a door, saying:

"It's I, papa."

And Monsieur de Noirmont's sharp voice replied:

"Well! what is it now?"

The pretty minx opened the door of her father's study, passed her head only through the opening, and said:

"Are you busy? I have come to introduce someone."

"Who is it?"

"A new lady's maid who has been engaged for me, and who has just arrived."

"The idea of disturbing me for a lady's maid! What have I to do with such matters? Really, Ernestine, you wear out my patience."

"Oh! don't be cross with me, papa! But as mamma is away, you must see my new maid; I can't manage the house all alone!"

"Well! bring her in," rejoined Monsieur de Noirmont in a gentler tone; "where is she? let us have it over."

Ernestine led Louise into the room; the girl cast down her eyes, and felt that she was trembling, for Monsieur de Noirmont's voice was far from being as sweet as his daughter's.

After scrutinizing for some time the village maid who stood before him, Monsieur de Noirmont asked her:

"How old are you?"

Before Louise could reply, little Ernestine exclaimed:

"She is seventeen; isn't she very tall for her age, papa? and isn't she lovely? I like her so much! Her name is Louise; she has never been in service, but I am glad of that, because I can train her according to my ideas."

Monsieur de Noirmont with difficulty restrained a smile, provoked by his daughter's speech.

"It seems to me," he said, "that this girl is too much of a child to be in your service."

"Why so, papa? On the contrary, see how sensible she is! Besides, I tell you that I will train her, and Comtois has had only the best reports of her."

"All right, if she suits you.—What part of the country do you come from?"

"From Gagny, monsieur," replied Louise tremulously.

"Gagny? Why, that is very near Paris. Your parents are laboring people, no doubt?"

"Yes—yes, monsieur," faltered Louise, in an almost unintelligible voice.

"And instead of keeping their daughter at home, they send her out to service in Paris!—However, it seems to be the custom in the country! and still people extol the morals of the rural districts! But you seem modest and respectable, my girl, and I am glad to believe that your conduct will not belie the promise of your face. Besides, I know Comtois, and I rely upon his prudence. Go, go!"

Monsieur de Noirmont motioned to them to leave him; but his daughter ran to him and kissed him; then she hastened from the room with Louise, and closed the door, saying:

"That's over; I was sure that it would come out all right."

Young Ernestine next took Louise to a pretty little room which was to be her own. The sweet child made sure that her new maid was provided with everything that she needed, and displayed so much interest in her that Louise, who was deeply touched, thanked heaven for bringing her to that house.

The first day was employed by Ernestine in giving instructions to Louise, and she, not knowing how to lie, frankly confessed to her young mistress that she was entirely ignorant of the duties of her position, and that she must beg her to be as indulgent as possible. Ernestine repeated emphatically that she would have no difficulty in training her and that she need not worry.

In Monsieur de Noirmont's family, the valet ordinarily waited at table, unless there were many guests at dinner; so that the duties of the lady's maid were limited to waiting on the two ladies, assisting them to dress, and working almost all the time for them, or at some household work.

Louise could sew very well; she was active and clever, and she very soon learned what was expected of her; moreover, Ernestine taught her to embroider, to make tapestry, and to do innumerable little things that women do; things which are unknown in villages, but which it is essential to know in Paris.

Louise made rapid progress, and Ernestine said to her father:

"Oh! if you knew how much I like my maid!"

"Is she so very clever?" inquired Monsieur de Noirmont.

"Clever—yes; but she knew nothing at all; I have shown her everything."

"What do you say? that girl knew nothing?"

"What difference does it make? When I show her anything, in two days she does it better than I do. Oh! I am sure that mamma will congratulate me for engaging her."

Louise's modest and serious manner eventually won Monsieur de Noirmont's good-will as well as his daughter's, and he spoke to her less coldly. Comtois was delighted with his new fellow-servant, and the cook was never tired of extolling her extreme sweetness of temper. As for Ernestine, although she sometimes lost her patience and cried out, when her maid was awkward about dressing her, the next moment she would run to her and kiss her, and beg her not to be offended by her quick temper. In fact, each day that passed increased her affection for Louise, and the latter would have been happy in her new position, had not the thought of Chérubin constantly filled her mind. But she was beginning to lose all hope of seeing him in Paris, for she very rarely left the house, and only to do errands for her young mistress in the shops nearby.

Louise had been in Ernestine's service three weeks, when her mistress said to her one morning:

"Mamma is coming home at last! Papa has just told me that she will be here in three days. I am awfully glad, for she has been away nearly six weeks, and I long to see her. Oh! what joy! Then I shall have everything I want. And mamma will like you too; I am sure that she will be as pleased with you as I am."

Louise made no reply, but she felt deeply moved; she could not understand her own perturbation when she learned that she was to see Madame de Noirmont.

XXI

Chérubin followed Daréna's advice; he wrote a very amorous, but very timid, note for the young woman he had seen at the play. On the following day Daréna called upon his friend in good season and found him finishing his lovelorn espistle.

"Are you writing to the lovely foreigner?" asked Daréna, dropping into an easy-chair.

"Yes, my dear fellow, I have just finished my letter, which you have promised to forward to its destination."

"Parbleu! cannot one do anything with money? Do not all obstacles vanish before it? Valets, maid-servants can be bribed, duennas and concierges corrupted. I will spend money in profusion."

As he spoke, the count slapped his pockets, then exclaimed:

"But in order to spend it, I must have it, and I find that my pockets are empty."

Chérubin went to his desk and took out several rouleaux of gold pieces, which he handed to Daréna, saying:

"Take this, my dear fellow, take this; don't spare it. Reward generously all who help to forward my love."

"You do not need to give me that injunction; I will play the magnificent, the Buckingham! After all, you are rich, and if you did not use your fortune to gratify your wishes, really it wouldn't be worth while to have it. Is your note very ardent?"

"Why, I think that it is very honorable——"

"Honorable! that's not what we want, my dear friend.—Come, read me what you have written, and let me see if it's all right."

Chérubin took up the letter and read:

"'I ask your pardon, madame, for the liberty that I take in writing you, but ——'"

Daréna's roar of laughter interrupted Chérubin, who inquired:

"What are you laughing at? Isn't it all right?"

"Ha! ha! ha! Your innocence is enchanting; one would think that it was a letter from a boy to his aunt on her birthday. Let's hear the rest."

Chérubin continued:

"'But I should deem myself most fortunate if I might have the pleasure of making your acquaintance. My family is well known, I am received in the best society, and——'"

"Enough! enough!" cried Daréna, rising. "That won't do, my dear fellow; you are on the wrong track!"

"Do you think that my letter is too bold?"

"On the contrary, it isn't bold enough! She would laugh at you when she read it."

"Remember that this is the first time I ever wrote a billet-doux, and I don't know how they are usually expressed."

"Take your pen again and write what I dictate."

"All right, I prefer that."

Chérubin seated himself at his desk again and Daréna dictated:

"O woman more than adored! I burn, I wither, I languish! Your eyes are the flame, your smile the brazier, my heart the conflagration! You have set fire to my whole being. A word of love, of hope, or I will not answer for the consequences—I will kill myself at your feet, before your eyes, in your arms! Derision! damnation! if you do not answer!"

Chérubin ceased to write.

"Great heaven, my dear count!" he exclaimed; "why, that is horrible!"

"It is what you need."

"And then, I must admit that I don't clearly understand the letter."

"If you understood it, the charm would be destroyed."

"Why not write simply, as one speaks?"

"Because three-fourths of the women, who are impervious to seduction by what is simple and natural, are delighted when a man seems to have lost his head for love of them. Trust me; this note will deliver the heart of the lovely Pole into your keeping. Sign that and give it to me."

Chérubin did as he was told.

"By the way," said Daréna, as he took the letter, "don't mention this intrigue to your Monsieur de Monfréville."

"Why not?"

"In the first place, because an intrigue with such distinguished persons as these Poles requires to be conducted with the utmost secrecy. Monfréville is very inquisitive and very talkative; he would want to see the lovely foreigner and that would spoil everything."

. "But you are very much mistaken; Monsieur de Monfréville is neither inquisitive nor talkative; on the contrary, he is a most sensible man, and he gives me excellent advice."

Daréna bit his lips, seeing that it was useless for him to try to destroy Chérubin's good opinion of Monfréville.

"Monfréville, sensible, virtuous!" he retorted in a sarcastic tone. "At all events, he hasn't always been; I remember a time when he was the greatest ne'er-do-well; nothing was talked about but his conquests. To be sure, it was fifteen or eighteen years ago. When the devil grows old, he turns hermit. For my part, I am not changed, at all events; as I always have been, so I propose to remain; I prefer that. However, my dear fellow, I tell you again that, if I consent to act for you in your love-affair with the young Pole, I do it solely on account of my friendship for you; but you understand that the slightest indiscretion would compromise me. I demand secrecy, or I will have nothing to do with it."

Chérubin swore that he would not mention his new conquest to a soul, and Daréna left him, promising to return as soon as he should have anything to tell him.

Daréna had hardly left his young friend, when Jasmin entered his master's presence. The old servant's manner was important and mysterious, and at the same time showed much satisfaction with the errand he had to perform. He tried to walk on tiptoe, as if he was afraid of being overheard; he went close to his master, nearly falling upon him because he lost his balance trying to lean over him, and said, with an expression at once serious and comical:

"There's a woman here, monsieur, who wishes to speak to us—that is to say, to you—if you are alone."

Chérubin could not help laughing at his old servant's expression and at the malicious meaning which he tried to impart to his message.

"Who is the woman, Jasmin? Do you know her?"

"Yes, monsieur, I recognized her from having seen her in her mistress's antechamber; you go to the house sometimes."

"What do you say?"

"Why, yes, she's a lady's maid. Oh! she doesn't come on her own account, it's her mistress who sends her—I know all about it. Many of them used to come to see monsieur le marquis, your father, before he was married. There was sometimes a line waiting in our little salon. Ha! ha! I used to toy with all the maids."

"Well, from whom does this one come?"

"Didn't I tell monsieur? From Madame de Valdieri."

"The pretty countess! Show her in at once, Jasmin."

Chérubin was very curious to know what Madame de Valdieri could possibly want of him. Jasmin went to call the maid, a tall, stoutly-built girl of some twenty years, with red cheeks and rather an attractive face, who seemed not at all abashed at calling at a gentleman's apartments. After ushering her into his master's room, the old servant, imagining doubtless that he had gone back to the time when they used to stand in line at Chérubin's father's door, essayed, as he left the room, to put his arms about the waist of the pretty lady's maid; but his foot slipped, and, to avoid falling, he was obliged to cling tightly to her, whom he had intended simply to caress; luckily the girl was firm on her legs, and able to sustain the weight of the old fellow, and she merely laughed in his face as he slunk from the room in dire confusion.

As soon as Jasmin had gone, the maid took from the pocket of her apron a tiny scented note, which she handed to the young marquis, saying:

"Madame told me to hand this to monsieur, and to request an immediate answer."

Chérubin quivered with pleasure as he took the note, and while the maid discreetly stepped back, he eagerly read the pretty countess's missive, which contained these words:

"You are not agreeable; I have not seen you for several days. To make your peace with me, will you give me a moment this morning, and tell me your opinion of some verses which have been sent to me? I shall expect you at one o'clock."

Chérubin was beside himself with joy; he read that pleasant epistle once more, then said to the maid:

"I accept your mistress's invitation with great pleasure, mademoiselle; I will be with her at one o'clock; I shall not fail."

"Then monsieur will not write his answer?" asked the maid.

Chérubin hesitated; he walked toward his desk, realizing that it would be better policy perhaps to seize the opportunity to write something agreeable to his charming friend; but he remembered that Daréna had just told him that he did not know how to write a love letter. Fearing that he might make some blunder, he tossed his pen aside, crying:

"No, I think not; I haven't time to write. Besides, I have too many things to say to your mistress; I should not know where to begin; simply assure her that I will not keep her waiting."

The maid smiled, made a pretty little curtsy, and seemed to be waiting for the young man to slip something into her pocket and take on her cheek an earnest of what he was to take from her mistress. But, finding that he did nothing of the sort, she shrugged her shoulders imperceptibly and left the room, taking pains, as she passed through the reception room, not to approach the old servant, who seemed inclined to try again to pull her over.

"The servant is terribly old," she said to herself, "but the master is very young!"

Chérubin was in an ecstasy of delight. Madame de Valdieri's note had caused him to forget the Polish lady altogether. At nineteen years it is common enough to think of present happiness only; the new love expels the old; it is not always necessary to be nineteen years old in order to experience that phenomenon; but can all these sentiments which are constantly replacing one another properly be called love?

Chérubin glanced at his clock; it was half after eleven; he was not to be at Madame de Valdieri's until one, but he proposed to make an extremely careful toilet. He rang for Jasmin, he rang for his other servant, he ordered several suits to be brought, and could not determine which one to wear. He had his hair dressed, crimped and curled, rising constantly to look in a mirror. He told his old servant to perfume his handkerchief, upon which Jasmin emptied several phials, smiling cunningly, and murmuring: "What did I say? Our *bonnes fortunes* are about to begin. We are going to have some sport now! We are quite good-looking enough for that."

As he dressed, Chérubin thought of the pretty woman with whom he was soon to be alone for the first time; he was not very composed in mind, for he was wondering what he should say to her. He was well pleased to have the assignation, but he regretted that Monfréville was not there to tell him how one should behave with a lady of the most fashionable set, who invites one to read poetry to her.

It was too late for him to consult Monfréville; the appointed hour was drawing nigh. Chérubin completed his toilet, but did not notice that Jasmin had saturated him with perfumery: his coat was scented with essence of rose, his waistcoat with patchouli, his handkerchief with Portugal water; and, in addition, all his other garments smelt of musk. He looked himself over, concluded that he was becomingly arrayed, stepped into his tilbury, and soon reached the countess's abode.

He was admitted by the same maid, and instead of taking him to the salon, she led him through several secret passages to a delicious boudoir, where the light was so soft and mysterious that one could scarcely see. However, after a few seconds, Chérubin's eyes became accustomed to that doubtful light, and he spied the pretty countess half-reclining on a couch at the back of a little curtained recess, which seemed intended to perform the functions of an alcove.

Chérubin made a low bow and said:

"I beg pardon, madame, but I did not see you at first, it is so dark here."

"Do you think so?" rejoined the fair Emma affectedly. "I don't like broad daylight, it tires my eyes.—It is very kind of you, Monsieur Chérubin, to consent to sacrifice a few moments to me—you are in such great demand everywhere!"

"It is a great pleasure to me, madame, and I—I—really I cannot promise to read poetry very well. I am not much used to it."

The countess smiled and motioned him to a seat beside her. Chérubin was exceedingly perturbed in spirit as he entered the delicious little recess and seated himself on the couch, which was not very broad, so that he was necessarily very close to the other person upon it.

There was a moment's silence. Emma, flattered by Chérubin's evident emotion and embarrassment in her presence, decided to begin the conversation, which she was not accustomed to do.

"How do you like my boudoir?"

"Exceedingly pretty, madame; but it seems to me to be a little dark for reading poetry."

The little lady arched her eyebrows slightly and rejoined:

"Do you like Madame Célival's boudoir better?"

"Madame Célival's boudoir? Why, I have never been in it, madame; I don't know what it is like."

"Oh! what a fib!"

"I assure you, madame——"

"You are lying!—However, I cannot blame you; discretion is the first condition one should exact in love."

"Discretion——"

"Oh! you play the innocent to perfection; but I am not taken in by that ingenuous air. Mon Dieu! there is such a strong smell of perfumery here—a mixture of scents. Have you essence of rose about you?"

"Rose? I don't know; it is possible. Does it affect you unpleasantly?"

"My nerves are so sensitive! but it will pass away."

The pretty countess lay back a moment, put her handkerchief to her face, and drew a long breath.

Chérubin looked at her, and dared not stir. There was another long pause; the young man would have liked to say a multitude of things, but, as he did not know how to express himself, he inquired at last:

"Is your husband well, madame?"

The pretty creature burst into laughter which seemed a little forced, and replied:

"Yes, monsieur, my husband is singing! So long as he is making music, that is all that he wants.—Mon Dieu! there's a smell of patchouli here, too, and musk. Ah! it gives me a sort of vertigo!"

And whether as a result of the vertigo, or for some other reason, the young woman half-reclined against Chérubin, so that her face almost touched his, and he would have had to move very little nearer to kiss her; but, deeply moved to find that lovely mouth so near to him that he could almost feel her breath, he dared not move a muscle, and finally he faltered:

"Madame, I believe that I was to read poetry to you."

The little countess abruptly raised her head and rested it on the back of the couch, as she replied with a touch of spite in her voice:

"Mon Dieu! what a memory you have, monsieur!—Well, take that album in front of you and read."

Chérubin took up an album that lay on a chair, opened it and saw a medley of drawings, poems, portraits—everything, in short, that one finds in a woman's album; and, after turning the leaves a moment, he glanced at the countess and asked timidly:

"What do you want me to read to you, madame?"

"Mon Dieu! whatever you choose, it makes no difference to me!"

Chérubin opened the album again, at random, and read:

> "Fair countess, on this page,
> You bid me pen some verse:
> Quick your commands engage;
> For you the universe
> Would rhyme.—But clear to see
> My lines good sense ignore.
> How could it other be?
> You've reft me of its store."

"Oh! that is that absurd Monsieur Dalbonne!" murmured Madame de Valdieri, twisting about impatiently on the couch. "He is forever writing such nonsense; he adores all women.—Are you like that, Monsieur Chérubin?"

"I, madame!" Chérubin replied in confusion; "oh, no! I—I—But I continue:

"'STORY OF A MOUSE.'"

"Ah! this is much longer."

The fair Emma, who evidently did not care to hear the story of a mouse read at length, and who thought that Chérubin was making sport of her, determined to resort to violent measures; she fell back on the couch, murmuring:

"Oh! I can't stand it any longer! these different scents set my nerves on edge; I am fainting!"

Chérubin uttered a cry of alarm, dropped the album, and gazed at the lovely blonde, who had chosen the most bewitching attitude that a coquette could devise in which to faint, and whose half-closed eyes wore an expression which did not indicate any very serious danger. But instead of admiring it all, Chérubin rose and ran about the room, looking for smelling-bottles and crying:

"Great God! you are losing consciousness, and I am the cause of it! I am so distressed. I will call for help."

"No, no, monsieur, just unlace me!" murmured the countess, with a sigh.

"Unlace you! Why, I don't know how; still, if you think——"

And Chérubin returned to the pretty creature, to do what she suggested; and she, seeing him lean over her, closed her eyes altogether, presuming that that would give him more courage and that he would succeed at last in behaving himself more becomingly; but, when he saw that the countess had closed her eyes entirely, Chérubin jumped back, ran to a bell cord and jerked it violently, and cried:

"She has fainted completely! what a bungler I am! As it's this perfumery that I have about me that has caused Madame de Valdieri's illness, of course she won't recover consciousness so long as I am here."

The maid appeared, vastly surprised to be summoned so suddenly. Chérubin pointed to her mistress stretched out on the couch, and said:

"Come quickly and attend to madame la comtesse. I am going away; the perfumery I have about me is what made her feel faint, so of course I must not stay with her. Pray tell her that I am terribly distressed at what has happened."

And Chérubin took his hat and hastened from the boudoir, leaving the lady's maid in utter amazement and the pretty little countess with her eyes wide open.

Chérubin returned home, cursing Jasmin for turning him into a perfumery booth. He found Monfréville waiting for him, and told him what had happened.

When the young marquis had concluded, Monfréville looked at him with a curious expression, and said:

"My dear fellow, I have always been perfectly frank with you, and I must tell you therefore that in this whole business you acted like an idiot."

"An idiot!" cried Chérubin.

"Yes, like the most idiotic of idiots! When a young and pretty woman deigns to receive you alone in her boudoir, it is with the purpose of having you make love to her, not to read. The poetry was only a pretext."

"Do you think so? Mon Dieu! I had that idea, too, but I dared not venture to think—But if she had not fainted——"

"Why, that was the time above all others when victory was in your grasp. What! a lovely woman tells you to unlace her, and you ring for her maid! Ah! my poor Chérubin, if this adventure becomes known, it will do you a deal of harm in society."

"Great heaven! you distress me! But I didn't know—However, I will repair my blunder; in the first place, the next time that I go to see the lovely Emma in her boudoir, I will have no perfumery at all; and then—oh! I will be very enterprising."

"I trust that you may be able to set yourself right with the countess, but I doubt it."

"Why so?"

"Because with women, especially coquettes, a lost opportunity never recurs. So I will bet that Madame de Valdieri won't speak to you again and won't make any more appointments with you."

"Do you think so? But what if I ask her for one?"

"She will refuse it."

"Oh! I can't believe that! What! just because I was afraid of making her ill by staying with her?"

"Poor Chérubin! what a child you are still!—But I'll tell you—let us go to Madame Célival's to-night; the little countess is usually there, and if she is, you will find out at once whether I am right."

Chérubin accepted this suggestion; he waited impatiently for the evening, for he was burning to see Madame de Valdieri again. He was convinced that Monfréville was mistaken, and he could not believe that he would be ill received because he had hurriedly left her when he discovered that perfumery was unpleasant to her.

The hour to go to the reception arrived. Monfréville called for his young friend, and they went together to Madame Célival's. The salons were already filled with people, but the young countess was not there, and Chérubin, who was on the watch for her and hoped to see her whenever the door of the salon opened, was restless and preoccupied to a degree that did not escape Madame Célival. The sprightly widow declared war on him and tried to keep him by her side; but at last Madame de Valdieri appeared with her husband.

Never had the little countess been dressed with better taste, with more grace and coquetry; never had she worn a costume which set off her charms to greater advantage; one would have said that the fascinating Emma had sworn to make more conquests than ever that evening, in order to be revenged for her discomfiture during the day.

All the men vied with one another in extolling the charms of the new arrival. Chérubin did not say a word; but he could not tire of gazing at Emma, and he said to himself:

"And I was sitting beside her this morning—and we were alone in her boudoir—and her head was almost on my shoulder—and—Gad! I believe that Monfréville is right; I was a great fool."

Chérubin waited until the countess had received the homage which men hasten to lay at a pretty woman's feet. When Madame de Valdieri was no longer surrounded, he seized an opportunity to go to her, and said in an almost familiar tone:

"Well, madame, are you better this evening? Your indisposition had no serious results?"

The little countess bestowed a contemptuous glance on Chérubin, and answered in an ironical tone:

"I don't know what you mean, monsieur!"

"You don't know what I mean? Why, this morning——"

The countess rose, as if she did not choose to listen to Chérubin, and seated herself beside a lady with whom she speedily began a very lively conversation, judging from the frequent bursts of laughter with which it was interspersed.

The young man was speechless with amazement.

"What a tone! what an expression!" he said to himself as he took a seat in a corner. "One would think that she did not know me."

Monfréville, who had taken his place at a card table, was not at hand to console his friend, and Chérubin had been sitting by himself for quite a long time, when a hand was laid gently on his shoulder, and a penetrating voice said, almost in his ear:

"What are you doing here? sulking? Madame de Valdieri doesn't seem to treat you very well this evening."

"Ah! is it you, madame?"

"Haven't I guessed right, that you are at odds with the countess?"

"Oh! I assure you that you are mistaken; I am not sufficiently intimate with that lady to——"

"You are discreet—that is right, and it will be a recommendation with the ladies."

"Well, well!" thought Chérubin, "they all seem to be agreed on that point; Madame Célival says almost the same thing that the countess said."

The lovely widow seated herself for a moment by Chérubin's side, and said in a very low tone:

"You must have done something very bad, to be treated so—to be looked at like that?"

"I, madame? Why, I give you my word that I have done nothing at all."

"Bless me! how innocently he answers! One would take him for a little saint."

"Well, she asked me if your boudoir was prettier than—than hers. I told her that I knew nothing about it, and she told me that I lied; but you know that I told the truth."

"Ah! so she asked you if my boudoir was prettier, did she?" said Madame Célival in an irritated tone. "You admit then that you go to her boudoir? Ah! that little countess! But, on my word, I consider it very inquisitive of her to ask you if you had seen mine!—And you said no?"

"Why, I don't see how I could have said yes, madame; that would have been a lie."

"Great heaven! what an astonishing creature you are with your scruples! As if people never lied in society! Why, you must know that one is driven to it sometimes, that it is absolutely necessary. However, I propose that you shall make the acquaintance of my boudoir, so that you can answer that lady when she questions you again.—Come to breakfast with me to-morrow."

"Oh! how kind you are, madame!"

"Will you come? will you be allowed?"

"Will I be allowed! Am I not my own master, pray?"

"Perhaps.—I shall expect you then to-morrow, at twelve o'clock; and we will breakfast in my boudoir; so that you may have plenty of time to make its acquaintance, and to tell madame la comtesse what you think of it."

"Oh! I am willing to bet in advance that it is prettier than hers, and not so dark."

Madame Célival smiled, placed her hand softly in Chérubin's, and walked away, murmuring almost inaudibly:

"Until to-morrow!"

Chérubin, enchanted with his new assignation, incontinently forgot Madame de Valdieri's disdain; he recovered his spirits and his assurance, sought out Monfréville, who was at the card-table, and whispered:

"I have another, my friend."

"Another what?"

"Why, another appointment, in a boudoir, for to-morrow."

"With the same person?"

"No, with Madame Célival."

"You are a lucky dog! Pray try to carry it off better than before."

"Oh! make your mind easy! I shan't put on any perfumery at all this time.

—Are you going to play much longer?"

"Yes, we are just beginning a game of whist; I shall play two rubbers at least."

"I will leave you then; I am going home to bed."

"I don't see why you should be tired."

"Madame de Valdieri keeps looking at me with that contemptuous expression; I prefer to go."

So Chérubin disappeared from the salons and went home, thinking exclusively of Madame Célival, and engrossed by the appointment she had made with him for the next day.

XXII

THE PLUMS

One wakes early when one is in love and has an assignation with the object of one's love. It is not absolutely certain that Chérubin loved Madame Célival; indeed, it is probable that he felt for all his conquests only those fleeting desires which all young men feel in the presence of a pretty woman; a form of disease with which we often continue to be afflicted when we have attained the age of maturity, and of which it is very pleasant to be unable to cure oneself as one grows old. But Chérubin was still too inexperienced to be able to draw distinctions in his sensations; he believed himself to be passionately in love with Madame Célival.

He was no sooner awake than he rang. Jasmin, despite his years, was always one of the first to answer his master's bell; but Chérubin did not desire his services again to assist him to dress.

"You made a fine mess of it yesterday, Jasmin," he said.

"What did I do, monsieur?" asked the old servant, dismayed by Chérubin's irritated manner.

"Why, you drenched me with perfumery, Jasmin; you put it on all my clothes; I was a regular walking scent-bag."

"Did not monsieur smell good?"

"Why, yes! I smelt too good—that is to say, too strong! In fact, I went to people's heads. Nervous ladies can't endure that sort of thing, and you are responsible for a lady's fainting away. It was exceedingly unpleasant."

Jasmin was in despair. To repair his blunder of the previous day, he suggested putting camphor in all his master's pockets, because he had been told that that was very good for the nerves, and he supposed that it would cure the illnesses caused by perfumery. But Chérubin would not have it; he expressly forbade Jasmin to perfume him in any way, and he was obliged to lose his temper in order to deter his old servant from slipping lumps of camphor into his pockets.

When his toilet was completed, Chérubin assured himself that he did not smell of anything at all; and, while waiting for the hour at which he was to go to Madame Célival's, he thought about the lovely widow and went over in his mind what he could say to her. The thing that worried him most was the breakfasting with her.

"When you breakfast with a lady you're in love with," he said to himself, "I wonder if you should eat, if you should satisfy your appetite? Mon Dieu! I forgot to ask Monfréville for instructions on that point. I'm afraid I shall make more stupid blunders.—But after all, what is it that I am always blamed for? For being too timid. If I don't eat, I shall look like a fool; on the other hand, if I eat and drink freely, it will give me assurance and presumption. Yes, I certainly must eat."

The breakfast hour arrived at last. Chérubin betook himself to Madame Célival's; his heart throbbed violently as he followed the maid to the boudoir, but he said to himself:

"Well, I won't be timid to-day, at all events, and I'll eat a lot."

The fair widow's boudoir was a charming retreat, hung on all sides with violet velvet. A soft, thick carpet covered the floor, and the threefold curtains allowed very little light to enter.

"Evidently these ladies are very fond of the darkness," thought Chérubin, as he entered the room; "but I am not to read poetry to-day, and I can see well enough to eat breakfast. And then, I understand—the darkness should make one bolder—that is the reason, no doubt, why these ladies expel the daylight from their rooms."

Madame Célival was awaiting Chérubin; her dress was simple, but well adapted to display her good points to advantage: her lovely black hair fell in long curls on each side of her face, and the amaranthine bows that adorned the dainty little cap she wore gave even more animation to her eyes, which were full of fire.

The fascinating widow gave Chérubin such a pleasant welcome that any other than he would at once have felt at his ease. He did what he could to overcome his embarrassment, and the most judicious thing that he did was to stand in rapt contemplation of the charms of his hostess.

"Well, Monsieur Chérubin," said Madame Célival, after a moment, "what do you think of my boudoir? not so pretty as the countess's, I suppose?"

"Why, yes, madame, yes, I assure you, I like yours quite as well—in fact, I think it even prettier."

"Oh! you say that to flatter me!"

"But they are equally dark."

"A bright light makes my eyes ache; I detest it."

"But, madame, you should not dread being seen; when one is so lovely ——"

Chérubin dared not go on; he was tremendously surprised that he had said so much; but Madame Célival, to whom the compliment seemed quite natural, replied with a smile:

"Really! do you think me lovely? Oh! but it costs you men so little to say things that you don't mean!"

And, as she spoke, Madame Célival leaned carelessly on the cushion of the violet velvet couch on which she was half-reclining, and her bosom rose and fell rapidly as she gazed at Chérubin, who was sitting on a chair by her side; he lowered his eyes, dared not look at her, and held his peace.

After a long pause, Madame Célival, finding that Chérubin did not speak, exclaimed:

"But I am forgetting our breakfast! Perhaps you are hungry?"

"Why yes, madame, I am very hungry," Chérubin at once replied.

"And it seems that your appetite deprives you of the power of speech," said Madame Célival with a smile. "Mon Dieu! why didn't you remind me? I don't want to see you fall dead from starvation. Please ring that bell."

Chérubin pulled a cord and a maid appeared.

"Serve breakfast," said Madame Célival.—"We will breakfast here," she added, turning to Chérubin, "because then we shall not be disturbed by anybody; if any unwelcome visitor calls, they will say that I'm not at home. Do you think that I have done well?"

"Oh, yes, madame, it will be much pleasanter!"

Madame Célival smiled again; perhaps she thought that their tête-à-tête would become pleasanter; but this is mere conjecture.

The maid quickly laid the table with two covers. Chérubin noticed that she placed the dessert on a small table beside the large one, which was covered with dishes.

Then Madame Célival dismissed her, saying:

"If I want you, I will ring.—And now," said the fascinating brunette, offering her hand to the young man, who continued to gaze at her admiringly, "take your seat, monsieur le marquis, and excuse me for treating you so unceremoniously; but this is not a formal breakfast."

Madame Célival's informal breakfast consisted of a *terrine de Nérac*, a stuffed partridge, small birds *aux pistaches*, and a superb dish of crabs; and on the small table were pastry, preserves, and a compote of plums, for dessert; lastly, several decanters of choice wines indicated that the hostess did not propose that her young guest should retain his self-possession unimpaired.

Chérubin was seated beside Madame Célival, who helped him to everything, but ate very little; by way of compensation, the young man ate for two. After he was at the table, he felt much less embarrassed, more inclined to talk; he concluded that he had guessed aright, and that to eat and drink freely would give him assurance; so he did honor to everything that was set before him and drank whatever was poured into his glass.

Madame Célival was very lively; she knew the art of keeping the conversation from flagging; and she seemed delighted by the way in which her companion did honor to the breakfast.

"Really," she said laughingly, "I am not surprised that you didn't say anything just now, that you seemed so taciturn! It was because you were dying of hunger."

"It is true, madame, that I have an excellent appetite; and then, with you, it seems to me that one must needs always be hungry."

"Oh! I don't feel sure whether I ought to take that for a compliment or not! There is a proverb which would rather work against me."

"What is the proverb, madame?"

"As you don't know it, I won't tell you.—Now, we will proceed to the dessert; I had it put within our reach, so that we need not ring; all we have to do is to change tables. Don't you think that that is pleasanter?"

These last words were accompanied with such a tender glance that Chérubin was greatly confused; to recover his self-possession, he hastily pushed away the table on which they had breakfasted and replaced it by the smaller one on which the dessert was all set out.

Madame Célival, who was desirous that the breakfast should come to an end, made haste to serve her guest, and offered him everything. Chérubin scrutinized the compote of plums and asked:

"What is that?"

"Plums. Do you mean to say that you don't know this dish?"

"Mon Dieu! no, I never saw it before. At my nurse's we never ate it."

Madame Célival laughed heartily.

"At your nurse's!" she repeated; "that is lovely! an excellent joke! One would think, to hear you, that you had remained out at nurse to this day."

Chérubin bit his lips; he thought that he had made a foolish speech, and was overjoyed to find that she took it for a good joke. He accepted the plums which Madame Célival offered him.

"Well!" said the lovely widow, after a moment, "how do you like what you never had at your nurse's?"

"Very well! delicious!"

"Will you have some more?"

"With pleasure."

Madame Célival served him again to plums, and he said, as he ate them:

"But you are eating nothing, madame."

"Oh! I am not hungry."

"Why not?"

"Why not! what a strange question! Because women aren't like men, and when they have anything on their mind, they live on their thoughts and their feelings, and those are all they need."

These last words were uttered in a tone of annoyance, for Madame Célival was beginning to think that Chérubin passed an unduly long time at the table; however, she continued to offer him the different dishes, like a woman of breeding, who knows how to do the honors of her house.

"Thanks," said Chérubin, "but I like the plums better than anything."

"Very well, take some more."

"Really—if I dared——"

"You are not going to stand on ceremony, are you? I shall be offended."

Chérubin remembered that he must not be timid, that it was that which had been so harmful to him. So he helped himself to plums; in a moment he took some more; and as Madame Célival laughed heartily over his passion for plums, and he was delighted to entertain her, he did not stop until the dish contained no more.

The lovely widow seemed very well pleased when the plums were exhausted, and the words: "That is very lucky!" escaped from her lips; but they were almost inaudible, and Chérubin did not hear them.

Meanwhile the pretty hostess had softly moved her chair away from the table; she drank a few spoonfuls of coffee, placed her cup on the mantel, then resumed her seat on her couch, saying to the young man, in a voice that went to his heart:

"Well! aren't you coming to sit by me?"

Chérubin began to understand that the time had come when he must turn his attention to something besides plums; he left the table and walked about the salon, admiring divers lovely engravings, the subjects of which, while not too free, were well adapted to appeal to the passions. He went into ecstasies before Cupid and Psyche, the river Scamander, and an Odalisk lying on her couch; and finally he seated himself beside Madame Célival, who said to him:

"Do you like my engravings?"

"Yes, all those women are so lovely—especially the Odalisk!"

"The painter has hardly clothed her; but to enable us to admire her beauty, it was necessary to show her to us unclothed. That is allowed in painting; artists have privileges; we pardon everything in talent—or in love."

These last words were accompanied by a sigh. Chérubin looked at the lovely widow, and she had never seemed to him more alluring; for her eyes shone with a fire that was at once intense and soft, and her half-closed lips seemed inclined to reply to many questions. The young man ventured to take a hand which was relinquished to him without reserve; he gazed fondly at that soft, plump, white hand, with its tapering fingers; he dared not put it to his lips as yet, but he pressed it tenderly, and not only was it not withdrawn, but a very warm pressure responded to his. Encouraged by that symptom, Chérubin was about to cover that hand with kisses, when he suddenly felt a sharp pain in the intestinal region.

Chérubin was thunderstruck.

"What's the matter?" queried Madame Célival, amazed to find him holding her hand in the air, without kissing it.

"Nothing, oh! nothing, madame!"

And the young man tried to dissemble a wry face caused by a second pang, less sharp, it is true, but followed by internal rumblings which portended a violent tempest.

Meanwhile, being completely engrossed by his sensations, and disturbed by the thought of the possible sequel, Chérubin ceased to take any part in the conversation and dropped Madame Célival's hand on the couch.

"In heaven's name, what is the matter, monsieur?" murmured the pretty widow, in a half-reproachful, half-melting tone. "You seem distraught, absent-minded; you say nothing to me. Do you know that that is not agreeable on your part?"

"Mon Dieu, madame, I assure you that nothing is the matter; you are mistaken."

And Chérubin did what he could to mask another contortion; he was attacked by gripes which fairly tortured him; he realized that he had the colic, and not for anything on earth would he have had Madame Célival guess what had happened to him.

However, it is not a crime to feel indisposed! But we weak mortals, who seek sometimes to exalt ourselves to the rank of gods, we blush because we are subject to all the infirmities of the simplest of God's creatures; there are times when we are sorely embarrassed to be at once the man of the world and the natural man. Poor Chérubin found himself in that predicament; the plums were playing him a very treacherous trick.

Madame Célival could not misunderstand the young marquis's tone. Piqued, too, because she could no longer read in his eyes either affection or desire, she exclaimed after a moment:

"Evidently, monsieur, you find it dull with me."

"Why, madame, I swear to you that that is not true—far from it; but——"

"But you would prefer to be with Madame de Valdieri, wouldn't you?"

"Oh, no! that is not where I would like to be at this moment!"

"Indeed! where would you like to be at this moment, monsieur?"

Chérubin did not know what to reply; he endured with difficulty another sharp pain, and felt the cold perspiration standing on his forehead. He cut a very sad figure at that moment, and did not in the least resemble a lover.

Madame Célival looked at him; she compressed her lips angrily, and cried:

"Oh! what an extraordinary face you are making! Such a thing was never seen before—by me, at all events. Come, monsieur, speak, explain yourself; something is the matter, certainly."

And the fair widow, still impelled by the tender sentiment which spoke in Chérubin's favor, walked toward him and would have taken his hand; but he hastily drew back, faltering in a stifled voice:

"Oh! don't touch me, madame, I implore you!"

"What does that mean, monsieur? I beg you to believe that I have not the slightest desire to touch you," retorted Madame Célival, offended by the alarm depicted on the young man's face. "But, monsieur, I am justified in being surprised by the ill humor that has suddenly taken possession of you; I did not expect that I should—er—frighten you by showing you what pleasure it gave me to entertain you.—Ha! ha! it is most amusing, on my word!"

Instead of replying to what she said, Chérubin abruptly sprang to his feet, muttering:

"Excuse me, madame, excuse me—but an appointment I had forgotten—I absolutely must go."

"What, monsieur! you made an appointment when you knew that you were to breakfast with me! That is extremely courteous of you! You cannot make me believe that it is so urgent that you must go at once."

"Oh! yes, madame, yes! it is horribly urgent; I cannot postpone it any longer. Adieu, madame, adieu!"

And Chérubin, after running madly about the boudoir three times, in search of his hat, spied it at last, seized it, rushed at the door, threw it open with such force that he nearly broke it, and fled through all the rooms of the suite, as if he were afraid of being pursued, leaving Madame Célival aghast at his manner of taking leave of her.

Chérubin reached home at last cursing the plums and the ill-fortune which seemed to pursue him in his love-affairs.

Toward evening Monfréville called upon his friend; he was curious to know if he acquitted himself more creditably at his last assignation than at the first. When he saw the young marquis, still pale and exhausted, he smiled and said:

"I see that your good fortune was complete this time, and that you won a grand victory."

Chérubin looked at his friend with such a piteous expression that he did not know what to think. After carefully closing the door of his apartment,

Chérubin told Monfréville what had happened in his second amorous tête-à-tête. Monfréville could not keep a sober face as he listened to the story; and although Chérubin did not share his merriment, it was a long time before he could restrain it.

"So you consider it very amusing, do you?" said Chérubin, with a sigh.

"Faith, my dear fellow, it is very hard not to laugh at the plight in which you found yourself."

"Agree that I am very unlucky."

"It is your own fault. When you breakfast tête-à-tête with a lady, you should not stuff yourself with plums, especially after you have already eaten heartily, as you seem to have done."

"I did it to give myself courage, nerve!"

"What you did give yourself was very agreeable."

"Well, no such accident will happen in my next tête-à-tête with Madame Célival; I shall have better luck next time."

"Oh! don't flatter yourself that you will obtain a second assignation from the fair widow. You are ruined in her esteem, as well as in the little countess's. That makes another conquest that you must abandon."

"Do you think so? How unfair! Does a woman cease to love us because we are suddenly taken ill?"

"Not for that reason, but because you behaved so clumsily."

"What would you have done in my place?"

"I would have said frankly that my breakfast was disturbing me, that I was feeling very sick; then she would have understood and excused my departure."

"Oh! I would have died of shame rather than say that!"

"That is very poor reasoning, my dear fellow; remember that a woman will forgive everything except contempt or indifference to her charms."

Chérubin was very much cast down during the rest of the day; it seemed to him that there was a sort of fatality about his love-affairs, and he was afraid that it would continue to pursue him. But that same evening Daréna came to his house, to apprise him of the results of his negotiations with the charming woman he had seen at the Cirque.

"Victory!" cried Daréna, bringing his hand down on the young marquis's shoulder; "it's going on finely, my friend; your business is in good shape."

"Well, have you obtained an appointment for me?" inquired Chérubin, with an almost frightened expression.

"Deuce take it! not yet; such things don't go so fast as you think; the young Polish countess is closely watched, surrounded by duennas and Cerberuses."

"Is she a Polish countess?"

"Yes, the Comtesse de Globeska, wife of the Comte de Globeski, a man of high social position who had to flee from his country because he was accused of high treason. He's as jealous as a tiger! he's the kind of fellow that talks of nothing but stabbing his wife if she should give so much as one hair to a man!"

"This is terrible!"

"It's of no consequence at all! Women haven't the slightest fear of daggers; on the contrary, they love to defy danger. I succeeded in getting your letter to the fair Globeska. It was a hard task; I had to scatter gold lavishly, and I did so; in fact, I borrowed some, as I had not enough. I know that you will make it up to me, and I thought that you would not blame me for being zealous in the service of your love."

"Oh! far from it, my dear Daréna; I thank you. But did the pretty Pole write me a word in reply?"

"No, she didn't write you; perhaps she doesn't write French very well—that is excusable in a foreigner; but women abound in self-esteem; they are afraid of being laughed at if they make a mistake in grammar; in fact, the enchanting Globeska replied by word of mouth, and what she said is worth all the billets-doux that ever were written."

"What did she say?"

"She said to her maid, whom I had seduced—I mean that I bribed her with money: 'Say to this young Frenchman who has written me, that I share his passion. Since I saw him, I dream of him all the time, even when I am not asleep.'"

"Did she say that? Oh! what joy!"

"Let us finish: 'I am bound to a tyrant whom I detest. Let this Frenchman devise some way to carry me off, and I am ready to go with him—I will throw myself into his arms.'—Well, what do you say to that, my lucky Lovelace? I should say that you had turned her head!"

"Yes, my friend, I am very glad; for I feel that I like that young woman better than all the rest. With her it seems to me that I shall be more at my ease than with the women in fashionable society, who always intimidate me."

"You will be very much at your ease, I promise you; the Poles are very unceremonious."

"But she talks about my carrying her off. Can that be done? Is it allowable to carry off a man's wife?"

"Oh! what a child! In the first place, you don't ask leave; and secondly, you see that she herself wants it done. Never fear, I will look after the abduction; I make that my business."

"My dear Daréna, how much I am indebted to you!"

"But the main point is to know where I shall take your charmer. You will understand that it would be neither proper nor prudent to bring her to this house, where your servants will see her, and——"

"Oh! certainly not. But where can we take her then?"

"Nothing can be simpler. All that we have to do is to hire a little house near Paris, in the suburbs, in some lonely and quiet spot. Do you wish me to attend to that too?"

"Oh, yes! I beg that you will."

"Very good, I will hire a house. If it isn't furnished, I will send some furniture. Give me some money; I shall want quite a great deal."

Chérubin ran to his desk, took out some bank-notes, and handed them to Daréna, saying:

"Here, here are two thousand, three thousand francs—is that enough?"

"Yes; but you may as well give me four thousand at once; I must not fall short. Now, let me manage the affair. I will make sure of a house, first of all, and have it arranged to receive your inamorata; then I will watch for a favorable opportunity; as soon as it comes, I will abduct the lady, then I will come here and tell you. All that you will have to do will be to pluck the fruit of the victory, and that will not be an unpleasant task."

"It is delightful!"

"But, above all, not a word of this to Monfréville, or I will have nothing more to do with it."

"Never fear, that is understood."

"When your charmer has escaped from her tyrant's hands, I will take care to order a dainty repast sent to your little retreat. It is always essential that a lady should find something to eat when she arrives."

"Yes, my friend, order a supper. But no plums, I beg! No plums! I have a horror of them!"

Daréna stared at Chérubin in amazement as he replied:

"Never fear. I was not aware of your aversion for plums; they are said to be very healthful."

"If I see any on the table, I shall run off at once."

"All right—don't get excited. I will see that none are served."

And the count left his young friend, after pocketing the bank-notes.

"Well," said Chérubin, "this conquest shall not escape me, and it will make up to me for all that I have lost."

XXIII

A FAMILY INTERIOR

As Ernestine had announced to Louise, Madame de Noirmont returned home on the day that she was expected. Her arrival was a festal occasion for Ernestine, who flew to meet her mother the instant that she caught sight of her, and threw herself into her arms. Madame de Noirmont responded lovingly to her daughter's caresses; it was easy to see that she was touched by them, and that she was genuinely happy to be at home once more.

Monsieur de Noirmont did not rush to meet his wife; such tokens of affection were not in accordance with his nature; he feared that, by indulging in them, he should compromise his dignity. However, when he learned that she had returned, he went to her room and greeted her pleasantly, but did not kiss her.

"Did you have a pleasant journey, madame?"

"Yes, thanks, monsieur."

"And how is your aunt, Madame Dufrénil?"

"She is much better, monsieur; her health is entirely restored. But it was time for me to return, or I should have been really ill with ennui, from being away from my daughter so long. I was very sorry that you did not allow me to take her with me, monsieur."

"The result of that, madame, is that you have the greater pleasure in seeing her again, and I trust that it will make you love her dearly."

With that, Monsieur de Noirmont saluted his wife and returned to his study.

When her husband had gone, Madame de Noirmont drew her daughter to her and pressed her to her heart again and again:

"Your father thinks that I do not love you," she murmured. "Do you think so too, my love?"

"Oh, no! indeed I don't, mamma," cried Ernestine. "But papa doesn't think so, either; I am sure of it. I know that you love me; and why shouldn't you? am I not your daughter?"

Madame de Noirmont's features contracted nervously; her brow darkened, and she hastily extricated herself from Ernestine's arms. But the cloud soon vanished and she drew the girl to her again, saying in a melancholy tone:

"Oh, yes, yes! I love you dearly!"

"I have never doubted it, mamma, and if you have sometimes—as you had just now, for instance—moments when my caresses seem tiresome to you, I am sure that it's just because you have a headache, or because you're thinking about something else; but you don't love me any less, do you?"

"No, of course I never love you any less. Did the time seem long to you while I was away?"

"Oh! yes, mamma! But luckily I have had a new maid for three weeks. Father must have written you that he discharged the other one, didn't he?"

"Yes, dear."

"Oh! I like the new one ever so much better! If you knew how nice she is! and not a bit stupid, nor vulgar! She speaks very correctly, and yet she came right from her village; she has never lived out, but she learned her duties instantly."

"Who brought her here?"

"Comtois. He had excellent recommendations."

Madame de Noirmont smiled at the serious tone in which her daughter spoke.

"My dear girl," she replied, "I know that we may rely on Comtois.—What is your new maid's name?"

"Louise—Louise Fré—Frénet—I never can remember her other name. But no matter, she's a very nice girl, I tell you, mamma; I am sure that you will like her too. I am going to call her, to show her to you. She's very shy, that is why she hasn't come to pay her respects to you."

"Mon Dieu! my dear love, I have plenty of time to see your maid; there is no hurry about it."

"Oh, yes! I want you to see her right away, mamma."

Ernestine rang a bell; in a moment the door opened and Louise appeared in the doorway, timid and with downcast eyes.

"Did madame ring for me?" she murmured.

Madame de Noirmont scrutinized the girl, whom she then saw for the first time; she was struck by her beauty, by the dignified expression of her features, by her modest and reserved demeanor, by her whole aspect, which was not what one ordinarily sees in a lady's maid. She could not tire of looking at her.

Ernestine leaned toward her mother and whispered:

"Well! what do you think of her?"

"Lovely, my child, lovely; she has an air of distinction too; no one would think that she was a servant."

"I didn't flatter her, did I?—Mamma thinks that you are lovely, Louise," continued the girl; "she likes you too. I told you that she would like you."

Louise made a curtsy and murmured:

"Madame is very kind; I will do my best to satisfy her, and mademoiselle too."

"I don't doubt it, my child," replied Madame de Noirmont; "everything prepossesses me in your favor, and I am convinced that my daughter is not mistaken in all the good that she has told me of you."

While Ernestine's mother was speaking, Louise raised her eyes and looked at her. At sight of that beautiful, noble and stern face, of that pale and haughty brow, of those great black eyes wherein one could always detect a melancholy expression, the girl felt deeply moved and impressed; her heart beat violently, whether with pleasure or fear she did not know; she could not define her feelings, but she did not speak or move. For some moments after Madame de Noirmont ceased speaking, she continued to listen; they motioned to her that she might retire, and she remained. At last Ernestine had to touch her arm and say: "You may leave us, Louise," before she came to herself and left the room, casting a last furtive glance at Madame de Noirmont.

After a few more words concerning the new lady's maid, Madame de Noirmont turned all her attention to taking up the threads of her usual domestic occupations, and to superintending her daughter's education and her studies with the different teachers who came to the house to give her lessons.

Madame de Noirmont's life was very regular; she rarely went out and received few visits; she devoted herself to her daughter, overlooked her studies and read a great deal: that was her greatest pleasure, her most agreeable means of distraction.

Monsieur de Noirmont passed the whole day in his study; his wife and daughter saw little of him before dinner. At that repast they met, and not infrequently some old friend of Monsieur de Noirmont dined with them, but they very rarely had more than one guest. During dinner Madame de Noirmont talked very little, while her husband discussed politics or economic matters with his guest. Ernestine alone did anything to enliven the party. She succeeded very well; her childish sallies and observations often made her mother smile; and even Monsieur de Noirmont, despite his gravity, could not always keep a sober face. In the evening, the ladies worked, made tapestry, or sang, and the men played chess or backgammon. When there were no guests at dinner, Monsieur de Noirmont often went out in the evening to some party or reception; sometimes his wife and daughter accompanied him, but rarely. Madame de Noirmont preferred to remain at home with Ernestine; and when her husband was not there, she seemed less serious, less pensive, and she manifested her affection for Ernestine more freely.

Louise's duties were very pleasant in that family, where the ladies did not go to balls and received very little company. Comtois alone waited at table. The young lady's maid assisted the ladies to dress; then, during almost all the remainder of the day, she worked in her room, making dresses for mademoiselle or keeping the linen of the household in order. In the evening, she served at tea, then looked to it that her mistresses had everything in their room that they required. This was not very wearisome, and Louise sometimes told Ernestine that they did not give her enough work to do; but the girl would reply, with a smile:

"What makes you work so fast? We no sooner give you a piece of sewing to do than it is done. Mamma says that your activity and skill are most unusual. Other lady's maids don't work so fast, I promise you!"

Louise felt a thrill of pleasure whenever she was told that Madame de Noirmont was pleased with her. And although that lady always preserved a grave and serious manner with her servants, which made the slightest approach to familiarity impossible, she felt drawn to love her, and it seemed to her that it would be a source of deep grief to her if she should now be compelled to leave her.

Meanwhile three months had passed since she came to Paris, and she had not once seen Chérubin. But since Madame de Noirmont's return, Louise, engrossed by the desire to please her, had felt her love-pangs less sharply; although she still loved her old playmate as dearly as ever, another sentiment had glided into her heart, to distract her thoughts from her troubles.

Monsieur Gérondif had called several times to inquire of Comtois what Louise's employers thought of her, and each time the old servant put forth all his eloquence in praise of the young lady's maid and begged the professor to thank old Jasmin for the present he had sent them. Monsieur Gérondif went away overjoyed that he had brought Louise to Paris, although Chérubin, entirely absorbed by his *bonnes fortunes*, had forgotten about going to see Nicole.

One morning, when Monsieur Gérondif called at Monsieur de Noirmont's to ask Comtois if they were still content with Louise, the valet replied:

"Yes, indeed; Mademoiselle Louise is a model of virtue and industry. If you would like to see her, monsieur, she is alone at this moment; the ladies have gone out to do some shopping. She is working in her room, and there is no reason why you should not go up and bid her good-morning."

Monsieur Gérondif joyfully accepted the proposition; he followed Comtois, who led him to Louise's chamber and left him with her.

Louise manifested the keenest delight at sight of the tutor, for she would have an opportunity to talk with him about all those who were dear to her. Monsieur Gérondif, who was, like most pedants, a conceited fool, took to himself a pleasure of which he was the pretext simply; he believed that he had kindled a tender sentiment in the breast of the pretty lady's maid, and he smiled as if he would dislocate his jaw as he took his seat beside her.

Louise began by inquiring for her adopted mother.

"She is perfectly well, and she is overjoyed that you are in such a fine position in Paris," replied the tutor, lying with imperturbable coolness; for he had not been to the village since Louise left it.

"And Monsieur Chérubin?" continued Louise, "is he pleased to know that I am in Paris as he wished? Hasn't he any desire to see me? Doesn't he ever speak to you about me? Did he send you here to-day?"

The tutor scratched his nose, coughed, spat, wiped his forehead, all of which operations required much time with him, during which he considered what he should say. Having made up his mind at last, he said to Louise:

"My dear child, it rarely happens that childish loves come to a good end. I might cite Paul and Virginie and a thousand other examples *ad hoc*; I prefer to tell you *ex abrupto*—which means, without preamble—that you are making a mistake to give any further thought to Monsieur le Marquis de Grandvilain, because that young man never gives a thought to you. In the first place, when you came to see him at his house—when you came to Paris with Nicole——"

"Well, monsieur?"

"Well, the young marquis was at home; but as he didn't want to see you, he gave his concierge orders to tell you that he was away."

"O mon Dieu! is it possible?"

"Amid the debauchery in which he is plunged, how do you expect him to remember a young country girl with whom he used to play puss-in-the-corner, and other more or less innocent games? He has become a great rake, has my pupil; he has a lot of mistresses. It isn't my fault. He receives so many billets-doux that it's perfectly scandalous, and I should have left his house before this if my financial interests did not oblige me to close my eyes,—which however, does not prevent my seeing whatever happens."

Louise put her handkerchief to her eyes and faltered:

"So it's all over—he doesn't love me at all! Who would have believed it of Chérubin?"

"One must believe everything, expect everything from a beardless youth," replied the tutor.

Then, drawing his chair close to the girl's, and laying his hand on her knee, Monsieur Gérondif tried to assume a mellifluous voice and began, weighing his words:

"I have made the wound, and it is for me to apply the balsam, otherwise called the remedy.—Lovely Louise, although young Chérubin has not been true to your charms, there are others who will be too happy to offer incense to them, to cultivate them. I go straight to the point: I love you, divine maiden! and I am not fickle, because, thank heaven, I am a grown man. I have not come to make any base propositions to you—*retro, Satanas*! which means: I have only honorable views. I offer you my hand, my heart, my name, my rank and my title; but we will wait two years before we marry. I will try to restrain my passions for that length of time, which I require in order to amass a tidy sum of money. You will contribute your wages, your savings; they are much pleased with you here, and it is probable that you will receive a handsome present at New Year's. We will put it all together and buy a little house in the outskirts of Paris; I will take a few pupils to keep my hand in; we will have a dog, a cat, chickens, all the pleasant things of life, and our days will be blended of honey and hippocras."

During this harangue, Louise had pushed away the hand that Monsieur Gérondif had laid on her knee, and had moved her chair away; and as soon as he had finished speaking, she rose and said to him in a courteous but determined tone:

"I thank you, monsieur, for condescending to offer me, a poor village girl, without name or family, the title of your wife; but I cannot accept it. Monsieur Chérubin no longer loves me; I can understand that, monsieur, and indeed I was mad to imagine that, in Paris, in the midst of pleasures, living in the whirl of society, he would remember me. But it is altogether different with me! I have not become a great lady, and the image of the man I love can never be effaced from my heart. I love Chérubin; I feel that I shall never love anybody else! So, monsieur, it would be very wicked of me to marry another man, as I could not give that other my love."

Monsieur Gérondif was greatly surprised by this speech; he recovered himself, however, and replied:

"My sweet Louise, *varium et mutabile semper femina*; or, if you prefer: '*souvent femme varie, bien fol est qui s'y fie.*'—Woman changes ever; he is a great fool who trusts her.—The latter lines are by François I; I prefer Beranger's.—Tiresias declares that men have only three ounces of love, while women have nine, which enables them to change oftener than we do; and yet, with only three ounces, we do pretty well."

"What does all this mean, monsieur?"

"It means, my dear love, that you will do like the others: you will change; your love will pass away."

"Never, monsieur."

"Never is a word that means nothing at all in love. However, you will have plenty of time to think about it, as I give you two years for reflection. Until then, allow me to hope."

"Oh! it is useless, monsieur."

"I beg pardon; by hoping one lives content, and I cling to my hope. Adieu, fair Louise; continue to behave becomingly; your remuneration will be increased doubtless, and I shall continue to put mine aside; and, as a very trivial but very shrewd popular proverb says: 'Let's let the mutton boil!'—I lay my homage at your feet."

Monsieur Gérondif took his leave, and Louise was at liberty to weep without restraint. She did not bestow a thought on the tutor's offers, she thought only of Chérubin, who no longer loved her, who had ceased to think of her, and who had mistresses. She had been afraid for a long time that he had forgotten her; but now she was certain of it, and it is a far cry from fear to certainty, in love.

The return of Madame de Noirmont and her daughter forced Louise to conceal her tears. She hastily wiped her eyes and tried to dissemble her depression, for she felt that she must not betray the secret of her heart.

On that day Monsieur de Noirmont went out after dinner. Ernestine remained with her mother, to whom, as they worked, she said whatever came into her head, especially as she saw that it was one of her moments of good humor. When Madame de Noirmont smiled at her daughter's speeches, the latter was so delighted that she often laid her work aside to throw her arms about her mother's neck, who sometimes held her lovingly to her heart for some moments.

Louise, for whom they rang to order tea, entered the salon at one of the times when Madame de Noirmont's arms were about her daughter; and the sweet child, in her joy at being so fondled, cried out:

"See how happy I am, Louise! see what a dear, good mother I have!"

Louise stood still in the middle of the salon; she was glad for Ernestine's happiness, and yet, in the touching picture before her eyes, there was something that hurt her, she did not understand why. Two great tears escaped from her eyes; but she turned quickly, so that they might not see her weeping.

Meanwhile Madame de Noirmont had resumed her grave demeanor, and Ernestine had had to return to her seat. Louise served the tea as quickly as possible, then left the room, fearing that her sadness would be noticed.

Despite all her efforts to be calm, Louise was still crying when Ernestine entered her room to ask her some question, before going to bed. Seeing that Louise's face was wet with tears, her young mistress ran to her, and said with the most touching interest:

"Mon Dieu! crying, Louise! What's the matter?"

"Oh! excuse me, mademoiselle. I know that I should not weep here, where everyone is so kind to me; but I could not help it!"

"Have you some reason for being unhappy? You would not cry like this for nothing. Louise, I insist on knowing why you were crying."

"Well, mademoiselle, it is because, when I saw you in your mother's arms to-night, the picture of the happiness you enjoy made me feel more keenly than ever the misery of my position. Oh! mademoiselle, it isn't envy that makes me say it! I bless Heaven for making you so happy; but I could not help crying when I remembered that my mother never kissed me, that I shall never be able to throw my arms about her!"

"What's that you say, my poor Louise? Doesn't your mother love you?"

"It isn't that, mademoiselle. But listen, I am going to tell you the truth, for I don't know how to lie. And then, I don't understand why I should make a mystery of it; you won't be any less kind to me when you know that I am a poor girl, abandoned by her parents."

"Is it possible? you haven't any parents?"

"At all events, mademoiselle, I don't know them."

Thereupon Louise proceeded to tell Ernestine the story of how Nicole had been employed to take care of her, and of the kindness of the village people, who had kept her and treated her like their daughter, when they found that she was abandoned by her mother.

Ernestine listened to the story with the deepest interest. When Louise had ceased to speak, she kissed her affectionately, saying:

"Poor Louise! Oh! how glad I am you have told me that! It seems to me that I love you even more since I know that your parents have abandoned you. And that dear, good Nicole! those kind peasants! Ah! what splendid people they are! I will tell mamma all about it to-morrow! I am sure that it will interest her too."

"Oh! that isn't worth while, mademoiselle; Madame de Noirmont may not like it because I have told you about my troubles."

"I assure you, on the contrary, that, for all her serious manner, mamma is kind and good; and, besides, she likes you very much. She has said to me several times that your manners were just what they should be, and that is great praise from her, I tell you!—Well, good-night, Louise, sleep soundly, and don't cry any more. If you haven't any parents, you have some people here who love you dearly and who will take good care of you."

Ernestine left Louise, to go to bed, and the latter felt less unhappy when she saw her young mistress's affection for her—an affection which she shared with all the sincerity of her soul.

The next morning the Noirmont family met at the breakfast table. Ernestine had not seen her mother since the preceding night, because a headache had kept Madame de Noirmont in bed later than usual; but her father, who rarely appeared at breakfast, had just taken his seat, when Ernestine, after kissing her mother, said in a mysterious tone:

211

"I have something very interesting to tell you this morning, and I am glad papa came to breakfast, to hear what I am going to say."

"Really?" said Monsieur de Noirmont, smiling, and in a tone of mild raillery. "From the way in which you say that, I imagine that it must really be something most serious."

"Why, yes, papa, it's very serious! Oh! you look as if you were laughing at me, but when you know what it is, I'll bet that you will be as touched as I was last night when I found poor Louise crying!"

"What! is it something about Louise?" asked Madame de Noirmont, with an air of deep interest; "can it be that anything has gone wrong with her? I should be extremely sorry, for the girl is a very good girl indeed, and seems to deserve our kindness."

"This is what it is; listen. Louise didn't want me to tell you; but I am very sure that you won't blame her for it; it isn't her fault."

Monsieur de Noirmont, whose interest was aroused by this exordium, said impatiently:

"Come, my child, go on, explain yourself."

"Well, papa, last evening, when Louise came to the salon to serve the tea, she found me in mamma's arms, and we were kissing each other."

"That is well, my daughter; what next?"

"At night, when I went up to bed, as I couldn't find a fichu that I wanted, I went to Louise's room to ask her where she had put it. I found her crying hard, and I asked her why she was crying. She replied, sobbing: 'Oh! mademoiselle, because, when I saw you in your mother's arms to-night, I felt more keenly than ever my misfortune in never having been kissed by my mother, and in being only an abandoned child.'"

"An abandoned child!" murmured Madame de Noirmont, whose face instantly became deathly pale.

"But," said Monsieur de Noirmont, "if I am not mistaken, Comtois told us that the girl's parents lived in the outskirts of Paris—I don't remember in what village."

"Yes, papa, that is what Comtois was told when Louise was brought here; but that was a lie that her friends thought they ought to tell. Louise thought it was better to tell the truth."

"She is right. But call your maid, Ernestine; I want to hear the whole story from her own lips. It has roused my curiosity. And you, madame—are not you

212

curious to hear this girl's story?"

Madame de Noirmont replied with a few almost unintelligible words; it was as if she were oppressed by some secret suffering, which she was doing her utmost to conceal.

Meanwhile, Ernestine had not waited for her father to repeat his request; she had run off to call Louise, who soon appeared before the assembled family.

Monsieur de Noirmont looked at her with more interest than he had previously displayed; Ernestine smiled at her affectionately; Madame de Noirmont lowered her eyes and became paler than ever. From the disquietude that had taken possession of her, from the anxiety that could be read upon her features, one would have taken her for a criminal awaiting judgment.

"Come, Louise, come nearer," said Monsieur de Noirmont, motioning to her; "my daughter has told us of what you told her last evening. Do not tremble, my child; we shall not reproach you for telling us what was not true when you entered our service."

"Oh! it was not I, monsieur!" murmured Louise.

"I know it, it was the person who obtained the situation for you, who thought it his duty to tell that falsehood.—So you do not know your parents, my poor girl?"

"No, monsieur."

"Where were you brought up?"

"At Gagny, monsieur."

"At Gagny. Ah! that's it; I had forgotten the name of the village that you told me when you came here.—And the people who brought you up?"

"A kindhearted peasant woman, Nicole Frimousset. She was nursing Monsieur Chérubin de Grandvilain at the time."

"Indeed! so this woman was the young Marquis de Grandvilain's nurse?"

"Yes, monsieur, he is my foster-brother, and in my childhood we played together all the time."

"Very good! But that doesn't tell us how you went to Gagny."

"Mon Dieu! monsieur, it was a lady—my mother, I suppose—who carried me to dear Nicole's, and begged her to take me to nurse. I was then a year old; she left some money with Nicole and went away, saying that she would come again. The next year she sent a little more money by a messenger from Paris;

but she didn't come to see me, and no one ever after came to inquire for me."

"But what was the lady's name; where did she live?"

"Nicole didn't think to ask her any of those questions; for she could not dream that she would abandon me, that she would never come again. The messenger from Paris did not know who the lady was who hired him on the street, he could not tell my good nurse anything."

"But was no paper, no mark found on you or on your clothing?"

"Nothing, monsieur, absolutely nothing."

"That is very strange.—Don't you agree with me, madame?"

As he asked this question Monsieur de Noirmont turned to his wife, whom he had not looked at while questioning Louise; Ernestine, whose eyes followed her father's, uttered a piercing shriek.

"Oh dear!" she cried, "mamma has fainted!"

Madame de Noirmont's head had fallen against the back of her chair; she had in fact lost consciousness, and the livid pallor of her face made her condition seem most alarming.

They hastened to her assistance; Ernestine wept and lamented as she kissed her mother again and again. Louise shared her distress; she lost her head, did not know what to do, and did not hear what was said to her. But Monsieur de Noirmont, who retained all his presence of mind, called Comtois, and, with his assistance, carried his wife to her room and laid her on her bed.

After some time, Madame de Noirmont came to herself; but there was a look of gloom and anxiety in her eyes, which indicated that the cause of her trouble still existed. She turned her eyes slowly on her husband and her daughter; then, as she caught sight of Louise, who was a little farther away and who seemed to share the general anxiety, she closed her eyes and let her head fall back on the pillow.

"Mamma, dear mamma, how do you feel now?" cried Ernestine, squeezing her mother's hand.

"Better, my dear, I feel better."

"What was the cause of your sudden illness, madame?" asked Monsieur de Noirmont with interest. "You gave us a terrible fright."

"Why, I have no idea, monsieur. I had a sudden feeling of suffocation; then a cold perspiration broke out all over me, and I lost the use of my senses."

"You didn't feel well this morning, you had a headache," said Ernestine.

"Yes, that is true," replied Madame de Noirmont hastily. "I felt poorly this morning, and that is the cause, no doubt——"

"And then Louise's story must have grieved you, made your heart ache. That probably made you worse."

"Do you wish me to send for the doctor, madame?"

"No, monsieur, it is not necessary; I need nothing but rest and quiet—and a little sleep, perhaps."

"We will leave you, then."

"But I shall be close by," said Ernestine, "and I will come at the slightest sound."

Madame de Noirmont seemed most desirous to be left alone. All the others went away, Ernestine still deeply moved because she had seen her mother in a swoon, and Louise very much cast down because she feared that the story of her misfortunes had touched her mistress too deeply.

Madame de Noirmont passed the rest of the day in her room; she kept her bed and expressed a wish to be alone. The next day passed in the same way; and for several days she did not leave her bed.

She refused to see a doctor, however, and declared that her trouble required no other remedy than rest.

But from the first moment of her illness, it was evident that Madame de Noirmont's humor had changed: she hardly spoke; sometimes her daughter's presence seemed irksome to her; she answered her curtly and received her caresses without warmth. As for Louise, while her mistress kept her room, she persistently declined her services on the pretext that she did not require them.

Poor Louise was greatly distressed.

"Madame your mother," she said to Ernestine, "will not let me wait on her, or even go into her room. I am afraid that I have displeased her, mademoiselle; perhaps she does not like to have in her house a girl whose parents are not known."

Ernestine tried to comfort her, saying:

"You are wrong. Why should you think that mamma has anything against you? No, it is this trouble of hers, it's her nerves that make her depressed and irritable. Why, she even pushes me away now when I kiss her, and she doesn't kiss me; that makes me unhappy too, but I am sure that mamma still loves me."

As she spoke, the sweet child shed tears, and Louise mingled hers with them, for she could think of no other consolation to give her.

Madame de Noirmont made up her mind at last to leave her room, and she went down to the salon. The first time that Louise saw her, she longed to ask about her health, but she dared not; her mistress's eyes seemed to avoid hers, and she did not display her former kindliness to her. For the merest trifle, Madame de Noirmont lost patience, scolded and became angry; sometimes she gave Louise ten contradictory orders in the same minute. The poor girl lost her head, was bewildered, did not know what to do, while Ernestine gazed at her mother with a surprised and grieved expression, when she saw her treat her protégée so harshly.

Sometimes, however, a violent change seemed to take place in that strange creature; after speaking sharply and severely to Louise, Madame de Noirmont, remarking the poor girl's heartbroken expression, would suddenly change her tone; her eyes would fill with tears and follow Louise's every movement; then she would call her in a gentle, affectionate, even tender voice, and the girl would return instantly, joyous and eager; but her mistress's face would already have resumed its stern expression, and she would motion her away, muttering curtly:

"What do you want? I didn't call you."

Several weeks passed in this way. One morning, Madame de Noirmont, who seemed even more thoughtful than usual, said to her daughter when she came to kiss her:

"Really, I don't propose to keep your maid; the girl is good for nothing; we must dismiss her. We will pay her two or three months' wages more than is due her. Tell her, and advise her to return to her village; I think that she made a great mistake in coming to Paris to seek employment. Do not try to change my decision, it would do no good."

Ernestine was in despair; she was very fond of Louise, and it would be a real sorrow to her to part with her; but her mother had spoken in such a stern and decided tone that the poor child dared not reply. She said nothing, but lowered her eyes with a sigh, and left the room to perform the distressing duty with which her mother had entrusted her. As she left her mother's apartment, Ernestine met Monsieur de Noirmont, who came up to her and kissed her, and said, observing her sorrowful air:

"What is it, my child? You look as if you had been crying!"

"It's nothing, papa."

"You know, Ernestine, that I do not like evasions or mysteries; I insist upon knowing at once what makes you unhappy this morning."

"Well, papa, it's because mamma is going to send Louise away, poor Louise, our maid, who is so sweet, and whom I love so dearly. But mamma doesn't like her any more; she says that Louise isn't good for anything; but Louise works just as much as she ever did, and she sews like an angel. But as mamma insists, I am going to tell Louise, so that she——"

"Don't go to her, my child, it is not necessary; Louise will stay in this house."

"But, papa, when mamma told me——"

"I tell you the opposite, my child, and I am the only master here."

Ernestine said no more, for her father had assumed a severe expression which in him denoted that he had formed a resolution which no one could change. Monsieur de Noirmont then went to his wife and said to her in a cold and impressive tone:

"Your humor is very capricious, madame, as anyone may see by the way in which you treat your daughter sometimes; but you extend it to defenceless servants also, and that is what I cannot endure. This young Louise, who came here to wait upon Ernestine, is honest and virtuous; her appearance is as becoming as her manners; I think that it would be difficult to find another so satisfactory; and yet you propose to dismiss her, madame—you expect me to turn a good girl out of my house, because, for some unknown reason, she has ceased to please you; because your fanciful humor makes you more difficult than ever to serve!—No, madame, that shall not be; I propose to be just before everything, and this girl shall remain in my house, because it would be unjust to send her away."

Madame de Noirmont had not a word to say in reply; she hung her head and seemed completely crushed.

PART IV

XXIV

THE POLISH INTRIGUE

Chérubin did not see Daréna for a week; he fretted and fumed with impatience, fearing that his intrigue with the pretty Pole had fallen through altogether; and, as is always the case, he became immeasurably more enamored of the object of his passion as his fear of not possessing her increased. It was for the purpose of giving him time to reach that climax of passion, that Daréna, who was thoroughly acquainted with the human heart, had allowed several days to elapse without going to see him.

At last Daréna appeared at the hôtel de Grandvilain one morning, hurried and breathless, like a man who had galloped twelve leagues without a halt. He pushed old Jasmin aside and almost knocked him down, when that worthy retainer attempted to tell him that he did not know whether he could see his master, who had not yet risen.

"I don't care whether he's up or in bed, he is always visible to me,"replied Daréna imperiously. "Learn, you old donkey of a valet, to know the persons whom your master is always delighted to receive."

As he spoke, Daréna rushed into the young marquis's bedroom, leaving Jasmin propped against the wall, muttering in a voice that trembled with wrath:

"Old donkey! he called me an old donkey! He's an impertinent knave. The Grandvilains, father or son, never called me that. He's not a donkey, but I have an idea that he's a much more dangerous animal!"

Daréna reached Chérubin's bedside and pulled the curtains aside, crying:

"Up, Joconde! up, Lovelace, Richelieu, Rochester! The moment of triumph has arrived at last!—Sapristi! I can fairly say, my dear fellow, that I have made myself ill for you! Ouf! I can do no more!"

And Daréna threw himself on a couch, and mopped his face with his handkerchief.

"But what has become of you during these eight long days that I have not once seen you, and have not known what to think of your silence?" asked Chérubin, looking closely at his friend. "I thought that you had forgotten me."

"Ah! that is just like a man—a young man! Because things are not done on

218

the instant, you think that you are forgotten. Do I ever forget my friends? Am I not absolutely devoted to you? If you have not heard from me for a week, it is because I had nothing to tell you; but I have been on the lookout, watching and waiting for the moment to act. It has come at last; I have acted, and the fair Globeska is in our power."

"Is it possible? Oh! do tell me how you did it, my dear Daréna?"

"Parbleu! by my ordinary method: I scattered money about. I know no other way, especially as it always succeeds. Dress, and meanwhile I will tell you how it all came about; but don't call your valet; you will understand that I can't talk about it before a witness. I have already compromised myself enough—but damn the odds!"

Chérubin rose and began to dress, saying:

"Go on, I am listening; I shall not lose a word."

"You know that the pretty Pole lived with her husband in furnished lodgings in the Marais; I succeeded in effecting the delivery of your billet-doux by bribing a lady's maid and two concierges. The Comtesse de Globeska replied that she was mad over you and asked nothing better than to leave her tyrant. That was all very well, but how were we to abduct the young woman from a man who left her no more than her shadow? It was very difficult. Seven days passed thus; Monsieur de Globeski did not leave his wife for an instant. At last, yesterday, I learned from a concierge, by a further use of money, that the Polish count had decided to leave Paris, and that he was going to take his wife to Norway; of course, if we had had to pursue our conquest to Norway, it would have taken us too far. I instantly formed my resolution, saying to myself: 'He shall not take her!'

"I learned—still by the lavish use of money—that the post-chaise was to call for our Poles at eight in the evening. I arrived just before the hour; the carriage came and stopped in front of the house, and I went boldly up to the postilion and led him aside.

"'I adore the woman who is going with you,' I said. 'I am going to follow with two friends to a lonely place on the road, one or two leagues from Paris; we shall pretend to attack you, and fire a few shots with pistols loaded with powder only. You will stop; we will open the carriage door and seize the young woman; then you will start off at full speed with the old gentleman, and if he shouts to you to stop, you will pay no attention until you have galloped at least two solid hours.'

"You will understand, my dear Chérubin, that I should not dare to make such a proposition as that to a postilion, without supporting it by convincing arguments. I handed him a thousand-franc note, and he turned his back, saying:

"'What do you take me for?'

"I added five hundred francs. He remarked that it was a very ticklish business! I added another five hundred. He agreed to everything. That's the way things are done in Paris. I went off to choose two rascals on whom I could rely, in consideration of five hundred francs, which I gave to each. I also hired a post-chaise. When the Comte de Globeski started off with his wife, we followed; and, about two leagues from here, between Sèvres and Chaville, in a place where nothing grows but melons, we discharged our pistols. The bribed postilion stopped. It was dark, and everything went off as I had arranged. We kidnapped the young woman. The old Pole defended her like a genuine demon; indeed, he inflicted a slight dagger wound on one of our men in the scuffle, which forced me to disburse three hundred francs more. However, we captured the divine Globeska, and I took her to the house I have hired, where she passed the night and is now awaiting you."

"Oh! what a series of events, my dear Daréna! But great heaven! this stealing a woman from her husband, and by force! Suppose it should be known? Isn't it a crime?"

"Bah! are you going to have scruples now?—At all events, there was no other way, and then, if worse comes to worst, I am the only one compromised; but my friendship is of the sort that defies danger."

"And the pretty Pole—where have you taken her?"

"To a little house that stands all by itself near Barrière de la Chopinette; I could find nothing better. And then I considered that to go into the country, at a distance from Paris, would incommode you too much. The house I have hired is in a spot where very few people pass; the outlook is not very cheerful, but what do you care for that? You aren't going to shut yourself up with a woman, to look out of the windows at people passing, are you? Isn't one always happy when with the person one loves?"

"Oh, yes! of course; but in what quarter is this Barrière de la Chopinette?"

"In the quarter of La Poudrette, and of lonely promenades, in the direction of Ménilmontant. However, we can go there in a cab. Remember, my dear fellow, that your charmer is waiting for you; I told the concierge of the house to order as toothsome a breakfast as he can procure in that quarter, and some superfine wines. Make haste and finish dressing—put on your best clothes, perfume yourself——"

"Perfume myself? Indeed, I shall not; perfumery makes me sick."

"As you please, but put on your armor. Lucky Chérubin! you are about to possess one of the loveliest women I have ever seen; and her Polish accent, too, is most fascinating."

"And she loves me, you say? she has admitted it?"

"Parbleu! how many times must I tell you? In fact, I should say that her conduct was quite sufficient proof of it."

"She didn't weep when she was kidnapped?"

"Weep! She danced—she adores dancing, it seems. By the way, I need not tell you that I have nothing left of the funds you advanced me. The postilion and my men to pay—the hire of the post-chaise and the house—and all the people I bribed. In fact, you owe me fifteen hundred francs."

"Fifteen hundred francs!" exclaimed Chérubin, as he walked to his desk; "it costs a lot to abduct a woman!"

"To whom are you telling that? to me, who have abducted a hundred perhaps, in the course of my life? Indeed it was in that way that I spent a large part of my fortune; but it is a princely pleasure all the same, in which everybody cannot indulge."

Chérubin handed Daréna the sum that he required, and said:

"I am ready."

"Very good; send out for a cab; you will understand that we can't go to your *petite maison* with your tilbury and your groom. You should never take your servants into the secret of a mysterious intrigue like this; such people are too fond of talking."

"You are right.—Holà! Jasmin!"

The old servant appeared, still with a long face, and cast an angry glance at Daréna. Chérubin ordered him to send for a cab.

"Will not monsieur take his cabriolet?" queried Jasmin, with an expression of surprise.

"Evidently not!" cried Daréna, laughing at Jasmin's face; "as your master orders a cab, he doesn't propose to take his cabriolet. Off with you, old ruin, and make haste, if you possibly can."

"Old ruin!" muttered Jasmin, as he left the room. "Still another insult—and I must swallow it all! I am very much afraid that this ne'er-do-well will ruin my young master. I should like to know why he makes him take a cab, when he has his own tilbury and cabriolet."

However, Jasmin did his errand; the cab was summoned. Chérubin went downstairs with Daréna, and they both entered the vehicle, which Jasmin looked after, with a far from pleased expression, as it drove away.

Daréna told the driver where to take them. After quite a long drive they stopped in front of a shabby house outside Barrière de la Chopinette, on the outer boulevards.

"Here we are!" said Daréna, jumping out of the cab.

Chérubin looked at the house, which had but one floor above the ground floor, with two windows on the front.

"This isn't a very handsome house!" he exclaimed.

"It is very fine inside," replied Daréna. "The principal thing is that it's isolated; the devil himself would be in it if the husband should unearth you here! My dear fellow, when you run off with a woman, you must take the greatest precautions. And after all, what do you care about the house? It's the woman that you come here to see. For my part, I should have been perfectly happy in a shepherd's hut, with the object of my love.—Send the cab away; I am going to ring."

Chérubin made haste to pay the cab-driver, who returned to his box and drove away.

Daréna pulled a wire beside the low door that gave admission to the house. A little fellow of some thirteen years, with an impudent expression, whose knavish and insolent bearing harmonized well with a very dirty costume, answered the bell, his cap over his ear, his blouse flapping in the wind, and his hands black with dirt. He bestowed a glance of intelligence on Daréna, who recognized little Bruno, the same urchin of whom Poterne had tried to make a monkey, and who, on his side, had conceived the idea of appropriating the skin which he had used in studying his character. Later Poterne had found Bruno, who had squandered his disguise; the business agent took the liberty of thrashing the boy, then forgave him, and charmed by the happy talents which young Bruno manifested, determined to employ him again when the opportunity should present itself. In the scheme which had been devised to dupe Chérubin, it was necessary to station some intelligent person, who could be trusted, in the house which had been hired. Poterne instantly thought of the urchin, to whom he did not pay much, and who had all the qualities essential to forward their designs.

"Ah! this is the concierge's son," said Daréna, glancing at Bruno as they entered the house, and leading Chérubin through a sort of vestibule, toward the staircase. "Where's your father, my boy? is he away?"

"Yes, monsieur, he had to go to a place ten leagues from here, to see my aunt, who is very sick."

"And you are keeping the house?"

"Yes, monsieur."

"Has the lady who slept here had everything that she wanted?"

"Oh, yes! monsieur; don't you be afraid; that lady hasn't wanted for anything. She's upstairs. By the way, she says that she's beginning to get tired of being all alone."

"Patience! monsieur here has come to keep her company.—How about the breakfast; is it ordered?"

"Yes, monsieur; and it will be fine, I tell you. I was the one that went to the restaurant——"

"This little rascal is overflowing with intelligence," said Daréna, turning to Chérubin, "and I recommend him to you in case you need anything.—Well, my dear friend, here you are with your charmer now, and I will leave you."

"What! you are going to leave me?" cried Chérubin, almost in an offended tone.

"Why, I don't see that there is anything more for me to do here; the rest is your business. You are going to breakfast tête-à-tête with a little foreigner, who is mad over you. Would not a third person be in the way?"

"Oh, yes! of course. Well, then, au revoir."

"Au revoir, my dear marquis, and may love crown you with its sweetest favors!"

Daréna smiled, almost ironically, as he shook hands with Chérubin; then he flashed a glance at Bruno and left the house, closing the door behind him.

Chérubin felt intensely excited when he found himself in that strange house, in a quarter which was entirely unfamiliar to him, with no other company than a boy who stared at him with a sly expression, as he cracked nut after nut which he took from under his blouse.

The vestibule had two doors, both of which were open, disclosing the interior of two rooms, in one of which the only furniture was several rickety tables, and in the other, one table and a wretched cot bed; the windows on the boulevard were supplied with iron bars, but entirely unprovided with curtains.

Chérubin, who had seen this at a glance, reflected that Daréna had not spent much money in furnishing the house. Then he turned to Bruno, who was still breaking nuts, sometimes with his teeth and sometimes with his feet, and humming at intervals a tune of which nothing could be heard save: *tu tu tu tu tu tu tu r'lu tu.*

"Where is madame la comtesse's apartment?"

"Whose?" queried the ex-bootblack, looking up with an insolent expression.

"I ask you where the young lady is, who has been in this house since last night?"

The boy thrust his tongue into his cheek,—a street Arab's trick when he proposes to lie—and answered:

"Oh, yes; the young foreign lady, who was kidnapped, and who slept here —*tu tu tu r'lu tu*—she's upstairs, on the first floor, in the finest apartment in the house, where she's sighing and having a stupid time—*tu tu tu r'lu tu!*"

Chérubin asked no further questions; he went upstairs—there was but one flight—and stopped at a door, the key of which was on the outside. His heart beat very fast at the thought that he was about to stand in the presence of the young Pole who had consented so readily to leave her husband and go with him; but he remembered how pretty she was, and he decided to knock.

"Come in," cried a voice, "the key's in the door."

Chérubin recognized Madame de Globeska's accent; he opened the door and found himself face to face with the young woman.

Chichette Chichemann wore a very simple costume, into which a few odds and ends of lace, flowers and fur had been introduced, in an attempt to set it off; but they produced the contrary effect in the eyes of a good judge. But Chérubin was not as yet an expert in such matters; moreover, a man in love pays no heed to such details. What impressed him at once was Chichette's pretty face, over which was perched the same velvet toque that she wore at the Cirque; and as he entered the room she greeted him with a pleasant smile, crying:

"Ah! here you are; that's very lucky! for I was beginning to be awfully bored, all alone here!"

Encouraged by this greeting, Chérubin seated himself beside the young woman, and said to her in a very tender tone:

"Ah! madame, then you will pardon what my excessive love has led me to undertake? You have consented to trust my honor, to fly from him who—from him who—that is, from that gentleman who looked so ugly and who assuredly is not worthy to—to——"

Chérubin had never said so much at one time; he stopped, for he did not know how to finish his sentence. But Chichette gave him no time; she instantly replied:

"Yes, yes! I've fled from my tyrant. But let's talk about something else."

"She doesn't want me to talk about her husband!" said Chérubin to himself; "she wants me to talk about something else—my love, no doubt. She is charming.—And so," he continued aloud, "you do not regret having entrusted to me the care of your happiness, and being here at this moment, far from your native country [*pays*]?"

"My pays? oh, yes, I always regret my little pays! but I hope to see him again some day. Let's talk about something else."

"Ah! how kind you are, madame! how lovely you are! If you knew how—I —I—I love you!"

It required a great effort on Chérubin's part to say that, and he dared not look at the young woman, fearing that she would consider his declaration rather abrupt. But Mademoiselle Chichette, far from seeming offended, began to laugh idiotically, and replied:

"Yes, yes! I know. Ha! ha! It's nice to love, and you have very fine eyes. Ha! ha! I'd like right well to laugh with you."

And the so-called Polish countess, who seemed, in truth, much inclined to laugh, and who showed some very pretty teeth, looked at the young man in a meaning fashion, and did not tell him to talk about something else. For a moment Chérubin was tempted to kiss his enslaver, who almost offered him her fresh, pink cheeks; he confined himself to taking a hand, which he laid upon his heart and pressed it hard.

Chichette, tired perhaps of having her hand pressed to Chérubin's heart, said to him, still laughing:

"How your thingumbob goes tick-tack! It's like a big clock."

"Oh! it is emotion, madame; it is pleasure; it is——"

"Aren't we going to breakfast?" cried Chichette suddenly; "I'm hungry, I can hear my belly crying; it goes *flouc-flouc*!"

These words brought Chérubin back to less romantic thoughts; he ran to the door, opened it, and shouted:

"I say, young one—what about that breakfast?"

"Here it is, monsieur, here it is! Right away, smoking hot!" replied Bruno;

"the restaurant man's just this minute come."

And a moment later a wine-shop waiter came up the stairs with the young concierge. They laid a table with two covers; they produced a basket filled with bottles, with seals of all colors; they covered the table with freshly opened oysters, and placed several covered dishes on another table. At sight of the oysters the so-called Pole indulged in the most plebeian demonstrations of delight, and began to dance about the room, crying:

"Ah! oysters! I like oysters so much! I'd let myself be hamstrung for some oysters."

Chérubin was amazed to hear Madame de Globeska express herself in such terms, but he attributed it to her ignorance of the language.

The waiter was too much accustomed to such expressions to be surprised. As for young Bruno, he contented himself with thrusting his tongue into his cheek again and muttering:

"Thanks! that's a fine sort of talk! This game will get spoiled!"

The breakfast was served. The waiter left the room with the urchin, and they took care to close the door behind them. Mademoiselle Chichette did not wait for Chérubin to escort her to the table; forgetting all the lessons she had had in behaving like a comme il faut person, she ran and took her seat in front of one of the covers, crying:

"Let's eat! let's eat! Oysters! ah! that's good!"

"She seems to be very hungry!" thought Chérubin, as he took his seat at the table. And he made haste to supply the young woman with oysters; but she did not wait for him to select them for her; she put them out of sight with wonderful rapidity, then held out her glass, saying:

"White wine, please; I'm very fond of white wine too."

Chérubin filled her glass with a white wine from a bottle which had been supplied with a long cork, to give it the appearance of sauterne; but it looked as if it were not drinkable with anything but oysters.

The young man considered that they were very badly served, generally speaking: the plates were the commonest china, the covers had not the ring of silverware, and the linen was very far from being fine. The wine, too, despite its yellow seal, seemed to him decidedly poor; but his conquest thought it delicious; she swallowed oysters, emptied her glass, called for more oysters and held out her glass to be filled, without any perceptible interval. Chérubin could not keep up with her; not until there were no more oysters on the table did Mademoiselle Chichette conclude to make a little pause.

"I will call the little concierge and tell him to take these things away," said Chérubin.

"No, no, I'll take 'em away myself!" replied Chichette; she rose, and with a turn of the hand cleared the table of plates and shells, and brought two of the covered dishes. The young man tried in vain to prevent the lady from performing that task; she would not listen to him, and did not resume her seat until it was all done.

"Mon Dieu! how it distresses me to see you take all this trouble, madame la comtesse!" said Chérubin; "but you seem to have been brought up to household duties. In Poland, young ladies receive a less frivolous education, I see, than in France; and your noble parents did not disdain to teach you these little domestic details. They are dead, doubtless—your noble parents?"

"Yes, yes! Let's talk about something else! Let's see what's in this dish. Ah! how good it smells! It's rabbit! Oh! I'm so fond of rabbit!"

Chérubin did not fully agree with his inamorata; he did not like rabbit himself, and he found that the breakfast which had been ordered for him did not at all resemble what he ordinarily ate at restaurants in Paris. But his companion was much less particular than he; she helped herself to the rabbit and seemed to enjoy it hugely; she even exclaimed from time to time:

"It's mighty well fricasseed!"

Chérubin offered her some wine with a different seal. Chichette drank red as well as white, then uncovered another dish, and shouted, leaping up and down in her chair:

"Ah! chowder! Oh! I'm glad of that! I'm so fond of chowder!"

"It seems to me that she's fond of everything!" thought Chérubin; "she certainly has been very well brought up; she doesn't play the prude!"

Chichette voted the chowder delicious; she helped herself several times without waiting for Chérubin to offer it; she was particularly enthusiastic over the sauce; finally she began to lick her plate, unwilling apparently to leave the least particle of the sauce which she liked so much.

The young man was thunderstruck when he saw the Comtesse de Globeska put her plate to her mouth and run her tongue over it; but he concluded that custom in Poland permitted such behavior. When Chichette noticed that her companion was watching her, she realized that she had made a blunder, and instantly replaced her plate on the table, saying:

"Oh! that was just a joke! I won't ever do it again! But let's see what's under that other cover."

Chichette uncovered the last dish, which contained fried fish. She uttered a joyful exclamation:

"Ah! gudgeons! fried gudgeons! Oh! I'm so fond of fried fish!"

"I am delighted, madame, that you find all these things to your taste," said Chérubin, serving his charmer to gudgeons; "but really you are not hard to suit; to me it seems that our breakfast is not worthy of you. Evidently there are no good restaurants in this quarter."

"Oh, yes, yes! at La Courtille."

"At La Courtille! I don't know that place; did your husband take you there to dinner sometimes?"

"My husband! Oh! let's talk about something else. I'd like something to drink; gudgeons make you thirsty in a minute."

Chérubin hastened to supply his guest with a wine decorated with a different seal, which she drank and declared excellent. The young man would have liked to lead the conversation back to his love, but his conquest was so busily engaged in eating and drinking that he dared not divert her from an occupation in which she seemed to take so much pleasure; and then he recalled his breakfast with Madame Célival and said to himself:

"I ate heartily to drive away my bashfulness. Perhaps this pretty Pole is doing the same; but God grant that she doesn't end as I did!"

When there was no more fish, they passed to the dessert, which was very modest, consisting only of biscuit, cheese and dried fruit. Again Chérubin anathematized the restaurant keeper; but Chichette continued to declare everything excellent; she stuffed herself with figs, raisins, and biscuit; she drank several glasses in succession to wash it all down; and at last she stopped eating and leaned against the back of her chair.

"It's strange," she said, "but I'm not a bit hungry now."

"It would be much stranger if she were!" thought the young man, as he moved away from the table in order to approach his companion.

Having placed his chair close beside Chichette's, he ventured to take her hand.

"How fortunate I am," he said in a hesitating tone, "to be—to be with you! What a lucky chance it was that led me to the theatre where you were; for, but for that, I should never have met you; and yet, my friend, the gentleman who was with me that evening says that we were born for each other.—Do you think that, madame?"

Chichette rose hurriedly, saying:

"I am rather full; it's funny, for I didn't eat very much."

She walked several times around the room. Chérubin went to her and said:

"Do you feel ill?"

"Oh, no! it will pass off."

Chichette sat down again, not on her chair, but on an old couch, covered with spots, the cushions of which looked as if they were stuffed with chips. The girl stretched herself out on it, however.

"I say, this is mighty comfortable," she said.

Chérubin gazed amorously at her and cried:

"Oh, yes! there certainly was sympathetic attraction in our meeting. My tutor, Monsieur Gérondif, explained it to me once. He took a little piece of agate, rubbed it hard on his coat sleeve, then held it toward a straw, and the straw instantly jumped at the stone and clung to it.—'Thus the magnet attracts iron,' said my tutor; 'thus sympathy draws together two hearts that were made to love and understand each other.'—Ah! madame, I am not a Pole, but I love you as dearly—more dearly, perhaps; for my inexperienced heart feels a craving for love, and if—and if——"

Chérubin paused, because it seemed to him that his words were accompanied by a dull, rumbling sound. That sound came from the couch. He had noticed that his pretty companion closed her eyes while he was speaking, but he supposed that it was from modesty. However, desirous to learn the cause of the noise he heard, he approached the young woman and saw with surprise that she was not only asleep, but was snoring heavily.

The unfortunate lover gazed for some time at his sleeping enslaver; but the snoring became louder with every instant; ere long it was like the breath of a forge bellows, and Chérubin gradually drew away; he felt that his amorous desires were vanishing; for a woman who is snoring like a Swiss inspires infinitely less passion than one whose breathing is soft and light.

Chérubin seated himself on a chair.

"She is asleep," he said to himself; "she is even snoring. Evidently my remarks did not interest her much, as she went right off to sleep while she was listening to me! It's very strange! This young woman has such manners and uses such language—If Daréna hadn't assured me that she was a Polish countess, I should have thought her something very different. The idea of going to sleep while I was talking to her about my love! If that's the way she is mad over me!—Great heaven! what snoring! Jacquinot used to snore, but not so loud as that. Perhaps I ought to wake her—and kiss her; but she is sleeping so soundly, it would be too bad. And then, I believe that listening to that monotonous noise is putting me to sleep too."

Chérubin dropped his head on the back of his chair; he closed his eyes, and in a moment, he was in the same condition as Mademoiselle Chichette, except that he did not snore.

Let us leave the young couple asleep, and see what the engineers of this whole intrigue were doing.

On leaving Chérubin, Daréna had gone in search of his friend Poterne, who, still dressed as a Polish count, was waiting for him at a restaurant in Ménilmontant. The two gentlemen sat down to breakfast and discussed their plot.

"It goes as if it were on wheels," said Daréna. "Chérubin is now with the girl, whom he thinks that I kidnapped for him! I trust that Chichette won't make any slips of the tongue. But no matter! with that accent of hers, anything will go; and besides, a lover never pays any attention to idioms!"

"Was my little Bruno at his post?"

"Yes; he is supposed to be the concierge's son. That boy has the look of a famous scamp."

"He has a lot of intelligence; he'll go a long way!"

"So I believe."

"Besides, for the last act of our comedy, it will be better to have nobody there but a boy, who won't interfere with us at all. And then, too, it will be much more probable that I was able to force my way into the house, if there's nobody but a boy to guard it; for we must strike the great blow now. A few thousand-franc notes, by the way, are all right; but they're gone too soon. We have an opportunity to obtain a good round sum and we mustn't let it slip; it won't come again."

"You are perfectly right, Poterne. What we are going to do to-day is not strictly honorable; but, after all, the little fellow is rich; sixty thousand francs won't ruin him."

"You don't want me to ask for more?"

"Oh, no! we mustn't flay him. It's understood then—in two hours you will go to the house."

"Why not earlier?"

"My dear Poterne, how impatient you are! we must give the lovers time to breakfast and to abandon themselves to the joys of love. Deuce take it! everybody must amuse himself, after all; and consider, Poterne, that by leaving them together longer, you will inevitably take them *in flagrante delicto!* That is much the shrewder way. You are supposed to be the husband; your wife has been spirited away, and you find her in her ravisher's arms; you bellow and roar and swear that you will kill them both—your wife especially! Chérubin pleads for mercy for her, and you refuse to accord it unless he signs notes of hand for sixty thousand francs.—You have some stamped paper, haven't you?"

"Oh! I have all that I need. But suppose the young marquis defends himself, suppose he refuses to sign?"

"Nonsense! a mere boy! You must threaten him with prosecution for abducting your wife; you will have your dagger, and you can still insist on killing her; Chérubin is too generous not to try to save her."

"I agree with you there."

"In all this, Monsieur Poterne, take good care not to hurt anybody! Your dagger isn't sharp, I trust?"

"Oh, no! there's no danger."

"And when you speak, assume some kind of an accent, so that he won't recognize you."

"I will be careful, and I will do a great deal in pantomime."

Everything being arranged, the gentlemen breakfasted and conversed at great length; ordered a pipe and cigars, and smoked to pass the time away.

More than two hours passed. Poterne replaced his green spectacles on his nose, saying:

"Now I can go and finish up our business."

He rose; Daréna did the same.

"Yes, it is time; let us go."

"But I don't need you," said Poterne; "besides, you mustn't go into the house with me, it would be imprudent. If Chérubin should see you, he would call on you to help him."

"I know all that, you old sharper; but you don't imagine, I presume, that I am going to let you go off all alone with notes for sixty thousand francs in your pocket? No, my dear fellow, I love you too dearly to lose sight of you. I propose to watch you into the house; I know that it has but one door; I shall keep my eye on that door, and if it should occur to you to run away too fast, I promise you that you will soon be overtaken."

"Oh! monsieur le comte! you have suspicions that hurt me terribly!"

"Why, no, it's simply *savoir-vivre*, it's the way of the world, that's all! Off we go."

The two worthies passed the city wall to the outer boulevards, and walked toward Barrière de la Chopinette. When they were within three hundred feet of the house where he had left Chérubin, Daréna stopped and said to his companion:

"Now, go on alone, illustrious Poterne, and manage the business gracefully; remember that the whole thing must be carried through with the courtesy and formality which betray men of breeding."

Poterne went on to the house and knocked softly at the door, which Bruno opened.

"Are they upstairs?" queried Poterne in a low voice.

"Yes."

"Have they had their breakfast?"

"It went up more'n two hours ago."

"And they haven't called since?"

"Not a call; and they don't even make any noise—you can't hear 'em move."

"All right."

Poterne pulled his enormous hat over his eyes, made sure that his spectacles were secure, stuffed bunches of flax into his mouth to fill out his cheeks, and walked toward the stairs. He stole cautiously up, reached the door, saw the key outside, and said to himself:

"How imprudent lovers are! what a childish trick!"

He turned the knob softly, then rushed into the room, shouting:

"Ah! traitor! guilty wife! I have caught you! You must die!"

Poterne expected shrieks of despair, as he had arranged with Chichette; but, hearing nothing at all, he walked farther into the room and was thunderstruck to see the lovers sound asleep at an extremely respectful distance from each other.

"Sapristi!" said Poterne to himself; "and I hoped to catch 'em in flagrante —as monsieur le comte said. They are amusing themselves by sleeping! If that's the way the young man makes love! Chichette must have made some stupid blunder. But no matter! I must act; besides, I surprise them together, that's the main thing; and if they're asleep, it's because it suits them to sleep."

Thereupon Poterne began to rush about the room with shrieks and imprecations. He pulled Chichette's ear and she awoke; he pinched her arm and she shrieked with him. Chérubin opened his eyes and saw that man, whom he recognized as the Comte de Globeski, storming and blaspheming and drawing from his breast a sort of dagger with which he threatened the young woman. Chérubin realized at once that his charmer's husband had run them to earth. He trembled and turned pale, and faltered:

"O mon Dieu! we are lost!—Don't kill her, monsieur, I entreat you! Kill me rather—although I have respected your wife's honor."

"Yes, yes, I will have my revenge, *per Diou!* Bigre! Ah! you think, villain, to steal my wife from me!" screamed Poterne, stamping on the floor. "*Tarteiff sacre mein Herr!* On the high road—stop my cab—no, my carriage.—Ah! madame, you shall die by my hand—on the honor of a Polish count!"

Chichette did not seem greatly alarmed; she continued to yawn and rub her eyes; Poterne passed her and pinched her with more force; whereupon she gave a loud yell and exclaimed:

"Oh! how stupid that is! I don't want you to do such things to me!"

Poterne began to roar so that Chérubin might not hear what Chichette said. He brandished his dagger with one hand, while with the other he stuffed the flax back into his mouth, whence it had almost escaped. But Chérubin had lost his head; the presence of that man, whose wife he believed that he had abducted, his outcries, his oaths, and the dagger he was brandishing, terrified the young man beyond words. Poterne, seeing that he was in a condition to submit to whatever terms he might impose, took the notes from his pocket, placed them on the table, found a pen and inkstand and presented them to Chérubin.

"If you wish to save this guilty woman, god dem!" he said, "there is only one way to appease my wrath."

"Oh! speak, monsieur, command—All you choose."

"Fill out these notes of hand—here are four of them—make them twenty-five thousand francs each. *Per Diou!* that is too *poco!*"

"Notes of hand—for a hundred thousand francs?"

"Yes, signor."

"Oh! you want me to——"

"If you hesitate, sapermann! I will kill this guilty wife of mine, I will kill you, I will kill everyone in the house—fichtre!—and then myself."

"Oh! no, no, I do not hesitate, monsieur. I will make them for whatever sums you say."

"Good! then you will make them for thirty thousand francs each.—Come! write and sign—*per Dio!*"

Chérubin seated himself at the table; he took the pen in his trembling hand and cast a sorrowful glance at his conquest, who had thrown herself on the couch, where he believed that she had swooned, whereas she was simply trying to go to sleep again. But Poterne returned to his side, ground his teeth and swore blood-curdling oaths. The young lover at once began to write; he had already filled out the body of one note, and was about to sign it, when they heard a loud noise below; then steps rapidly ascended the stairs, the door was thrown open, and Monfréville appeared, followed by old Jasmin, who uttered a cry of joy at sight of his master.

"Ah! here he is!" he cried; "God be praised! they have not destroyed him!"

Chérubin felt as if he were born again when he saw his friend; he threw himself into his arms, while Monfréville, observing his confusion and bewilderment and pallor, asked him:

"Great God! my dear fellow, what are you doing here, in this house—this den of thieves, to which a little rascal refused to admit me?"

"Ah! my friend, the fact is that—that I have been very guilty!" Chérubin replied in a voice broken by sobs. "I abducted madame—this gentleman's wife; that is to say, it wasn't I who did it—Daréna abducted her for me. Monsieur is a Polish count, and he insisted that I should give him my notes for a hundred and twenty thousand francs, or else he would kill his wife! Ah! how glad I am to see you!"

While Chérubin was speaking, Poterne, who was very ill at ease, tried to sidle toward the door; but Jasmin had stationed himself in front of it, after taking pains to lock it.

As he listened to his young friend, Monfréville looked about the room in keen scrutiny. He examined Mademoiselle Chichette and the supposititious outraged husband, who acted as if he wished to crawl under the table. Chérubin had no sooner finished speaking than Monfréville ran up to Poterne, snatched off his hat and spectacles, and raised his cane threateningly.

"This creature a Polish count!" he exclaimed; "why, it's that vile Poterne, the agent of that contemptible knave Daréna! They plotted together this infamous scheme to extort money from you!—Ah! I am strongly tempted to break my cane over this cur's shoulders!"

"Poterne!" cried Chérubin; "is it possible? Poterne!"

"Why, yes," said Jasmin, "it's the dealer in preserves and dogs and turtles. Ah! my dear master, I suspected that they meant to take you in again; and that that man who called me an old donkey was fixing up some treacherous scheme to catch you."

When he saw Monfréville's cane in the air, Poterne fell on his knees.

"Mercy, monsieur," he faltered, "all this was only a joke—nothing else; it was a comedy!"

"A jest, you villain! But your notes of hand were properly stamped! Oh! we know now what you are capable of, you and your worthy friend, Comte Daréna, who has fallen low enough now to blush at nothing, and in whose eyes all methods of procuring money are all right. We agree not to treat you as you deserve. Go and join your confederate, and tell him that this young man is able now to judge him as he is, and that if he should ever presume to show his face at the hôtel de Grandvilain, the servants will be instructed to turn him out."

"Yes, indeed, I will undertake to do it!" said Jasmin. "He called me an old ruin too! but an honest ruin is worth more than a sharper in perfect repair."

Monsieur Poterne did not wait to hear any more; he picked up his hat and spectacles, hastily opened the door, and fled; but he was not so quick that he did not receive the toe of Jasmin's boot in his posterior; and the old servant said to him at the same time: "There, you thief; take that for your preserves!"

Monfréville walked toward Chichette, who had remained on the couch, without speaking or moving; he could not help smiling at her expression.

"And you, madame la comtesse," he said, "in what shop do you usually work?"

"I make Italian straw hats on Rue de Grenétat. It wasn't my fault; they promised me a lot of money if I'd make believe I was monsieur's wife; and I consented so I could put it by and marry my little pays."

Mademoiselle Chichette drew her handkerchief and looked as if she were going to weep; but Monfréville reassured her by saying:

"I have nothing against you, my girl; don't cry, and go back to your Italian straw hats. But believe me, it is much better for one in your trade to dance the cancan than to play the great lady."

Mademoiselle Chichette blew her nose, made several curtsies, then left the room with a shamefaced air, not venturing to glance at Chérubin.

"And now, my friend," said Monfréville to the young marquis, "I think that we too may quit this wretched barrack. I believe that there is nothing to detain us here longer."

"Oh, no! and I am so happy, my dear Monfréville, after having such a terrible fright! I will tell you the whole story; but first tell me how you succeeded in learning that I was here, and how you happened to arrive so opportunely."

"That's easily done; do you see that cab at the door?"

"Yes."

"It's the same one that brought you here. I called at your house after you left; I found Jasmin very uneasy; he told me that you had gone away in a cab with Daréna, whose frequent visits of late, together with his air of mystery, had aroused my suspicions! I asked Jasmin if he had called the carriage himself, and when he said yes, I asked him to take me to the cabstand. There we waited more than two hours for your cab to return. It appeared at last. I gave the driver twenty francs and told him to take us to the place to which he had taken you; he asked nothing better, and he brought us to this house. Knaves are very shrewd, my dear boy, but luckily there is a concealed power shrewder than they, who defeats the most cunningly devised schemes at the moment when their authors deem themselves most certain of impunity. Some call that power Providence, others chance, fatality, destiny, luck. I don't know what name to give it, but I bow before it and am only too glad to believe that, if there are people here on earth inclined to do evil, there is a power on high, ever on the watch to prevent or repair it."

Chérubin pressed Monfréville's hand affectionately; then they left the house on the outer boulevard, which even little Bruno had abandoned, for they saw no sign of anybody. They entered the cab with Jasmin, upon whom they were almost obliged to use force, because the old fellow insisted on riding behind.

When they reached home, Chérubin told Monfréville how Daréna had managed the affair, and how he had urged him above all things to preserve the most absolute secrecy about it.

"I am not surprised," said Monfréville, "that he urged you not to mention it to me; he knew that I would not be taken in by the story of a Polish countess who was anxious to be abducted by a young man whom she had seen just once, at the theatre."

"He said that you set yourself up now as a man of strict virtue, to make people forget your former conduct; he declared that you used to be famous for your love-affairs, your conquests, and that your principles then were much less severe than they are to-day.—Forgive me—I am only repeating what he said."

Monfréville's brow had grown dark; his face wore an expression of deep sorrow, and he was silent for some time. At last, fixing his eyes upon Chérubin's, he said in a melancholy tone:

"It is true, my friend, that in my youth I did many foolish things, and I have some serious faults with which to reproach myself. But I was so cruelly punished that I was cured in good season. That does not prevent me from being indulgent to others, because I am well aware that it is a part of our nature to be subject to passions and weakness, and to be led astray by them sometimes. Some day, Chérubin, I will tell you a story of my young days, which has had an influence on my whole life. You will see that these love-affairs, which we treat so cavalierly at twenty, sometimes have very bitter results."

"Thus far," said Chérubin, with a sigh, "I haven't been lucky in my love-affairs, and my amorous adventures have not afforded me much enjoyment!"

XXV

A GRAND DINNER

After Monsieur de Noirmont expressed in such decided terms his resolution with respect to Louise, Ernestine's mother said not a word to indicate that she still thought of dismissing the young woman; on the contrary it seemed that, having made up her mind to submit to her husband's desire, Madame de Noirmont had recovered from her apparent prejudice against Louise. She still treated her with a coldness which sometimes approached severity; but the tone of her voice, sharp and curt at first, often softened so far as to seem almost affectionate. One would have said that she was vanquished by the charm with which the girl's whole personality was instinct, by her timid obedience, by the eagerness with which she waited on her mistress, so that the latter was sometimes, in spite of herself, drawn on to love her.

Louise did not know that Madame de Noirmont had thought of sending her away. Ernestine and her father alone were aware of the circumstance, and the former, when she learned that her mother's determination would not be carried out, had concluded that it would be useless to mention it to Louise, that it would grieve her to learn that she was so far from having succeeded in winning her mistress's favor by her zeal, that that mistress had intended to dismiss her. As for Monsieur de Noirmont, after making his wishes known, he was not the man to mention such domestic matters to anybody on earth.

But a thing that was easily noticed, and that Louise saw, together with all the rest of the household, was that Madame de Noirmont became more depressed and gloomy every day. A smile never appeared on her lips; she avoided society; visits annoyed her and were a burden to her; spending almost all the time in her apartment, she ordered the servants to say that she was out, or not feeling well, so that she might not be disturbed in her solitude; even her daughter's presence seemed sometimes to oppress and irritate her. The sweet-tempered Ernestine, who had done nothing to forfeit her mother's affection, was sometimes very much distressed at being treated so coldly by her; when she went to Madame de Noirmont, to kiss her, she would push her away impatiently, or receive with listless indifference the marks of her affection; thereupon the girl would turn away, forcing back the tears which rose to her eyes, but which she would not allow to appear, for fear of angering her mother.

Louise, seeing her young mistress furtively wipe her eyes, would say to her:

"You are unhappy, mademoiselle, and I am very sure that it's because your mamma hasn't kissed you for some time past."

Whereupon Ernestine would reply, with a deep sigh:

"That is true; I don't know what mamma can have against me; it's of no use for me to try to think what I can have done to displease her; I can't remember anything. But for some time she hasn't called me her dear child or taken me in her arms. It isn't possible, though, that she doesn't love me, is it, Louise? It's her health that makes her like this; her nerves are out of order; she doesn't complain, but I am perfectly sure that she is sick; besides, anyone can see that she has changed a great deal lately."

"That is true, mademoiselle, I have noticed it too. Yes, you are right, it's because madame isn't well that she is more melancholy and doesn't caress you so much. But why don't you send for the doctor?"

"Several times I have said to mamma: 'You are pale, you must be suffering; you ought to send for Monsieur Derbaut, our doctor;' but mamma always answers in a provoked tone: 'Nothing's the matter with me; it's useless to have the doctor, I don't need him.'"

The two girls exchanged their ideas thus, seeking a way to make themselves useful, one to her mother, the other to her mistress; for they both loved Madame de Noirmont, despite the harshness and capriciousness of her temper, which so often made her unjust; Ernestine loved her with all the clinging affection of a child who refuses to see her mother's faults; Louise with a respectful devotion which would have led her joyfully to undertake the most painful task, if it would have earned her a smile from her mistress.

But Madame de Noirmont seemed carefully to avoid giving Louise any opportunity to wait upon her; only in her husband's presence, and when it was impossible for her to do otherwise, would she give her an order or two, or take something from her hand. The young lady's maid, who would gladly have anticipated her mistress's slightest wish, sometimes followed her with her eyes, in the hope of making herself useful to her; but if Madame de Noirmont caught Louise's glance fastened upon her, her own expression would become sterner, and she would instantly motion to her to leave the room.

One day, madame was in her room, as usual, holding a book of which she read very little, because her thoughts absorbed her so completely that she could give no attention to anything else. Ernestine was seated at a little distance, embroidering, and from time to time glancing furtively at her mother, in the hope of meeting her eyes and of obtaining from her a smile, which had become a very infrequent favor. Madame de Noirmont turned to her and said, holding out the book:

"Ernestine, bring me the second volume of this; you will find it in the library, on the second shelf at the left."

The girl rose quickly, took the book and left the room, eager to obey her mother. Having found the volume for which Madame de Noirmont had asked her, she was about to take it to her, when she found her drawing-master, who had just arrived, waiting for her in the salon. Ernestine gave Louise the book and told her to take it to her mother; then she sat down by her teacher to take her lesson.

Louise took the book and went to her mistress's room. When she was about to turn the knob, she felt that she was trembling; she was so afraid of offending Madame de Noirmont, who had not sent her on that errand. However, she went in.

Madame de Noirmont was seated, her head fallen forward on her breast. She did not raise her eyes when she heard the door open, for she had no doubt that it was Ernestine; and Louise reached her side and handed her the book without daring to utter a word.

But at that moment, impelled by an outburst of maternal affection, she took the hand that offered the book and squeezed it in her own, murmuring:

"My poor love, you must have thought me most unjust to you of late, and you think perhaps that I no longer love you! Do not think that, my child; I still love you as dearly as I ever did; but you cannot understand what is taking place in my heart, and what I suffer. No, you will never know——"

At that moment she raised her head and drew the girl toward her, meaning to kiss her. Not until then did she recognize Louise. She was speechless and motionless with surprise; a terrified expression appeared on her face, from which all the blood receded, and she raised her eyes to heaven, faltering:

"O mon Dieu! and I called her my child!"

"Forgive me, madame, forgive me," murmured Louise, terribly alarmed at her mistress's condition. "It was not my fault, it was mademoiselle who sent ——"

Madame de Noirmont struggled to master her emotion, and rejoined in a sharp, stern tone:

"Why did you come into my room? Did I call you? Why are you here? To try to surprise my thoughts, my secrets?"

"O madame—mon Dieu! can you believe it?"

"Have I not constantly found your eyes fastened on me of late, mademoiselle—following, watching my slightest movements? What makes you act so? Have you some hidden motive? Come, speak, mademoiselle."

"If I have offended you, madame, it was entirely without intention; if my eyes have sometimes rested on you, it is because I would have been happy to anticipate some wish of yours, to do something that would please you, to earn a word or a kind look from you; that was my motive, when I ventured to look at you. And then too it was a joy to me, madame; but I will do without it, since you forbid it."

Louise bent her head before her mistress; she was almost on her knees, and her voice trembled so that she could hardly finish what she was saying.

Madame de Noirmont seemed deeply moved; one would have said that a conflict was raging in the depths of her heart; she rose, paced the floor, walked away from Louise, then toward her. She gazed at her for a long, very long time, but not with a stern expression; her eyes were filled with tears. Suddenly she ran to the girl, who had remained on the same spot, with downcast eyes and afraid to take a step; she took her hand and drew her toward her—but almost instantly pushed her away again, saying sharply:

"Go, mademoiselle, go; I have no further need of you."

Louise obeyed. She left the room, saying to herself:

"Mon Dieu! what is the matter with her, and what have I done to her?"

A week after this incident, Monsieur de Noirmont informed his wife that he proposed to give a great dinner. He named the persons whom he had invited, fifteen in number, and added:

"I had an idea of inviting young Marquis Chérubin de Grandvilain too; but I asked him to come to see me, and he has never come; and so, as he has not shown the slightest desire to associate with an old friend of his father, we will not have him."

Madame de Noirmont could not conceal the annoyance which the announcement of that function caused her. But Monsieur de Noirmont continued in a very curt tone:

"Really, madame, if I should leave you to follow your own desires, we should have no company, we should live like owls. I am not a fool—a devotee of pleasure; but still, I don't propose to live like a hermit. Besides, madame, we have a daughter, and it is our duty to think about her welfare; before long it will be time to think of marrying her, of finding a suitable match for her; meanwhile we must not keep her sequestered from society, of which she is destined to be an ornament some day. Poor Ernestine! you refuse every opportunity that offers to take her to balls or receptions or concerts. You are ill, you say. I cannot compel you to go out, madame; but, as your health confines you constantly to the house, we will entertain; such is my present determination, madame."

Madame de Noirmont made no observation, for she was well aware that as soon as her husband had made up his mind to do a thing, nothing could divert him from his resolution; and Monsieur de Noirmont left her, having requested her to give the necessary orders so that everything might be ready for the dinner, which was appointed for the Thursday following.

Madame de Noirmont resigned herself to the inevitable; when the day drew near, she gave her orders and superintended the preparations for the banquet. Ernestine, when she learned that they were to entertain many guests and give a grand dinner, rejoiced greatly and looked forward to it with the keenest pleasure. Pleasures and amusements had become so rare in her life, that every departure from the customary monotony seemed a blessing. Louise hoped that the dinner would afford her an opportunity to make herself useful, to display her zeal, and she shared her young mistress's childlike joy.

At last the day came when the interior of that house, ordinarily so placid, was to echo with the voices of a numerous company. From early morning there was a great commotion in the Noirmont mansion; the master of the house alone spent the day as usual, working tranquilly in his study, awaiting the hour when the guests were to arrive; but Madame de Noirmont issued orders, overlooked the preparations, made sure that everything that she had ordered was at hand. Ernestine followed her mother about, dancing and laughing, anticipating great pleasure for that day.

"You must make yourself very lovely for the dinner," she said to Louise, "because you are to wait at table with Comtois; that is the custom when we have company."

"Never fear, mademoiselle," replied Louise; "I don't know whether I shall be lovely, but I promise to do my best to wait at table well, so that madame your mother will be content with me."

But, a few moments before it was time for the guests to arrive, Madame de Noirmont said to her daughter:

"Ernestine, I don't want your maid to wait at table; tell her that she may remain in her room; we shall not need her."

Ernestine could not understand her mother's whim; she looked up at her and said hesitatingly:

"But, mamma, usually, when we have company—you know——"

"I do not ask for your comments, my child; do what I tell you."

Ernestine obeyed her mother; she went sadly to Louise's room, where she found her finishing her toilet.

"Do you like me in this dress, mademoiselle?" inquired Louise; "is it suited to my position?"

"Oh! yes, yes, my poor Louise, you look very pretty!" replied Ernestine, heaving a deep sigh; "but it was not worth while to take so much pains with your toilet, for mamma doesn't want you to wait at table; she says that you can stay in your room."

Louise's face expressed the disappointment caused by that command;

however, she did not indulge in a single murmur.

"I will obey, mademoiselle," she replied; "doubtless madame your mother has good reasons for wishing me not to do it. Ala! I am afraid that I can guess them: she doesn't like to see me; my presence annoys her; I will obey, she shall not see me."

Ernestine did not feel equal to contradicting her; for, knowing that her mother had once intended to dismiss Louise, she believed that the girl had guessed aright. She simply pressed her hand, then left her, because the time had come when the guests would probably begin to arrive.

Monsieur de Noirmont had invited more men than ladies; however, the wife of a certain advocate arrived with her husband; she was a tall, large woman, of much pretension, very fond of listening to herself talk, but, to balance matters, little inclined to listen to others.

Another lady, young and rosy and affable, formed a striking contrast to the first; she was the wife of a solicitor, who had just married in order to pay for his office. The advocate had married the tall lady so that he could afford to wait for clients. In society nowadays a marriage is a matter of business, seldom of sympathetic sentiments.

A few serious men, two young exquisites, and Monsieur Trichet, whom we have met before at Madame Célival's, completed the party. Monsieur de Noirmont received his guests with his customary phlegmatic manner. Madame de Noirmont, who had made the best of it and had resigned herself to receive all that company, tried not to allow her ennui to appear; she did the honors of her salon with much grace; she forced herself to smile; she was able, when she chose, to address a pleasant word to each guest; and they were all the more pleased because they were not used to it.

Ernestine recovered her spirits when she saw that her mother seemed to have recovered hers; at her age small vexations are soon forgotten; she loved company, and of late she had had so few opportunities to enjoy herself, that she joyfully seized every one that presented itself. As the young lady of the house, she listened to those complimentary remarks which it is not safe to believe, but which are always pleasant to the ear. They said that she had grown and improved; they did not say it to her, but they said it to her parents loud enough for her to hear. Madame de Noirmont listened indifferently to the compliments paid to her daughter, but Monsieur de Noirmont was enchanted by them.

Monsieur Trichet was the same as always: talking all the time, determined to know everything, taking part in every conversation, and with his ear always on the alert to hear what was being said in all the corners of the salon; that man was kept very busy in company.

Comtois announced that dinner was served, and the whole company adjourned to the dining-room. They took their seats and began to eat, with the silence of good breeding, which is sometimes maintained until the dessert.

The first course was still in progress when Monsieur de Noirmont, not being served quickly enough, looked about the room and said to Comtois:

"Where is the maid? why is she not assisting you? I am not surprised that the service is so slow! What is she doing, pray? Didn't you tell her that she was to wait at table?"

Comtois was sadly embarrassed; when he called Louise, she told him what orders she had received from her mistress. He twisted his tongue about, and answered half audibly:

"Monsieur—I—madame said that—that it was unnecessary for——"

Monsieur de Noirmont did not allow Comtois to finish his sentence; he rejoined shortly:

"Tell Louise to come at once; she must help you serve."

Comtois did not wait for the order to be repeated, especially as he was very glad, in the bottom of his heart, to have the girl assist him.

Madame de Noirmont looked at her plate and turned ghastly pale; Ernestine gazed anxiously from her father to her mother; and Monsieur Trichet, who had comments to make on everything, exclaimed:

"Ah! so you have a lady's maid who doesn't want to serve at table? You are perfectly right to compel her to do it. Servants are amazing nowadays! If we listened to them they would do nothing at all, and we should pay them high wages! I am curious to see your lady's maid."

Louise's arrival put an end to these remarks. The girl was much embarrassed when she received the order sent through Comtois; she hesitated to follow him at first, but Comtois said:

"You must come, mademoiselle; monsieur says so, and when he gives an order, you must obey."

So Louise decided to go with the valet. The thought that she was going to vex her mistress by obeying her master's commands caused her very great distress; so that she entered the room with downcast eyes and with her cheeks flushing hotly. But she was all the prettier so, and most of the guests seemed impressed by her beauty.

"Upon my word," said Monsieur Trichet, "this girl would have done very wrong not to show herself! I have seen few servants so pretty.—What is that you are saying, Monsieur Dernange? Oh! I hear you: you said: 'A Greek profile.'—True, very like it. But Greek or not, it is very distinguished for the profile of a lady's maid."

The two young men did not make their reflections aloud, like Monsieur Trichet, but they seemed not to weary of gazing at Louise, and they were delighted to have their plates changed by her.

The tall, pretentious lady cast a disdainful glance at Louise and muttered:

"I cannot understand how anyone can call a servant pretty!"

"That girl is fascinating!" cried the other lady; "and she has such a modest air! Everything about her speaks in her favor."

"Oho!" said Monsieur Trichet, "it isn't safe to trust to such airs; they're often very deceptive. I know what I am talking about; I have had two hundred maids, and they have all stolen from me."

Madame de Noirmont made no reply to all these reflections inspired by the sight of her pretty lady's maid. But it was plain that she was suffering, that she was holding herself back, that she was doing her utmost to appear calm and amiable as before.

Ernestine was no longer in a merry mood, for she saw that something was wrong with her mother.

As for Monsieur de Noirmont, content to be obeyed, he turned his attention to his guests and did not observe his wife's pallor.

The subject of conversation soon changed however, and Madame de Noirmont was able to breathe a little more freely.

Louise performed her duty as well as she could, lowering her eyes when she passed her mistress, not daring to look at her, and taking care never to stand opposite her.

But suddenly Chérubin's name fell on the girl's ear. Monsieur Trichet, speaking of a reception at the Comtesse de Valdieri's, observed:

"The young Marquis de Grandvilain was not there. I have noticed too that he doesn't go to Madame Célival's any more. That seems strange to me, for everybody knows that the little marquis was making love to those ladies; he is still too new at the game to conceal his feelings; he used to stare at them too much—it was absurd."

At that moment Louise had in her hands a plate of chicken with olives, which she had been told to carry to the advocate's tall wife. But when she heard Chérubin's name, Louise forgot what she was doing; she dropped the plate on the pretentious lady's shoulder, and a large portion of chicken with olives fell on that lady's dress.

"What a stupid idiot you are!" cried the tall lady, with a savage glance at Louise. "If you don't know how to pass a plate, you should stay in your kitchen."

Louise stood like a statue, confused and distressed. The men, thinking her prettier than ever, tried to excuse her; Ernestine rose hastily and wiped the lady's dress, which it did not even occur to Louise to do. As for Madame de Noirmont, when she heard Louise called stupid and an idiot, her eyebrows contracted and her eyes shot fire for an instant; she half rose, then fell back in her chair, as if she were dead. Monsieur Trichet, who was beside her, exclaimed:

"Madame de Noirmont is certainly ill.—Do you feel ill, madame?"

"It is nothing, I hope," said Madame de Noirmont, rising; "just an ill turn; I will go and take a breath of air."

Ernestine was already beside her mother; she supported her, gave her her arm, and they left the dining-room together.

This episode caused Louise's awkwardness to be forgotten, although the tall lady continued to grumble about her dress; but nobody seemed to listen to her. After ten minutes Madame de Noirmont returned to the table. She was still very pale, but she insisted that she no longer suffered. The dinner came to an end dismally enough; the accident that had happened to the mistress of the house had dispelled all merriment.

They returned to the salon. The men conversed among themselves, and the tall lady thought of nothing but her damaged gown. Madame de Noirmont forced herself to smile as she listened to Monsieur Trichet; Ernestine kept her eyes on her mother, and the young men looked frequently toward the door, disappointed that the pretty lady's maid did not appear again. A game of whist was organized, but it was not kept up very long, and the guests took their leave well before midnight, because Madame de Noirmont was ill and must need rest.

It was two hours after midnight. All the members of Monsieur de Noirmont's household had long since withdrawn to their apartments, and should have been buried in slumber. Louise, still excited by the emotions of the day, had just closed her eyes, thinking of Chérubin, who was said to have been in love with two women.

Suddenly someone opened the door of her room, and entered cautiously, holding a light. Louise opened her eyes and recognized Madame de Noirmont, in her night dress, as pale as she had been at dinner; she walked to the bed after pausing to listen and make sure that no one was following her.

"Mon Dieu! is it you, madame?" cried Louise; "can it be that you are ill? that you need my services?—I will get up at once."

"Stay where you are, and listen to me."

As she spoke, Madame de Noirmont went to the door and closed it, then returned to the bed, sat down beside it, took Louise's hand and pressed it in both of hers, saying in a broken voice:

"Louise, you must leave this house, unless you want me to die—to die of grief. Oh! my suffering has been horrible! and I feel that I shall not have the strength to endure it any longer."

"What! can it be that I am the cause of your suffering, madame? Indeed I will go; yes, be sure of it. Mon Dieu! if I had known it sooner, I would have gone long ago and spared you much annoyance. Forgive me; for, far from seeking to make you unhappy, I would give my life to prove my zealous attachment to you. But no matter—I will go."

"Poor Louise! then you do not hate me—me who have treated you so harshly, who have never said a kind or gentle word to you?"

"Hate you, madame? Oh! that doesn't seem possible to me; it seems to me that it is my duty to love you.—Oh! pardon—I forget that I am only a poor servant."

"A servant—you! Ah! that is what is killing me, that is what I cannot endure! You, a servant in my house! O my God! I was very guilty, I know, since Thou hast inflicted this punishment on me; but to-day it was too heavy. —Great heaven! what am I saying? I am losing my wits.—Louise, my poor child, you have believed that I detested you, that that was the reason why I was constantly trying to keep you away from me, have you not?—Ah! if you could have read in the depths of my heart!"

"Is it possible, madame, that you do not dislike me? Oh! I am so glad!"

"Listen to me, Louise. You ought not to be a servant; you ought to be rich and happy, poor girl! You have suffered enough for faults committed by others; your lot will soon be changed. Here, take this letter which I have just written, and hand it to the person whose name is on the envelope, to whom you will go at once on leaving here. I do not know where the—the person to whom I am sending you lives now, but you can learn by going to Monsieur Chérubin de Grandvilain's house; he is his friend, and he will tell you at once where he lives. You know Monsieur Chérubin's house, do you not?"

"Oh, yes! I have been there twice, madame.—And the person to whom I am to give this letter?"

"That person will—at least, I think so—restore you to your father."

"To my father! O my God! What, madame! I shall find my parents? Do you know them, madame?"

"Ask me nothing more, Louise; what I am doing now is a great deal. I swore that I would never write to this person; but since I have seen you, I have felt that it was wicked, very wicked, to deprive you of your father's caresses; for he will be happy to recover you! Oh, yes! I am sure that he will surround you with love and care."

"And my mother, madame—you say nothing of her? Shall I not see her too? Oh! it would be so sweet to me to hold her in my arms!"

"Your mother? Oh, no! that is impossible; your father will conceal her name from you—he must. If, however, he should disclose it, remember that a heedless word would kill her!—But I have said enough. To-morrow, at daybreak, before anyone in the house is up, you will go away; you promise me that, Louise?"

"Yes, madame, I promise."

"That is well; and now, kiss me."

"May I?"

Madame de Noirmont's only reply was to put her arms about Louise's waist, strain her to her heart, and hold her so a long time, covering her with kisses. The poor girl was so happy that she thought that she was dreaming, and she prayed heaven not to wake her.

But Madame de Noirmont, whose eyes were filled with tears, made a superhuman effort, and extricating herself from the arms that enlaced her, deposited one more kiss on the girl's forehead and hurriedly left the room, saying in a voice overflowing with affection:

"Do not forget anything of all that I have said to you!"

Louise lay in a sort of trance; the kisses she had received had made her know such unalloyed happiness that she tried to prolong it; she dared not reflect, or seek to solve the mystery of Madame de Noirmont's conduct; but she repeated again and again:

"She loves me! oh, yes! she loves me, for she held me to her heart a long while, and she said: 'Don't forget anything that I said to you!'—Ah! I shall never forget those words; I shall remember them all my life."

Louise did not close her eyes during the rest of the night. As soon as the day began to break, she rose, dressed hastily, made a bundle of her clothes, placed in her bosom the letter that Madame de Noirmont had given her, and, softly opening the door, left her room, stole noiselessly through several rooms to the staircase, and so down to the courtyard; she knocked on the concierge's window, he opened the gate, and at daybreak she stood in the street.

XXVI

FEAR

Since his adventure with Chichette Chichemann, Chérubin had been less quick to take fire; or, rather, he had begun to understand that what he had taken for love was simply those desires which the sight of a pretty woman arouses in a man's heart; desires which are certain to be renewed often in a wholly inexperienced heart, whose sensations have the charm of novelty.

But the checks he had met with in his amorous essays had made Chérubin even more shy and timid; instead of taking advantage of the lessons that he had received to bear himself more gallantly in a tête-à-tête, poor Chérubin was so afraid of being unfortunate or awkward again, that the bare idea of an assignation almost made him tremble. On the other hand, as love, at his age, is the first joy of life, the young marquis, not knowing how he could procure that joy, became sad and melancholy. At twenty years of age, with a noble name, a handsome fortune, with good looks and a fine figure; in a word, possessed of everything that is supposed to make a man happy, Chérubin was not happy; he lost his good spirits and even his fresh coloring. He no longer had that bright, ruddy complexion which people used to admire in him; for it is useless to try to conceal the fact that, while excessive dissipation sometimes destroys the health, excessive virtue may produce the same result; excess in anything is to be deplored.

The young marquis no longer visited the Comtesse de Valdieri, or Madame Célival, because the frigid greeting he received from those ladies was equivalent to a dismissal; but he sometimes met them in society. When he did, it seemed to him that all the ladies looked at him in a strange fashion, that they whispered together and even went so far as to laugh when he appeared. All this tormented and disturbed him; he told his troubles to his friend Monfréville.

"Do you suppose that that little countess and Madame Célival have been saying unkind things about me?" he said. "I don't know what I have done to them."

"That is just the reason!" replied Monfréville, with a smile. "I beg you, my young friend, do not persist in this apathy, which is ill-suited to your years. You have everything that a man needs, to be agreeable to the ladies; form other connections. Have three or four mistresses at once, deceive them all openly, and your reputation will soon be reëstablished."

"That is very easy for you to say, my dear Monfréville, but, since my misadventures, I am so afraid of being—er—awkward again with a woman, that it makes me shudder beforehand. It is enough to kill one with shame and despair! I prefer not to take the risk. And yet I feel that I am terribly bored."

"I can well believe it—to live without love, at your age! when one has not even the memory of his follies! that is perfectly absurd. But if you are afraid that you are not yet sufficiently enterprising with a great lady, why, my friend, make a beginning with grisettes and actresses. I assure you they will train you quite as well."

"Yes, I thought of that at first; and last week, happening to meet Malvina —you know, that lively little ballet girl?"

"Yes."

"Well, I spoke to her. At first she called me Monsieur Jack Frost; but when I told her that I wasn't as cold as she thought, she said: 'To make me believe that, you must prove it.' And she invited me again to breakfast with her—at six o'clock in the morning—and we appointed a day."

"Good! that is excellent!"

"Oh, yes! but the day came long ago, and I didn't go."

"Why not?"

"Because I reflected that I had no more love for Malvina than for the others, and that I should no doubt make as big a fool of myself with her as I had done at my previous tête-à-têtes."

"You were altogether wrong! your reasoning is ridiculous! The idea of reflecting about an amourette, a passing fancy! But stay—didn't you tell me once of a grisette, a girl who worked in a linen-draper's shop near by, and who used to ogle you? she even told you her name, I believe."

"Yes, my friend, that was little Célanire, with the fair hair and the nose *à la Roxelane.*"

"Well, there's your chance; ask Mademoiselle Célanire for a rendezvous. Judging from what you have told me, she won't refuse you."

"That is what I did, my friend. The day before yesterday I saw the young grisette in the street; when she found that I was walking behind her, she pretended to make a misstep; then she stopped and clung to me to keep from falling."

"That was very clever."

"So I thought; after that, we talked, and finally she agreed to meet me that evening on Boulevard du Château d'Eau, a long way from her quarter, for the express purpose of not meeting people who might recognize her."

"That was very prudent; grisettes think of everything. Well, how did matters go at that meeting?"

"Mon Dieu! my friend, I didn't go there either. As I was about to start, I made the same reflections that I had made concerning the little dancer. Then I was afraid and I stayed at home."

"Oh! this is too much, my poor Chérubin! If you give way to such terrors, there is no reason why you should not be bewildered by them all your life! In old times, the old women would have said that someone had cast a spell on you, and they would have sent you to see some famous exorcist. For, in the good old days, spells were cast and destroyed frequently; indeed, it was not uncommon to see prosecutions based upon such affairs, and to see the judges order an inspection, in order to make the man prove his innocence, who attempted to make so many honest people forfeit theirs. But those barbarous days have passed—for they really deserve to be so called. Now, we know no better sorcerer than a pretty woman to discover whether a man is in love or not. So that I persist in referring you to such a one."

Monfréville's words did not console Chérubin in the least; he continued in his state of depression and self torment; but one morning there came to his mind a thought that roused and revivified him: he thought of Gagny, of young Louise, of his kindhearted nurse, who loved him so dearly; it occurred to him to revisit his childhood home. In his melancholy and his ennui he remembered those who loved him; in the whirl of dissipation he had forgotten them! Such cases are too common; they do not speak well for our hearts, but why did Nature make us like that?

Chérubin said nothing to any of his household; he took neither Jasmin nor Gérondif, but ordered his cabriolet, bade his little groom climb up behind, and started, after obtaining minute directions as to the shortest way to Gagny.

With a good horse it is not a long drive. Chérubin arrived at Villemonble in a short time. His heart beat fast as he drove through the village, for he recognized the country where his childhood had been passed, and a large part of his adolescence. His heart was very full when he spied the first houses of Gagny; he felt such a thrill of pleasure, of happiness, as he had not known since he went to Paris, and he was amazed that he could have allowed so long a time to elapse without returning to the village.

He recognized the square, the guard house, and the steep street leading to his nurse's house; he urged his horse and drew rein at last in front of Nicole's door. It was only three years since he had left it, but it seemed to him a century, and he scrutinized everything about him to see if anything had changed.

He alighted from his carriage, crossed the yard where he had played so often, and hastily entered the room on the ground floor, where the family usually sat. Nicole was there, working, and Jacquinot asleep in a chair; nothing was changed; one person only was missing.

Nicole raised her eyes, then gave a shout. She gazed earnestly at the fashionably dressed young man who had entered the room; she was afraid that she was mistaken, she dared not believe that it was Chérubin. But he did not leave her long in uncertainty; he flew into her arms, crying:

"My nurse! my dear Nicole! Ah! how glad I am to see you again!"

"It's him! it's really him!" cried the peasant woman, who could hardly speak, she was so overcome by joy. "He has come to see us, so he still loves me, the dear boy! Forgive me for calling you that, monsieur le marquis, but habit is stronger than I am."

"Call me what you used to call me, dear Nicole. Do you suppose that that offends me? On the contrary, I insist upon it, I demand it."

"Oh! what joy!—Wake up, Jacquinot, my man, here's our *fieu* Chérubin come back, and in our house again."

Jacquinot rubbed his eyes and recognized the young marquis, but dared not offer him his hand. But Chérubin warmly grasped the peasant's rough and calloused hand. He, in his delight, ran off, as his custom was, to bring wine and glasses.

Chérubin seated himself beside Nicole; he kissed her again and again, then glanced about the room and said:

"What a pity that someone is missing! If Louise were here, my happiness would be complete. Is she still in Bretagne—a long way off? Doesn't she mean to return?"

"Oh, yes, my boy," murmured the peasant woman with evident embarrassment. "But you do still care for us a little bit, my dear child, although you have got used to finer folks than we are?"

"Do I care for you! Indeed I do! I understand why you ask me that, dear Nicole; I have been an ungrateful wretch, I have acted very badly. To think of not coming once to embrace you in three years! Oh! that was very wicked of me. I planned to do it very often, but one has so many things to do in Paris! Society, and all the amusements that were so new to me—it all bewildered me. You must try to forgive me."

"Forgive him! How handsome he is! how handsome he is!"

"And then, it seems to me that if you had wanted to see me, there was nothing to prevent your coming to Paris, to my house.—You know well enough where it is."

"Why, we did go there, my dear child, we went there twice, Louise and I. We asked to see you, and the first time they told us that you were travelling; the second, that you were at some château and would be away a long while."

"That is very strange! In the first place, it isn't true; I have not left Paris since I first went there, I have not travelled at all; and then, I was never told that you came."

"The idea! I told the concierge to tell you."

"Ah! I will look into this, and I will find out why they presumed to conceal your visits from me."

"Bless me! that made Louise and me feel very bad, and we said: 'As long as he knows we've been to see him but couldn't find him, and he don't come to see us, why, we mustn't go again, because perhaps he don't like to have us come to his house in Paris.'"

"Not like it, my dear Nicole! The idea of thinking that of me! And poor Louise too! But why did you send her to Bretagne, instead of keeping her with you?"

"Louise in Bretagne!" exclaimed Jacquinot, who returned to the room just then with a jug of wine and glasses. "What's the sense of making up stories like that to deceive my friend monsieur le marquis?"

"What! Louise is not in Bretagne!" cried Chérubin. "Why, Monsieur Gérondif has been telling me that for two years. What is the meaning of that lie?"

"Oh! dear me, my boy!" said Nicole, "I'll tell you the whole story, for I don't like to lie! And then, the more I look at you, you look so good and gentle, I can't believe that you've got to be a rake, a seducer, as Monsieur Gérondif told us!"

"I, a rake, a seducer! Why, that is not true, nurse, it is horribly false! On the contrary, people laugh me in Paris because they say I am too bashful with the ladies. And to say that I am a rake! That is abominable! And my tutor dared to say such things?"

"My dear child, I am going to tell you the whole truth. Monsieur Gérondif, who came to see us often and seemed to admire Louise's beauty, came one day about nine or ten months ago, and offered the child a fine place in Paris, which he said that you wanted her to take."

"Ah! the liar!"

"Louise liked the idea of going to Paris, because she said that that would bring her nearer to you, and she hoped to see you once in a while."

"Dear Louise!"

"So she accepted; but while she was packing her clothes, monsieur le professeur whispered to me: 'I am taking Louise away to remove her from the designs of my pupil, who means to make her his mistress.'"

"What an outrage!"

"'And if he comes here, make him believe that she's been with a relation of yours in Bretagne a long time.'"

Chérubin rose and paced the floor; he was so suffocated by wrath that he could hardly speak.

"What a shameful thing! to say that of me! to invent such lies! But what could his object have been? Do you know where he took Louise?"

"Oh! to some very fine folks, so he told us."

"But who are they?"

"Bless me! I didn't ask that, my dear child, because I had so much confidence in the schoolmaster."

"So you don't know where Louise is? Oh! I will find out! I will make him tell me!—I am dying with impatience; I wish I were in Paris now.—Adieu! my dear Nicole! adieu, Jacquinot!"

"What, going already, my *fieu*? You have hardly got here!"

"And he hasn't drunk a single glass!"

"I will come again, my friends, I will come again—but with Louise, whom I am wild to find!—Ah! Monsieur Gérondif! you say that I am a rake! We will see! They have all looked upon me as a child hitherto, but I'll show them that I am their master!"

Chérubin embraced Nicole, shook hands with Jacquinot, and, turning a deaf ear to all that those good people said to pacify him, he returned to his cabriolet, lashed his horse and drove rapidly back to Paris.

On reaching home, he at once summoned Monsieur Gérondif, Jasmin and the concierge. From the tone in which he issued the order, and from the expression of his face, the servants did not recognize their master, ordinarily so mild and gentle. The groom went to call the tutor, who had just finished dressing, although it was midday. He went down to his pupil, thinking:

"Monsieur le marquis undoubtedly wishes me to teach him something. Perhaps he wants to learn to write poetry. Mademoiselle Turlurette tells everybody in the house that my verses are so fine! I will have him begin with free verses; they are certainly easier to write, most assuredly."

But on entering the apartment of the young marquis, whom he found pacing the floor with an impatient and angry expression, the tutor became anxious, and began to think that he had not been summoned to give lessons in poetry. Jasmin, who did not know where he was, his master was scowling so at him, stood motionless in a corner, whence he dared not stir, and the concierge, who was fully as terrified as the others, remained in the doorway, afraid to go in.

Chérubin addressed the latter first; he bade him come nearer, and said to him:

"A short time after I first came to this house, a worthy countrywoman, my nurse, came to see me, with a young girl. They came twice; they were most anxious to see me; and you told them, the first time, that I was travelling, and the second time, that I was at the château of one of my friends. Why did you tell that falsehood? Who gave you leave to turn away people who are dear to me and whom I should have been glad to see? Answer me."

The concierge hung his head and answered:

"Faith, monsieur, all I did was to follow the instructions Monsieur Jasmin gave me; and I thought he was only carrying out monsieur's orders."

"Ah! it was Jasmin who told you to say that, was it? Very well; you may go; but henceforth take your orders from me alone."

The concierge bowed and left the room, delighted that he had come off so cheap.

Old Jasmin turned purple; he twisted his mouth, like a child about to cry. Chérubin walked up to him and said in a tone in which there was more reproach than anger:

"And so, Jasmin, it was you who ordered my dear Nicole and Louise to be turned away? It was you who arranged matters so that the people who brought me up must inevitably think me proud and unfeeling and ungrateful!—Ah! that was very ill done of you—and I don't recognize your kind heart in that business."

Jasmin drew his handkerchief and wept.

"You are right, monsieur!" he cried; "it was a shame, it was downright folly, but it wasn't my idea; I should never have thought of it. It was your tutor who told me that we must prevent your seeing Nicole and little Louise, because it would be very dangerous for you. As Monsieur Gérondif is a scholar, I thought that he must be right, and I did what he told me."

While the old valet was speaking, Monsieur Gérondif scratched his nose with all his might, as if to prepare for the attack that he was about to undergo; and in fact it was to him that Chérubin turned after listening to Jasmin, and there was the ring of righteous anger in his voice as he cried:

"So all this comes from you, monsieur? I should have suspected as much. —So it was dangerous for me to see the people from the village, who love me like their own child!"

Monsieur Gérondif threw one of his legs back, puffed out his chest, raised his head, and began with abundant assurance:

"Well, yes, my illustrious pupil! and I consider that I was right. *Non est discipulus super magistrum.*—Listen to my reasons: You left the village and the fields with great regret; you might have been tempted to return thither, and it was necessary to remove that temptation—always in your interest. The *Sadder*, abridged from the *Zend*, which contains all the tenets of the religion founded by Zoroaster, ordains that every man must make a strict examination of his conscience at the end of each day; and mine——"

"Oh! I am not talking about Zoroaster, monsieur! Was it in my interest too, that, at the time of your last visit to the village, you told Nicole that I had become a rake and a seducer in Paris; that I intended to make Louise my mistress; and that it was absolutely necessary to find a place for her in Paris, and to make me believe that she was in Bretagne?"

Monsieur Gérondif was petrified; he could think of no quotations to make; he hung his head and did not know which leg to stand on; while Jasmin, when he heard what the tutor had said of his young master, ran to the fireplace, seized the tongs, and prepared to strike Monsieur Gérondif:

"You dare to tell such infamous lies about my master!" he exclaimed; "to slander him like that! Let me thrash him, monsieur! I believe that I can do that with as much force as I had at twenty years."

But Chérubin stopped Jasmin, and said to the tutor:

"What were your reasons for lying so, monsieur?"

"To tell the truth, my noble pupil, I do not know;—a temporary aberration, a——"

"Well, I shall find out later. But, first of all, where is Louise?"

"The young and interesting foundling?"

"Come, come, monsieur, answer me, and no more lies; where is Louise?"

"In an honorable family, I venture to flatter myself; I obtained her a situation as lady's maid with Madame de Noirmont."

"A lady's maid! my foster-sister! You have made my old playmate a lady's maid!—Ah! that's an outrage!"

"The wages are good, and I thought that, as she has no fortune——"

"Hold your peace! Poor Louise! so this is the reward of your sworn attachment to me!—But she shall not remain another day in that position. Jasmin, call a cab at once, and you, monsieur, come with me."

Monsieur Gérondif did not wait for the order to be repeated; he followed Chérubin, who took his hat and hastened downstairs. Jasmin called a cab, the young marquis stepped in, ordered Monsieur Gérondif to take his place beside him and to give the driver Madame de Noirmont's address. The tutor obeyed and they drove away.

Chérubin did not open his mouth during the drive, and Gérondif did not dare even to blow his nose. When the cab stopped in front of the Noirmont mansion, Chérubin said to his tutor:

"It was you who brought Louise to this house; go now and find her. Say to the persons in whose service she is that she is not to work any more, that she has found a friend and protector; say whatever you choose, but remember that you must bring me my friend and sister. As for her, simply say to her that I am here, waiting for her, and I am perfectly sure that she will instantly make her preparations to come to me. Go, monsieur; I will stay here and wait."

Monsieur Gérondif jumped out of the cab, blew his nose when he was on the sidewalk, and entered the house at last, saying to himself:

"Let us do it, as there is no way to avoid it! The little one will not be mine

—unless, perhaps, later—no one knows. Perhaps he will endow her, and I will imagine that she's a widow."

Chérubin counted the minutes after the tutor entered the house; he leaned out of the cab door and did not take his eyes from the porte cochère; for he momentarily expected Louise to appear, and that hope was constantly disappointed. At last two persons left the house and came toward him; they were Monsieur Gérondif and Comtois. The professor's face wore a most woebegone expression; he rolled his eyes wildly about as he approached Chérubin: but the latter did not wait for him to speak.

"Louise!" he cried, "Louise! why hasn't she come with you? Didn't you tell her that I was here?"

"No, my noble pupil," replied Gérondif, with an air of desperation, "I did not tell her, for I could not. If you knew!"

"I don't want to know; I want Louise—I came here to get her. Why doesn't she come down? Do they refuse to let her go? In that case I will go up myself ——"

"Oh, no! nobody refuses anything; but she has gone already, and that is why she doesn't come down with us."

"What do you say? Louise——"

"Has not been at Monsieur de Noirmont's for four days; she went off one morning, very early, before anyone in the house was up."

"Ah! you are deceiving me!"

"No, my noble pupil; but as I thought that perhaps you would not believe me, I requested Comtois, Monsieur de Noirmont's confidential valet, to come with me and confirm my story.—Speak, incorruptible Comtois; tell the truth, the whole truth, and nothing but the truth."

Comtois stepped toward Chérubin, and said, saluting him respectfully:

"Since Mademoiselle Louise has been in our family, we had never had anything but praise for her behavior. Her modest manner, her sweetness of disposition, won all our hearts. Mademoiselle Ernestine de Noirmont treated her more as her friend than as her maid; madame was the only one who, for some unknown reason, was a trifle harsh with Mademoiselle Louise.—Well, last Friday, the day after a large dinner-party that we gave here, the girl went away. She took nothing with her but a little bundle containing her clothes— not another thing. Mademoiselle Ernestine was terribly unhappy over her going; but we supposed that Louise had decided to return to her province because she was disappointed that she had not been able to win madame's

258

favor. That is the exact truth, monsieur. However, if you will take the trouble to go upstairs, you can see Mademoiselle Ernestine, or my master and mistress, who will tell you just what I have told you."

Chérubin did not deem it necessary to question Monsieur or Madame de Noirmont; Comtois had no motive for lying to him, and in his eyes could be read his personal regret for Louise's departure.

"She must have returned to Gagny, beyond any question," cried Gérondif, scratching his nose.

"To Gagny!" exclaimed Chérubin, in despair; "why, I have just come from there! You forget that I have been there this morning, that I am just from Nicole's house, and that Louise has not been seen there."

"Perhaps you may have passed each other on the road."

"Why, he says that it was four days ago that she left the house!—four days, do you understand? What has become of her during all that time? Does it take four days to travel four leagues?"

"Not usually—but, if she stopped often on the way."

"Ah! it was you who induced Louise to leave the village, where she was safe from all harm. It was you, monsieur, who brought her to Paris. But remember that you must find Louise, that I must know where she is, what has happened to her in the four days since she left this house; and if she has met with any misfortune—then all my wrath will fall on you!"

Chérubin leaped into the cab, gave the driver Monfréville's address, and hastened to his friend. He longed to confide his troubles to him, for he knew that his friendship would not fail him when he went to him to claim his aid and support.

Monfréville was at home; when his young friend appeared, deeply moved and intensely excited, he instantly questioned him concerning the cause of his agitation. Chérubin told him all that he had done since morning: his visit to the village, his conversation with Nicole and her disclosures of Monsieur Gérondif's conduct regarding Louise, and finally the girl's disappearance from the house in which she had taken service. When he had finished his narrative, he cried:

"I must find Louise, my friend, I must find her, for I know now how dearly I love her. Poor Louise, it was to be near me, it was in the hope of seeing me, that she accepted that place in Paris. Nicole told me all, for Louise still thought of me, she never let a day pass without speaking of me, and I, like an ingrate, let three years pass without a sign that I remembered her!"

"That is true," said Monfréville, "and to-day you are in the depths of despair because you don't know what has become of her! But from all that you tell me, it seems to me that this girl is worthy of your love, and that it would be a great pity that she should fall into some trap, that she should be victimized by some miserable villain. Is she pretty, did you say?"

"She was lovely at fifteen, and Nicole told me that she had improved every day."

"The deuce! poor child! If she is very pretty and has lost her way in Paris, it's very dangerous. As for your tutor, there is a very natural explanation of his conduct: he was in love with Louise, no doubt, and deemed it prudent to keep you from seeing her, which was sure to happen sooner or later. For a pedagogue, that was rather clever."

"In love with Louise! the insolent old idiot!—But where shall I look for poor Louise—where can I hope to find her now?"

"That will be rather difficult, perhaps; but rely upon me to help you, to guide you in your search. You must set your servants at work; we will not spare money, and that is a powerful auxiliary in all the emergencies of life."

Chérubin thanked his friend warmly for lending him his assistance, and they began their search the same day.

While these things were taking place at Monfréville's apartment, Monsieur Gérondif stood in the street, as if turned to stone by his pupil's anger and threats. Comtois had long since returned to his duties and the tutor was still in front of the porte cochère. He decided at last to go his way, saying to himself:

"The Scripture says: 'Seek and ye shall find.' I am going to seek you, Louise, but I probably shall not find you."

XXVII

THE LITTLE DOG FANCIER

We left Louise at the moment when, in compliance with Madame de Noirmont's wishes, she left the house before anybody had risen.

Thus Louise found herself in the street at a very early hour. She had her bundle of clothes under her arm, and in her breast that letter, of such inestimable value, which would perhaps enable her to find her father.

When she was at a sufficient distance from the house that she had left, her first thought was to learn the name of the person to whom Madame de Noirmont had sent her. She took out the letter and read this address:

"For Monsieur Edouard de Monfréville. To be delivered to him in person."

"Monsieur de Monfréville," said Louise; "I have never heard of that gentleman. But Madame de Noirmont said that he was a great friend of Chérubin, and that they would give me his address at Chérubin's house. So I will go there. Oh! I shall not ask to see him! I know that he no longer cares for, that he doesn't choose to know me any more; and besides, as he has three or four mistresses at once, why, I haven't any desire to see him either."

The girl heaved a sigh as she spoke, for her heart was by no means in accord with her words; but she started toward Faubourg Saint-Germain, saying to herself:

"I must not think any more about my old playfellow; I will think only of what Madame de Noirmont said to me last night."

Louise at last reached the street on which the hôtel de Grandvilain stood. When she realized that she was so near Chérubin's abode, she stopped and began to tremble:

"As Chérubin wouldn't admit us," she thought, "when I came with his dear old nurse, perhaps they'll shut the door in my face. They will think that it is he whom I wish to see, and that will make him even more angry with me. Oh dear! what am I to do?"

And instead of going toward the house, Louise retraced her steps, walking very slowly. But in a moment she stopped again and said to herself:

"But I must ascertain this Monsieur de Monfréville's address! Suppose I should wait until someone comes out of the house? Yes, I think that that will be the better way. I shall not be so afraid to speak to someone in the street. But it is still very early; people don't get up at this time in these fine houses. I will walk back and forth, and wait; there's no law against that, and, besides, not many people are passing yet. If I should see him come out, I would hide so that he might not see me. But I could look at him, at all events—and it is so long since I saw him!"

Louise had been walking the street for some time, looking in vain for somebody to leave the house, when two persons came toward her from a street near by. They were not arm in arm; indeed, one of them allowed his companion to keep always a few steps in advance, as if a certain residuum of respect kept him from putting himself on a level with the other. The first wore a long coat lined with fur, very stylish and sadly soiled, and a hat which was almost new, but which seemed to have received a number of blows; he had a cigar in his mouth; the second wore his huge umbrella hat and nut-colored box-coat, a pair of shockingly dirty trousers, and boots which were not made for him and in which his feet and legs seemed fairly to dance. In addition, he had a black eye and a bruised nose.

Daréna and Poterne had passed the night at a party where they had played cards until daylight, and had indulged in a fight before separating. Daréna had chosen to pass through Chérubin's street on his way home; he always took that road by preference, a fancy which did not please Poterne, who muttered as he followed him:

"If your former friend the young marquis should meet us, he might pay me a few more compliments behind, and I can do without them."

"Bah!" retorted Daréna, "you always look at the dark side. For my part, I would like to meet Chérubin. I would go up to him with a laugh, and I would say: 'Who ever heard of friends falling out for a jest? I obtained your introduction to a charming girl; instead of being a Pole, she was an Alsatian, but what's the difference? And, faith, it isn't my fault that you went to sleep in her company!'—I'll bet that he would shake hands with me, and all would be forgotten."

"Hum! I don't think it! If you knew how his friend Monfréville gave it to

262

you!"

"Ta! ta! mere empty words! nonsense! I am above all that!"

The two worthies were walking on when Poterne, spying Louise standing a few steps from the hôtel de Grandvilain, upon which her eyes seemed to be fixed, put his hand on Daréna's arm, saying:

"Look—yonder, at the right."

"Bigre! what a pretty girl! What in the devil is she doing there, in rapt contemplation, before the door of Chérubin's house? Do you know, Poterne, that girl is perfectly bewitching! The more one looks at her, the more charms one discovers."

"Yes, and it's not Parisian style; however, she's something more than a peasant. She has a bundle under her arm—do you suppose she has just arrived from the provinces?"

"She is still staring at the house. I certainly must find out what she is doing here."

"What are you going to do?"

"I don't know yet, but I am a Frenchman, and a lady's man before everything; and I am bound to aid and protect the fair sex. Forward, and you will see. Walk beside me, idiot!"

Daréna and Poterne crossed the street and walked toward Louise; when they were near her, Daréna stopped and said in a loud tone:

"Monsieur Poterne, as we are passing through this street, suppose we stop and bid our good friend, Marquis Chérubin de Grandvilain good-morning? this is his house. You know that he is constantly asking us to breakfast with him."

Poterne enveloped himself closely in his box-coat and replied:

"It's too early as yet; no one is up in the marquis's house."

These words were not lost on Louise, who started at the name of Chérubin. She approached Daréna and said to him timidly:

"Excuse me, monsieur, but as you are a friend of Monsieur de Grandvilain, who lives in this house, perhaps you know Monsieur de Monfréville also?"

At that name Poterne made a wry face; but Daréna replied as amiably as possible:

"Yes, my lovely maiden, I know Monfréville; indeed, I am intimately acquainted with him. Have you business with him?"

"I have a letter for him, but I do not know his address, and I was told that I could learn it at Monsieur Chérubin's; but, although I know Monsieur Chérubin, I dared not go into his house."

"Ah! so you know my friend Chérubin, mademoiselle? In that case he must have spoken to me about you, for I was his most intimate confidant."

"Oh, no, monsieur!" replied Louise sadly, "he would never have spoken to you about me, for he has forgotten me; he doesn't want to see us again. I am Louise, Monsieur Chérubin's friend in childhood."

"Young Louise!" cried Daréna; "who was with Chérubin, at his nurse Nicole's, at Gagny?"

"Yes, monsieur."

"You see that I am well informed, mademoiselle, that I did not deceive you when I said that I was the marquis's friend."

"Oh, yes! I see that, monsieur."

During this dialogue, Poterne sauntered up to Daréna and whispered:

"There's a chance to make a turn here."

Daréna retorted with a blow of his elbow in the ribs, muttering:

"So I see, you fool!"

Then, turning to Louise, he continued:

"Mademoiselle, if you do not wish to call at my friend Chérubin's, it does not seem to me fitting that you should remain in the street. In Paris, you see, there are certain proprieties that one must always observe. Young and pretty as you are, you must not expose yourself to the risk of being insulted by some scoundrel. Take my arm; you are my friend's foster-sister, his playmate, and I naturally declare myself your protector. Pray take my arm."

"Oh! how kind you are, monsieur!" replied Louise, timidly putting her arm through Daréna's. "Are you really going to take the trouble to take me to Monsieur de Monfréville's?"

"I will take you wherever you choose—to the king if you have anything to say to him.—Poterne, why don't you take mademoiselle's bundle?"

"You are too kind, monsieur, but it does not trouble me."

"No matter; I will not allow my friend Chérubin's foster-sister to carry a bundle when she has my arm."

Poterne had already taken the bundle from Louise's hands; and she, confused by so much courtesy, walked on with her arm through Daréna's, while Poterne followed, feeling the bundle to find out what there was in it.

As they walked along, the girl told Daréna how she had left Gagny to enter Madame de Noirmont's service, and her grief because Chérubin had forgotten her; in fact, she omitted nothing save the visit Madame de Noirmont had paid to her during the night.

"And what do you propose to do at Monfréville's?" asked Daréna, fixing his eyes on Louise's lovely ones.

"I am going to give him a letter which was given to me for him."

"To induce him to reconcile you and your dear friend Chérubin, no doubt?"

"Oh! no, monsieur! it's about something that he alone knows about."

Louise said no more, deeming it improper to admit a third person to the secret of what Madame de Noirmont had said to her. Daréna paid little heed to that matter; he was thinking what he should do with Louise. Suddenly he remembered the little house on the outer boulevard, which he had hired for the Polish intrigue, and which was still in his possession, as he had been obliged to take it for six months. Turning to Poterne, he said with a wink:

"Monsieur de Poterne, my friend Monfréville is still living in his *petite maison* on the boulevards, outside the wall, is he not?"

"He is, monsieur le comte," replied Poterne innocently. "But Monsieur de Monfréville often goes away on short journeys about the neighborhood; I can't vouch for it that he is at home now."

"At all events, we will take mademoiselle there. If he is absent, we will consider what Mademoiselle Louise, my friend Chérubin's foster-sister, can do until his return. Ah! there's a cab; let us take it, for it's a long way from here to Monfréville's."

Poterne summoned a cab, and Louise entered it with her two chance acquaintances; the girl was entirely unsuspicious; she was convinced that the gentleman who had offered her his arm was a friend of Chérubin, and in her eyes that title was enough to banish suspicion.

The cab stopped in front of the house near Barrière de la Chopinette, which had been occupied since the abortive Chichemann affair by little Bruno alone, whom they left in charge. Daréna whispered a word in Poterne's ear, and that gentleman took pains to enter first. Louise remained with Daréna, who wasted a long time paying the cab-driver. At last he ushered the girl into the house, the boy having received his instructions.

"We wish to speak with Monsieur de Monfréville," Daréna said to Bruno. "Here is a young lady, my intimate friend Marquis Chérubin's foster-sister, who is most anxious to see him."

Bruno eyed Louise impertinently as he replied:

"Monsieur de Monfréville's away; he'll probably come back to-morrow or next day; if anybody wants to wait for him, he told me to offer his room to any of his friends who might come to see him."

Louise was in despair; she looked at Daréna and murmured:

"The gentleman is away; what shall I do?"

"In the first place, my child, you must go upstairs and rest," said Daréna; "then we will see, we will consider. Come, follow me without fear; in Monfréville's house, I act as if I were at home."

Louise went upstairs with Daréna, who, to dispel every shadow of fear from her mind, made a show of treating her with the greatest respect, and kept always at a considerable distance from her. She was rather surprised that the person to whom Madame de Noirmont had sent her should occupy a house of such humble appearance, and so modestly furnished; but she had not told her that he was rich, she had simply said that he could tell her who her father was, and that was why she was so eager to see him.

"My lovely maid," said Daréna, after a moment, "you know no one in Paris—except Chérubin; and you do not wish to go to him to ask for shelter, I presume?"

"Oh! no, monsieur!"

"To return to Gagny and then come here again would be a waste of time; besides, if you travel alone, you expose yourself to a thousand encounters that are most annoying to a young lady. It seems to me, therefore, that the best thing for you to do, in view of your position, is to wait here until Monfréville returns."

"Here, monsieur! alone in this house, with nobody but the little boy I saw downstairs," replied Louise, with a shudder of dismay; "oh! I should not dare."

"Alone, my child? no, indeed. If that were the case I would not make the suggestion; but there is a concierge here, Monfréville's confidential servant, a most respectable person. That little fellow is her nephew; she probably is not far away, and he is watching the house during her absence."

"Oh! that is a very different matter! If there is a respectable woman here, and she is willing to look after me until Monsieur de Monfréville returns

_____"

"Wait; I will go down and see what has become of her."

Daréna hurried downstairs and said to Poterne:

"You will send this little rascal away instantly and find a woman between forty and sixty years of age, who has a face that is somewhere near respectable; that will give the girl confidence, and she will stay here. I am not sorry to get rid of Monsieur Bruno anyway, after he admitted so readily those people who ruined our last affair."

"A respectable woman," said Poterne—"I don't know any such. How in the devil do you expect me to find anything of the kind at La Courtille?"

"Where you choose—nonsense—a dealer in old clothes—a fortune-teller —a charwoman—and teach her her lesson."

Daréna returned to keep Louise company and told her that the concierge had gone to the central market, because there was no market in that quarter, but that she would soon return.

Meanwhile Poterne began by discharging Monsieur Bruno, who was much displeased to be turned out-of-doors, and who ventured to indulge in some far from respectful gestures as he withdrew. But Poterne did not amuse himself watching Bruno's antics; he went about to the neighboring wine-shops, and from house to house, inquiring for what he wanted. At last, after two hours search, he found it. He returned to the house with a woman of about fifty years, tall as a grenadier, with a cap on her head which certainly had not been washed for a year, and a dress the color of which was no longer distinguishable; a pimply face, blear-eyes and a nose smeared with snuff completed her portrait.

"This is Madame Ratouille, Monsieur de Monfréville's confidential servant," said Poterne, presenting his companion.

Madame Ratouille, to whom Poterne had given careful instructions, curtsied very low to Daréna and greeted Louise most affably, assuring her that the house was at her disposal, and that her master, Monsieur de Monfréville, would approve of her having urged the young lady to wait for him. Madame Ratouille, being extremely loquacious and anxious to play her part well, because she had been promised six francs a day and all that she wanted to eat, lost herself in a sea of words intended to prove to Louise that she would be out of reach of insult in that house. The girl, feeling certain that Madame de Noirmont could not have sent her to any but respectable persons, thanked Madame Ratouille warmly, and consented to await Monsieur de Monfréville's return under her care.

Daréna passed some time with Louise; Poterne seized the opportunity to show the new concierge over the house, where she was supposed to have lived for a long while. He urged her not to talk too much, for fear of making some slip, and above all things not to allow anyone to have access to the girl who was placed in her charge; then he went away with Daréna, who bade Louise adieu, informing her that he would come the next day to find out whether his friend Monfréville had returned, and whether she had everything that she needed.

When they had left the house, Poterne said:

"This girl has fallen into our hands to make up to us for the Polish intrigue. She is a fascinating creature! It is impossible that young Chérubin should not adore her; indeed, you have often told me how much he used to talk about his little playmate—a proof that he hasn't forgotten her, as she thinks; but we mustn't let him have her except for her weight in gold."

Daréna made no reply; he seemed to be thinking deeply, and Poterne did not dare to disturb him; he proposed to have the management of the affair in his own hand.

The next day Daréna made a careful toilet and went with Poterne to the little house. While he talked with Louise, Poterne remained below, talking with Madame Ratouille, who assured him that the girl had not had a moment of ennui as she had played cards with her all day.

Daréna remained with Louise until nightfall; when he went away with Poterne, he was as silent as on the day before.

The following day passed in the same way; but Poterne observed that his dear friend was becoming more and more coquettish in his attire. Madame Ratouille continued to play cards with Louise, who thought that Monsieur de Monfréville was very slow about returning. But Daréna said to her every day:

"Be patient; he must return at last, and as you have waited for him so long, it would be absurd to go away just at the moment of his return."

But Louise was beginning to be disturbed; it seemed to her that the gentleman who came every day to keep her company, no longer addressed her with the same respect or kept so far away from her; she considered that he gazed at her too often and too long; and she had observed some things in Madame Ratouille's manners and speech which materially diminished her confidence in that woman.

On the sixth day, when they left the house, where they had remained later than usual, Poterne, surprised to find that affairs were still at the same point, said to his companion:

"I say! what's your plan? When shall you see the young marquis? What fairy tale do you propose to tell him on the subject of the girl?"

Daréna puffed himself up and replied in a fatuous tone:

"I have changed my mind! This girl is decidedly too pretty to turn over to another man; she pleases me. I had forgotten what love was, and she has revived that sentiment in my dilapidated heart! Louise shall be my mistress; and then, later, when I am tired of her, we will see."

"That's a fine idea!" cried Poterne. "Is that the way you hope to earn money? Fall in love—you! why it's pitiful! just because you have a few gold pieces in hand, and because you have been lucky at play these last few days. But it will soon be spent; and if you miss this opportunity——"

"Poterne, if you don't stop annoying me, I'll break this stick over your back! I mean to possess that child; perhaps it is only a whim, but it suits me to gratify it. She's a little jewel, is this Louise, not a false one, like the one you sold to Chérubin. To-morrow, you will order a delectable repast, with wines which you will be kind enough not to purchase at La Courtille; you will order it sent to my villa near Barrière de la Chopinette; I will dine with Louise, and I will sleep there. As to you, if Madame Ratouille tempts you, I turn her over to you."

"Sapristi! I should prefer five years at Toulon!"

"You heard me, Poterne: a dainty feast at the little house to-morrow."

"And you think that this young Louise will consent to——"

"Why not, when I have induced her to drink a few glasses of champagne? And if she doesn't consent, why, I will do without her permission. For six days now I have been darting burning glances at her, and if she hasn't understood them, so much the worse for her! it isn't my fault, and I have no desire to take it out in sighs."

"Well," thought Poterne, as he followed Daréna, "he has taken it into his head, and anything that I could say would do no good."

While all this was taking place, Chérubin and Monfréville were searching Paris, making inquiries, asking in all directions if anything had been seen of a young woman, of whom they gave an exact description. All of Chérubin's servants too had taken the field; Monsieur Gérondif started out as soon as he had breakfasted and did not return until dinner-time, swearing that he had travelled twelve leagues during the day in search of Louise. Jasmin had gone to Gagny to inquire whether by any chance Louise had returned there; but the girl had not been seen, and Nicole, when she learned that the whereabouts of her adopted child were unknown, shed tears, cursed the tutor, who was responsible for Louise's going to Paris, and swore that she would find him and beat him if her child was not found.

Two days passed and no trace of her had been discovered; toward the end of the third day, Chérubin had just left Monfréville, to return home, in despair over the non-success of his search, when, as he crossed the Pont Neuf, his eyes happened to fall on a small boy, leading an ugly dog, which he offered for sale to the passers-by.

The young dog fancier's face bore altogether too noticeable an expression of craft and mischief not to attract the attention of a person who had seen it before. Chérubin instantly recognized the little scamp who was watching the house to which Daréna had taken the so-called Comtesse de Globeska; and, without any very clear idea in what way that encounter might be of service to him, he walked toward Monsieur Bruno, who recognized him and seemed delighted to see him.

"Ah! it's you, is it, monsieur? I recognize you!" said Bruno, staring impudently at the young man; "you're the man they tried to gull with a German woman who made believe she was a Pole! Don't you want to buy my dog? It's a terrier; he'll bring things back better'n I do, for I never bring anything back at all. Six francs! that's not a high price. I found him yesterday and I'm selling him to-day; we're both hungry, and that's why I'll let you have him so cheap."

"Ah! so you sell dogs now, eh?" said Chérubin.

"Well! I've got to do something, as those fellows turned me out-of-doors. You know who I mean—your friend that's such a bully, and that old thief of a Poterne. You see they've taken another girl to the little house yonder, but she's a very different kind from the Alsatian; she's a mighty sight prettier."

A sudden thought flashed through Chérubin's mind; he led Bruno aside, put twenty francs in his hand, and said to him:

"Here, that's for you; and ten times as much more if you will help me to find the woman I am looking for."

"Twenty francs! My eyes! what luck! I never had so much money at once. The dog's yours."

"Now answer my questions. Daréna and Poterne, you say, have taken a young girl to the house outside the barrier?"

"Yes, in a carriage, an old cab."

"How long since? do you know?"

"*Pardi*, yes! I was there when they brought her. It was—let me see—a week ago to-day."

"A week—and we have been looking for her three days; oh! it must be she! Is this young lady pretty?"

"Lovely, and she don't look like a country wench like the other. They made her believe that she was at a Monsieur de Monfréville's house; then that old vagabond of a Poterne went off and found, I don't know where, an old woman to play concierge; and they kicked me out."

"Did they call her by name before you?"

"Wait a minute—I remember now that, when they arrived, Monsieur Daréna said, as he brought the girl into the house:

"'This is my friend Marquis Chérubin's foster-sister.'"

"It is she! Ah! the villains! I'll make them give her back to me! Poor Louise! in that infamous Daréna's hands for a week! God grant that I may arrive in time!"

"Take me with you. If you appear at the door, they won't let you in."

"I'll break the door down."

"Oh! it's too strong; but I promise you that I'll find a way to make them open it."

"Come, then, come; I will double the reward I promised you, if Louise is under my protection soon."

"Ah! a fine trick! They'll kick me out, will they? Thanks! I guess I'll have a little revenge.—Go on, Boudin, I give you your liberty—go find a dinner."

Bruno released his dog. Chérubin hesitated a moment, uncertain whether he should inform Monfréville of his discovery; but every instant's delay made him more and more fearful that Louise would fall a victim to some plot, and he felt that he had sufficient resolution and courage to rescue her, single-handed, from the dangers that threatened her. He took a cab with Bruno, and was driven first to his house, which was not far away; he took a pair of pistols, determined to make use of them, if necessary to rescue Louise; then, without a word to any of his people, he returned to the cab, which conveyed him and Bruno to Barrière de la Chopinette.

It was dark when they reached the outer boulevard. Chérubin quivered with impatience, rage, and fear of not finding Louise. Little Bruno, who thought of everything, said to him:

"Have the cab stop before we're very near the house. If they should hear it, it would put them on their guard."

Chérubin realized the wisdom of that advice; he alighted with Bruno, ordered the driver to wait for him, and walked toward the house with his little companion. The shutters were closed on the ground floor and first floor; but through the poorly joined boards it was easy to see that there were lights on both floors.

"There's somebody there!" said Chérubin, his heart beating violently.

"Yes. Now is when we need to be cunning, in order to get in. Wait, and don't breathe. Have your pistols all ready to frighten them when the door is open. You'll see how I pull the wool over their eyes."

And Bruno knocked on the door, beginning at the same time to whistle and hum his favorite tune: *Tu tu tu tu r'lu tu tu tu.*

Poterne was at table with Madame Ratouille, on the ground floor; Daréna had gone upstairs, where he had ordered Louise's dinner to be served, announcing his purpose to dine with her. He had just declared his love to Louise, who, terrified and trembling, began to understand that she had fallen into a trap, and implored heaven to come to her aid.

On the ground floor, where there was no talk of love, they ate much and drank even more. Madame Ratouille's eyes had grown so small that they were invisible, and Monsieur Poterne's tongue was beginning to thicken, when Bruno knocked on the door.

For some time no one answered; at last Poterne's voice inquired:

"Who's there?"

"It's me, Père Poterne; it's your little monkey, Bruno; please let me in."

"What do you want, you scalawag? what have you come here for? We are not in need of you. Away you go!"

"I came to get a Greek cap that I forgot to take; I'm sure I can find it, for I know just where I put it. Let me get my cap and I'll go right away."

"You annoy us. Go somewhere else and get a cap. Leave us in peace."

"If you don't let me get my cap, which is in your house, I'll knock on the door all night, and I'll make row enough to bring the watch here."

That threat convinced Poterne; he opened the door, grumbling:

"Well, come in and find your Greek cap; and make haste to clear out."

But instead of the small boy whom he expected to see, Chérubin darted into the house, with a pistol in his hand, the barrel of which he held against

Poterne's chest, saying in a low voice, but with fire flashing from his eyes:

"If you make a sound, I'll kill you!—Where is Louise?"

Poterne was so frightened that he could barely murmur:

"Upstairs—with Daréna."

Chérubin asked no more questions; he darted forward, rushed upstairs, and with a kick forced the door of the apartment on the first floor. He was no longer the weak, timid young man, who could neither speak nor act, but a Hercules whom nothing could withstand. As he entered the room he saw Louise struggling and doing her utmost to repel Daréna, who was trying to take her in his arms. Chérubin rushed upon the man who sought to outrage Louise, and seizing him about the middle of the body, lifted him up and threw him violently across the room, against the table on which the dinner was served.

Daréna had no time to grasp what had happened, or to defend himself; his head struck the corner of the table, his chin broke a plate which cut his face, and he fell, murmuring Chérubin's name.

"Chérubin!" cried Louise, staring at her rescuer, afraid to believe her eyes, but shedding tears of joy. "Is it possible? It is he! it is you!"

"Yes, Louise, it is I, Chérubin, your friend, your brother—so overjoyed to find you! But come, come! Do not stay any longer in this infamous house! As for you, villain, if there is any heart left in your body, and if you wish to have the honor of dying by my hand, come to my house, and you will find that the young man whom you believed to be so shy and timid, knows how to use a sword and a pistol."

Daréna could not reply, for he was unconscious.

Chérubin took Louise's hand and led her away; on the lower floor they found Madame Ratouille still at table, while Poterne was trying to hide in a butter firkin, and Bruno stood guard at the door. Chérubin did not stay an instant with Daréna's confederate; he led Louise from the house, and told Bruno to call the cab to the door; he did so, and they entered. But, before they drove away, Chérubin took a handful of gold pieces from his pocket and gave them to Bruno, saying:

"Take this; you have earned it by doing a good deed; I hope that it will bring you luck, and that you will try to become an honest man."

The cab drove off. Chérubin held both of Louise's hands in his; and for some time those two, who had not met for three years, were so pleased and happy to be together again, their hearts were so full, their emotion so intense, that they could exchange only incoherent words and broken sentences.

"It is really you, Chérubin, who saved me," said Louise. "So you did still think of me?"

"Why, Louise, I have been searching Paris for three days, looking everywhere for you, ever since I learned that you had disappeared from Madame de Noirmont's. I have not lived, I have not had a moment's peace of mind!"

"Can it be true? Then you still love me, Chérubin?"

"Love you, my Louise! Ah! more than I ever did—I realize it now! I let a long while go by without going to see you, it is true; you must have thought me indifferent or ungrateful; but I always intended to go to see you, if Monsieur Gérondif had not told me that you were in Bretagne, where you were so happy that you did not mean to return to Gagny."

"Oh! the liar! And it was he who drove me to despair by telling me that you never gave a thought to your old playmate, that you had no desire to see her again."

"The miserable villain! why, that was perfectly horrible!"

"And it was not true, and you do still love your poor Louise? Oh! how happy I am!"

This time the drive from the barrier to his house seemed very short to Chérubin. He alighted, led Louise into the house, and took her up to his own apartment. She followed him trustfully; she was with the man she loved—that was the only thought in her mind.

Jasmin, who had come up to his master's apartment with a light, uttered a cry of joy when he saw the girl, and Chérubin briefly explained to him how he had found her.

"So it was that blackguard Poterne again—the preserved turnips fellow!" cried Jasmin; "and his master—another rascal! Do you know, monsieur, it has occurred to me several times that they were mixed up in this."

"Louise will remain here. I do not propose that she shall leave me," said Chérubin; "I am too much afraid of losing her again. She will have apartments in this house; but meanwhile she will occupy mine to-night. Jasmin, you will have a room prepared for me upstairs."

"Yes, my dear master."

Louise tried to object to that arrangement; she disliked to disturb Chérubin and said that the smallest room in the house would suffice for her; but

Chérubin paid no heed to her, and Jasmin went to carry out his orders.

The young people were left alone. It seemed that Chérubin would never tire of gazing in admiration at Louise. She was so lovely, so charming, so fascinating, in his eyes, that he cried:

"And I forgot you for all those creatures that I thought that I loved. Ah! Louise, there is not a single one of them who can be compared with you!"

The girl told her friend all that she had done since she left the village; she concealed from him none of her thoughts; she had no secrets from him. When she reached the time of her entering Madame de Noirmont's service, she told him of all the incidents that had marked her life there; then, suddenly putting her hand to her breast, she made sure that she still had the letter which she was to deliver to Monsieur de Monfréville, and which Daréna was trying to make her give up to him when Chérubin arrived so opportunely to rescue her.

"I will take you to Monfréville to-morrow," said Chérubin, "for it is too late to-night to send for him to come here. Madame de Noirmont told you that he would tell you who your father is; but, my dear Louise, let us swear that, whatever happens, we will never part again. If you have no parents, I will take the place of them both; I will be your protector, your friend, your——"

Chérubin did not know how to finish, but he took Louise's hand and covered it with kisses. The girl was so happy to find that her old playmate still loved her, that she gladly took the oath that he requested. They did not weary of telling each other of their love, and of swearing that they would love each other always. Then they recalled their childish delights, their first games, the happy moments that they had passed together, those days, so brief and so blissful, which they might perhaps know again.

To two people who love each other sincerely and who have not seen each other for a long time, the hours pass rapidly and unnoticed. Jasmin had long since come to inform his master that a room had been prepared on the upper floor, and Chérubin had dismissed him, making ready at the same time to follow him. But he resumed his conversation with Louise, he let his eyes rest in unalloyed delight upon hers, which were filled with emotion and love. They exchanged more oaths of never-ending love and thought no more about parting.

Suddenly a neighboring clock struck two.

"Mon Dieu! it is very late!" said Louise; "two o'clock! I would not have believed it! My dear, I am keeping you from sleeping; we must say good-night, but only till to-morrow."

"Very well," said Chérubin, "I will leave you to sleep, Louise. Good-night

—since it must be."

And the young man gazed lovingly at the girl—and did not go away. At last he added with some embarrassment:

"Louise, before we part, won't you let me kiss you? I have not dared to do it since I found you; and yet, in the village, we used to kiss very often."

The girl saw no reason why she should deny the friend of her childhood the sweet privilege which she used to accord him, and her only reply was to walk toward him. Chérubin threw his arms about her and pressed her to his heart; but his kiss was no longer the kiss of a child. Louise realized her imprudence too late; how can one shun a danger which one does not anticipate? And then there are sins which it is so pleasant to commit, and Chérubin swore so earnestly that he would always love her!—He had ceased to be bashful!

XXVIII

MONFRÉVILLE'S LOVE-AFFAIRS

Daybreak found Chérubin still in Louise's arms; the apartment made ready on the floor above had not been required. But when morning came, the young man crept softly upstairs, so that his servants might think that he had passed the night there. About nine o'clock he rang for Jasmin and bade him go down and see if Mademoiselle Louise had risen and could receive him.

The old servant eagerly performed his errand and returned with a radiant face to inform his young master that his dear friend had risen, that she was as lovely and fresh as a rose, and that anyone could see that she had slept soundly all night.

Chérubin smiled at Jasmin's perspicacity, and went down at once to Louise.

The girl wept and hid her face on her lover's breast; but Chérubin said to her in the tone which speaks true love and which reaches a woman's heart so quickly:

"Why should you regret having made me happy, when I propose to employ my whole life hereafter to make you happy? We will never part, you will be my faithful companion, my beloved wife."

"No," replied Louise, weeping, "you are rich and of noble birth, and you cannot marry a poor girl without father or mother. I shall love you as long as I live, but I cannot be your wife; for perhaps a day would come when you would be sorry that you had given me that title, and then I should be too wretched."

"Never! and it is very wicked of you to have any such idea!—But there's the letter that you are to deliver to Monfréville—that should inform you who your parents are. I will throw myself at their feet, and they will have to consent to my becoming your husband."

Louise sighed and hung her head.

"But am I worthy *now* to find my parents?" she replied. "It seems to me that I no longer dare to deliver the letter to that gentleman; perhaps I should do better to destroy it."

Chérubin succeeded in allaying her fears; he decided to write to his friend and to send him the letter that the young woman dared not carry to him. So he at once wrote Monfréville the following letter:

"My dear friend:

"I have found my Louise; she is an angel who will embellish my life. She cannot be another's now, for she is mine. O my dear Monfréville, I am the happiest of men, and I was not frightened this time. But then, I have never loved other women, and I adore this one.

"Madame de Noirmont gave my Louise a letter for you, and told her that you could tell her who her father was; and it was while she was looking for your house that she fell in with that villainous Daréna, who took her to his *petite maison*, making her think that she was in your house. Luckily, I arrived in time! I send you this letter, my friend; come to us quickly, and tell us what you know. But if Louise's parents would try to part us, do not make them known to her; for henceforth we cannot exist without each other."

Chérubin signed this letter, enclosed with it the one that was given to Louise, and sent them both to his friend early in the morning.

Monfréville was alone when Chérubin's letter was brought to him, and he lost no time in reading it. When he saw Madame de Noirmont's name and learned what she had said to Louise, he trembled and turned pale, and his eyes instantly rested on the enclosure; he glanced at the superscription and exclaimed:

"Yes, she has written to me; I recognize that writing, although it is a long while since my eyes last rested on it. Great God! what can have induced her to write to me, after swearing that she would never look upon me except as a stranger, that she would wipe the whole past from her memory? And this girl that she sent to me—Ah! if I dared to hope!"

Monfréville broke the seal of Madame de Noirmont's letter. Before reading it, he was obliged to pause again, for he was so excited that his eyes had difficulty in distinguishing the letters. At last he made an effort to recover himself, and read:

"Monsieur:

"When, disregarding your oaths, you left me to lament by my child's cradle a fault which you made no motion to repair, I swore that you should never know that child. And more than that, I confess that I included her in the hatred which filled my heart thenceforth for my seducer; I abandoned my child to the village people in whose care I had placed her, and I determined never to see her again. Later, my position made it my duty to keep that oath. My father, who, thank heaven, never knew of his daughter's wrongdoing, disposed of my hand; married, a mother, and the wife of a man no less severe on the question of honor than jealous of his reputation, I should have wrecked my daughter's happiness, Monsieur de Noirmont's, and my own, if, by a single imprudent step, I had exposed myself to the suspicion of a youthful indiscretion. To tell you that I was happy would be to deceive you; can a mother be happy, when she has spurned one of her children from her arms? I often blamed myself for the caresses that I gave my daughter; for I said to myself, in the depths of my heart, that I had another daughter who had an equal claim to my affection, and that I had cast her out!—My remorse was not sufficient, evidently, and Heaven had a more terrible punishment in store for me! A few months ago, while I was out of town, a young woman was taken into my household as lady's maid. Her sweet disposition, the charm that emanated from her whole person, soon won all hearts. I myself felt drawn toward her. But conceive my situation when I discovered that that girl, brought up in the village of Gagny, by the good-nature of a peasant-woman named Nicole, was the same child whom I had abandoned to that woman's tender mercies years ago! My daughter under my roof in a servile capacity! a servant in her mother's house! Ah! monsieur, could I endure that ghastly position of affairs? Constantly tempted to throw myself into Louise's arms, to strain her to my heart; then, remembering my husband, my other daughter, the honor of a whole family—I felt that I must find a way out of that situation or die. At last I went to Louise; I could not force myself to confess that I was her mother, but I implored her to leave the house, and the poor child yielded to my entreaties. But, deeply touched by the attachment to me which she has manifested, I have determined to give her a father. That child, whom, on your return to France, you vainly implored me to make known to you, is Louise, the lovely and virtuous maid who will hand you this letter. Give her a father, monsieur; as for her mother, you must not mention her name to her, but her heart will doubtless lead her to divine who she is.

"AMELIE DE NOIRMONT."

When he had finished reading this letter, Monfréville abandoned himself to the wildest delight; he ran his eyes over Madame de Noirmont's missive again, for he feared that he was the plaything of a delusion; he was too happy to think that Louise, whose beauty and virtue and sweet temper everyone joined in extolling, was the daughter whom he was ardently desirous to find. But soon he recalled something that moderated the exuberance of his joy; he remembered Chérubin's letter, took it up and read it again, and a melancholy expression stole over his face.

"Heaven did not choose that my happiness should be without alloy," he murmured, with a sigh; "doubtless it is to make me expiate my sin; but after being so guilty myself, there is nothing left for me to do but to forgive."

Louise and Chérubin were still together; they were impatiently awaiting

Monfréville's arrival, and their impatience was blended with a secret fear which they could not clearly define.

At last, Jasmin announced: "Monsieur de Monfréville."

Louise, deeply agitated, lowered her eyes; Chérubin ran to meet his friend, but stopped short when he saw his serious, even stern, expression, and faltered, offering him his hand:

"Haven't you received my letter, my friend?"

Monfréville did not touch the hand that Chérubin offered him; he turned his eyes on the girl who stood, trembling, at the farther end of the room; and, as he gazed at her, he felt that his eyes filled with tears. But, struggling to conceal the emotion that he felt, he seated himself a few steps from Louise, who still kept her eyes on the floor, and motioned Chérubin to sit, saying:

"Yes, I have received your letter; and I have read the one from Madame de Noirmont, who tells me that mademoiselle was adopted by the same good woman who nursed you."

"Well, my friend, is it true that you know Louise's father, that you can help her to find him? But do you think he will make her happy, that he will not put any obstacles in the way of our love?"

Monfréville glanced at the girl again and said in a faltering voice:

"Yes, I know mademoiselle's father."

Louise raised her eyes at that, and looked at Monfréville with a thrill of hope and of filial affection, crying:

"You know my father? Oh! if it should be true, monsieur, that he would deign to love me—to——"

She could not finish the sentence; her voice trembled and the words died on her lips.

"Before answering your questions," Monfréville continued, after a moment, "it is necessary that I should tell you an anecdote of my youth. Please give me your attention.—I was just twenty-two years old; I was independently rich, absolutely master of my actions and with very little control over my passions. I loved a young lady belonging to an honorable family. She had no mother to watch over her, and during her father's absence, my love succeeded in triumphing over her virtue. Believe me, it is very wrong to abuse a sentiment you have aroused, in order to induce the person you love to forget her duties; and it rarely happens that one is not punished for it!"

Here Chérubin lost countenance and dared not look at Monfréville, while

Louise, pale and trembling, felt the tears falling from her eyes.

"Soon after," continued Monfréville, "being obliged to visit England on business, I went away, promising the victim of my seduction that I would soon return to ask her father for her hand. But when I was away from her, inconstancy, too natural in a young man, led me to forget my promise. But I received a letter in which she told me that she was about to become a mother, and that I must hasten back to her, if I wished to save her honor and repair the wrong I had done. Well! I left that letter unanswered; I had another intrigue on hand! Two years passed. I returned to France, and, remembering the woman whom I had abandoned in such dastardly fashion, and the child who did not know its father, I resolved to offer my name and my hand to her to whom my conduct had been so blameworthy. But it was too late—she was married! As she was married to a man of honorable position, I felt sure that she had succeeded in concealing her weakness from all eyes; but I was wild to know what had become of my child. After many fruitless attempts, I succeeded at last in obtaining a secret interview with the woman who had loved me so well; but I found only an embittered, implacable woman, who, to all my entreaties, made no other answer than this: 'You abandoned me when I implored you to come home and make me your wife and give your child a father. I no longer know you! I desire to forget a sin for which I blush; and, as for your daughter, all your prayers will be wasted, you shall never know what has become of her.' This decree, pronounced by an outraged woman, was only too strictly executed. Sixteen years passed. I renewed my prayers at intervals, but in vain: they were left unanswered. And now, Chérubin, you know the cause of the fits of melancholy which sometimes assailed me in the gayest circles; of that instability of temper for which I am noted; sometimes, amid the noisy amusements of society, the thought of my child would come to my mind, and the wealth that people envied, the good-fortune that I seemed to enjoy—ah! I would willingly have sacrificed them to hold my daughter in my arms just once! But to-day my desires are granted; to-day, a friend of her whom I once loved so dearly, has deigned to restore my child to me at last! But O my God! when I should be so happy to recover her, must I needs learn at the same time that she is guilty? that seduction, which wrecked her mother's happiness, is the lot of my child also?"

Monfréville had not finished when Louise and Chérubin threw themselves at his feet. With their faces bathed in tears, they kissed his knees, and Louise held out her arms, murmuring tremulously:

"Forgive me, father—forgive us! Alas! I did not know my parents, and Chérubin was everything to me!"

Monfréville opened his arms and the lovers threw themselves upon his heart.

"Yes," he said, as he embraced them, "yes, I must forgive you, for henceforth I shall have two children instead of one."

XXIX

CONCLUSION

Some time after that day which restored a father to Louise, Monsieur de Monfréville, who had publicly acknowledged her as his daughter, bestowed her hand on Marquis Chérubin de Grandvilain.

And on the wedding-day, Nicole came to Paris, doubly happy to be present at the ceremony which sealed the happiness of him whom she still called her *fieu*, and of the child to whom she had, for a long time, been a mother.

And Jasmin, who seemed to have recovered all his youthful vigor, absolutely insisted upon discharging fireworks in the courtyard for his master's nuptials; but stout Turlurette opposed it, recalling the accidents that had happened at the time of Chérubin's birth. So that Jasmin confined himself to firing a few rockets, with which he burned off what little hair he had left.

As for Monsieur Gérondif, Chérubin, after bestowing a tidy little sum upon him, requested him to seek other pupils. The tutor, finding himself possessed of a round sum, determined to make a name for himself in Paris; he founded a Latin journal, wrote a tragedy, gave a course of lectures on universal knowledge, and tried to compel ladies to dress without corsets. After some time, having succeeded only in squandering his capital, he was very glad to return to Gagny and resume his post as schoolmaster.

As the result of his fall among plates and glasses, Daréna was permanently disfigured, so that he dared not show himself in respectable society; he abandoned himself more freely than ever to his taste for debauchery, and after a wild orgy and a night passed at play with some low wretches, whose money he had won, he was found in the street, dead and stripped clean.

Thus ended a man born in good society, brought up in opulence, and well educated, but reduced to the lowest social level by his vices.

After losing his intimate friend, Monsieur Poterne became a dealer in return checks at the doors of theatres, and in that occupation he received several beatings because one could never get into the theatre with the checks that he sold.

Little Bruno took advantage of the advice and the money that Chérubin gave him; abandoning the practice of stealing dogs to sell, he set up a little shop, did a good business and became an honest man; he often said that it was easier than to be a knave.

Louise was a happy wife and a happy daughter. Monfréville never told her her mother's name; but when she went into society, where she was warmly greeted as young Marquis Chérubin's wife, she sometimes met the Noirmont family. It was with the keenest pleasure that she embraced Ernestine, who always manifested a warm affection for her. Then her eyes would seek Madame de Noirmont's, who, on her side, was always on the watch; and when, concealed behind the throng, their eyes met, their glances were eloquent with all the love that a mother's and a daughter's hearts can contain.

As for Chérubin, he became a model husband; it is even said that he was faithful to his wife; that young man was always different from other people.